Broken Heart Attack

Broken Heart Attack

Braxton Campus Mystery Book 2

James J. Cudney

Copyright (C) 2018 James J. Cudney
Layout design and Copyright (C) 2019 by Next Chapter
Published 2019 by Gumshoe – A Next Chapter Imprint
Cover art by Cover Mint
This book is a work of fiction. Names, characters, places, and incidents are the product of the author's imagination or are used fictitiously. Any resemblance to actual events, locales, or persons, living or dead, is purely coincidental.
All rights reserved. No part of this book may be reproduced or transmitted in any form or by any means, electronic or mechanical, including photocopying, recording, or by any information storage and retrieval system, without the author's permission.

Acknowledgments

Writing a book is not an achievement an individual person can do on his or her own. There are always people who contribute in a multitude of ways, sometimes unwittingly, throughout the journey from discovering the idea to drafting the last word. *Broken Heart Attack: A Braxton Campus Mystery* has had many supporters since its inception in September 2018, but before the concept even sparked in my mind, my passion for writing was nurtured by others.

First thanks go to my parents, Jim and Pat, for always believing in me as a writer, as well as teaching me how to become the person I am today. Their unconditional love and support has been the primary reason I'm accomplishing my goals. Through the guidance of my extended family and friends, who consistently encouraged me to pursue my passion, I found the confidence to take chances in life. With Winston and Baxter by my side, I was granted the opportunity to make my dreams come true by publishing this novel. I'm grateful to everyone for pushing me each and every day to complete this second book.

Broken Heart Attack was cultivated through the interaction, feedback, and input of several beta readers. I'd like to thank Shalini G, Lisa M. Berman, Rekha Rao, Laura Albert, and Nina D. Silva for providing insight and perspective during the development of the story, setting, and character arcs.

- A special call-out goes to Shalini for countless conversations helping me to fine-tune every aspect of the setting, characters, and plot. She read every version and offered a tremendous amount of her time to advise me on this book over several weeks. All the medical points were reviewed with Shalini to be sure I covered them appropriately. I am beyond grateful for her help. Any mistakes are my own from misunderstanding our discussions.

- Nina also read all of the versions and provided in-depth and varied feedback on character relationships, actions, and personality traits. She's a keen eye for knowing what will and won't work. She messaged back and forth for weeks to keep me focused and provide the motivation to challenge myself. Many thanks!

- Much appreciation for Lisa who has become a fantastic friend and confidante in the last few years. I appreciate all her time and effort into reading my books before launch. She always finds those items I miss, and I'm grateful more than I can say.

- A huge welcome to Laura for joining the team with this book. Laura provided lots of ideas for how to grow the characters, but she also found a few dozen proofreading issues which made my life so much easier. I'm truly thrilled to be working with her this time around.

- A big welcome to Rekha for joining the team with this book. Rekha read and reviewed the entire novel over a weekend and provided helpful comments on scenes that worked well and some that needed more pop. Thank you!

Much gratitude to all my friends and mentors at Moravian College. Although no murders have ever taken place there, the setting of this series is loosely based on my former multi-campus school set in Pennsylvania. Most of the locations are completely fabricated, but Millionaire's Mile exists... I only made up the name and cable car system!

Thank you to Creativia / Next Chapter for publishing *Broken Heart Attack* and paving the road for more books to come. I look forward to our continued partnership.

Welcome to Braxton, Wharton County
(Map drawn by Timothy J. R. Rains, Cartographer)

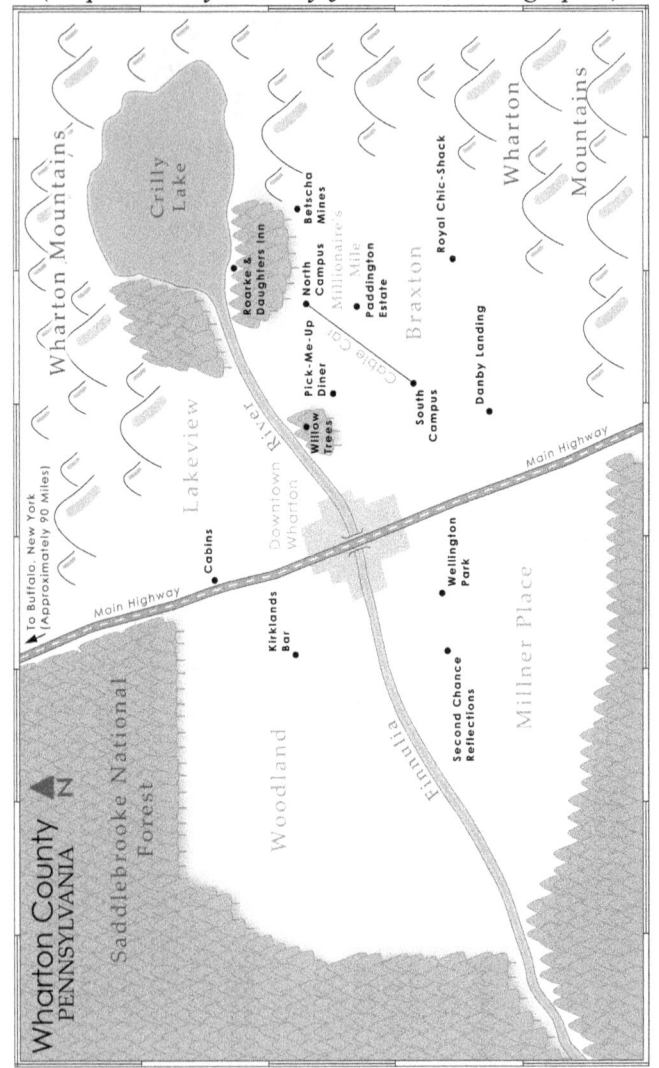

Who's Who in Braxton?

Ayrwick Family

- *Kellan*: Main Character, Braxton professor, amateur sleuth
- *Wesley*: Kellan's father, Braxton's retired president
- *Violet*: Kellan's mother, Braxton's admissions director
- *Emma*: Kellan's daughter with Francesca
- *Eleanor*: Kellan's younger sister, owns Pick-Me-Up Diner
- *Hampton*: Kellan's older brother
- *Nana D*: Kellan's grandmother, also known as Seraphina Danby
- *Francesca Castigliano*: Kellan's supposedly deceased wife
- *Vincenzo & Cecilia Castigliano*: Francesca's parents, run the mob
- *Alexander Betscha*: Nana D's cousin, doctor

Braxton Campus

- *Ursula Power*: President of Braxton, Myriam's wife
- *Myriam Castle*: Chair of Communications Dept., Ursula's wife

- *Fern Terry*: Dean of Student Affairs
- *Connor Hawkins*: Director of Security, Kellan's best friend
- *Maggie Roarke*: Head Librarian, Kellan's ex-girlfriend
- *Yuri Sato*: Student, Dana's friend
- *Craig 'Striker' Magee*: Student
- *Arthur Terry*: Fern's son, works at Paddington's Play House

Paddington Household

- *Millard Paddington*: Brother to Eustacia
- *Eustacia Paddington*: Sister to Millard
- *Gwendolyn Paddington*: Sister-in-law to Eustacia and Millard
- *Jennifer Paddington*: Daughter of Gwendolyn
- *Timothy Paddington*: Son of Gwendolyn
- *Ophelia Taft*: Daughter of Gwendolyn, Married to Richard
- *Richard Taft*: Married to Ophelia
- *Dana Taft*: Ophelia and Richard's daughter
- *Lilly Taft*: Ophelia and Richard's daughter
- *Sam Taft*: Ophelia and Richard's son
- *Brad Shope*: Nurse
- *Bertha Crawford*: Housekeeper

Wharton County Residents

- *April Montague*: Wharton County Sheriff
- *Marcus Stanton*: Braxton Town Councilman
- *Officer Flatman*: Police Officer
- *Finnigan Masters*: Attorney
- *Buddy*: Works at Second Chance Reflections
- *Tiffany Nutberry*: HR Employee
- *Lindsey Endicott*: Friend of Nana D & Paddingtons

Chapter 1

March weather in Wharton County, Pennsylvania was as unpredictable as a cutting jeer from Nana D. Although bound to happen, the actual impact boasted an infinite range unlike any missile I'd ever seen launched. There might be a blizzard worthy of a Christmas snow globe furiously shaken by an overeager child, or spring could be testing its feverish desire to burst through the frozen soil with an unparalleled zest for life. While thunder rolled above me in a murky gray sky, I read my nana's latest message for the third time wondering if she realized the extent to which she could confuse people and make them want to cry—all in a single, random meandering text.

Nana D: *Can't stand these old whiners. Save me. You better not be late. Did you get a haircut yet? I've seen more attractive farm animals than you lately. Sometimes I can't believe we're related. Made you a special dessert. Why didn't you talk me out of this stupid race? I'm proud of you for coming back home. What's an emoji again? I need to find us both dates. Do I swipe right or left if I'm interested in a man? Hurry up. Hugs and kisses.*

Since we enjoyed torturing one another in a loving yet competitive way, I ignored my grandmother's craziness hoping it'd lead to a conniption fit in front of her friends. That wind-up Energizer bunny desperately needed a case of extra-strength Valium while I craved the warmer, drier weather as my drug of choice. Instead, I stared depressingly at an over-stuffed storm cloud threatening to torture us again. We'd already suffered through a nasty four-day bout of torrential rain that made everything feel like soggy bread. And in case it wasn't obvious, no one liked soggy bread. Now that I thought about it, my entire week had felt like soggy bread mischievously sprinkled with a side of unrelenting and peculiar death.

Fresh off accepting a new job as a professor at Braxton and unravelling my first murder case, I was hopeful for some relaxation. Unfortunately, everything morphed into swiss cheese with holes the size of the Grand Canyon. No, I wasn't a police detective or private investigator. I got lucky solving the murder of two colleagues before our county's crabby sheriff finally nabbed the misguided culprit, yet that wasn't the most scandalous thing about my recent return home after a decade's absence.

When I told my in-laws that I was leaving Los Angeles and moving back to Pennsylvania, I learned through an ordinary, everyday conversation that my supposedly dead wife, Francesca, wasn't really dead. Nearly two and a half years ago, I'd been led to believe she'd perished in a car accident when a drunk driver plowed through a red light at a dangerous intersection. No longer true! *'Alive today, gone tomorrow. Hey, I'm back again. The after-life wasn't too fun, so I changed my mind about dying. Just not for me!'* Maybe things happened like that in the menacing world of my in-laws, *The Castigliano Family*, but definitely not in mine.

The car accident had been staged by Francesca's parents after someone tried to kill my wife as revenge for a multitude of mob faux pas. My in-laws sat at the helm of a ruthless LA crime syndicate, and somehow Francesca—who never told me anything about this aspect of her life while she was *alive*—had gotten caught up in their web of deception. The only way for them to protect Francesca and our young daughter, Emma, was to fake Francesca's death.

My emotions had been incredibly erratic and raw for the last five days since learning the truth. I couldn't tell anyone except my sister, Eleanor, who'd been present when Francesca showed up. And just as easily as my no-longer-dead-wife had materialized, she vanished again under the dark iron curtain that was the protection of her parents. Was there a handbook for dealing with a wife who'd come back from the grave? Had I been kidnapped and brainwashed by a cult performing some maddening initiation rite? Seriously, what did I do in the past to be saddled with the mother of all gut punches? Sadly, I had no answers but as far as priorities went, my presence was imminently required elsewhere for a different kind of brutal torture.

I was currently driving to visit my almost seventy-five-year-old grandmother, Nana D—known to everyone else as Seraphina Danby—who'd declared her intent to run for Mayor of Wharton County in a surprise press conference earlier that week. Five-foot-tall, less than a hundred pounds wet—mostly from her wild, henna-rinsed red hair taking up nearly half her height—and full of boat loads more sarcasm than me, Nana D was preparing for her first major campaign activity. I'd promised to organize all her '*old, whiny*' volunteers for the mayoral race since none of them knew where to begin.

Although a proper tea would be served at Nana D's, I popped into The Big Beanery, Braxton's charming and crowded South Campus student café, and ordered an extra-strong, extra-tall salted caramel mocha to go. I drooled at the pastry counter despite knowing Nana D had baked something delicious I'd undoubtedly consume like a pig from a trough. I scanned the room searching for any of my students who might've been hanging out with their friends or reviewing class materials in study group but only saw one person I recognized who was not a student by any means.

What was Dean Terry doing on campus on a Saturday? While waiting for my overly complex coffee and assuming she sat by herself, I moseyed over to the table to brighten her day. That's the kinda guy I was. Although I was a mere three inches shy of a full six-feet, my colleague tipped the other side of the scale and unwisely chose to keep her hair extremely short. Built like a quarterback who'd recently eaten way too much salt, the dean had been using her thick, towering presence to intimidate students for nearly twenty-five years at Braxton. Once you got beyond the surface, she was truly a pussycat.

After getting used to the idea of being colleagues, I refrained from calling her Dean Terry and addressed her by her first name. With a smile, I said, "Good afternoon, Fern. Don't you ever take a break?" She'd almost been awarded the coveted presidency of our well-regarded institution last week. The Board of Trustees had surprisingly gone with someone else and instead offered her a leading role on the committee that would convert Braxton from a college into a university over the next two years. She was disappointed, but once we reconnected and realized we could make a huge difference together, Fern quickly got on board with the decision.

"Kellan, so nice to see you. I'm meeting my son for brunch. He's stepped outside to fix an issue with the school's *King Lear* production." Fern's tone had more verve than I was ready to handle at that time of day. Although I'd always known her academic and disciplinarian side, I'd recently connected with the dean on a more personal level finding we had a lot in common. Between our mutual love of black and white films and traveling cross-country by train, we were destined to develop a stronger friendship. Where was that love when she'd raked me over the coals for something my frat had done while I was a student ten years ago?

As far as I recalled, Fern only had one son who'd graduated high school with me. Instead of going directly to college, he'd moved to New York City to become an actor before returning three years later to obtain his bachelor's degree. "How is Arthur? I haven't seen him in years," I said pushing away wavy, unruly dirty-blond hair from my three-day unshaven face. Nana D had astutely remarked I was overdue for a haircut but since I hadn't been to a barber in Wharton County in a decade, I'd no idea where to go. Eleanor had tried to convince me to let her trim it, but that would never happen. A steady grip with a pair of scissors and erring on the side of caution were not her strong points.

"Arthur's directing Braxton's play this semester. Unfortunately, it means he's working for a tyrant, but he's dealt with far worse on Broadway, I'm sure." Fern shrugged her shoulders, then offered me a seat. My mouth watered over the gooey cinnamon roll sitting on her plate inches away from my nimble fingers.

"No, I shouldn't. I have to be somewhere but thought I'd say hello," I noted, preparing to leave while Arthur returned from his phone call and stormed up to the table. Hints of a ferocious dog came to mind when his alarming expression and cold, dark pupils centered on his unsuspecting mother.

"That woman is a miserable old cow, Mom. I don't know how you cope working with her every day," Arthur snarled. He was tall with round and puffy features like his mother but instead of a gray pixie-cut, thinning, sandy-colored hair was combed over in a failed attempt to hide what was inevitably going to happen relatively soon. Although he was thirty-two like me, early crow's feet and cavernous lines had already begun to dominate his face. "Oh, wait… Kellan Ayrwick, is that you?"

I nodded. "I can only imagine you're speaking about my wonderful boss, Myriam Castle. I'd appreciate any tips you might have for dealing with that venomous barracuda!" It'd spilled from my lips before I could stop my verbal diarrhea. Myriam was one of my least favorite people. Ever. I'd barely known her for three weeks, but every interaction left me bristled and inflicted with a rash the size of Texas. Between her nasty, chirpy tone and inciting way of quoting Shakespeare, it often felt like a nails-on-chalkboard episode of *Twilight Zone* or a sinister case of *Candid Camera*. I waited for someone wearing a demon mask to jump out and yell surprise, but sadly, it never happened. I would've popped that charlatan right in the schnoz for messing with me.

"If only." Arthur sat forcefully on the chair wiping wet hands across his jeans. He'd regrettably gotten caught in the deluge without an umbrella. "Run. That's all I can say when it comes to that—"

"Now, Arthur. We all know she can be difficult, but let's not say something you'll regret," Fern interrupted while patting her son's forearm. "Remember, this is your opportunity to get into directing and away from acting. Isn't that what you said you wanted?" Fern fretted like a mother hen trying to calm her little chick. I'd rarely seen this side of her, but she handled her son with aplomb and tact.

"I know, Mom. Myriam's squashed the entire opening scene we'd been rehearsing for days. Now I have to re-block the stage before tomorrow's dress rehearsal." He grunted and took an aggressive bite out of his grilled cheese sandwich. His canine teeth resembled a ravenous vampire's fangs.

Arthur answered an incoming call from someone named Dana on his cell phone. Since he and Fern were busy and my coffee grew colder on the counter, I excused myself to leave. I pretended not to hear Fern gasp when Arthur told Dana he also wanted to kill some woman for what she'd said at last night's rehearsal. I felt bad for Arthur who'd have to find a way to work with the corrosive woman, or she'd make his life miserable.

When Myriam had become the new chairman of our department, I suddenly took direction from her since I was teaching a full course load on broadcasting writing, television production, and history of film. We'd held our first supervisory meeting this week where she'd made things exorbitantly clear—once my father officially retired as the president of Braxton College in the coming days, I no longer had anyone to protect me. I might've been granted a one-year contract, but Myriam articulately clarified the new president—her wife, Ursula Power—could override it.

I grabbed my coffee and took off for Nana D's. She owned and operated Danby Landing, an organic orchard and farm in the southernmost section of Wharton County. At one point in the county's history it had the largest acreage of any homestead, but Nana D had sold off a large chunk after my grandpop passed away. As I turned onto the dirt path leading to her farmhouse, I quarantined thoughts of my back-from-the-dead wife and loony boss and focused on the next irrational mess I had to deal with.

When I pulled up at Danby Landing, my six-year-old daughter raced out of the house and jumped in my arms. I swung Emma from side to side and kissed her cheeks. She'd slept at Nana D's the previous night, so they could have a fancy slumber party—no boys invited apparently.

"Daddy! We made smores last night. I got to ride the tractor with Nana D's farmhand this morning. He has a daughter my age. Can I play with her? When are we going to the zoo?" Emma asked, unable to control her glee. Her crimped dark-brown hair was pulled into pigtails, and she wore an adorable pair of denim overalls Nana D had sewed the previous week. Emma inherited her mother's olive-tinted skin which made me unable to forget my wife's enchanting beauty.

"That sounds like fun, baby girl!" I sat her on the swinging bench next to me to spend a few minutes together before dealing with the old whiners. We played a few rounds of *Cat-in-the-Cradle* and discussed the sleepover before Emma decided to drag me inside the house. While she poured herself a cup of juice and turned on a video, I trudged into the den to be terrorized.

There were four others in the room besides my nana, all of whom I'd met in the past. It was a meeting of the founding members of Braxton's Septuagenarian Club: Nana D, Eustacia Paddington, Gwendolyn Paddington, Millard Paddington, and Lindsey Endicott. They'd formed the group years ago upon turning seventy to celebrate a revival of their youth. They'd initiated at least forty new members and ran amok trying to reclaim any remaining independence from their family who'd locked them in nursing homes or taken away their driver's licenses. Nana D was the ringleader and caused the most disturbances around town. '*Not my monkey, not my circus,*' I often reminded myself when anyone begged me to stop her from whatever trouble she'd brewed up.

"If it ain't the little bedwetter," taunted Lindsey Endicott, a seventy-six-year-old retired attorney whom Nana D and Eustacia Paddington were both dating. His bright pink polo was two sizes too small and revealed way too much of his rotund beer belly. As soon as he'd sold his law practice, he'd opened a microbrewery in one of the well-frequented downtown shopping areas. The only problem was that he was his best customer and had never learned when or how to cut himself off.

"Aw, he hasn't done that in years, right, Kellan?" said Eustacia. Her electric-blue track suit fit properly, but she obviously wasn't wearing anything underneath it. I shook my head in disbelief at the multitude of oddly-shaped age spots and diverted my sight anywhere but in her direction. She continued, "I remember when he had that awful problem. Poor Seraphina had to change the sheets whenever that boy stayed over."

Could this get any more embarrassing? I'd been three years old and had a nervous bladder. I'd gained full control of the situation for close to three decades at this point. "Cut it out, you two. I'll toss your little blue pills down the garbage disposal, Mr. Endicott. How'd you like that?" His eyes opened wide sending two giant, bushy eyebrows in every direction like ants in search of a morsel of food. "And you, Ms. Paddington... I'll slice several inches off your cane and see how you like hobbling around."

Millard Paddington, Eustacia's older brother—by less than a year, Irish twins as she often called them—blushed a shade of red I rarely saw anymore. He was the only truly gentle human being in the bunch. "Leave the boy alone, you rascals, or I'll swap Gwennie's high-blood pressure pills with Eustacia's gastrointestinal medication. Neither of you will know what hit you. Don't we have important business to attend to?" Millard was the tallest of the bunch, rail thin, and had lost his hair years ago. He'd grown a handlebar moustache and had almost perfected the curls, but the children at the library held a penchant for yanking on it when he'd read to them. Calling it *spotty* would be a generous description yet he seemed to enjoy all the attention from the boisterous toddlers.

Gwendolyn, or Gwennie as her fellow club members called her, had been married to Eustacia's and Millard's brother, Charles, who'd passed away the prior year. She was exceedingly prim and proper and had a habit of being hasty and judgmental. I'd luckily rarely been on the receiving end of it, but Nana D had to put the woman in her place many times in the past. Gwendolyn remained silent with her upturned nose looking as snooty as possible—old schoolmarm after tasting a rancid, sour grapefruit.

"As much as I'd love to keep getting roasted by the old timers' club, Mr. Paddington is correct. How can I help with Nana D's campaign?" I asked relaxing into the only remaining chair in the room which left me practically sitting inside the roaring fireplace. "What have you prepared so far?"

Silence. No one said a word, just looked back and forth at each other waiting for someone else to chime in. We continued like this for another five minutes until I finally got them to produce a list of the top ten changes they wanted to see happen in Wharton County. I was pleasantly surprised to discover at least six of them were pragmatic ideas others could get behind. The remaining four were not—free massages in the park by 'the hot little number at the Willow Trees Retirement Complex' and a new dating app called 'Let's Get Lucky' for the over-seventy crowd seemed a tad unnecessary and inflammatory to me. Then again, I might want those things in forty years, too. Whom was I to judge or put the kibosh on someone's late-in-life carnal desires? I won't even mention the other two ideas.

While I assigned everyone tasks, Gwendolyn excused herself to use the powder room. "I'm borrowing your cane, Eustacia. I'm not feeling too steady on my feet the last few days."

As Gwendolyn walked down the hall, Nana D teased, "I'm sorry I don't have a chamber pot, you old bat. Here we call it a restroom! No one says powder room anymore." Was Gwendolyn avoiding her responsibilities or was the absence a coincidence? As if she were privy to the conversation going on in my head, Nana D turned and said, "She always does that. When she returns, Gwennie will rush out saying she has to deal with an emergency. Just like Millard whenever I asked him to sleep over. That's the reason things didn't work out between us. He was selfish when it came to intimate things like—"

"No, Nana D. Please stop. I can't listen to it," I said once my insides cringed and turned to Jell-O. "We've talked about this many times. I don't want to hear anything about your love life. And in return, I won't bother you with anything about mine."

"Does that mean you have a love life to speak of? Because last time we chatted, your ability to flirt and any awkward sex appeal you still clung to had disappeared the way of the pony express," she replied while kissing her finger, touching her derriere, and making a sizzle sound. Her tiny noise erupted into a room full of irritable senior citizens hooting at my expense.

"I'm only here for a little while, Nana D. You need to use your time wisely, or I might not help you win the mayoral race." I filled Gwendolyn's box with campaign promotional flyers and walked out the front door to load them in Lindsey's car. He'd carted the gang over to Nana D's given he was the best driver in the whole group. When I got to the porch, I heard Gwendolyn on her phone as she shuffled to the far corner.

Gwendolyn said, "Well, if you can't make it, then I'll find someone else to take your ticket. It's not the first time you've disappointed me, and I'm sure it won't be the last. I've sponsored this production of *King Lear*. The whole family is supposed to be there in support of our generous donations. Maybe you're not cut out to be a member of this clan anymore."

I watched the sourpuss expression on her face deepen until it was her turn to speak again. When she did, even I got the chills from her icy tone and unexpected threat.

"You remember that when I'm no longer around. Family is supposed to look out for one another as they get older. Not throw them to the curb like trash. Maybe I need to make another trip to the lawyer to look over my will again." A few seconds later Gwendolyn shouted into the phone, "You've always been useless. I've got a good mind to take you down right now. We'll see how you like it when things don't turn out as you expected." Then she hung up and struggled with the clasp on her vintage 50's-style handbag. She finally got it open, flung her phone inside, and agitatedly clutched it to her side.

I'd already stepped onto the porch and couldn't sneak back inside without her noticing me. As she turned around, Gwendolyn sneered. "You eavesdropping on my call? What kind of manners did your nana teach you, Kellan? I've got a good mind to—"

"I'm sorry. I was bringing this box to the car and didn't know you were out here," I said cautiously holding my free hand up and balancing the box against my chest with the other. I felt bad for interrupting her privacy but was shocked at what she'd said on the phone. "Is everything okay?"

"No, my awful family keeps taking my money but refuses to do anything nice for me. I'm about to learn how dreadful one of them truly is. What are you doing tomorrow?" she asked in a raspy voice.

Other than preparing for classes and trying to contact Francesca, who'd left me no number to reach her when she absconded with her mother to New York, nothing was planned. "Spending time with my daughter and helping Nana D prepare for her upcoming debate with Councilman Stanton."

"Well, find yourself a babysitter. You're coming with me to Braxton's dress rehearsal for *King Lear*. One of my useless kinsfolks canceled and I have an extra ticket." Gwendolyn wiped a speck of dust from her eye. A woman like her never cried about family. She just complained about them to anyone who'd listen. Or even those who didn't.

"I'm sure they love you. Maybe it's a misunderstanding," I said, sympathetic for her plight. Nana D had mentioned several times how Gwendolyn's kids had either abandoned her or gotten into trouble ever since their father had passed away. Her husband, Charles, had been the family's center of gravity while he'd been alive, but now they all treated her like a burden or an ATM machine.

"That's certainly a load of petrified cow dung! They'd be happier if I kicked the bucket on the drive home tonight. I'm concerned one of them might be trying to kill me. Something ain't right with how I feel lately. Going to the doctor on Monday to find out." She steadied herself against the doorjamb and huffed loudly. "Stupid ungrateful beasts. If I find out one of them has been gaslighting me, I'll have them arrested. No two thoughts about it. We might be family, but they're all a bunch of vultures."

Gwendolyn went back inside to corral the rest of the Septuagenarian Club. I rubbed my temples, loaded the box into Lindsey's car, and returned to the house. After everyone left, Nana D pulled me into the kitchen away from Emma's curious ears. "Did I overhear Gwennie tell you someone in her family is trying to murder her?" Nana D asked with a peculiar twitch in her left cheek.

"Yes, I assumed she was upset about one of them not going to the show. I guess I'll be going with you now," I sighed as if the weight of the world rested on my shoulders. I loved my nana, but her friends were harder to handle than standing upside down catching a greasy pig in a mud slide.

"No, brilliant one. That's where you're wrong. Something is definitely whackadoodle in that family. She's been acting strange for weeks. I wouldn't be surprised if one of those Paddingtons was trying to kill Gwennie. You're gonna help her figure out which crazy one it is before they succeed, right?"

Chapter 2

After leaving Nana D's farm, Emma and I went shopping at a local bookstore. An hour later and a hundred dollars deeper in debt, we exited the charming literary wonder set between the two Braxton campuses with our hands full of recycled bags stocked with books. I'd snagged a copy of the debut novel in a new mystery series that had caught my eye. Next stop, the Pick-Me-Up Diner for an early dinner and much-needed therapy session with my sister. Since she was the only person I could talk to about Francesca, Eleanor would have to suffer through endless conversations about what to do next.

When we arrived, I made Emma put on a hard hat in case she bumped into any of the construction in the currently-being-renovated Pick-Me-Up Diner. Emma joined Manny, Eleanor's chef, who was in the kitchen testing new recipes even though the place wasn't accessible to the public. It still needed a final inspection on Wednesday morning before allowing in any paying customers.

"She seems to be adjusting well," Eleanor said pulling her dirty-blonde, curly hair into a bun on the top of her head and wrapping a scrunchie around to hold it in place. While our older siblings had inherited our father's tall and lanky body structure, Eleanor and I split the dominant Danby and Betscha traits in resemblance of our mother. Eleanor got saddled with wider hips and shorter arms than she'd liked, and I ungraciously accepted untamable hair and a tiny, button nose that refused to properly balance my glasses. "Still haven't said anything to Emma, right?"

"No, I wouldn't know how or where to begin. I'm living in one of your daytime dramas lately," I teased my sister even though it hadn't felt like a laughing matter. I loved Francesca, and the day I buried my wife was the worst day of my life. I was having trouble believing her reappearance wasn't a dream.

"Tell me again exactly how the Castiglianos pulled this off?" When Eleanor had met my mother-in-law to pick up Emma, Cecilia sent my daughter upstairs in my parents' log cabin, aka *Royal Chic-Shack* as we all called it, while she told Eleanor to wait in our father's study. A few minutes later, Cecilia snuck Francesca into the small, private office nestled in the far corner and locked the door. Eleanor shockingly learned that Francesca was alive, and I was summoned home immediately.

"I had less than one hour with her, then Cecilia whisked Francesca away to New York refusing to provide any way to reach her. All communication must go through my controlling in-laws," I replied. It was like a Woody Allen movie playing out in front of me, not my own life. "I'm hoping to see her again when they return tomorrow."

"You're seriously telling me Francesca's been hiding out at the Castigliano mansion for over two years?" Eleanor asked with bright eyes and an exaggerated amount of air blown through her lips to push rogue bangs away from her forehead. "Diabolical!"

"Yes, the whole macabre series of events happened quietly and quickly. A few days before the fake car accident, Francesca had been kidnapped by a rival mob family, the Vargas gang. I never knew about it because I'd been away on a film set. Her father's goons killed one of their men, and as retaliation, the Vargas mob captured Francesca. When he found out what'd happened, Vincenzo instructed his henchmen to do whatever it took to return his daughter."

"But how did she end up faking her death? You've never explained that part," Eleanor asked while peering through the small window in the kitchen door to verify Emma was still helping Manny prepare dinner and not listening to our conversation.

"The only way Vincenzo could protect her was to stage an accident that looked like she'd been killed by the Vargas family's newest driver. He bought off a local cop who poured alcohol all over the other guy's car and had the medics attempt to rescue Francesca. They never caught the driver because there never was one. When the police called to tell me about the accident, Francesca was in the room with them trying to convince her father to find another solution."

"I can't believe she'd hurt you like this. Painful." Eleanor acted as if it were her wife who'd lied and disappeared. I knew she was empathetic, but no one could understand the impact to my world.

"I remember seeing a few random thugs checking out the accident. They must have been there to ensure Francesca looked dead and to report my reaction. Vincenzo eventually convinced the Vargas family that he'd suffered enough by losing his daughter. Everyone agreed to call off their turf war and carefully observe proper boundaries in the future."

"Does she have to stay dead forever? What kind of life is that?" Eleanor asked.

"I wish I knew. We only had time to agree on not telling Emma for now." It'd made me so happy to see my wife, but my body filled with an intense anger I'd never experienced before. "Francesca's been secretly watching our daughter at the Castigliano mansion whenever Emma slept over. When I told the Castiglianos I was moving back to Pennsylvania, Francesca freaked out. It meant she could no longer watch Emma from a safe, comfortable distance."

"That's why she came back from the dead *now*?" Eleanor said without blinking for a long time.

I nodded. Francesca tried to abide by her father's rules and stay hidden, but when the possibility of never seeing her daughter again became a reality, she snuck onto the plane with her new fake identity to convince me not to take Emma away. Francesca had worn a costume, dyed her hair, and sat far away in coach from Emma—Cecilia had undoubtedly flown first class. "I have no idea what to do next. I can't let this impact Emma, but if her mother's alive, shouldn't she get to be part of her life?"

"Only if it isn't dangerous. What about you? Are you thinking about getting a new identity and disappearing somewhere to rebuild a life together?" Eleanor looked disappointed and worried that I would leave town again.

In the forty-one minutes Francesca and I had together, all of which were supervised by my mother-in-law, we only discussed what to do about Emma. "I haven't thought about it. Right now, I just want to find out what she's been doing the last two and a half years. I don't even know if we're technically still married, or how any of this works."

"Don't you still want to be married to her? You loved Francesca so much," Eleanor asked while hugging me.

"I'm overwhelmed. I want to reclaim what we once had, but she lied to me. She ended something intimate and passionate. We were great together, and now, it feels strange to be around her." I paused to keep my emotions from exploding. "The new Francesca has short blonde hair, wears colored contact lenses, and speaks differently. I don't know whom my wife is anymore, Eleanor."

My sister leaned in to hug me, but we were interrupted by my ringing cell phone. I looked at the screen and groaned. What did my boss want with me on a Saturday evening? I wanted to ignore her but needed a temporary break from thinking about Francesca's re-appearance in my life.

"Good evening, Myriam. How's your weekend?" I asked in as calm a voice as I could muster. Eleanor patted my shoulder, then went into the kitchen to check on Emma and give me some privacy.

"I've no time for small talk. I'm trying to fix gargantuan issues with our upcoming *King Lear* production. I suddenly remembered you were supposed to drop off your course recommendations for next semester. You seem fond of keeping me waiting for you to get your job done properly," Myriam said haughtily. Her normal appearance backed up the narcissistic attitude, too—she always wore immaculately cut power suits and kept her short, spiky gray hair perfectly styled. I'd suspected at one time it was a wig, and if I ever had the chance, I'd rip that sucker off to test my theory. It didn't matter that she was old enough to be my mother, the viper needed to be taken down a notch or two.

While Myriam was correct about the deliverable, we'd agreed on Monday being the due date. It was only Saturday. I'd completed them that morning but hadn't planned to submit them until the last minute as retaliation for her giving me such a short deadline. It was the only way I could irritate my boss without crossing any overt boundaries. "Certainly. I thought we could discuss them in our weekly meeting next Tuesday. I'd be happy to email them to you tomorrow."

"That simply won't do. I need time to review before we meet, and I'm in rehearsals all day tomorrow. I distinctly asked you to get them to me in advance, but it seems you struggle with listening as well as punctuality. '*Better three hours too soon than a minute too late.*' Wouldn't you agree?" Myriam told me to hold on, then shouted at someone in the theater about annunciating properly.

"As you like it," I replied naming the Shakespearean comedy from where her line came.

"Now you seem to understand who's the boss. Drop it off in thirty minutes at Paddington's Play House. And don't dawdle.

I'm sure it'll take me hours to revise and comment on it," Myriam replied with a growl before hanging up.

As I tapped my fingers on the diner's dusty table, I considered my options. If I stood my ground, Myriam would continue to itemize everything she'd felt was an influential enough reason to push me out of Braxton. If I let her obnoxious attitude roll off my shoulders like it meant nothing, she might eventually tire and bore of chiding me every moment of every day. Before I acted too severely, it'd be beneficial to have my first official meeting with Ursula to understand her perspective on the situation.

Eleanor agreed to drop Emma off at our parents on her way home since our mother was remaining in for the evening. Our father had an out of town golf game that weekend which meant our mother planned to curl up with the latest regency romance novel from her favorite author—her sister, Deirdre.

A few minutes later, I pulled into the South Campus parking lot and grabbed the printed course outlines and film suggestions from my briefcase. As I entered Paddington's Play House, someone shouted terse stage directions at the actors and loudly dropped a prop. It sounded like something made of glass when I heard the earth-shaking shatter as it hit the stage. I ambled around the lobby hoping whatever commotion was stirring up inside the theater would settle down.

Paddington's Play House had been built by Charles, Millard, and Eustacia's father in the late 1940s while his children were young. None of the other colleges had a theater program or entertainment venues, and the Paddingtons were determined to always be first in every endeavor. Built in the shape of a large octagon that resembled Shakespeare's Globe Theater, it seated up to one-thousand guests. Unlike the original Globe Theater, there was no standing room. A large cathedral ceiling with reclaimed wood beams, antique gilded and cushioned seats, and plastered walls painted an ivory white offered a charming and bespoke atmosphere. The college played four shows a year, one of which was always a Shakespearean production to properly celebrate the Bard.

I admired the inlayed, two-toned natural wood flooring as I descended into the seating area hoping the ruckus had died down. Arthur and Myriam attempted to co-direct several reticent actors on stage. They both waved their hands furiously and stomped across the narrow expanse demonstrating what the actors should've been doing. I was too far away to hear their words or see the expressions on their faces, but it was obvious they provided contradictory direction.

Two female voices startled me from the corner. A dark brunette in designer jeans and low-cut red blouse said, "He told me how pretty I looked earlier. I think maybe I have a chance."

"Get out. He's too old for you, Dana. Why would you be interested in him?" the thin, taller girl with a pasty complexion and nasal voice replied. She'd pulled her neon-green hair up under a baseball cap and was dressed in a pair of old, ratty sweats.

Dana said, "I know he's not exactly the hottest guy and he might be a little on the older side, but he's hilarious. And he knows so many famous people." She swooned as she spoke, then looked toward the stage. As her head turned, she caught sight of me.

I nodded in her direction. "Excuse me, would you know when they'll take a break? I need to drop something off for Myriam Castle."

"Ugh, you better wait until she's done. Dr. Castle doesn't like to be interrupted," Dana said.

"We're about ready to do a scene change. I'm the set designer, Yuri," the girl wearing the sweats replied. Now I understood why she looked more casual than the rest. "She's Dana. You are?"

I remembered seeing the name *Dana* on Arthur Terry's cell phone earlier. Could she have been talking about having a crush on Arthur? Dana could barely have been nineteen or twenty-years-old, and he was my age. "Kellan Ayrwick. I'm one of the professors here at Braxton."

"Awesome sauce. Let's head up together. They'll be done by the time we get to the front. Just wait in the front row until I climb on stage to change the set," Yuri said.

Dana followed. "I'm handling props for the show. I'm not an actress, but I love everything about the theater." Her bouncy walk and flashy grin demonstrated vast excitement over working on the show.

"You must be a student at Braxton?" I asked remembering Myriam had indicated everyone who worked on the play had to be a current or former Braxton attendee. They'd first cast any performers and hired all back-of-the-house roles from currently enrolled students. If there was a special need or talent not in existence at the school, they'd solicit help from alumni.

"Sophomore. Studying drama and psychology. I want to work on Broadway one day, but my parents forced me to take something practical as a back-up. It's not like I'll ever need to get a real job. My family's loaded," Dana said shrugging her shoulders.

She looked familiar, but I couldn't place her. "What did you say your last name was?"

"Um, Taft, but my mother's family has the money. You must know the Paddingtons. They own this place," Dana said with a slew of pretentiousness that hadn't gone unnoticed by either of us.

That's why she looked familiar. She had the same patrician face and narrow jawline as Eustacia and Millard. "I've met a few of your family members. What branch do you hail from?"

"Grandmother is Gwendolyn Paddington. Grandfather passed away last year, but my parents are still around. Do you know Richard and Ophelia Taft? The grand dame is named for Grandmother's favorite Shakespearean character." Dana leaned against the side wall while Yuri scattered toward the stage once the scene finished.

"I saw your grandmother earlier today. She was visiting my nana," I replied. If Dana was related to Gwendolyn, she might be one of the family members possibly trying to do away with the difficult matriarch. "You must spend a lot of time with your grandmother, too?"

Dana rolled her eyes, but she'd never be able to compete with me. I was king of that move. "Grandmother is hard to take. She cares more about what things look like than what's under the surface, you know what I mean?"

I shrugged my shoulders. "Different generations, I suppose. They expect all the skeletons in our closets to stay hidden. I heard she's not been feeling too well lately." I wasn't convinced anyone had been trying to kill Gwendolyn, but it wouldn't hurt to poke around.

"She is kind of old. Ever since Grandfather passed away, she's gotten worse. Grandmother keeps reminding everyone she's paying for this whole show." Dana seemed like a typical college girl with a large chip on her shoulder. Kids her age thought anyone over forty was old. Wait until she started to see the world without rose-colored glasses.

"Are you worried about something happening to her?" I asked.

"She's a tough old bird, but yesterday she could barely get through brunch. Everything tires her out quickly in the last few weeks," Dana said while adjusting the straps on her blouse and checking her reflection in a compact mirror. "Looks like they're done on stage."

As Dana marched up the stairs, Myriam waved me over. "Don't just stand around making me wait. Do you have the course outlines?"

After handing them to her, I said, "How's the show going?" Tomorrow's dress rehearsal would only be open to family and select faculty. Students were on Spring Break this week, but if they were involved in the theater, they had to stay on campus.

"Like a root canal without any pain relief. I never should have hired Arthur Terry, but like other people around here, he was forced upon me." Myriam slid her tortoise-shell glasses an inch down her nose, pointedly stared at me, then sighed. Even the ruffles on her royal-blue blouse seemed to fluster.

"Is Arthur a bad director? We went to high school together, you know," I said ignoring her dig about how I'd gotten my job at Braxton. She took every opportunity to belittle me or my family.

"He's new to the role. Actors often think they can easily transition from in front of the camera to behind the camera. His Broadway experience is lackluster." Myriam walked away from me and descended the stairs. "Don't dally, follow me."

I had a gnawing urge to mock her as I trailed behind but decided to set a good example in case anyone was watching. As Myriam sat in the front row, I noticed Dana cornering Arthur on the opposite side of the venue. She'd placed her hand on his right arm and soon began to rub his shoulder. The girl was on a mission, but Arthur didn't appear highly responsive or remotely interested.

"If you didn't hire Arthur, who did?" I asked.

"Gwendolyn Paddington insisted I offer him the opportunity. Some people don't understand the value of hard work and earning their positions." Myriam pulled a red marker from her briefcase and crossed out items on the outlines I'd given to her. "No, no. This won't do. You need to be more creative." As the ink bled on the paper like a murder scene, her forehead wrinkled in spades.

"Gwendolyn's always been active in the arts like her father-in-law from what I understand. She assumed responsibility as the patron of Paddington's Play House when he died." She'd also been a savagely brutal and vocal art and theater critic before retiring several years earlier.

"She's one to put her nose where it doesn't belong." Myriam stared at me waiting for a response. When I didn't share one, she said, "We're done. Expect feedback on Tuesday. You may leave."

I had little energy to argue with the monster and chose to say my goodbye. As I walked down the center aisle, a pale and disheveled Arthur joined me. "Ugh, those Paddingtons are truly going to drive me insane. I can't win with any of them. One day they'll be begging me to do something for them instead of the other way around." He pulled at his hair and sneered as we entered the lobby.

"It sounds like things aren't going so well with the show. I'm sorry to hear it," I said to Arthur hoping empathy might calm him down.

"If it's not Dana playing her little games or Gwendolyn thinking she can control me, it's the confusion with that other one. And on top of it all, I can't find any way to win with that witch, Myriam. I should never have come back home," Arthur grunted.

I couldn't agree with him more about returning to Braxton if I'd tried to. Which other Paddington was causing him trouble? "Myriam mentioned Gwendolyn insisted you take this job. I would've thought you were on good terms."

Arthur laughed wildly as he opened the door to step outside. "Maybe a long time ago, but not after what she did to me. I'm gonna take a cigarette break before I do something I regret. Is it a bad thing that all I dream about is squeezing my hands around Gwendolyn Paddington's neck until her every breath has expired?"

Chapter 3

After my trip to Paddington's Play House, Emma and I ate dinner and settled in for a movie. Emma convinced my mother to give up reading Aunt Deirdre's latest romance novel about Casanova and his voluptuous lover, Torrentia, who was dying of consumption, and instead watch an animated film about dogs ruling the world. An hour later, I lost count of how many times Emma inquired if we could get a puppy. We only convinced her to stop asking us once my mother agreed to make ice cream sundaes. Emma wasn't a big dessert connoisseur like me, but she loved butterscotch crunch. After I tucked my best girl into bed, I fell asleep dreaming about giant dogs headlining an astoundingly different production of *King Lear*. Even Myriam was present in the strange oddity, barking and all, as a wrinkled Shar-Pei playing the Fool advising Gwendolyn's Dalmatian version of Lear.

On Sunday morning, while my mother took Emma with her to church, I went for a run at Grey Sports Complex, Braxton College's sprawling athletic facility. As I ran the third loop around the indoor track, I remembered that I'd forgotten to re-schedule dinner with Maggie Roarke, my ex-girlfriend from college days. We'd recently met up again and were supposed to get together last Tuesday, but once Francesca showed up, I'd canceled citing the need for a couple more days to get Emma settled. Maggie asked me to call her this weekend to pick a new date. I hadn't done it yet, but I also no longer knew what I should do since Francesca was alive. Again, I stress a need for a handbook on dating protocols when you have a dead-not-so-dead spouse.

My mother-in-law and I had planned for Francesca to arrive this morning at ten o'clock. Since my mother would be at church and a subsequent banquet celebrating Lent, and my father wasn't coming home from his trip until late afternoon, it'd give us the entire house to ourselves to discuss the situation. I finished the run, showered, and arrived home as their limo pulled up. Cecilia and Francesca slipped through the back door and met me in the living room. Francesca lagged behind a bit.

When Francesca and I had met in California, she had long, flowing jet-black hair and wore makeup in muted, natural colors. With her new appearance, she'd cut her hair into a short bob, dyed it an interesting platinum blonde, and wore brash pinks and reds on her face. Even her clothing was different. She truly was a whole new woman, but not one I found as attractive. I didn't mean strictly in terms of beauty and sex appeal. Francesca's attitude seemed colder, more distant.

"How was New York?" I asked reaching for her hand as we sat on the couch.

"It was fun. I didn't get out much, but it felt good to see another city again." Francesca turned to her mother and said nervously, "Can you give us a little time alone?"

Cecilia agreed. "We only have forty-five minutes before we need to leave for the airport. I'll make a cup of tea in the kitchen." As she left the room, her overly sweet perfume lingered in the air. I'd always hoped she'd explore something other than Chanel Number Five, but Cecilia Castigliano was a creature of habit worthy of Mario Puzo's Vito Corleone.

When Francesca smiled, memories of our past flooded back. "Did you miss me?" she asked.

What kind of a question was that? I'd missed her for two years, three months, and fourteen days. Did she mean since I'd found out she was alive earlier that week? Since the day I saw what I thought was her dead body? Since I cradled our daughter and wiped away her tears every night for a month upon learning her mother had been killed?

"I don't know how to answer that question. Of course, I do, but where do we go from here?" I held myself back from saying too much too quickly. Staring at her nostalgic and hopeful face only made it hurt worse.

"I've apologized many times, Kellan. I had little choice in what my father did. If I try to resume my previous identity, they'll be too much damage. Not only will the Vargas family kill me, but they'll go after you and Emma, my parents, and anyone I know as part of their revenge." Several tears cascaded down her withdrawn cheeks in painfully slow motion. As I stared into the new blue color of her weary eyes, I sighed. She asked, "Do you still love me?"

I had given so much thought to how I felt since her return, but as awful as it sounded, would it be better to continue pretending for Emma's sake that her mother had truly died? Francesca inched closer to me and tickled my forearm the way she'd do every night before bed to relax me. There was still an intense connection, but it was enveloped by fear and apprehension. Would I always need to look over my shoulder to protect myself from what the Castiglianos had done? "I will never stop loving you. But how do we make this work?"

After we discussed various options and talked about how much Emma had grown, Francesca said, "I have to fly back to LA today. I want you to come with me... we can figure out a solution... maybe run away together. Or we can live together in secret in my parents' house... when Emma's old enough, we can tell her the truth. My father has to find a way to end this war, so I can come out of hiding."

I started to respond, but Cecilia stepped back into the room. "You know that will never be an option, bella. There are still many members of the Vargas family who are alive and angry they couldn't exact revenge against us the way they wanted to. A few don't believe you were accidentally killed by their driver. They don't see your death as a proper balance to everything."

I stood from the couch and reflected on the six years I had with Francesca before our happy world ceased to exist. All the parties we'd attended with my Hollywood colleagues. The quiet nights at home watching Emma sleep in her crib. The romantic, moonlit walks to the beach. Then I recalled the sleepless nights after Francesca died. The dark night I spent trying to understand how a drunk could get behind the wheel of a car and kill another human being. Or the tears I kissed on Emma's face the first day of school when the teacher asked why her mommy wasn't dropping her off anymore.

"Francesca, I can't do this to Emma. She can't be forced to keep secrets and live a life in hiding." Emma was undoubtedly my priority in all this chaos.

"I can't give up ever seeing her again, Kellan. We have a perfect solution back in LA. I can watch her grow up, and maybe one day in the future, I'll be able to actually talk to her." When Francesca began to sob, it was Cecilia who comforted her. I wanted to hold my wife, but I held back.

"We should go. Let's give Kellan time to come to the right decision. He'll return to LA, I'm certain of it. He's in shock, bella." Cecilia patted her daughter's back and offered me a cold, angry stare.

"I promise to give this some thought. How can I reach you, Francesca?" I asked knowing I could never abandon my family. As much as they frustrated me, I couldn't say goodbye to Nana D, my parents, Eleanor, or other siblings even if it meant I could be with Francesca again.

"You can't," Cecilia said sharply before ushering my wife toward the back door. "I expect you to return to LA soon, Kellan. You have two weeks to figure this out before I make the decision for you."

Before I could object, they snuck out the garage door and into the waiting limo. I could've stopped them, but I was too distressed thinking about all the pressure and the veiled threat of a decision being made for me. I paced the floor for at least ten minutes searching for a compromise, but nothing seemed plausible. In a moment of sheer frustration, I grabbed the door handle ready to pull the entire door off its hinges, but Emma's voice stopped me.

"We're home, Daddy. I brought you a red velvet cupcake," she said while running up to hug me. I basked in her innocence and love before she bounded up the steps to her room raving about a new cartoon someone had discovered at the church banquet.

I lifted my head and saw my mother staring back at me. "You look like someone just stole your favorite blanket, my son." And with that, she pulled me against her, squeezed as hard as she could, and kissed my cheek. "I'm always here if you need to talk, Kellan. Even though I sense there's something weighing heavily on your mind, I know better than to push you."

Just a few words from my mother helped me realize despite some of the awful situations going on around me, I still had loads of love and support in my life. She offered to take Emma shopping for the afternoon to buy some new spring clothes, then encouraged me to attend the *King Lear* dress rehearsal with Nana D and the Paddington family. Although I wasn't in the mood for heavy drama, I changed into a suit and dashed to the theater in a daze.

The performance started at two o'clock which meant I had at least thirty minutes to find Nana D and Gwendolyn to get my ticket. When I entered the lobby, there was a sea of guests meandering around aimlessly. Arthur entered the lobby and called approximately three-hundred guests to attention by instructing everyone where to look on their tickets for the assigned seat number. As people filed into the venue, the noise level grew more tolerable and I could freely move around without feeling every nook and cranny of every weirdo in the joint. First up was texting Nana D to find out where I'd be sitting. If she sat me next to some new Tinder blind date she'd coordinated...

Me: *Where are you? It's like a blue-haired Neil Diamond concert in here today.*
Nana D: *More like a wannabe Lady Gaga gig. Don't you know any current pop references?*
Me: *Given the number of septuagenarians, I assumed they wouldn't know whom she was.*
Nana D: *You know what happens when you ASS-U-ME, don't you, Kellan?*
Me: *That was weak even for you. Epic FAIL! Where's my ticket?*
Nana D: *I left it at the Box Office. Wasn't sure you'd show. Go get it. Now.*
Me: *Yes, chief. On my way. You're feisty today. Too much bran? Not enough veges?*
Nana D: *Pop a cork in it and get to your seat. You ain't seen nothing yet, brilliant one.*

I waved to Fern while passing by other colleagues whose names I'd failed to remember. As I approached the ticket window, Maggie looked up, smiled, and dropped a bag of programs to the floor. Her flawless alabaster skin was a perfect offset to rich brown hair and eyes that tempted everyone to fall in love with her.

"I didn't expect to see you here today," I said debating whether to lean in and hug her. Maggie made the decision when she stepped forward and kissed my cheek.

"I volunteered to hold tickets for anyone picking them up at will call. Then I'm seeing the show with Connor. He's finishing at the office and should be here any minute," Maggie said while stepping away from me. The fresh lavender smell of her skin comforted and teased me.

Did she consider it a date? The last time Connor and I had talked, my former best friend told me he'd been in love with my former girlfriend for years and planned to get to know her better. I hadn't seen either in a decade, so I didn't feel comfortable stopping them from taking a chance. Maggie could date whomever she wanted. Okay, except Connor. There, I said it out loud.

"Oh, sounds fun. I believe you might be holding a ticket for me," I noted timidly trying to keep myself from thinking about Maggie in any way other than as a friend.

"Oh, yes. Nana D dropped it off a few minutes ago. Come on back, it's inside the office. As I followed Maggie through the door, she asked me not to close it all the way. "It sometimes gets stuck, and you can only open it from the outside."

I found a small, wire wastepaper basket in the narrow hallway and wedged it between the door and its frame to prevent it from closing. "How've you been? I'm so sorry about canceling dinner last Tuesday."

Maggie smiled and placed her hand on top of mine. "Emma comes first. We have plenty of time to get to know each other again, right?"

Her warm touch reminded me of a finely spun silk scarf caressing my palm. Every cherished moment in our past together vied for control of my attention. A flood of heat surged through my torn body. I almost got lost in the moment, but a loud thud interrupted my thoughts. "What was that?" I asked turning around.

"Oh no, the door must've closed," Maggie moaned rushing past me and kicking the rolling wastepaper basket out of her way. She tried opening the door, but it wouldn't budge. I looked at the clock and verified we had several minutes before the show began. My phone chimed.

Nana D: *A brilliant person once told me to use my time wisely. I think you should heed the same advice. I'll let you out when the show starts. Go get her, tiger.*

"I think we'll be fine. It appears fate in the form of a nosy old woman who will be properly punished has intervened," I said shaking my head.

"Nana D?"

"Yep."

"She saw me struggle with the door earlier. I might've said something about it being broken."

Perhaps Nana D had a point, but what could one really do with such a short amount of time? All I could think about was that silly game we played in junior high school. As I remembered the name, Maggie said, "It's like we've been locked in the closet to play *Seven Minutes in Heaven.*" When she walked by me to access the back-office area, her skin flushed a deep shade of crimson.

"Are you saying being locked in here with me is like heaven?" I felt cheesy using the line, but so much of our past connection revolved around humor and acting silly. "It must be a thoroughly different game at thirty-two than it was at twelve, right?"

Maggie giggled and handed me my ticket. "It's been a long time since we actually kissed. Do you remember that night we got locked in the library?"

I did. "It was the night we first said I love you to one another."

A huge part of me wanted to take a few steps closer to Maggie to see if the touch of her lips against mine would ignite the same intensity it had years ago. It seemed like she was struggling with a similar longing and began leaning toward me.

When we met in the middle, we stood staring at one another for what felt like an eternity. Who would make the first move? I didn't think I was strong enough since I couldn't split my focus between her and Francesca. Foolishly, I asked, "Are you sure about this?"

The chemistry between us temporarily broke when the door busted open. I had just enough time to back two steps away before Connor saw us.

"Ah, did you get locked in again?" Connor said in a hesitant voice while squinting with concern. His all-black suit, dark and stormy complexion, and striking facial features made us both do a double take. Maggie because of his general sexiness according to all woman and half the male population, me because Connor had been a frequent weight-lifter who could easily knock me out with a single punch.

I released a bunch of hot air from my mouth. "Yes, thank you. I needed to get my ticket. I'm meeting Nana D and her friends."

As I rushed past, Connor stopped me. A musky cologne consumed the remaining oxygen between us in the small passageway. "It's good to see you. We should grab a beer sometime soon now that you're living in Braxton." His thick, rich Caribbean accent was more noticeable than normal.

"I like the sound of that," I mumbled while giving him an awkward thumbs-up sign. Was I back in college again? As I took off toward the double doors opening into the venue, Nana D winked. "Sorry, kiddo, I tried. But that man is one hot piece of beef we can't ignore. Pity I'm not ten years younger."

While we searched for our seats, I gagged over Nana D's comment. I also told myself Connor's interruption was a good thing. I couldn't get involved with Maggie until I knew what was going on with Francesca. Nor if Maggie and Connor were seriously interested in one another. They deserved a chance since I'd blown mine years ago.

I sat in the front center row between Nana D and Gwendolyn. To Gwendolyn's right was Eustacia, then Millard. Lindsey was on the other side of Nana D, which annoyed Eustacia since they were still involved in some sort of quirky, repressed love triangle. I apparently took after Nana D way more than I wanted to admit.

Gwendolyn leaned over to me. "I'm glad you came to your senses and attended the show. My son-in-law, Richard, was the one who canceled. That's whom you overheard me talking with yesterday."

"I'm sorry he's missed out. I hope you two can patch things up," I replied noticing Gwendolyn didn't look well. Her hands shook more than normal, and her breathing seemed labored.

"Richard's a pain in my ass. Always has been. I'll fix him one day, but right now, I'm more concerned about my son, Timothy," she spit out with a clear sense of frustration and mixed-emotions.

"I guess we never stop worrying about our kids, huh?" Emma's future reaction to learning her mother was still alive had frightened me to a point I'd never reached before as a parent.

"Timothy and I had a long talk last night. Important stuff. The relationship between parents and their children is never easy, Kellan. I've got a few pieces of dead fruit of my loins hanging around, and I intend to clear those limbs off the tree soon enough. Sometimes we don't know our family as well as we think we do. There's something everyone's hiding these days, even in your brood, too. I'm sure you'll find out soon enough." As Gwendolyn sat up straight with her back firmly pressed against the seat, I wondered what she'd meant by her last few comments. Was she talking about disinheriting them or evicting them from the house? And what did it have to do with my family?

I looked around to see whom else I knew. Dana and Arthur stood on the far corner of the stage embroiled in an animated discussion. I could hear people behind me chattering about this being Dana's first big role on a college production. I turned my head to the side and saw whom I thought was likely her mother,

Ophelia, whispering to someone directly behind me. I couldn't turn around further without it looking obvious, so I'd have to try again during the intermission. I heard Ophelia say, "It's not like she has anything else going on in her life. She's certainly my laziest child."

Ophelia could give her mother, Gwendolyn, a run for her money when bad-mouthing her own children. Just as the other person behind me was about to respond, Myriam stepped to the stage, organized her notes on the podium, and introduced the debut performance of *King Lear*. The first half lasted about an hour and kept everyone entertained. Despite their differences, Arthur and Myriam pulled off an engaging performance full of wit, depth, and intelligence.

When intermission began, I stood to stretch in such a way I could see who was behind us. I was clearly able to tell Ophelia and Jennifer were sisters given their shoulder-length, chestnut-brown hair, sparkling green eyes, and golden-tan complexion. Ophelia was the older of the pair, probably early to mid-fifties, but it was evident only in a few fine lines beginning to develop around her mouth and on her forehead. She probably wore top-tier designer clothes only released on this year's fashion runway and had been to the salon moments before the show. To say she'd recently had a lengthy blow-out would be over-stating the obvious. How did hair triple in size to such an all-consuming degree?

Jennifer was less bold in her appearance. Instead of faint hints of aging, the contours of her face were smoother and softer with a penchant for dark, moody colors. She was an inch taller than her sister putting her closer to my range, but she since wore heels we were practically the same height. Jennifer dressed more casually covering up her svelte figure with a stylish black A-line dress and silver wrap.

When Nana D and her friends stepped into the aisle in search of the restroom, I listened in to Jennifer's and Ophelia's conversation. Jennifer said, "Mother has been particularly difficult the last few weeks. Every time we have one of her little chats, it's an inquisition. I'm forty-seven years old and do not need her relentless judgment."

Ophelia nodded in agreement. "Awful. I know we're supposed to love our parents, but it's time for her to get with the program or take her final bow."

"You said it. I wish she'd learn to be kinder and more open-minded. I feel like she's always miserable and never thinks about what's best for us. It's constantly what she wants," Jennifer sniped.

"That's why Timothy avoided it all today. He's the only one in the family who didn't show up," Ophelia said. Timothy was the middle brother, but I hardly knew anything about him nor had I ever met the man as far as I could recall. While Timothy and Jennifer didn't have any kids, Ophelia had two others besides Dana. I'd just never been introduced to either of them.

"Except your husband. Where is Richard these days… off galivanting again?" Jennifer accused with a gaze that seemed to penetrate right through Ophelia's skin and scratch at her iron composure.

"He's meeting with clients. At least I can keep a husband around. Still waiting for mother's approval, are you?" Ophelia continued their vicious barbs against one another. "You know the only way to control her is to stand up to her. Mother doesn't like it when we all stick together or say *no* to her."

Jennifer stood as if to walk away, then chose not to. "Maybe we should all confront her and tell her it's time to let go of Father's money and give us our inheritances."

"Let's discuss it another time. I need to talk with Dana before the second half. Can you get out of my way?" Ophelia demanded while waving both hands furiously.

When Ophelia went searching for Dana, and Jennifer wandered closer to the stage, I strolled to the lobby to hunt for Nana

D. I couldn't find her but saw Gwendolyn talking to a man in his fifties. They looked like they were arguing. As I approached, it appeared like he grabbed hold of her wrist with intensity. Gwendolyn almost spilled her drink from the pressure he'd applied. By the time I reached her, he'd already walked away.

"Are you okay, Mrs. Paddington? It looked like that man was harassing you," I asked scanning the room to see if he was still nearby.

"That was my son, Timothy. He needed to talk to me for a minute. Have you seen Brad around?" Gwendolyn asked appearing like she was about to fall apart.

"I don't know anyone named Brad," I responded as Nana D walked up with a younger guy.

"Brad is Gwennie's nurse. She can't find the travel bottle with her medicine in her purse. I called him earlier to drop it off." Nana D introduced me to Brad, a fit guy in his mid-twenties wearing skinny jeans and a heather gray sweater.

"I'm right here, Mrs. Paddington. Here's your medication." Brad handed her several pills.

"You'll have to explain to me how we screwed this up earlier. I thought you'd put the bottle in my purse. But I don't have time to discuss it right now. I'm coming right home once the show ends," Gwendolyn noted before tossing the pills into her mouth. From the brief glimpse I had, there were three tablets ranging from small to large sizes and coated in different colors. Brad waited for her to swallow them, reminded her to take a sip of her iced tea to wash them down, and then disappeared probably used to being dismissed as one of the servants who knew his place in the household.

"Should we take you home? I'm like your older brother. You should listen to me," Millard said.

"Nah, I'll be fine. Just lost my breath for a few minutes. Let's go sit down," Gwendolyn replied.

We all scrambled into the theater and took our seats. Jennifer and Ophelia had already returned and stood near one another but were clearly not speaking. While Eustacia held her sister-in-law's glass, Lindsey helped Gwendolyn get seated. Nana D introduced me to Ophelia's two other children, Sam, a senior at Braxton, and Lilly who'd graduated two years earlier. Neither noticed their grandmother profusely sweating or her inability to get situated without nearly falling. The Paddingtons were a strange family. Everyone seemed to care enough to show up, but no one looked fond of one another.

When the lights blinked several times, Myriam stepped onto the stage to announce intermission was over and the show was about to begin. A few seconds later, the theater went dark. The actors portraying King Lear and the Fool appeared on stage for one of my favorite sets of witty and revealing dialogs. Midway into the scene, something bumped my right shoulder. I looked to the side only to notice Gwendolyn leaning into me. I whispered, "Is the performance that boring?" but she didn't answer.

I nudged her arm thinking she'd fallen asleep, but that didn't rouse her either. I shook her more forcefully. Gwendolyn wouldn't respond. I activated the flashlight on my cell phone and shined it on her face. It appeared Gwendolyn had passed out after the lights went down. I pressed my fingers into her cool and saturated neck searching for her carotid artery. I couldn't find a pulse, nor could I find any sign of life. I leaned over to Nana D and said, "I think Gwendolyn just died in her seat!"

Chapter 4

Interrupting a live theater performance was not an easy task. While my stomach revolted over finding another dead body and having it physically leaning against me in the dark, I made use of my extensive grasp on the English language to delicately inform the actors we needed to stop the show. As Lear emphatically cursed the weather surrounding him, I'd been forced to shout over him from a few feet off center stage. First came the boos and sounds of people hushing my disturbance. Then the actor portraying Lear turned to me in full character questioning if I were the impetuous and virulent storm about to hit the stage. Thankfully, once the lighting director moved the spotlight to my seat, the entire troupe could see I was serious about someone needing medical attention.

Myriam assumed control of the stage and directed all the guests to quietly and orderly file into the main lobby. Nana D volunteered to call 9-1-1 as I kept Gwendolyn's family from rushing up to check on her. I knew the woman had passed away, and while I hadn't truly given credence to her suspicions about someone in her family trying to kill her, it was important to prevent what could be a crime scene from contamination. I'd learned that tenet many times over in the past from our county sheriff.

Eustacia moaned loudly and turned to Lindsey for comfort. Millard, her brother, stepped to the side aisle to provide some space, but I was too focused on Ophelia's daughters to listen to his conversation. A tear-stained Jennifer breathed in and out in an almost panicked mode but soon gained control of her composure. Ophelia kept looking toward two of her children to see how they were reacting, but she didn't appear to be shocked or devastated by her mother's passing. Dana was still back stage and probably hadn't known who'd fallen ill or what'd stopped the performance.

"The ambulance is on its way," Nana D said in a soothing but despondent voice. "My poor friend, Gwennie. She wasn't feeling well earlier, but I didn't know it was so serious."

I wrapped my arms around my grandmother who'd leaned against me for comfort. "She did have a little spell out in the lobby earlier. I'm wondering if she had a heart attack or a stroke."

Maggie stood closer to the stage tilting her head in a way I knew she was telling me everything would be okay. I always could read her expressions as though I were inside her mind, too. Connor arrived within a few seconds desperate to take control of the situation. As the head of the Braxton Campus Security Office, he'd be the first on the scene even if he hadn't been on a date with Maggie. After checking Gwendolyn's pulse, Connor pulled Nana D and me aside. "She's definitely gone. I'm so sorry for her family," he said with sorrow while resting a hand on Nana D's shoulder.

"Connor, you need to check for evidence right away," whispered Nana D while tugging on his sport coat. "Gwennie told me someone was trying to hurt her in the last few weeks. She knew something was wrong. We should've done something sooner about it."

"Nana D, I'm sure the coroner will check for any sign of something unnatural happening." I didn't want to stir the pot when we were already in an awkward state.

Connor's gaze opened wide. "Are you saying you think someone tried to kill her today, Mrs. Danby?" He looked at me for confirmation, but I shrugged my shoulders. I was distracted first by everything going on, then by Arthur's wide grin while talking on his cell phone near the stage steps.

Nana D explained that her friend had been feeling fine up until the prior month when she began having dizzy spells and feeling short of breath. Gwendolyn initially thought it was a touch of the flu or a bad winter cold. After nearly four weeks, Lindsey and Nana D had convinced Gwendolyn to listen to Brad who'd wanted to schedule an appointment with her doctor. In the last two weeks, she'd vomited several times and her skin tone had grown paler each day. She'd even felt disoriented in her own house but blamed it on lack of being able to keep down any food or get a full night's sleep.

"Did she tell you she thought someone was trying to hurt her?" Connor asked.

I nodded. "She mentioned something funny was going on at the Paddington mansion and planned to address it with her family after the doctor's visit."

As the paramedics arrived, I stepped to the side to let them work. Connor returned to Maggie who waited with him while he made a phone call. Nana D sat a few seats further away near Millard, Eustacia, and Lindsey. The Septuagenarian Club had lost one of their founding members and comforted one another in a way no one else could. While Nana D placed something inside her oversized purse, she nodded at me and pointed toward the stage.

Arthur ended his phone call, then spoke with Myriam who appeared quite rattled. Arthur disappeared behind the curtain prompting Myriam to approach me with a scowl plastered on her face.

"You seem to find yourself in the middle of everything these days, Kellan. Ever since you returned to Braxton, '*Death, that hath suck'd the honey of thy breath,*' follows you like a ghost to Hamlet's conscience," Myriam criticized before clearing her throat.

"Romeo said that while putting Paris in the tomb, I believe, didn't he? You're mixing the Bard's greatest tragedies." I wanted to ask Myriam what her outlandish fascination was with Shakespearean quotes, particularly at inappropriate times, but I was interrupted by Ophelia. I felt sufficiently satisfied about getting in at least one dig.

"I recognize that line. How fitting, my mother loved Romeo and Juliet. She died of a broken heart from missing my father the last year," Ophelia said with a faint smile, then sighed. She ran a few fingers through the many layers of her voluminous hair and adjusted a diamond earring. "Myriam, tell me, how has Dana's work been on the show thus far?"

I tuned out while they discussed Ophelia's youngest daughter's participation in *King Lear*. Was this the time to bring up such a topic? Ophelia had as much tact as Myriam had kindness in her bones. I glanced toward Ophelia's other two children noticing Lilly, the eldest, listening as her brother, Sam, spoke to their Aunt Jennifer.

Lilly seemed disinterested in the conversation and kept leaning away to look at the paramedics as they attended to her grandmother. Perfectly styled, ruler-straight ebony hair cascaded down her back against a stuffy, jade-green silk blouse that belonged on someone older like Gwendolyn or Eustacia. It was pulled tightly across her ample chest and disappeared into high-waisted pants that forced her to walk erect like a model balancing a book on the top of her had. Angular features stood out against hollow cheeks and widely-set eyes that furiously darted from side to side. It made her appear gaunt and sickly, but also as though she thought she was more important than the crowd surrounding her.

Other than once witnessing Lilly berate a barista at The Big Beanery over a weak café au lait, all I'd known about her was that she'd survived a skiing accident that had occurred years earlier while her college roommate hadn't been so lucky. During winter break in their junior year, they'd been competing on one of the more treacherous slopes in the Wharton Mountains. Lilly had fallen into her friend who tumbled down the mountain and careened directly into a large fir tree. Lilly eventually stopped herself before she encountered the same fate but couldn't recall what had prompted her to fall. There had been another friend, a boy they'd both dated that year, who was supposed to ski with them but had gotten food poisoning the night before. I'd heard the story from Eleanor who'd been a part-time ski instructor on the mountain. She always felt there was more to the event than what Lilly had told everyone.

Myriam excused herself to meet with the cast about the next rehearsal. Ophelia rushed off citing a need to use the restroom, but it was clear she didn't want to be left alone to talk with me. I'd only met her moments before yet knew enough to recognize a blow-off when I saw one. My gaze returned to Jennifer who was hugging Lilly and Sam before leaving the theater. Lilly walked toward her sister, Dana, and they both vanished into the lobby laughing presumably about something funny one of them had just said. Dana wore a low-cut magenta top with her bare shoulders and midriff showing as though it were the middle of spring or summer. Though the room was heated, the chill in the air couldn't be ignored. Dana wore too little clothing for this event in my opinion. Despite being a red-blooded American man, I believed there was a fine line between dressing sexy and inappropriately.

Sam disappeared in a corner several rows away from everyone. The distant, withdrawn look in his bright green eyes revealed intense pain over losing someone he'd loved. Nana D had often remarked how sweet and kind he'd always been to her in the past. '*Not like a typical pompous or irascible Paddington,*' she'd quip whenever visiting Gwendolyn and he'd been home. Sam's slight build and babyface made him appear younger than a college senior. His neatly combed, straw-colored blond hair and delicate features reminded me of a Norman Rockwell painting. There seemed to be a maturity and quietness about him unlike his siblings.

He smiled despite my interrupting his solitude. "I'm so sorry about your grandmother, Sam. I lost my grandpop several years ago. I still remember it like it were only yesterday."

"Thank you, I'm in a bit of shock," Sam replied shifting back and forth on the heels of his feet. "We spent a lot of time together. We both loved the theater so much."

"Mrs. Paddington was a prominent supporter of the arts. I'm sure she will be missed. How's your family holding up?" I asked hoping to learn more from someone on the inside.

"Do I know you, I mean, have we met… never mind." Sam looked perplexed at my words but responded in a gentle voice. "Mom's strong. She and Grandmother didn't get along very well, but I know she'll collapse at some point. Aunt Jennifer is a mess, even said she had to leave before everyone noticed how awful she looked. I wish I could go, but Lilly is my ride back home."

"Were your sisters close to her, too?"

"Not particularly. Grandmother could be difficult if you didn't know how to handle her. She respected honesty and directness. I learned that early on and tried to always remain on her good side," Sam said looking weary and as if he'd become desperate to leave. "I'm sorry, I didn't get your name."

"I apologize," I responded, realizing I'd forgotten to introduce myself. Although I knew whom he was, he hadn't a clue why I still hung around. "I'm Kellan Ayrwick, Seraphina Danby's grandson. I was sitting next to Mrs. Paddington when she, um… fell ill. I'd met her many times through my grandmother. They've been best friends for over fifty years."

Sam smiled nervously, then pulled back as if he'd felt awkward having any moment of positivity given the circumstances. "Or frenemies from what I hear, too. Ayrwick, you said?" A look of confusion clouded his face as he processed our conversation.

I nodded. "Yes, they've had their ups and downs in the past. I wonder if it was a heart attack or if anything else was going on with her health."

Sam pulled out his phone. "I should go. Nice to meet you. I appreciate you being there for her just now... you know... when..."

"I understand. You're welcome," I replied. Sam rushed away leaving me concerned why his mood further soured near the end of our conversation. He exited into the lobby, then took off through the front doors by himself. So much for waiting for a ride from his sister, Lilly.

While none of the Paddingtons seemed like potential killers, they were all mysterious and disparate from one another. The family certainly had enough money. I couldn't be sure about the younger generation's personal lives or spending habits. I'd have to ask Nana D, or maybe Millard and Eustacia could fill in the blanks. It wasn't any of my business, but if one of them had purposely caused Gwendolyn's death, I should let Sheriff Montague know.

The paramedics informed everyone they were going to remove the body soon. It was a polite way of indicating it was time for us to leave the building since no one would want to see Gwendolyn being tucked into a black body bag. Nana D was watching everyone else get into Lindsey's car, holding her purse strangely so that it wouldn't fall. As I unlocked my SUV's door, Sheriff Montague's motorcycle pulled up. She parked near the entrance and removed her helmet, then went inside. I'd never seen the woman wear anything fashionable before today. Now she'd had on designer black jeans and knee-high gray leather boots. Under her open form-fitting rain coat, a purple silk blouse and cream-colored scarf stared back at me. Perhaps she had a personal life like the rest of us and didn't live in a dark cave despite my theory she were a hermit or a troll.

"Kellan, I need to speak with you," whispered Nana D before I pulled the SUV's door shut. Nana D ran around to the other side and snuck into the passenger seat. "Shh, don't say anything."

I had no idea what Nana D was trying to hide, but she opened her purse and pulled out a half-empty glass with a straw sticking out the top. She'd wrapped a piece of cloth over the top, so she wasn't touching anything. "What is that?" I asked fearing the worst.

"Gwennie's iced tea. She hadn't finished it, and I was afraid the cleaning staff would throw it out." Nana brimmed with excitement about why she'd kept the glass.

"I don't understand. What's that for?" I grabbed the glass careful not to touch any surface with my fingers.

"Evidence. You need to have this tested to see if someone drugged Gwennie," Nana D said bluntly while slapping my arm with her free hand. "Do I have to do *everything*?"

"Even if someone put something in her drink, you've contaminated it. Why didn't you leave it there?" I slapped my forehead in disbelief with my free hand.

"Don't be absurd! I used my handkerchief and didn't touch anything. I told Connor it was a suspicious death, but I didn't know if he'd call that lazy sheriff."

"Well, April Montague is here now. What are you planning to do with the glass?"

Nana D pulled back. "Me? I can't be involved in this. I'm running for Wharton County Mayor. You need to take it from here. Someone's gotta protect Gwennie now that she's gone."

There are days I wish my nana was an eccentric old woman who liked to sit home and play Yahtzee or do needlepoint. Maybe talk to herself or twenty cats about the price of a bottle of unpasteurized milk prior to the Great War. But Nana D wouldn't let the barn cats indoors and she had a lactose intolerance—neither of those things were possible. Nor was she ever the type to act her age. Instead, I had a super-charged nana who interfered in everyone's business and thrust herself into every possible kind of trouble. Is this what I'd turn into when I reached her age? I'd have to warn Emma to put me in a home far away from everyone.

"Nana D, I can't hand a glass of iced tea to the sheriff and demand she run lab tests on it. One, she already dislikes me. Two, it will make her angry that I took evidence away from a crime scene. Three, she'll accuse me of trying to go around her to solve another crime. Four, she'll—"

"That's what's wrong with you, Kellan. You think like you're stuck inside a box. Life's not about staying within four perfect walls or coloring within the lines." Nana D held her hands making the shape of a square with her fingers, then zoomed it in and out of my face. "It's blurry kinda like your vision, Magoo. I'm sure you're smart enough to realize that sometimes you can get away with anything you want by claiming you didn't know any better."

"That might work for a meddlesome member of the Septuagenarian Club, but I highly doubt Sheriff Montague will believe me if I said I didn't know any better when it came to contaminating evidence."

"Fine. If you don't want to help me, poor Gwennie's soul will roam around Braxton unable to properly pass over to the other side because she didn't know who killed her. *Tsk tsk.*" Nana D pursed her lips and shook her head. "Such a good woman. Stuck in between like those *Beetlejuice* characters. You don't want Eleanor to have to host a séance, do you, Kellan? Think of the dangers in doing that—"

"Are you trying to guilt me into finding Gwendolyn's killer? She might not have been murdered. This could have been a normal, natural death. Seriously, why don't you let the sheriff poke around and if something seems off, we can come up with a better plan later on? They're going to have to do an autopsy anyway."

"Kellan Michael Ayrwick! I am wiser and more experienced than you. I am your elder by a couple of years. I have a right to—"

"More than a couple years, if you're trying to be an honest candidate for mayor," I said unable to stop myself. That's when Nana D slapped my cheek and almost caused me to bang the iced tea glass into the rearview mirror. "Ouch. Uncalled for!"

"Totally called for. My point is... you better do something about this, or I will disown you."

"No, you won't."

Nana D rolled her bright bug eyes. Now I knew where I got it from. She continued to taunt me saying, "Fine, you're right. I won't disown you, but I will set you up with every available harebrained girl in this town. I'll have you fending off more cougars and petty criminals than that fool of a district attorney currently in office. She's next on my list as soon as you understand I'm right about testing this iced tea."

Nana D had it out for every branch of Wharton County's government. "Ugh, go away, Beelzebub," I said with a grimace while re-positioning the glass, so I could keep it hidden under my coat. "I'll find a way to fix your mistake." While Nana D went back to her own car whining "*I don't make mistakes,*" I walked toward the side entrance of Paddington's Play House.

As I scurried through the hallway in the backstage area, I saw Dana talking to Arthur. I stood for a moment to listen to their conversation.

"I can't believe she's gone," Dana said. "I know she's my grandmother, and I'm supposed to be upset, but she was always so cruel to me. It's better off this way. Now I'll finally get some of my own money and won't have to listen to my family anymore."

Arthur responded, "She was a royal pain, wasn't she? No offense, but the world's a much better place without Gwendolyn Paddington. She got what she deserved."

They stopped speaking, and in fear they might catch me listening, I kept moving. When I made it to the curtain, I looked down at the seating area. Only the paramedics were still around. I waited for them to roll the stretcher with the body through the main aisle before I snuck down the stage stairs. What had my days come to? I was helping my nana sneak evidence back into a potential crime scene, so the sheriff could find it on her own accord.

I quickly put the glass into the seat's cup holder and rushed up the stairs toward the stage. As I stepped behind the curtain and tucked the handkerchief in my pocket, I noticed the sheriff looking in my direction. I wasn't sure if April saw me, but I knew it wouldn't be ideal to get caught handling evidence. Connor pointed to the iced tea glass, then the sheriff called to an officer standing at the side of the room. A few seconds later, she bagged and labeled the glass. I wasn't sure how I'd have gotten her to inspect the glass if they hadn't done it on their own, but luckily it wasn't a concern now. Instead of returning to my car, I stopped next door at The Big Beanery for a cup of coffee and a pastry filled with as much sugary cream or jelly as I could find. I'd earned it. As I entered through the door, my phone beeped.

Connor: *I covered for you, but you better explain what was going on with that glass and why you sneaked it back into the theater.*
Me: *I owe you dinner. I promise, there's a valid explanation. Call me when you're done flirting with your girlfriend. Give the sheriff a hug from me.*
Connor: *Watch it, or I'll tell her the truth about you. She and I are not dating, Purple Panty Boy.*

Connor liked to use my dreaded nickname from college days, but I was too distracted dealing with another dead body. It brought me tumbling back to thinking about Francesca. As I settled into the corner table trying to keep myself from ordering a second dessert, Maggie walked into The Big Beanery. Why did thoughts of the two greatest loves of my life always come in pairs since I'd come back home?

Chapter 5

"Hey, stranger. Didn't I just see you a little while ago?" Maggie said in a coy tone with a large smile displaying bright white teeth.

"Yes, but that was before the drama. Although I feel bad for the Paddington family, I'm glad to see you again." Between the unexpected death and my determined attempt to avoid memories of Francesca, I'd originally thought being alone was the best thing for me. Sharing an afternoon cup of coffee with Maggie changed my mind.

"What happened?" she asked signaling to a server for a large decaf. When it was delivered, I handed the kid a ten-dollar bill and told him to keep the change. I didn't want to be interrupted again.

"I'm not sure if there's any merit to Gwendolyn Paddington's fears, but if the sheriff or coroner find anything concerning, we might have another murder in Braxton. I'm starting to think it's all because I returned home."

Maggie cocked her head like I'd spoken some foreign language. "Perhaps you're being a little self-involved with that theory? You had nothing to do with the other deaths, and I'm fairly certain even if someone killed Gwendolyn, it wasn't because of you."

"I didn't mean it that way. I'm not saying people are dying because I came back, I just meant—"

Maggie playfully tapped my right hand. "I was teasing." Her fingers lingered, making me think back to what might have happened when we were stuck in the Box Office before Connor's interruption. "Gwendolyn was in her mid-seventies. There's every chance it could've been a heart attack or something else normal. Let's wait until we hear if this is anything suspicious."

"I know. I just got strange vibes from her family. Do you know much about them?"

Maggie shook her head. "Since I've only been back for the one semester, I never had a chance to interact with Lilly. I helped Sam find a book on some rare plants and flowers several weeks ago, but we barely spent much time together. Dana and I have had a few interesting encounters in the library."

"Really… such as?" I asked guessing it related to an intimate discussion with Arthur. "Do tell!"

"Dana is extremely boy crazy. When she gets a crush on someone, she goes to great lengths to capture his attention. Last month, she claimed to be in love with one of my student workers and snuck into the archive room. I still don't know how she got in without anyone seeing, but she'd arranged a picnic lunch and was wearing minimal clothing."

"Was the student worker with her?"

"No, Jordan kept saying he was worried about an upcoming exam, so I finally told him to quit bugging me and leave. He mentioned accidentally leaving the door to the archive room unlocked which is how I found Dana crying and drinking from a nearly empty bottle of wine. I suspect Jordan was afraid to meet her, so he rushed out and forced me to be the one to find her."

"Dana sounds like she's a bit of a troublemaker," I said. Jordan Ballantine was a good kid I'd met earlier that month when he was a suspect on a murder investigation. He was also one of my students, and now that I remembered, he was Fern's nephew which made him Arthur's cousin. It seemed Dana liked to focus on guys in the same family.

"The next day, when I asked why he did that, Jordan claimed she was 'Jack Nicholson in *The Shining*' crazy. She'd been texting him to come find her and sending him compromising pictures. Apparently, she doesn't like to be told *no*." Maggie finished her coffee, then mentioned she was meeting Connor for dinner later that evening since their date at the theater had been preempted.

I thanked her for the information, suggested a day for our dinner the upcoming week, and pretended to be happy she had a date with someone else. As I finished up my coffee, Connor called. Had his ears been burning? I explained what Nana D had done, and he promised to keep our actions quiet assuming our fingerprints didn't show up on the glass despite our supposed intent to be careful.

"Next time inform Nana D that I listen when she tells me things. That grandmother of yours is going to outlast all of us," Connor jested.

"Did you learn any new information after I left Paddington's Play House?" I asked, curious whether he believed anything suspicious had occurred.

"The sheriff ordered an autopsy given the death happened in a public place when the deceased had just taken pills that might have been misplaced earlier that day. She wanted to know the exact cause of death before proceeding with anything else. April was angry the paramedics cleared the body before her team could investigate, but since it occurred so quickly, she couldn't say much."

"What happens next?" I asked, debating whether any delays were going to be an issue. If there was a killer, could they be hiding any additional evidence at Gwendolyn's home right now?

"The coroner and lab will be done tonight with preliminary observations on cause of death. Both agreed to rush their analyses, so the sheriff could get appropriate warrants to search the house. She's also inquiring with the family to understand if anyone thinks there's reasonable cause for this amounting to anything other than natural causes."

"Because of what Nana D said?"

"That's part of it. April also overheard people talking about an argument Gwendolyn had with her son, Timothy, in the lobby during intermission. That's also how she knew about the issue with the misplaced pills when the nurse showed up."

"I heard it, too. Something seemed odd in Gwendolyn's discussion with the nurse about misplaced pills."

"Don't put yourself in the middle of an investigation again, Kellan, if there's even a need for one. Please let the Sheriff's Office do their work," Connor grunted before hanging up.

I walked back to my SUV anxious to get home for dinner with Emma and away from the devastation of the afternoon. Although it seemed morbid at first, I'd bought my new vehicle from the estate of a friend, Lorraine, who'd been killed several weeks earlier. Her brother's highly discounted offer helped me maintain a connection to someone I'd cared for. When I asked my sister, Eleanor, whether it was a good idea, she consulted her Tarot cards and quickly learned I was meant to stay connected with Lorraine even though she'd passed over to The Great Beyond. It's not that I don't believe in spirits, but I've never met one before and honestly, it's just not my thing. I leave the supernatural and horoscope stuff to Eleanor. And if Lorraine ever showed up as a ghost riding shotgun in her former vehicle claiming she wanted to help solve Gwendolyn's murder, I'd sell the haunted SUV to the first interested party. As I started the engine, my phone chimed.

Nana D: *I forced Lindsey to tell me about Gwennie's will.*
Me: *Isn't that a violation of some law? Shouldn't he maintain her confidences?*

Nana D: *Lindsey's retired. He transferred the will with Gwennie's permission to another attorney a few years ago. Besides, we won't tell anyone else, will we?*

Me: *Most unbecoming for a mayoral candidate. What did it say?*

Nana D: *That hairdo of yours is unbecoming. At the time Lindsey worked on it, Gwennie and Charles had planned to leave everything to all three of their children, but something changed right around the time Charles died. Lindsey said Gwennie was keen on altering the will again.*

Me: *Who inherits now?*

Nana D: *Gwennie wouldn't tell Lindsey anything about the adjustment. Anyone could've killed her thinking they were still included in the will and set to inherit.*

* * *

As soon as I arrived home, my mother left to meet my father for dinner since he'd been away all weekend. I spent the rest of Sunday evening eating and assembling a puzzle with Emma. She'd chosen a collage of zoo animals at the bookstore earlier in the week. We baked peanut butter cookies in the shape of cows and sheep while play-fighting over who got to work on all the puzzle corners. I let her find three out of four corners, but never them all. It was important she knew the value of being a good loser.

Since Spring Break began at Braxton on Monday, classes weren't in session for the next week. I planned to spend a few hours on campus each day, but I also wanted to help get Emma settled in second grade at her new school. The school's principal and Board of Education had agreed to let her skip forward a year based on past exam results and a successful interview the prior week. I stayed for thirty minutes to watch her interact with other kids before leaving for Braxton. If I hadn't known better, my precocious and mature daughter was trying to push me out the door.

When I got to Memorial Library, I researched an upcoming digital project required as part of one of the courses I taught. After securing enough hours with the librarians for the whole class, I finished grading my last few papers in one of the reading rooms rather than trek back to my office on South Campus. Ten minutes later, Fern waved to me and asked if she could sit for a moment. I assumed the Dean of Student Affairs also didn't have off this week and was using the time to catch up on administrative functions. "What brings you to the library today? I can't imagine you're saddled with grading papers like me!"

"I'm reviewing the proposals from this year's student committee assigned to the cable car upgrades. There are some doozies in here, Kellan." Every year, the graduating class proposed three ideas for re-designing the interior of the cable car that ran from North Campus to South Campus.

"What do you think will win?" I asked recalling my own year's debacle over choosing a *Spartan 300* theme. A picture of me in a highly unflattering outfit still hung in the Alumni Office for all to see.

"Heaven help us, but the committee's favorite is an apocalypse caused by global warming and a cyber takeover," she sighed heavily. "What happened to the lighter sides of life? I'd even go for *Star Wars* again since it's become so popular."

"Good luck with that. How's Arthur doing since yesterday's incident?" I asked cautiously. After I'd overheard him backstage, I knew he was fine. It'd be eye-opening to learn what his mother thought.

"Oh, he's surviving." Fern squished together her lips and nose, then covered her face with both hands. "It was awful. I didn't care much for Gwendolyn Paddington, but I felt bad for her family. At least her death occurred in one of her favorite places. That's a comfort if nothing else."

"I interacted with them in the theater while the paramedics were onsite. Did Arthur know them well?" I asked hoping Fern would innocently share something valuable.

"Gwendolyn got him the job. She was very supportive back when he was in high school, but something changed in their relationship and she turned on him. He doesn't talk about it much anymore, but I know all about what she did to him afterward." Fern shook her head and made a *tsk tsk* sound.

My ears perked up. "I knew there was bad blood between them. Arthur mentioned it one day, but I didn't realize the feud had gone back so far."

"Well, he asked her to introduce him to her contacts in New York City when he moved there after graduating from high school. She'd been coaching the drama club back then and praised his talent, but she wanted him to get a degree at Braxton so he was a step ahead of everyone before taking his chances on Broadway."

"And things fell apart?"

"There was some sort of disagreement. She'd offered to introduce him to a few of her friends, but he was foolish. He'd gotten full of himself and used her name too much. He inherited those traits from his father. I should've left the man sooner, but unfortunately, I tried to make it work. Anyway, Gwendolyn chastised him for overstepping a boundary and blackballed him across the industry. She could be vicious. That's why he came back to Braxton to get his degree a few years afterward."

It made sense. I'd only seen him around campus twice my senior year, but he'd become suddenly snobby and difficult. "If she was angry, why did she give him the job directing the *King Lear* play?"

"Well, there's the reason I know, and there's the reason I suspect." Fern smirked and made a funny noise in her throat like she was frustrated with the whole series of events.

I laughed. "That sounds... confusing. Or intriguing."

"Myriam was stuck last-minute when the woman she thought was going to direct the show had to bow out after getting a national tour for an up-and-coming comedy revival. I happened to be meeting with her and Gwendolyn to discuss the plans for the production. I suggested that Arthur could pitch in knowing he hadn't been able to find a job for the last few months. The doting mom in me couldn't stop myself." A mixed look of pride and embarrassment overtook her calm and confident expression.

"So, what were the two reasons she said yes?"

"Gwendolyn felt bad about how hard she was on Arthur and wanted to give him another chance. She also despised Myriam more than anyone I know." In the brief moment before Fern spoke again, our eyes connected and part of me wondered whether Fern realized I might be the only one who disliked Myriam even more. "I suspect Gwendolyn wanted to witness Arthur and Myriam battle it out purely for her own entertainment. Not exactly mature, but she wasn't always the nicest of people."

"Based on what I know about her, she would do something like that," I responded. Could Gwendolyn have been wrong thinking it was her family trying to hurt her? Perhaps Myriam or Arthur exacted revenge on the unsuspecting and tetchy septuagenarian.

"Both women had been giving him a hard time while preparing for the show. Apparently, Myriam told Arthur this morning that she no longer needed his services and set him free with only two weeks' notice." Fern rubbed her fingers against the surface of the table while determining what to say next. "She's completely within her rights as the head of the drama department to make the decision. I'm not even sure who will represent the Paddington family anymore. I wondered if you might know whom I could speak with to convince Myriam not to push my son out."

Now I understood why Fern wanted to talk with me. "I don't know the Paddingtons all that well, but I suppose I could ask one of them." I wasn't exactly certain how it all came together. Gwendolyn was Braxton's patron for the art and theater program. She represented the Paddington family on all decisions regarding the Play House and its operations. Was it a formal position given to someone upon her death or a volunteer role within the family to look out for the campus and its creative endeavors?

I agreed to discuss it with Eustacia knowing I was meeting her and Nana D at the Paddington mansion for lunch that afternoon. When Fern left, I finished grading my papers for the remaining classes. I felt bad giving two students an 'F,' but one had clearly plagiarized an online database of essays written by an esteemed college professor. The other failed to visit the writing center which was a requirement for the assignment. I'd counted thirty-eight grammatical and spelling errors many of which would have been caught by a word processing program's spellchecker. Despite my education and experience, I still made a few mistakes now and again, but his paper was unreadable.

I drove to Millionaire's Mile, a mile-long street running parallel to the Braxton cable car system between the two campuses, where several enormous estates resided. The Paddington mansion was set between the Grey and Stanton properties and loomed over everything in the vicinity. The house had originally belonged to Eustacia's and Millard's parents, but when they died it was left to their son, Charles Paddington, even though he wasn't the oldest son. I never understood why and made a mental note to ask Nana D how that had all worked out years ago. Charles, Gwendolyn's late husband, had assumed responsibility for running the family businesses, Paddington Enterprises, for many years before turning it over to his son, Timothy. The conglomerate was comprised of a number of financial advisory firms, shipping warehouses and docks along the Finnulia River and Crilly Lake, and real estate investment and development holding companies.

Although I'd driven by the Paddington estate in the past, I was never invited through the gates to explore the crown jewel of all the homes in Braxton. The three-story estate had four separate wings and had been built in the early twentieth century using reclaimed materials from a Georgia manor house that was given up at auction. I parked in the small lot to the right of the main building and ambled up the cedar-chipped path. A large baroque fountain with at least six shooting sprays of water dominated the circle driveway. Home to several species of fish and floating water lilies, the crystal-clear bubbles resembled bottles of overflowing champagne. Robust gardens with shrubbery and trees shaped into forest animals adorned both sides of the house suggesting scenes of various famous paintings from the Gilded Age. They were encircled by a gentle stream of water filled with colorful flowers and sculpted rock collections.

I smiled at the beauty and obnoxious personality of the estate as I meandered the sprawling pathway and climbed the polished marble steps. Before I could knock or ring a bell, the door opened. An older, plump woman with gray curls, a pair of spectacles hung on a beaded chain, and a black and white uniform reminiscent of those I'd seen in early 1930s films introduced herself as Mrs. Crawford. "The Paddingtons are expecting you. Give me one moment to let them know you're here, Mr. Ayrwick." Even her charming accent had made the lucrative move from Georgia.

Before the woman could leave the large travertine-tiled foyer, Nana D stepped into the slippery space. It felt like an accident waiting to happen, especially for anyone using a cane. "Don't worry, Mrs. Crawford. I'll bring my grandson into the dining room. Isn't it time you took a break? I left you a peach crumble on the counter in the kitchen. Don't you be sharing that with anyone else! It's yours alone."

"That's generous of you, Mrs. Danby," Mrs. Crawford said beaming with a smile that had probably never seen the light of day in the Paddington mansion.

"I've told you before, please call me Seraphina. None of my friends call me Mrs. *Anything*, so you shouldn't either," Nana D replied guiding Mrs. Crawford down the west hall toward the kitchen.

"This place is enormous," I said walking behind her through the central section of the house. When we entered the Great Hall, it felt like it was the first time I'd ever seen light. A giant conservatory occupied the middle of the room offering so much brightness I could barely focus. I noticed dozens of exotic plants and trees scattered all around, many of which I was certain couldn't survive anywhere north of the equator. "Did we suddenly transport to the Amazon? Who's their gardener, Martha Stewart's South American doppelganger?"

Nana D grinned. "It is beautiful, but don't be juvenile. Millard has the green thumb. He's the designer and inspiration behind all of this. He hired lots of help over the years to maintain it, but there isn't a species in this room he didn't select himself from the original location."

Nana D had dated Millard for a few months sometime in the past while I'd lived in LA, but it didn't last long. I never understood exactly what'd happened to cause her to break it off, but she often mentioned his inability to be generous or treat women equally to men. He was charming and intelligent, but some old-fashioned sense of men being the dominant gender prevailed in his mind. Nana D tried to teach him how to be a modern man, but he simply couldn't abide by the new way of doing things.

"I could sit for hours and admire his imagination and creative genius. Does Millard live here, too?" I asked not knowing which of the Paddingtons had resided in the family home.

Nana D shook her head. "When Millard was passed over as the rightful heir, he moved out to allow Charles to occupy the family estate. His brother encouraged him to stay, but Millard felt their parents had made a decision for some reason and he had to abide by it."

"Where does he live?" I knew Eustacia had been invited to move in with Gwendolyn when it came time for in-residence assistance, but she never did. Eustacia was too proud to move back in with her brother's family and had bought a small upscale condo in the newly-built Willow Trees senior living retirement facility. She was surrounded by other sixty-five-plus inhabitants who kept her young at heart and full of spite.

"Millard has a few houses. He mostly stays in a cottage closer to the Wharton mountains. He prefers to be near nature, but he comes back every week to take care of this garden," Nana D noted. I wanted to ask why as the eldest he was never given the family estate, but it felt like too personal of a question. I'd barely been inside the palace and was already wondering who kicked out the rightful king. I blamed it on my love of English royalty and their order of succession.

"Does that mean only Gwendolyn's children and grandchildren live here?" I wandered around the immediate vicinity admiring the vivacious colors and shiny green leaves on all the lush foliage.

"Some, but not all. Why don't we head to the dining room and discuss it over lunch with Eustacia? She's staying here temporarily to help with the funeral arrangements and keep things running on the estate."

I followed Nana D through the Great Hall and exited in the back right down a long hallway covered in famous paintings and prints. I assumed they were copies, but I wasn't well-trained in that particular art medium. Given the wealth all around me, I wouldn't have been surprised if one or two were originals. When we turned down the final hall, I said, "How's Eustacia doing?"

"Tired. She didn't sleep last night, and it's hard to keep everyone under control. Let her tell you all about it, Kellan. Sheriff Montague was here earlier today and shared some news which confirms Gwennie's concern someone had been trying to hurt her." Nana D looked back at me with a heaviness I'd not seen in a long time. She pushed open the door into the dining room. "Drugs from some dirty hoodlum on the street killed her. It's looking rather scandalous and disturbing."

Chapter 6

"Kellan's here. I'll let Mrs. Crawford know to serve lunch in a few minutes," Nana D noted before leaving the room again. I didn't know whether to hug Eustacia or take a seat near her at the table as if I were a subject of hers. We'd known each other for years, but I barely knew much about her as a person. Occasionally, I'd run into her around town where we'd have a quick conversation, or that is, she'd chide me for something my nana had done, then direct me to get involved in sorting out the debacle. Eustacia and Nana D had some sort of symbiotic relationship where they often couldn't stand to be around one another but if ever two days went by without time for tea or gossip, the world might've come to an end.

"Did Seraphina tell you about the sheriff's conversation?" Eustacia pointed to a nearby chair.

I sat, then answered. "Not really. Just that it wasn't from natural causes."

"They found traces of street drugs in my sister-in-law's body. Gwennie's never taken any in her life!" She fanned herself with a cloth napkin she'd snatched up from beside the table's fine china setting.

"So, she was right to be concerned," I said with despair in my voice. "I'm sorry. How do you think it got into her system?" Could Nana D have been right to swipe that iced tea glass?

"It's rather unusual. Apparently, she consumed such a large dose of it yesterday, her heart couldn't handle the intensity. Dr. Betscha hadn't received the whole report from the coroner, but that was the preliminary finding."

"Do they know exactly when it was ingested yesterday?" I asked tentatively. "Or what it was?"

"Not yet. It had to occur while she was at Paddington's Play House. She wasn't feeling well yesterday morning. Nothing more unusual than we'd seen in the last month. Seraphina told me you were integral to solving those two murders a few weeks ago. Is that true?" Hope materialized on Eustacia's face as she searched for answers, but I knew nothing about the situation.

"I suppose you could say that, but it was very different than what happened to your sister-in-law. In the last murder, my father had been a suspect, and the victims had been people I knew well or was supposed to be interviewing as part of my job. The sheriff should handle this one, Ms. Paddington."

"Nonsense. If Seraphina says you solved the last murder, then you're capable of solving this murder. There are few things I will concede to that troublesome nana of yours, but she is one of my dearest friends. When she believes in someone, I believe in them, too. I might not like all the things that ninny does, but it's none of your dang business nor pertinent to this conversation, sonny boy."

Sonny boy? I felt like a child again. I needed to say something that would show her otherwise. "You did try to make it my business when you wanted me to stop Nana D from dating Lindsey, right?" I shouldn't have used an accusatory tone while saying the words, but I felt like I was being tricked or about to fall into a trap. So much for obeying our elders!

"Don't you start with me about what I did or didn't do. This is different. I'm not trying to stop Seraphina this time. I want her involved in solving my sister-in-law's murder. Gwennie was like a sister to me all these years. When Charles passed, I only had Millard left. As much as I love my brother, he's not exactly sentimental and open-minded. I want justice for Gwennie even if it means learning someone in our family goes to the pokey."

Nana D returned with the cook to deliver lunch. She'd told Mrs. Crawford to remain on a break and leave us in the room for the afternoon. While we had a delicious feast of butternut squash soup, rosemary-herbed Cornish game hens, and roasted Brussel sprouts, I considered everything Eustacia had told me. In the con column, I truly wasn't qualified to dig into the murder. I wasn't a family member, I wasn't a suspect, and I barely knew the victim. I also would get my rear end kicked from here to Timbuktu by Sheriff Montague if I went anywhere near another case of hers. In the pro column, I was a major crime buff. I did find the body in a manner of speaking, I had already seen a few suspicious behaviors, and the thought of digging into the Paddington family secrets excited me. I also would get my rear end kicked from here to Mars by Nana D if I didn't try to solve the case.

Since Mars was a lot longer of a journey than Timbuktu, and I was more afraid of Nana D than the sheriff, I settled on a compromise. "What if I agree to help, but you two are my front line of support on anything where the sheriff is involved. I value my life and freedom, and while I'm not afraid of her, she could make things miserable for me."

"Kellan, no grandson of mine would be scared to do the right thing. You're on the side of the law, and that nuisance of a sheriff needs to be more tolerant. If I'm elected mayor, she will learn to take direction from me." Nana slammed her fist on the table as further proof of her proclamation.

"Exactly. And Seraphina will be Wharton County's next mayor. Hey, that reminds me, don't we need to start preparing for your debate with Councilman Silly Man on Thursday?" Eustacia teased.

"Nana D, the sheriff doesn't take direction solely from the mayor. It's an elected position in Wharton County, not appointed by the mayor. I'm sure there's a partnership in that relationship."

"What? I thought I could fire that woman!" she scowled. "Or that fickle fish DA!"

"No. I think if you're gonna run for public office, we need to get you up to speed on how politics work in Wharton County," I said shaking my head for even trying to reason with the woman.

"Well, that's not good news. Okay, you're assigned to teach me how this county works, brilliant one. Let's start pulling our plan together this afternoon," Nana D said with a slight irritation to her voice.

Before I could reply, Mrs. Crawford knocked on the dining room door and asked if she could enter. All three of us responded, "Come in." We laughed when she arrived saying, "Well, that's a first. Usually Mrs. Paddington, that is, the last Mrs. Paddington, would tell me to go away the first three times I knocked. Pardon the intrusion, but there's someone here to see you, Ms. Paddington. New Mrs. Paddington, that is. Oh dear, this is complicated."

Eustacia smiled at Nana D. "Since Gwennie's not around anymore, God rest her soul, there's gonna be a few changes in this house... starting with an end to all the rudeness in this family." Eustacia turned to Mrs. Crawford, "First of all, you no longer have to knock when coming into the dining room. Second of all, what's your first name?" A bony finger wiggled in the maid's direction.

"Bertha, ma'am," Mrs. Crawford said hesitantly, nearly dropping a dish towel.

"Third, there's no more *sir* and *ma'am* while I'm in charge around here. I might not have control once we find the will and discover who inherits this place, but until then, I've got Gwennie's power-of-attorney, so things will be how I say things are gonna be. Got that, Bertha?"

"Yes, ma'am. I mean Ms. Paddington... wait... I'm not sure what to call you?" she said scratching her head.

I watched the entire conversation play out in front of me as though I were sitting at a tennis match. We had a murder to solve. We had a mayoral race to win. Bertha had said someone was here to see us. I attempted to interrupt the latest volley but got the look of death and a hand held up like a school crossing guard's stop signal from Eustacia.

"You can call me Eustacia. That's what everyone I know calls me except people who are trying to suck up to me for money." She looked generally in my direction then quickly turned back to Bertha.

"But I call you Ms. Paddington, and I'm not sucking—" I started to say but was stopped again.

Eustacia glared at me. "Didn't I give you the halt sign, Kellan? Learn your basics if you want to keep up with this crowd." Then she turned to Nana D with her thumb jabbing in my direction. "How do you tolerate the likes of that one? He's full of hot air, vinegar, and prissy fuss. Oh, never mind. It's almost like the two of you are cut from the same cloth, Seraphina."

Bertha's head jutted to the side as she took two steps backward. "Um, I'm sorry to interrupt, but I have Brad Shope here to see you."

"Isn't that Gwennie's live-in nurse? What's he want? Bring him in. He might be able to help explain a few things," Eustacia demanded while pouring herself another glass of white wine. She spoke so quickly and assuredly, I wondered if she'd been a drill sergeant in the past.

There are days when I want to pack myself in a box and ship it anywhere but Braxton for another forty years. It's almost like once people turned seventy, they decided it's their right to do and say whatever they wanted. Now that I'd agreed to help solve

Gwendolyn's murder, I'd have to deal with not only one ornery septuagenarian but a second who from first glance might be far worse than my nana. Why couldn't I have stayed back in Los Angeles? Oh right, the Castiglianos...

Before Bertha brought Brad into the room, I asked Eustacia to explain his role in caring for Gwendolyn. He'd been hired the previous year after Gwendolyn's husband, Charles, died from pancreatic cancer. Weeks had gone by where Gwendolyn laid in bed all day, ate the bare minimum, and stopped taking her normal medications. Although Bertha had done everything she could to help, nothing had changed. Over the winter while no one noticed, Gwendolyn finally forced herself out of bed and wandered the vast property all alone. She'd become disoriented, fallen into the stream breaking her leg, and suffered from hypothermia. Her family subsequently moved her to an outpatient facility rather than nurse her back to health themselves. Once she'd begun recovering from her injuries and the death of her husband, Gwendolyn moved back into the family estate. Brad followed suit as a private nurse she'd hired after meeting him through a friend who'd also been in recovery at the outpatient facility.

Brad stepped into the room and offered his condolences to Eustacia. He wore an untucked plaid shirt and mid-rise, stone wash jeans. His face was slightly rounded as though he still had some baby fat to lose while his dimples probably drove all the girls crazy. Mahogany brown hair was spiked at the top and shaved close to the skin on both sides of his head. I'd been considering a similar style for myself for whenever I found time to choose a new barber. "I apologize for interrupting your lunch, but I finished packing all my things. I thought I'd check in before leaving this afternoon," noted Brad in a quiet voice.

Nana D asked him to take a seat at the table across from her. "Have you eaten lunch?"

"Not yet. I've been cleaning up Mrs. Paddington's room to organize everything before I left. I assume I should review any final items with Bertha?" Brad had a gentle demeanor and good manners. Although on the shorter side, he looked strong and capable of handling his role as a nurse and physical therapist.

Eustacia asked Bertha to bring an extra plate and insisted Brad have something to eat. "Do you have somewhere else to go? I'm not sure how your role works when a client passes away."

Brad explained that he'd only worked at clinics and rehabilitation facilities in the past. This was his first in-residence, private client. He'd surrendered his apartment the previous year when Gwendolyn hired him to move in and take care of her. I decided to ask him a few questions while the opportunity presented itself. After explaining whom I was, I said, "What type of services did you provide for Mrs. Paddington?"

Brad took a large bite, swallowed, and answered me. "It changed in the last few weeks. At first, I ensured she did her physical therapy each day to get her walking again. It's different being at home where things are spread out further and harder to reach. The rehabilitation facility does its best to duplicate home environments, but it's not usually enough."

"Especially in this place, right?" Nana D joked while adjusting the braid on top of her head. "I still get lost at times despite coming here for years."

"True. For one thing, we had to move her to a downstairs bedroom, so she didn't have to climb the steps. Once she was able to walk on her own, we moved her back, and I prepared a new routine to help keep her body active but carefully protected from the possibility of another fall. I managed her medication and doctor appointments. We went for walks each day to keep up her spirit and flexibility. I suppose I became more of a confidante in the last few weeks once she needed less medical care."

"What pills was she taking? I recall someone mentioning she had high blood pressure," I noted while glancing at Nana D. From her smile, I knew she was happy about my prying into the details of Gwendolyn's health.

"Yes, she'd been taking those before I started working here. After the accident, the doctor added more medication to address increasing hypertension and high-cholesterol. I'd also suggested she consider an anti-depressant in the beginning to help get her mind in a better place. She was distraught over losing Mr. Paddington. And since her... well, never mind, that doesn't matter anymore."

Eustacia cleared her throat. "I'd appreciate you saying whatever's on your mind, Brad. My sister-in-law is gone, and I'm worried about how she was feeling these last few weeks. Did I miss any additional issues with her health?"

Brad shook his head. "No, I didn't mean anything... it's just... um, she was dismayed about her family and how they weren't bothering much with her anymore." He looked at the floor and went silent.

"It was good she had you to support her body and her mind. What can you tell me about your visit to the theater yesterday?" I said.

Nana D interjected. "I called him when Gwennie started to feel unwell. She was struggling to catch her breath."

"What pills did you give her when you showed up? Are you certain there wasn't a mix-up?" Eustacia asked abruptly.

Brad sat back with a nervous look on his face. His eyebrows raised and his lips stretched out thinly. "Did something else happen besides the heart attack? I gave her the normal afternoon medication, she'd just accidentally left them at home. She'd also been having a few panic attacks lately, which is why we were going to Dr. Betscha this week."

I looked toward Eustacia. "I'm sure her family is worried about how sudden this all seems to be. I'm helping them look into her last couple of weeks to ease their peace of mind." I knew Eustacia wanted answers, but she had to be more delicate in her approach.

"I understand. Mrs. Paddington was a special woman. I noticed a few things that didn't add up, but nothing too alarming. I don't mean any offense," he said looking at Nana D and Eustacia, "But at her age we unfortunately start to see the body having trouble keeping up with everything."

"You're telling me," quipped Eustacia as she stood reaching for her cane. At the top, a brass lion's head stared at me with a set of ferocious teeth as if to tell me to beware. "I take so many dang medications, I consider them my daily rainbow meal. Still looking for that leprechaun, though."

"Speak for yourself. I'm as healthy as a thoroughbred mare in the prime of her racing career," Nana D said with a chuckle. She was adamant about taking only herbal supplements and following holistic healthcare. At seventy-four, she *had* avoided every possible medication thus far.

If I let those two keep talking, we'd never get useful information. "Brad, can you provide a list of any medication she was taking? I think it would help the family feel a little better about her last few days. Also, if you don't have anywhere to move to, what are you planning to do?"

"Actually, I had that written out already for when we went to the doctor. As for my living situation, I'm planning to rent a room at the Roarke & Daughters Inn for a few days." He shrugged his shoulders and stood up to leave. I'd recognized the name of the bed and breakfast he'd mentioned. Maggie's parents and her sisters ran the charming ten-room inn near Crilly Lake.

"Nonsense," Eustacia whined while leading him toward the door. "You will stay here until you find your next job and a place to live. I could use a little help myself. Would that work?"

Eustacia was a lot smarter than she let others realize. If the autopsy revealed someone had been drugging Gwendolyn all along, Brad might be able to identify which member of the family had access to any medication or food where it could've been introduced. Or revealed if he was involved in trying to kill her. Having him onsite would be a helpful asset. Once Brad left, Nana D, Eustacia, and I focused on the upcoming mayoral debate.

For too long, Wharton County's current mayor, Bartleby Grosvalet, and Braxton's town councilman, Marcus Stanton, had been in office together running the show. In the last decade, the powerful duo had skated by in the polls winning via a narrow margin. Very few ever dared run against them, but their loyalists ensured both men garnered enough votes to push forth their dreary agendas. Mayor Grosvalet was in his seventies like Nana D, but he'd become a recluse since the last election and delegated many of his powers to Marcus. Nana D's biggest obstacles to winning would be her age and Stanton's experience as Grosvalet's right-hand man. The only way to gain support would be if she could reach the soul of the county by appealing to their need for change and growth in the future. We outlined Nana D's key points and scheduled practice-runs over the next couple of days.

I left to attend my first official meeting with Ursula Power. In my two previous interactions with the new president, I was extremely impressed with her candor and professionalism. I was a little concerned about being fired since my other job back in Los Angeles as an assistant director on the hit television show, *Dark Reality*, was in flux. The executive producer had recently canned my boss and informed me he needed a few weeks to decide whether I had a future at the network. I wasn't sure what I wanted to happen given everything else going on in my life but directing my own television crime series was still at the top of the options list. When were they going to call with an update?

I pulled into an empty South Campus parking lot given students were on break and entered the executive office building. Although my father would still be the president for another couple of weeks, he and Ursula were meeting daily to provide a smooth transition to the campus. He'd graciously moved into a smaller office on the first floor, so Ursula could settle in the second-floor corner suite. I swung by to say hello, but a student worker said outgoing president Wesley Ayrwick had already left the building.

Ursula hadn't yet hired a permanent assistant, but a cheerful temp notified her boss that I'd arrived. While the temp went to the small kitchenette, Myriam walked out and glared at me. "This was all your doing, wasn't it, Kellan?" Myriam said in a fit of semi-controlled rage. "I feel compelled to share with you of a line from this semester's theater performance. '*Come not between the dragon and her wrath.*' It will do you some good to remember that!"

It was rare I could find a hole in Myriam's quotations, but when I did, I felt the need to ride it like a hurricane's feverish winds. "I do believe you mean *his* wrath. I can appreciate you changing the actual line to suit your intended message, but a true historian would always leave the original message intact." Lear's warning to Kent was a passage I'd overheard during rehearsal the previous weekend otherwise I might not have noticed her slight alteration.

"That's preposterous! I changed only the gender and not the meaning of the line. I wouldn't expect someone like you to separate the little things from the big things. Obviously, you've less experience than I thought when it comes to grasping the semantics of the English language," Myriam sniped while turning toward the door to exit.

Ursula stepped out of her office obviously disgruntled. I'd never been certain of her age but guessed somewhere in her mid-forties, at least a decade younger than her wife. Given the frown lines I'd just seen for the first time ever, perhaps I was a few years off. "Myriam, I'll see you at home this evening. I can tell I made the right decision earlier about addressing the issue between you and Kellan," Ursula said smiling like Cheshire cat, then directing me to follow her into the office. I suddenly had the urge to ask those same hurricane winds to sweep me far away.

Chapter 7

What decision was Ursula talking about? My stomach felt ten pounds heavier, and it wasn't the strawberry cheesecake I'd eaten at the end of lunch. "How've your first few days been?" I sat in a tall wingback chair across from her desk. The room had been re-decorated with a pale gray wall-paper depicting a variety of Japanese maple trees. The pop of pinks and reds on the branches were a great contrast but also blended well with the cherrywood furniture and wrought-iron sculptures near the bay window.

When I'd first met Ursula weeks earlier, she had an ethereal quality about her. She truly could've been a model, but what made her even more charismatic was her genuine humility and intelligence. She accepted the cup of tea from her temporary assistant and smiled at me. "Braxton is the type of campus I dreamed about as a teenager. Unfortunately, I couldn't afford to live on my campus and worked too many jobs to cover tuition. I never had that classic college experience where I bonded with dormmates, snuck off to parties, and swung lazily in a hammock while reading *Jane Eyre* or *A Tale of Two Cities*."

I felt an incredibly warm sensation about Ursula's presence on campus. My father had been a strong president bringing in countless donations elevating the school from a small community college to the best in the county, but he often forgot to focus on the softer side of a liberal arts education—friendships, bonds, and memories. Ursula would be the one to make it happen, I could tell already.

"I remember them fondly, though now we often see students reading *Harry Potter* and *The Secret History* under the canopy of those golden yellow, red, and orange autumn trees." My stomach began to settle given the way Ursula handled herself and the conversation. "I'm excited about the opportunity to be part of the Braxton University team. Have you started diving into the proposed curriculum?"

We talked for twenty minutes about all the areas of expansion, in particular the communications department's overhaul. She was impressed by my experience and agreed with both my father's and the Board's decision to include me on the planning committee. As our time came to an end, I grew curious what she and Myriam had been discussing before I walked in. I was about to bring up the topic, but Ursula beat me to it.

"Kellan, I'm sure this might be awkward for you to answer, but I'd like to learn more about your relationship with Myriam. Please don't worry about her being my wife. I can easily separate work from personal, and I've known her for over twenty years. She has an advanced degree in quarreling and wrote a thesis on button-pushing. I still don't know when to successfully pick my battles." She gently shook her head and pulled her long, wavy blonde hair toward one shoulder.

Considering Ursula asked me directly what I thought of Myriam, I felt honesty was the best policy. However, I was nothing without my humor. "Let's not forget her special honorary certificate in obtuse Shakespearean zingers."

Ursula laughed so loudly the temp poked her head into verify everything was okay. When she went back to her seat, Ursula said, "Apart from all that, where do you see things going with Myriam? You've a one-year contract which I intend to honor. I make it a policy not to insert myself into professional relationships among colleagues unless necessary. Unfortunately, there've been a number of incidents between the two of you which are worrisome."

I nodded. "I agree with you. We aren't mixing well, but I assure you I intend to remedy our differences or keep them hidden at all times. I suspect you have something in mind to assist with the current volatility." I was a tad nervous what might come out of Ursula's mouth next given the curious look on her face and the accusatory remarks Myriam had made upon my arrival.

"I respect when someone cuts to the chase, so I'll do the same, Kellan," Ursula replied handing me a folder full of papers. "I had a call from Eustacia Paddington early this morning. Even in mourning, she's on top of important transitions. Besides calling to congratulate me on the new position and asking me to attend her sister-in-law's funeral service later in the week, she's proposed that you be made the temporary representative for the Paddington family on all things related to the Play House."

Some unintelligible sound emanated from my mouth before I could collect my thoughts. "I don't understand. She never said anything to me."

"Let me clear up any confusion. Gwendolyn Paddington partnered with our drama department to determine what shows we performed in the theater, worked with sponsors to offset any costs for set design and costumes, marketed our shows across the county, and mentored students beginning their careers. Apparently, there isn't anyone else in the family qualified to assume the role, so Eustacia suggested that you fill it until we could decide the future together as I settled into my new position at Braxton."

"Suggested or insisted?"

"I'm sure you can appreciate the fine line I need to walk. The Paddingtons donate a tremendous amount of money to Braxton. They have certain, shall we say, liberties to make decisions on the theater program and the Play House which has been named after them."

"What about Myriam? She oversees the drama department and operations at Paddington's Play House," I hesitantly said realizing why my boss had been so angry at me. "Isn't she a better choice?"

"I was planning to find an activity for the two of you to co-lead in the hopes it would encourage you both to get along better. When Eustacia made the suggestion for you to be the temporary patron, I struck a deal with her."

"But Myriam's the one with all the experience in theater. She has the Broadway connections and has been running everything for years." I sounded like I was whining but couldn't stop myself.

"And you have experience writing television scripts, directing shows, and working in Hollywood. You have a different but valid perspective, and you also have the ear of the Paddington family right now. As a team, I expect great things from your partnership with Myriam."

"Is this a proposal, or are you telling me this is requirement for my continued role at Braxton?" I kept my tone civil despite wanting to scream.

"I prefer to think of it as a mutually beneficial decision we've all made together with the best intentions for Braxton among our collective minds." Ursula stood, smiling at me. "I'm sure you see it the same way, too. Unfortunately, I have another meeting. I appreciate you making time for me."

Ursula indicated the papers in the folder outlined the Play House's budget, staffing, and general operations. I thanked the new president for her input, as Nana D taught me never to tease an animal until you knew how ferocious it could be. I'd initially put Ursula in the kind and gentle teddy bear category, but it might've been fallacious. If she could hold her own against Myriam, there undoubtedly must be a powerful stamina worthy of the grizzlies wandering the nearby Saddlebrooke National Forest.

As I left Ursula's office, the temp handed me an envelope. "Your father stopped by while you were inside meeting with Ms. Power. He asked me to give you this and said he found it on the floor in his office last night when he got home from his trip. He also mentioned something about you needing to explain what it meant." She turned and scampered away with a smug grin.

"I appreciate it," I mumbled wondering why my father wouldn't have given it to me when I got home. As I walked to the parking lot, I looked at the envelope. Written on the front in block print was: **TO MY DEAREST HUSBAND, KELLAN**. Now I understood why he had it delivered as soon as possible. Had he read Francesca's letter and known she was alive? I swiftly tore it open and read the contents.

In one week, it will be our eighth anniversary. Every night before I fall asleep, I think of how you looked when I walked down the aisle at the botanical gardens on our wedding day. You'd never been more handsome than you were that afternoon. The sun hit your face in such a way that you reminded me of an angel. I knew then I had to protect you from my family at any cost. I foolishly thought if you never knew their secrets, you'd never be in danger.

When the Vargas family kidnapped me, I honestly thought I wouldn't be rescued. I knew my father would do everything in his power to get revenge, but I said a silent, terrified goodbye to you and Emma as they locked me in a freezer filled with devices meant to torture me. Once my father's security team found me, I promised myself this would never happen again. I'm not telling you this because I want to hurt you or to make you feel guilty. I need you to understand that I made a decision to protect you and Emma above anything else.

My mother doesn't know I've written this note. I hope you find it hidden under the desk. I had only a few seconds to drop it in there as we were arriving. I am not giving up on us. I will find a solution to bring us back together. Don't give up on me. Remember the stars. We will always have a future.

I stared at Francesca's letter for what felt like an eternity but had only been a few seconds. I was pulled from my trance by a series of tears rolling across my cheeks onto the envelope and blurring out my name. She wanted me to remember the stars.

Francesca had referred to the night of our first anniversary. She'd asked me to meet her at the top of a mountain not too far from where we lived. When I arrived, she had a picnic set up with a late dinner. She told me to lie down on the blanket and stare up at the sky. She filled two glasses with sparkling cider, then handed me one. I glanced back at her with a confused look as she knew how much I loved champagne. Moments later, Francesca clinked my glass and told me she was going to have a baby. Then she encouraged me to look at the stars because one of them was our daughter waiting for us to love her. We must have pointed out dozens of stars that night talking about what kind of baby girl we wanted to have. In the end, Francesca told me she'd be happy no matter what the universe had given to us as long as she was healthy and happy. It was the beginning of our family and our future.

Remember the stars. I remembered them every year on our anniversary. We celebrated near them on each of Emma's birthdays. And the night Francesca died, I slept under them because there was nowhere else I could be by myself for the first time. But she never died. I tossed my head against the back of the seat and concentrated with soul-crushing focus. What was I going to do about our future?

Unfortunately, I couldn't think about it any longer because it was time to pick Emma up from her first day at school. When

I arrived, she boasted about how amazing it was and how she couldn't wait to go back. We had dinner with my mother since my father was working late with Ursula on an upcoming presentation. Emma went to sleep early, and I watched a few sitcom re-runs to distract myself from thinking about the reality around me. I ended up calling Cecilia and begging her to let me speak with my wife, but she put Vincenzo on the line. He heavily encouraged me to find my way back to Los Angeles quickly. He noted he wasn't in agreement with Cecilia who'd given me two weeks to decide how to proceed, but he would let his wife's decision stand only this one time.

* * *

I slept poorly that night trying to decide what to do about Francesca. Early on Tuesday morning, I texted Eleanor to check on the diner renovations, but she couldn't speak. She had a doctor's appointment and needed to finish preparing for the final inspection the next day before she could officially re-open. We agreed that I would stop by for dinner that evening to get her thoughts on the situation with Francesca.

After dropping Emma off at school, I went for a run to clear my head. I chose the Finnulia River path as the weather was finally starting to warm up in the high forties which meant I could leave the heavier thermal gym clothes at home. The air was also much cleaner and easier to breathe near the north end of town where the river emptied into Crilly Lake. Halfway through my return, I took a short break to stretch and drink some water near Maggie's family's inn. As I prepared to finish the final lag, a runner I recognized came toward me. I called out watching smoke from the crisp air funnel away from my lips. "You're Sam Paddington, right?"

He looked strangely at me on his approach, then stopped while still jogging in place. "It's Sam Taft. My mother was a Paddington. Not my father."

I hadn't forgotten, but I wanted to verify it with him. I knew his sister called herself Dana Taft, but I wasn't sure if they all shared the same father. Ophelia and Richard Taft had a complicated relationship from what Nana D had told me. "Oh, that's right. I forgot. Dana and Lilly Taft, your sisters. Now it makes sense."

He nodded. "Yes, we're all Tafts. You're Kellan, right?"

I asked him how his family was doing, and he noted they were all grieving in their own private ways. "I've spent a lot of time looking through photo albums and some videos we took years ago. I don't know what I'm gonna do without her," Sam replied. He wore a pair of navy-blue running shorts and a Nike t-shirt whose sweat stains clearly showed he'd been on the trail for a long time. Was he working off grief or guilt?

"It takes time. I still reminisce about my grandpop who's been gone close to ten years," I said feeling nostalgic for the past. "Looks like you know what you're doing out here."

"I'm a health nut. I've seen what poor diet and little exercise can do to people and don't want to throw away the future. I've got lots of hopes and dreams." Sam stopped jogging in place and checked his phone. He had something else in his pocket, but I couldn't tell what it was. I looked like a small cylinder or bottle filled with liquid. It almost reminded me of a tube of glue which seemed odd for him to be carrying on a run. He smiled when his phone beeped indicating he had a text message. I was too far away to see any of the words or name of the sender.

"Someone brightening your day?" I said noticing the change in his demeanor. "Girlfriend, I presume?" I knew it was nosy of me, but I had to find out a little more about him.

"Um, not exactly. Listen, I gotta go. I'm meeting my mom to help her plan the funeral service. Take it easy," Sam replied. It was the second time he looked awkward or nervous talking to me. I watched him take off toward the more treacherous path at a speed I could definitely not keep up with. Granted, he had ten years on me, but he was also most definitely at the top of his game.

Five minutes before I got home, my cell rang. "It's your grandmother. Get over to the Paddington estate pronto. That sheriff's crew is here with a warrant to search the house. Sheriff Montague is on her way here now," Nana D said in a clearly aggravated tone.

"Did you call a lawyer? What's she looking for?" I asked while speeding a little faster than I should've. I needed to shower before going to the estate.

"Eustacia called Lindsey. He may have retired years ago, but he'll know what to do. I can't read that mumbo jumbo legal speak. It could've said something about searching for a witch riding a broom in her pink polka-dot daisy dukes and sports brassiere for all I know, brilliant one."

"I'll be there in thirty minutes. Who's handling the Paddington legal affairs?" I pulled into the driveway and jogged up the back steps to the Royal Chic-Shack laughing about her unique expressions.

Nana D explained she didn't know which attorney was working for them anymore. I suggested she call Finnigan Masters who'd handled my parents' legal affairs over the last few years. I'd met him once before when I had to sign a document for them, but now that I was back in Braxton, I should re-connect with the man. I'd gone to school with his younger brother who'd become a professional hockey player. After a shower and change of clothes, I hightailed it to the Paddington estate.

Given how unlucky I'd been lately, of course the first person I ran into in the small parking area outside the mansion was April Montague. Her nearly translucent skin, brassy blonde Viking helmet hair, as I liked to call it, and high cheekbones were so prominent, I couldn't help but stare. "Good morning, sheriff. How's everything going today?" I said with the fakest smile I could muster. It sounded like I had marbles in my mouth given how much I didn't want to speak with the insufferable woman.

"I might have guessed you'd show up, Little Ayrwick. Please tell me you're here to mow the lawn or scoop off the algae and pond scum?" April taunted me wearing her favorite worn blazer and starched jeans. She was not one who should be casting judgment.

"I'm visiting an old friend, that's all. Ms. Paddington and I have some business to discuss about the upcoming *King Lear* performance. You might not know this, but I'm their representative on anything connected to the drama department or the Play House." I considered reaching my hand in her direction despite her callous wisecrack about gardening responsibilities. "What brings you here?"

"You've exceeded my expectations, I must say. Back for only three weeks and clearly embedded with the Paddingtons and the Stantons as if you were their trained pet. I hear you were even present when Gwendolyn died of that unfortunate heart attack the other day," Sheriff Montague said with a half-smile and sneer. Her jaw was set so tightly I thought she might chip a cap.

"Surely, it couldn't have been a heart attack if you're at the estate with a warrant to search the premises. Anything I should be concerned about?" I pinched myself in excitement for proving my point.

"Other than getting back into your car and driving off the property, so I can do my job? Last I checked, you didn't pass the Pennsylvania BAR. I see no reason for you to remain." She shut the passenger door to the sheriff's county vehicle. It was good to see her arriving in something other than her motorcycle. Although the thought of a woman riding a Harley excited me for some reason, picturing April Montague on it made me nauseous. Exorcist-level nauseous.

I tilted my head to the side and sighed. "I can't keep the Paddingtons waiting. Why don't we arrive together as a show of good faith? After you." I pointed toward the house like a flight attendant.

Once Bertha let us inside, we entered the foyer. "Kellan, it's so lovely to see you again," she said. After we hugged and exchanged thoughts about Nana D's peach crumble, Sheriff Montague interrupted. "I always said you had a gift for gab, Little Ayrwick. Since you know the place so well, how about you navigate me in the direction of my team."

I declined, having little energy to continue our banter. As the sheriff went off with Bertha, I located Nana D. "What's going on?"

"They showed up an hour ago with a warrant to search the place. Lindsey just got here and said it's all legal. They have reasonable cause that someone drugged Gwennie at the theater, but apparently they suspect something's been going on for weeks," Nana D said in a fury as we navigated the hallways toward the Great Hall. "I can't believe no one noticed what was happening."

"Lindsey knows one of the cops from past cases. He shared more than he should've, but I'm glad he did. There was something erratic or amiss with various counts and numbers in Gwennie's blood chemistry. Some whippersnapper hootenanny talk, if you ask me. All I know is what Brad said makes sense—he was right to bring her to the doctor this week. If only he had the chance."

"What exactly happened at the theater to cause her to finally succumb?" I asked filling with genuine concern for the whole family.

"An overdose of cocaine. Huge amounts in her body from the preliminary results of the autopsy. I have a call into Alex to find out what he knows." Alex, better known as Dr. Alexander Betscha, was Nana D's forty-year-old distant cousin, who served as a physician for most of Braxton's inhabitants.

"Did you learn whom the family's attorney is now? Where's everyone?" I looked back and forth.

"Nope. Ophelia's with Sam at the funeral parlor planning the services. I don't think Eustacia's called them yet. Dana lives on campus. Lilly comes and goes so much, no one ever knows where she is."

"What about Jennifer or Richard?" I asked.

"Richard's away. Jennifer doesn't live here. It was just Eustacia home when the cops showed up. She rang me, and I rushed over. That's when I contacted you and told her to call Lindsey."

Eustacia walked down the hall balancing on her cane and shouting at us. "Disaster. This entire town and family is a sheer disaster. Is that Kellan? What's he got to report? Did he figure out who killed Gwennie yet? What the devil is taking him so long?"

Unfortunately, Sheriff Montague was following Eustacia down the hall when she had her outburst. "Excuse me, Ms. Paddington. Can you explain why Kellan would be figuring out who killed Gwendolyn? First of all, he's not a member of the Wharton County Sheriff's Office. Second, how does he know it was murder when I haven't made it public knowledge. No one is to know anything about this crime until I say so."

It was at that moment I knew I'd be punished no matter if I had behaved or misbehaved. The world liked to torture me, which meant I had to find a way to accept it and move on. "Well, you see, Sheriff Montague, it sorta goes like this..."

Chapter 8

"Close your mouth. I'm getting tired of you showing up everywhere I am," the sheriff began to shout until another voice interrupted her tirade leading us to all turn around at the same time and see whom it'd come from.

Millard stepped into the hallway and demanded that everyone calm down. He ushered us back into the Great Hall where we all took seats near the palm trees and kidney-shaped pond. A submerged plant that looked like a Venus fly-trap floated past me as I walked by. "What's that one?" I asked wondering if it were about to snap at my fingers. How could I dunk the sheriff?

"Water wheel plant. Rare species, not usually in North America. I've been able to keep it alive through a proper feeding schedule," Millard noted. After what must have been a puzzled or concern expression appeared on my face, he continued, "They're carnivorous. I have to supply them with meat."

"How fitting," the sheriff added with a sinister glower in my direction. I also hear her mutter under her breath "*Must be a friend of Little Ayrwick's.*" Yikes, we really had it out for each other.

"How about we try starting this conversation all over again, sheriff?" Millard said.

"Please explain what is going on, Little Ayrwick," the sheriff said clearly frustrated and tired of my involvement in her cases and the vigor of the Paddington family.

"Gwendolyn told Nana D and I last Saturday she thought someone had been trying to hurt her. She wasn't feeling well and had some disputes with different family members. I didn't take it seriously at first, but when I went with them to the *King Lear* dress rehearsal the following day, I noticed a few peculiar behaviors and conversations. When she had the heart attack, it didn't feel right."

"I asked him to poke around and see if he could figure out what was going on. He's got my authority to be involved," Eustacia yelled in a cranky voice.

"And as the next mayor, I support it!" Nana rapped her knuckles on the wooden insert in the couch's arms as a misguided display of support.

"That's not how the law works, ladies," the sheriff replied in an authoritative tone. "Here's how this is going to proceed. All of you will be interviewed this afternoon. My team is collecting evidence around the estate. Your attorney will be notified of everything we take off property. If after these discussions I have any further questions, I will contact you directly. In return, not a single one of you will do anything to search for a potential killer nor discuss the case with anyone. At this point, we believe something suspicious led to Gwendolyn Paddington's death, but we have more tests to run, a full autopsy to complete, and an investigation to conclude."

"It might be important for you to know we've already started compiling a list of suspects who—" Nana D began but was told to be quiet.

"Can it, Mrs. Danby. All of you are to remain in this room until I call you into the front study for questions. Is that clear?" Sheriff Montague stood and left the room. A few seconds later, Officer Flatman, a young cop with hopes of making detective one day—something I definitely did not see happening soon given my past interactions with him—called Millard into the room. Nana D, Eustacia, and I decided to review our list of suspects, next steps, and theories while we waited. Lindsey was allowed to leave since he wasn't a member of the household or the family, but he was staying put until Finnigan showed up.

I narrowed my gaze at Eustacia and Nana D. "I've agreed to help you with this only because you're forcing me to do so, but I am staying out of April Montague's path. You will interact with her if there are any questions this time—not me. Is that clear?" Both nodded. "Okay. Who's tracking down the will to understand what motives might exist?"

Eustacia volunteered for that effort. "I've got power-of-attorney. Lindsey told me Finnigan Masters is the attorney he recommended to Charles years ago. Charles and Gwendolyn both had wills on file with him. All I need to do is talk with Finnigan later today when he comes by to discuss everything with me. He was in court and couldn't leave until three o'clock."

"Great, that will cover any motives for an inheritance. Who can talk with Bertha Crawford and Brad Shope to get a clearer picture of all of Gwendolyn's activities, meals, prescriptions and anything else the last few weeks?" I asked looking at Nana D. She'd already connected with both of them since she'd been hanging around the house to support Eustacia during her sister-in-law's death.

Nana D confirmed. "I'll find out what they know. I'll also get the full details from my cousin, Alex, about the autopsy. I owe it to Gwennie to help figure out what happened. And I need to teach that sheriff a lesson she won't forget. No one tells Seraphina Danby to *can it!*"

I rolled my eyes. "I'd like to meet the whole family again. Can you arrange a lunch or tea for tomorrow when everyone can come by, so we can carefully inquire about anything they might know?

Millard walked back in the room as I brought up the family meeting. "I'll handle that one. We have to discuss funeral arrangements with Ophelia anyway, so this will be a perfect opportunity to get everyone together." He indicated that Eustacia was next to meet with the sheriff. While she was gone, I told Millard and Nana D I'd chat with Arthur. He'd made a few disparaging remarks about Gwendolyn and had several run-ins with her in the past. As far as I was concerned, he should be on the suspect list.

By the time I finished writing out everyone's responsibilities, it was my time to see the sheriff. I luckily got away fairly unscathed but also hadn't learned anything new. She reminded me to stay out of the investigation which I, of course, agreed to do while crossing my fingers behind my back. At three o'clock, I left to pick up Emma at school. I'd been hoping to have a few minutes with Finnigan, but he was running late from court. I'd have to follow up with him in the future.

Emma and I stopped for a quick bowl of fruit for her and a coffee for me. We discussed her day before she had to go to a gymnastics lesson. I'd arranged for a friend of Eleanor's who had a daughter the same age as Emma to split today's responsibilities for drop off and pick up at the gymnasium. While Emma and I drove to her friend's house, she asked a few questions about her mother.

"Nonna Cecilia says I should still talk about her all the time. It helps keep the memory alive. How come you never talk about her anymore, Daddy?" Emma asked with a curiosity I didn't want to hear.

"When did she say that?" I sincerely hoped Cecilia wasn't forcing her demented plans behind my back. Although everyone complained about their mother-in-law, I knew for a fact mine was the worst.

"She called yesterday to see if I liked my new school. Did you know I can touch my tongue to my nose?" Emma demonstrated it for me and asked if I could, too. I tried but failed miserably. I ended up with drool sliding off my lips and a six-year-old daughter cackling like a goose.

"Does Nonna Cecilia call you often?" I asked preparing to block Cecilia's number from Emma's phone. I'd been against giving Emma her own phone at such a young age, but I realized she was a lot more mature than others. Since my daughter was often going back and forth between my house and her grandparents in LA, and now the same was happening between Nana D, Eleanor, and my parents' house in Braxton, it was useful to be able to reach her easily.

"Almost every day. 'Cept not today. She said she had a big meeting and couldn't use her phone where she was going." Emma changed the radio station as we pulled up to her friend's house. "We like rock music, Daddy."

"Okay, that's my favorite, too." While we waited for her friend, I told Emma that I missed her mother very much and hoped one day in the future to see her again.

"When you're in heaven?" she asked.

I nodded not knowing what else to say. Luckily the rear passenger door opened and Emma's new best friend jumped inside. I worked out the details with the girl's mother on when and where to drop Emma off, then drove to the gymnasium. It was a huge facility near the Betscha mines filled with authentic rock-climbing walls, rings hanging from the ceiling, balance beams, and tons of mats on the floor. I verified they were both in the beginner's class and only working on the mats today. I wanted to be present the first time Emma used any of the more intense or dangerous equipment. Thirty minutes later, I arrived at the diner to catch up with my sister.

"You look like you lost your best friend," Eleanor said while hugging me. "Your horoscopes this week keep warning about a devil consuming every ounce of energy you have left."

I couldn't agree more. But was the devil Cecilia? Francesca? Myriam? April? One of the Paddingtons? How was I supposed to know how to stop it from happening when I didn't know whom it was? "What should I be doing to prevent it?" I asked cautiously fearing the worst.

Eleanor asked me to cut the deck of Tarot cards a few times, then she displayed several in front of me sharing the story of my future. Or my past, I never knew what she was doing with all the numerology and astrology readings she forced on me. "Basically, you're screwed for the next two weeks. Someone's angry and you're going to feel the brunt of it," she said in a matter-of-fact tone.

"Tell me something I don't already know. That's just a fact of my life, sis."

We both guffawed, then talked about the renovations at the diner. She'd expanded the kitchen and closed up one of the small party rooms in the back corner explaining that no one had ever rented it. Rather than try to include more tables, she'd thought a better kitchen with more state-of-the-art tools and appliances would help drive customers to keep coming back.

"The inspector comes tomorrow morning. If everything goes well, we have a few minor things to finish up, then we can open next week."

"Not bad, only closed for two weeks. Are you and Maggie able to afford being offline this long?

"It was built into the cost of the loan. I think we'll be okay, but we can't let any delays get in the way." Eleanor's face relaxed as she spoke showing how much stronger she'd become in the last few years. There was a fair balance between confidence and humility that shined through.

I was proud of my sister. She'd been through countless discussions with my mother about why she hadn't settled down and gotten married. Eleanor explained she'd been trying but things weren't looking promising in that area of her life. Until she met the right man, the diner would be her partner. I felt obliged to ask about Connor.

"Yes, Connor called earlier today. We're planning to talk soon about what's going on between us. He's still interested, but he doesn't want to rush anything."

"I assume that's code for *scared to be in the middle of you and Maggie?*"

"Wouldn't you be?" Eleanor said using her '*I'm being serious*' tone and mean face.

"Only because you can be vicious when you go after something you desperately desire!" I teased.

"I'm a woman who knows what she wants and isn't afraid to go after it. I'm thirty-years-old and might not be married with kids, but I own a business and a small home. I'm on the board of the town community center, and I volunteer on several different committees in Wharton County. Life's good, but there can always be more. Why not throw myself at something when I want it?" There was a twinkle in her eye when she told me how she felt about herself these days.

I was excited for her becoming a big business woman around town. "You're pretty awesome, Eleanor. I don't tell you that enough."

"You're the best big brother around. Speaking of brothers, have you heard from Hampton at all?" Hampton, the eldest of the five Ayrwick siblings, was a lawyer married to a snobby, rich oil heiress.

I said, "Nope. I figured he'd call Dad first, then we'd know whatever surprise he had in store. How about Gabriel or Penelope?" Penelope is our second oldest sibling at thirty-four, married to Jack with twin boys about to enter their teenage years and a trouble-making step-daughter from Jack's first marriage—all of which I unabashedly hoped would wreak havoc with my sister's many OCDs.

"Penelope and I talked this morning. She made partner at that fancy New York City real estate firm. Gabriel is still a mystery," Eleanor said with a pang of sadness in her voice.

Nearly eight years ago, my youngest brother, Gabriel, announced he was transferring to Penn State to finish his degree having only been at Braxton for two years. That's when our father decided to accept the presidency Braxton had been offering to him for years—especially once they upped the ante until it was so sweet, even I might have passed on dessert for a taste of it. After Gabriel changed his mind on the transfer, he expected our father to withdraw from the job. Of course, he couldn't. Gabriel in his usual elegant manner left Braxton and decided never to come home again claiming our father had stabbed him in the back. He was too proud to attend the same school where our father was the head honcho. I can't say they ever got along, but I still don't know exactly what's kept him away for so long.

"I was thinking about hiring a detective to track down Gabriel. Maybe we could convince him to give Dad another chance," I said.

"Hire a detective? I thought that was your new job from what Nana D tells me about the search for Gwendolyn's killer. Aren't you running for sheriff, so you can be Nana D's sidekick when she wins the mayoral race?" Eleanor giggled like a school girl before standing up to plate some dessert for us.

I might have made an inappropriate gesture at her. "No, I'm not running for sheriff. That's not until next year, but you do have a point. I've picked up some more skills since returning home. I *could* track Gabriel down." Hmm… could I also run for sheriff? No, I wasn't qualified. Yet.

"What's going on with the Paddington case?" Eleanor asked as if I'd actually refer to them as cases. "I saw Jennifer today at the doctor's office. She's Gwendolyn's daughter, right?"

I nodded. "One of them, at least. Did you speak to her?"

"No, I've never met her before, but I recognized her from a few charity organizations we both worked on in the past. She was arguing with the receptionist." Eleanor scooped banana pudding between her lips practically drooling over the taste.

"That good?" I said with a cheer before shoveling down my own spoonful. "What was the disagreement about?"

"Money. She complained that some procedure was too expensive, and she'd lost her insurance when her last job ended. I'm not sure what it was about, but she seemed steamed no one had explained the costs to her before she saw the doctor."

At the risk of learning too much, I asked the question anyway. "What kind of doctor?" Fearing it was the gynecologist, I closed my eyes and covered my ears.

"You're such a baby! Yes, it was related to her lady parts. Honestly, Kellan. You're thirty-two-years-old and you have a daughter. You're gonna have to get used to talking about it someday." Eleanor dropped her spoon into the bowl and pushed it toward the end of the table. "Have you made any decisions about Francesca?"

Phew, I was glad she brought it up. I struggled to acknowledge out loud what was going on in my life. "Thank you for asking. I'm still in shock. Cecilia's playing games trying to manipulate Emma. And I found a letter Francesca left for me the day she came by."

"What did it say?" Eleanor reached out and patted my hand.

"She reminded me of wonderful times in our past. Just some personal things that made me realize I'll never stop loving her." My normally protected barriers began to weaken. I rarely cried, but in the last few days, I'd felt like the waterworks were always near the surface. "How can this be happening?"

Eleanor dragged me to the kitchen to wash our dishes thinking manual labor would be a good solution for improving my humdrum mood. We settled on not making any decisions until Cecilia's two-week deadline arrived, and even then, I would take control of the situation. Eleanor reminded me that I held the cards—not them.

When Emma arrived, we turned on some music and had a lively dance party. We also helped Eleanor finish setting up the rest of the diner in preparation for the inspection the following day. Maggie stopped by to check on progress but made it clear she fully trusted Eleanor to make all the decisions. As the silent partner in their new business venture, Maggie let Eleanor take the lead until her job at the library settled down. After introducing Emma to Maggie, Eleanor took my daughter into the kitchen to view the new equipment. I knew she was trying to give Maggie and me a few moments alone.

"She's gorgeous, Kellan. And so smart and kind. You must be an amazing father," Maggie said while hugging me. "She's a lucky girl."

As Maggie started to pull away, our favorite song came on the radio. An instrumental version of *'I'll Stand By You'* by The Pretenders accompanied us as we stood in an embrace beginning to sway back and forth like we had years ago. The street light poured in through the crackled window and illuminated her tender face. For just a minute, I saw a different future than the one I'd thought would always be present with Francesca. Lost in thought, I hadn't immediately realized my phone was ringing.

"I guess you need to answer that," Maggie said with disappointment.

I'd have let it go to voicemail for just about anyone, but I had to respond to Nana D's ring. I pulled the phone from my pocket as Maggie told me she needed to get going. When I watched her leave, my heart raced even faster. I forced myself to answer Nana D's call. "Hi. Everything okay?"

"No, Kellan, it's most definitely not. Finnigan told us what the cops found. We were right."

"What do you mean?" I'd been too distracted to think clearly.

"There wasn't anything in the iced tea. It's a good thing we saved that glass. It means the cocaine was introduced in the pills Brad gave to Gwennie. There was enough in there to kill a horse."

"That's awful. What else did you learn?" My head began to throb from overload of things taking up all my attention.

"Gwennie called last week to re-draft her will again with Finnigan."

"Did he say what changes were made?"

"No, that's the issue. Finnigan wrote up the revisions, but she asked him to leave the names blank. She planned to fill them in and send it back to him. That was the night before she died."

"Where's the will now?" I contemplated whether that approach was even legal, but Finnigan wouldn't have allowed it to happen if he had concerns. I'd need to validate that at some point. Maybe my brother, Hampton, would know the specifics of this type of law. Did I dare call him?

"Finnigan doesn't know. She might have put it in the mail, or it might not have been finalized. We're as confused as a fart in a fan factory on a humid day."

What did she say? I couldn't even permit myself to ask without conjuring up the most awful images and horrendous smells. I hung up with Nana D realizing the possible existence of two wills made the investigation a lot more complicated. What did it all mean? And was the sheriff looking at Brad as the guilty party for giving her the pills laced with cocaine?

* * *

"I must've dropped it in your office, Dad. I was going through some paperwork to change my mailing address and found it," I fibbed at breakfast the following morning when my father grilled me about Francesca's letter. I'd gotten home too late the night before to explain anything and had come up with the excuse overnight.

"What were you doing in my study? And under the desk no less." my father said curtly while sitting in the kitchen, drinking coffee, and eating a bowl of granola. He'd already dressed in his power suit for a big meeting on campus with the Board of Trustees to review the budget for Braxton's conversion into a university. "It's not that I don't want you in there, but it was odd."

I stared at him as he methodically collected several grains and a raspberry on the same spoonful before swallowing it. He'd always advised it was important to achieve the right balance in weight and taste with each bite. "I'm not sure, I probably bent down to pick up some loose change that fell from my pants and knocked the letter under the file cabinet portion. I had the letter in my pocket when I was thinking about my upcoming anniversary with Francesca. It's several years old." My brow began to sweat despite not having completed my morning run.

We chatted idly about the weather and Emma's new school. I could tell he was suspicious but had no way of knowing how the letter had wound up on the floor. Unless he had installed a security camera in his study in the past. A drop of sweat from my forehead splashed into my coffee. My father looked over and scratched his head. "Are you feeling okay, son?"

I nodded and mumbled something about it being too warm in the room. He offered to drop Emma off at school for me which was a big help since I needed to run a few errands, get in a workout, and meet Eustacia's family at noon for the family meeting Millard had organized for me to attend.

Once I kissed Emma goodbye and my father's car pulled down the driveway, I dashed into his study and combed every corner or crevice I could find. I waved in every direction to see if I heard a camera making any noise or moving to capture my picture. I made it appear like I was looking for a stamp. When I found one a few minutes later, I said out loud in case he was listening too, "Exactly what I needed to mail my change of address forms. I can always count on Dad to save the day." I even made a big show of holding out the stamp and admiring the latest design. Arthur or Myriam might cast me in their next production.

I found no cameras, but I wasn't as versed in the world of security as I needed to be. For all I knew he could've hidden something in a pen or a clock. Maybe even one of Emma's old teddy bears which sat on the shelf staring at me in judgment. I imagined it chastising me for lying to my family. For some reason, the bear sounded like Winnie The Pooh.

Chapter 9

Once all my tasks were completed, I pulled up in front of the Paddington estate at five minutes to noon. What does one wear when you plan to secretly grill the *loving* family of a woman who'd been murdered, but you aren't a detective? I'd settled on traditional clothing by choosing a pair of tan corduroys, a classic single-breasted blue blazer, and open-collared white dress shirt. If it weren't the Paddingtons I might have chosen something more comfortable like jeans and a t-shirt, but I wasn't completely clueless as to the need to impress a potential killer. Or should I have looked sloppy, so the perp ignored me? This new secret job of mine was more cumbersome and baffling than necessary.

Bertha led me to a new room I hadn't been in before. We turned left at the Great Hall and walked past a grand library and a game room, both decorated in mauve and gold wall-paper. She dropped me off in what I assumed to be Gwendolyn's office given it had a conference table and large, lavish desk in the corner. "The others will be in shortly," she said pulling the door closed behind her.

The room felt stuffy. Everything had been dusted recently as not a speck could be found. No personal items of any sort offered warmth or comfort. The lighting was minimal, and there was only one small window covered in thick, heavy drapery. I organized my thoughts as the grandfather clock's minute hand ticked by leaving me more unsettled with my approach. I reviewed the notes on my phone to ensure I had all the questions listed. I'd been intently reading when the door opened and spooked me back to reality.

Jennifer Paddington was the first to enter the room. Her slightly stooped posture and slow entrance felt awkward and unusual. Her normal elegance and confidence had been replaced by something darker. After a confused expression where she nervously scratched at the table's solid wood, Jennifer said, "Kellan, I didn't expect to see you in here. Uncle Millard told us we needed to discuss my mother's funeral plans. I'm sorry I'm late, did I miss that conversation?"

Hoping not to be caught off-guard as well, I shrugged my shoulders and asked her to take a seat at the table. I also thought I'd be interviewing the entire family in one meeting, but it seemed Millard had other plans. "I'm sure they'll be along soon enough. Millard and Eustacia asked me to swing by, so I could find out if anyone had input on the Paddington family's role in overseeing the Play House at Braxton," I managed to squeak out as a cover. If she thought I was there to solicit ideas as I temporarily stepped into the role of patron, it might relax her.

"Oh, I forgot about that. Mother was so active with the theater. Sometimes she spent more time with that crowd than her own family," Jennifer remarked with slightly pursed lips followed by a fake smile. I knew it was fake because she couldn't hold a gaze with me for more than a second at a time without blushing or coughing.

I considered her response, uncertain if she was being flippant or had seriously felt that way about her relationship with her mother. "She had a passion to support the arts. Were you close?"

"Mother wasn't someone you could easily be close to, Kellan. She loved us, sure, but we were often left to ourselves while she and Father kept busy running Paddington Enterprises, traveling to New York City for shows, and entertaining the more important people." Jennifer glanced around the room as if she were recalling previous times where her needs had been overshadowed by those of her parents. "I've never liked this room. It's cold. Empty. Don't you think?"

I sighed. "It's not an inviting space for cozy family time. I'm sorry things weren't so wonderful at home. I admired your mother's forthright approach, but I can see how it might be difficult being one of her children." I hoped there'd been a different, more private side to Gwendolyn, but it appeared that wasn't the case.

"There's nothing I can add of value to the Play House. It's not something I've ever been interested in. My nephew, Sam, and niece, Dana, were much more involved with Mother in that area. If that's all, I'm going to track down Uncle Millard. I don't have a lot of time today to—"

The door opened and in skulked Ophelia. "What's the purpose of calling us all together today? I'm handling Mother's funeral plans. There's nothing anyone else needs—" A knitted brow and an unflattering frown revealed her disgust before the words had even left her lips. She stopped short and adjusted the collar on her lavender silk blouse when she saw me sitting at the table. "Who are you?"

Jennifer moaned at the interruption. I attempted to reintroduce myself, but Ophelia turned away from me and focused on her sister. "Did you hear anything about Mother's will? I've called Finnigan Masters, but he hasn't returned my voicemail. It's quite irresponsible of him."

Eustacia walked in the room leaning on her cane for support until she reached the table. "Sit down, the both of you. Finnigan has no responsibility to discuss the will with either one of you. I have Gwendolyn's power-of-attorney. We're pulling everything together this week, so that we can determine when to have the formal will reading."

Jennifer took a seat at the table. Ophelia waved her hand at her aunt in a dismissive manner. "I don't understand why she left you in charge. You're not even her sister."

Jennifer said, "Behave, Ophelia. You know they've been close ever since Father died."

"My name is Kellan Ayrwick, Mrs. Taft," I said looking toward Ophelia. "We met the other day during the *King Lear* performance. I am a friend of your family—"

"Oh, yes, the guy Mother fell onto during the second half of the show. What are you doing here?" Her voice held enough contempt to rival any narcissist I'd met in the past, perhaps even Myriam.

"Kellan's here to discuss the Play House, but also to help me figure out which one of you drove poor Gwennie to her death." Eustacia sat taller in the chair unaffected by her accusation against someone in the family. She chose to go directly for the kill instead of gradually introducing the conversation.

"One of us? Are you mad, Aunt Eustacia? Mother died of a heart attack," replied Ophelia with a shriek in her voice. "What the devil are you talking about?"

"Didn't you know the cops were here searching the house yesterday?" Jennifer said shaking her head at her sister. "Maybe you shouldn't have gone off for a spa day in the middle of everything blowing up around us."

"No one cares what you think, Jennifer. You're one to talk. If anyone had it out for Mother, it's you. She's the one who pushed—"

"Why would you say that, Mrs. Taft?" I interrupted hoping to learn something of importance. It wasn't exactly my place to insert myself, but there were clearly problems in the Paddington family.

"Jennifer only visited Mother to get money out of her. She's kept herself distant from the rest of us except when she needed something or Mother forced her to attend a family function,"

Ophelia chastised while pouring herself a glass of sherry from the antique bar cart in the corner of the room.

Eustacia remained silent. I assumed she wanted me to witness the various antics and nasty behavior of her nieces. It was certainly an over-acted show reminiscent of a Kardashian family reunion.

"That's simply not true. You've been trying to get money out of her for years ever since that husband of yours disappeared," Jennifer reminded her sister while slapping her hand against the table.

"He hasn't disappeared. He goes out of town to do work for Paddington Enterprises. Besides, I have three children to take care of. You don't have anyone else!" Ophelia replied swiftly.

Jennifer looked away without any response. A bucket of rage flooded her face before she buried her focus on a family portrait behind the desk. It had been painted at least twenty years ago when Ophelia and Jennifer were in their late twenties or early thirties. I saw their brother standing between them prompting me to ask a question. "What about Timothy? I noticed him at the show last weekend. I guess he was sitting elsewhere? How's he handling your mother's death?"

Jennifer shrugged her shoulders. "I haven't heard from him."

"Neither have I," Ophelia added. "I doubt he attended the actual performance."

Eustacia cleared her throat. "The last I saw him was during the intermission. Has no one spoken to him? Surely he's aware what happened to Gwennie."

The room was silent when Millard entered. "I'm glad you started without me. I've been detained talking to Brad upstairs about a few things."

"Mr. Paddington, it's good to see you. Your family was just saying that no one's heard from Timothy since Gwendolyn passed away on Sunday. Were you able to get in touch with him?" I asked finding it odd that no one knew anything. I also knew minimal information about the man and would need to ask more questions privately when I had a chance.

"No, I thought you did, Eustacia. I left him a voice mail to be here at noon today. Is he not around?" Millard walked toward Ophelia and handed her an envelope. I couldn't see what was written on it, but it looked like something you'd get from a bank.

"No one's heard from him in three days?" Eustacia shouted in exasperation. As she stood from the table, her cane fell to the floor. I jumped up to help her re-gain her balance and be able to walk without falling. I looked around discovering no one else seemed to pay attention. This was not a family with an abundance of love. Gwendolyn's son was missing. Both her daughters were fighting about money. Millard was acting strangely given he'd agreed to setup the meeting today but showed up late and hadn't invited the whole family. What did he hand Ophelia?

"Where are Dana, Sam, and Lilly?" I asked.

Millard offered an apologetic look. "I should've mentioned it to you before. I didn't invite them today. I thought it best for you to meet Gwennie's children first, then we can follow up with the others."

I would have preferred to know that in advance, but it wouldn't help me to admonish him. I was certain no one reprimanded a Paddington. Ophelia announced she had to leave. Millard followed her out the door intent on discussing something before she left. Jennifer stood and thanked me for stopping by, then left. Eustacia and I looked at one another and laughed.

"How do you deal with them? I don't mean it offensively, but your family is more disruptive and bitter than mine," I said halfheartedly.

"It's always been like that, Kellan. My brother was the one person who kept everyone in line. When Charles passed away last year, Gwennie lost interest in controlling her children. Ophelia's husband is constantly in and out of the picture, I never know what's going on between them."

"They're still married?"

Eustacia nodded. "Ophelia claims Richard left her penniless, so she'd constantly ask her mother for money to cover expenses. Although, given she lives here and all the bills are paid for by the household budget, I'm not certain how much she needs to survive."

"Jennifer seemed shaken when Ophelia dismissed her needs because she didn't have any children to support."

"Jennifer's had a hard life. She's been engaged twice, both men broke it off. The first practically left her at the altar, poor thing. And the last time, well, that wasn't fair to her," Eustacia said wistfully while closing her eyes. "My dear niece had two miscarriages while they were engaged, and the louse walked away from her when he thought she couldn't give him any children."

"That's terrible," I said thinking about my sister. Though Eleanor had never been pregnant, wanting a child of her own had been a driving force in her life the last few years. "Is Jennifer still hoping to have a child?"

"I'm not the one to ask. We were close years ago but after the last broken engagement, she moved out of the house and keeps to herself," Eustacia noted while walking toward the door. "Did you learn anything of importance today?"

I shook my head. "Perhaps a little. I think we need to track down Timothy. I find it concerning he had a public disagreement with his mother moments before she died. He might have had access to put cocaine in her pills at any point before Brad brought them to the theater.

"As did Ophelia and Jennifer, as well as any of her grandchildren or anyone who had access to her medication closet," Eustacia explained looking back at the portrait above the desk with discerning focus. "We need to find out what was written in the will. Either someone killed Gwennie for the inheritance, or they were angry with her over something else. I can't think of another motive, can you?"

I told her I couldn't. When Eustacia left, Bertha stepped inside to escort me to the front door. As we walked the hallway, I asked, "Have you seen anything odd with Gwendolyn's behavior during the last few weeks?" I knew Nana D was going to talk with the staff, but since I was already there, I took advantage of the opportunity.

"Mrs. Paddington was distressed more than usual. She rarely said anything to me about them, mostly complained in general over their lack of consideration for her. But she did say something one afternoon," Bertha noted as we reached the front door. When I asked what she'd said, Bertha's face blanched. "That girl needs to be taught a lesson."

"Gwendolyn said that about whom?" I asked not understanding the comment.

"I think it was Jennifer. Gwendolyn had just hung up the phone with her when I announced lunch. Mrs. Paddington kept repeating the line, then told me call her attorney," Bertha explained before saying goodbye.

As I stepped down, I pressed accept on my ringing phone and said, "How did the inspection go?"

Eleanor grunted. "I failed. He told me the electrical work didn't meet code and that I couldn't open next week. I need help, Kellan."

This wasn't good news. "Did he give you a write-up of what needs to be corrected?"

"Yes, and it's way more than I can afford based on what the inspector suggested should be done. Apparently once I started construction by opening up walls and installing new appliances, I was responsible for bringing the kitchen up to current electrical code. I can't get this done without any money or time." Eleanor sounded infuriated. I couldn't blame her. I'd also be disheartened and worried if I'd sunk all my money into a new business that wasn't starting off in a good position.

"What does the contractor say?"

"He's gone already. He packed up yesterday when the work was done and told me to call him if I needed anything. When I tried just now, his phone was no longer in service."

I inquired how she'd located the contractor to begin with, but Eleanor mumbled something about the previous owners recommending him. Given the short time frame, she didn't bother with any additional quotes or references and foolishly trusted their judgment. Eleanor gave me the contractor's name, and I told her I'd find out what I could.

On the drive to Braxton to visit my mother, I thought through all the people who might be able to help Eleanor. I called the Play House to see if Arthur Terry was available. As the person responsible for running the *King Lear* production, he likely had an available carpenter or electrician who might be able to spare an hour and provide a quote and options for Eleanor. He didn't pick up the phone, but Yuri, the girl working on the stage design, promised to deliver my urgent message as soon as Arthur returned. My day was getting entirely too busy for what was supposed to be Spring Break.

I parked the SUV in the North Campus lot and briskly walked to the admissions building to visit my mother. Her assistant mentioned my mother was almost done updating a family who was about to take a tour of the campus. I waited in the lobby outside her door admiring the fancy new nameplate—Violet Ayrwick, Admissions Director. When she was done, my mother led me into her office, then closed the door. "Is there something you're keeping from your father and me, Kellan?"

I guess that meant my father had told my mother about the letter. "Not at all, why do you ask?"

"Oh, just wondering... your father mentioned finding something. You've been hanging out with the Paddingtons lately.

Nana D said you were running her campaign. Do you think that's a wise thing to do? She's almost seventy-five years old, honey. Nana D needs to rest," my mother reproached.

"Nana D's a lot sprier than you give her credit for, Mom."

"That's not what I'm worried about. I'm sure she can handle it, but do you think Wharton County will support her? She's not qualified to run for mayor. Marcus Stanton is going to destroy her reputation." My mother took a giant swig of water, then sighed heavily. "I wish my brother was home to help talk her out of it. He's been very quiet ever since he left on that month-long African safari."

"I understand, but when have you ever known Nana D to back down from a challenge? She's determined to fix Braxton while she still has enough energy and time." I'd already tried to convince Nana D not to take on the job, encouraging her to become a councilwoman when Marcus vacated his role to run for mayor. She wouldn't listen and had told me she had to *slap his bottom silly*. That was her frequent method for teaching people lessons—she comes from a different era.

"Just watch her closely please. She listens to you," my mother begged. We laughed for a minute knowing Nana D listened to no one but herself.

My mother brewed coffee while we talked. I asked her what she knew about the Paddington family. I remembered her telling me she'd gone to high school with Ophelia nearly thirty years ago.

"Ophelia's ruthless and mean, a bad combination. Many people say she's just like her mother, but there's a subtle difference. Where Gwendolyn was ornery and stubborn, Ophelia brandishes much more than a mean streak. That woman likes to get revenge on anyone who hurts her."

"It sounds like you speak from experience, Mom." I pictured an epic battle between my mother and Ophelia, not knowing who'd win. While my mother was sweet and gentle, she had a competitive side and could be stealthy.

My mother appeared to ponder the past before responding. "Not really. We were never friends or enemies. We didn't hang out in the same crowd. I had to help run things on the farm at Danby Landing after school. Ophelia went to a variety of social clubs and had a nanny who looked out for her."

"Do you know her husband?" I realized I still needed to find a way to meet him.

"Richard Taft used to be friendly with your father, and occasionally we'd see them at charity or sporting events around campus. He took an out of town job over a year ago last Christmas. I heard he and Ophelia may be considering separating which makes sense since I haven't seen him around at all."

"Has Dad not heard from him either?"

"No, he tried a few times, but after a couple of months, your father assumed Richard didn't want to talk anymore. There were a few unfortunate, public arguments between him and Ophelia."

"Do you think Ophelia is capable of killing her mother? From what I understand, she had little money left and was recently pressuring Gwendolyn to lend her some." I didn't like the way the woman had treated me or her family earlier that day, but there's a fine line between being a menace and killing someone. I didn't have enough information to hazard a guess if she was dangerous or just cruel.

"Oh, goodness. I don't know her that well now. I suppose under the right circumstances she could be vindictive enough. But surely someone wouldn't kill their own mother over money, Kellan." My mother looked at me with both judgment and concern.

"Don't worry, Mom. I'm not thinking about sending you to an early grave," I joked, then looked in the other direction while tapping my fingers together in a devilish way. "Besides, how else would I deal with Nana D if you weren't there to help me?"

My mother laughed and warned me to be careful. "I don't trust that family. I've never had any issues with them, but something's not right. Everyone seems out to hurt each other, even those older ones."

My mother told me that when their parents passed away, Charles, Millard, and Eustacia had a huge falling out over the distribution of assets. At the time and given the way things ran in the Paddington family, the eldest male inherited the bulk of the estate. For some reason, Millard was skipped over and everything had been given to Charles. Eustacia had pitched such a fit, her siblings stopped speaking to her for a year. My mother had no idea about the source of the blow-up.

"What happened when Charles died?" I asked.

"His son, Timothy, had been running the company for the last decade after Charles retired, but shortly before Charles passed away, he convinced the Board of Directors to place his son on temporary leave. Timothy had a substance abuse problem he'd been struggling with and was making some horrendous business decisions. I believe Gwendolyn kept the house because she was still alive, but I'm not certain of the other details or the current state of the family business," my mother indicated before telling me she had to prepare for a meeting.

Chapter 10

After I left the admissions building, the current state of Paddington Enterprises became my focus. Was Timothy still running the organization, or did he never come back from the forced leave of absence? I needed his help to fill in the missing pieces, but before I could do that, it was time to help Nana D prepare for her first debate with Marcus Stanton. I sent her a text indicating I'd be by for dinner after finishing up a few afternoon errands.

Nana D: *I want tacos. I'm feeling the need to have Mexican tonight.*
Me: *Are we cooking them ourselves, or am I bringing take out?*
Nana D: *Can't you make any decisions yourself, brilliant one?*
Me: *If I brought takeout, you'd tell me it was full of chemicals. If I bought all the ingredients, you'd tell me we had no time to cook since we're supposed to practice for your debate.*
Nana D: *Are you saying I never let you win? Margaritas, too.*
Me: *I think staying sober would be better for tomorrow.*
Nana D: *I wasn't asking your opinion. Don't be cheap. Get the good liquor. I'm out.*

I decided to compromise by picking up tortilla chips, tacos, and burritos at our favorite Mexican restaurant, but I'd also buy all the ingredients to make our own guacamole. I had a secret recipe with shallots, cumin, and bacon that couldn't be topped. As for the drinks, I knew I had no chance to stop her, so why bother? I'd make them as weak as possible or spill half of hers out when she wasn't looking.

* * *

I woke up Thursday morning with a hangover so painful my head had put out a foreclosure sign. My eyelids blinked several times in a row trying to read the clock on the far wall. Where was I? Nana D's couch. I then heard someone speaking and tried to understand the conversation.

"He doesn't look so well, Nana D," Emma noted and poked my cheek.

"That's what happens when you try to pull the wool over Nana D's eyes, baby girl. Don't ever forget that lesson," Nana D teased.

"Is he gonna throw up again? That was yucky," Emma shuddered.

"It's the only way to teach your Daddy who knows better. He likes to learn things the hard way. Always has, even at your age. Such a stubborn little boy," Nana D said with a sigh.

"I can hear you both." My left foot dropped to the ground with a thud. "Please explain to me what happened last night?"

Emma told me that we were all having a good time eating dinner, but she didn't understand why I kept switching out Nana D's glass with a different one. When she asked Nana D about it, my grandmother told Emma that the rules needed to change. It was time to swap out her daddy's glass with a different one Nana D had poured. It seemed at the end of the night, my nana had two margaritas and I had eight of them. Now I knew why I had the hangover from that place I told Emma never to speak of.

Emma went to the kitchen to get me a glass of water. "I'm the only person in the world whose nana purposely tried to get him drunk. Hardly seems fair, nor something you should be teaching

Emma, Nana D," I said feeling a dry pastiness in my mouth I hadn't felt in years.

"Oh, pish! All Emma knows is that you drank so much you almost wet the couch. I explained that she should never drink that much liquid before bed, so honestly, it was a useful thing for her to learn, Kellan. I hope *you've* also realized something from last night." Nana D handed me two aspirin and a cold rag, followed by a glass of something that smelled like rotten tomatoes and looked like the salsa we'd eaten the night before.

"What's this?" I asked feeling the contents of my stomach rising over the smell in the glass.

"Your hangover cure. I couldn't leave you feeling this bad all day long. I need your support at the debate." Nana D smiled at me like a gentle and innocent grandmother who wanted only the best for me.

"You're a wicked woman. I get it. Don't mess with Nana D. It won't happen again," I said before swallowing a large gulp of her concoction.

"Excellent. Then we're off to a good start today. Also, Timothy still hasn't turned up. Eustacia called an hour ago to tell me no one's heard from him in nearly four days."

"I'll see what I can find out after the debate," I said accepting the glass of water from Emma. I alternated between the water and Nana D's hangover cure until both drinks were gone. Within ten minutes, I felt like a new person. "You're a miracle worker."

When I came downstairs dressed and ready to go thirty minutes later, I asked Nana D, "Has anyone found out what's going on with either of the two wills?"

Nana D shook her head. "Eustacia was going to ask Bertha to go through the entire house to see if she could find anything. I unfortunately learned nothing from talking to her."

After dropping Emma off at school, we drove to the debate. As soon as we got back on the main road, my phone rang. Once we saw whom it was, Nana D put it on speaker, so we could both listen. Arthur called to offer the use of his stage contractor and an electrician who could stop by the Pick-Me-Up Diner on their break to give Eleanor a quote for the repairs. When I told him the name of Eleanor's contractor, he laughed wildly. "That man's a crook. I looked him up on a few websites when he applied at the Play House for a job. Steals from everyone, then doesn't finish the work. Eleanor should count herself lucky he accomplished what he did before vanishing!" Arthur suggested we should meet for coffee on Friday to catch up. We firmed up plans, then hung up.

As we entered the Wharton County Civic Center's parking lot, Nana D said, "I'm gonna crack down on these slipshod contractors and get them out of my county. By the way, might Arthur be a good catch for Eleanor? She could stand to get herself a date sometime soon. Between you and her, it's like an entire generation has given up on love."

I rolled my eyes for the umpteenth time at my grandmother. When I realized having her focus on setting up Eleanor would be a blessing in disguise, I gave in. "That's a possibility. Maybe you should try to help her out with a new romance?"

"Sounds like a deal. But don't think that gets you off the hook. You're still my primary focus right now. I've found a charming girl who works at the prison. Real chipper. Built like an ox, too. A security guard, I believe," Nana D casually mentioned as she popped open the car door and raced into the building before I had a chance to reply. Was she serious?

While Nana D and Marcus prepared with the moderator, Lara Bouvier, on stage for the upcoming debate, I made a list of things to inquire about once we were done. I needed to find out from the sheriff what she'd learned, not that she'd share easily. The debate kicked off with Lara introducing herself to the room. The local news station, WCLN, had planned to cover all three of the debates which meant the entire county could watch even though the attendance for today's first one was kept to a few hundred citizens ranging from members of the civic center to local merchant groups. Lara, a mid-forties divorcee, was the political correspondent at Wharton County's local news station who covered both national and regional politics in the area. She'd once been married to one of Judge Grey's sons, but it hadn't lasted long. Rumor had it—via the Septuagenarian Club—Lara was now getting hot and heavy with Marcus Stanton's younger brother, Niles, owner of Wharton County's prime real estate agency.

Marcus got the first question and dazzled the room by indicating his record for singlehandedly reducing the percentage of crime each and every year for the last seven years. When Nana D had an opportunity to counter, she went for the jugular. "Really? I may not have access to all the same metrics and phony details you've got, Stanton, but three weeks ago there were two murders in Braxton. Where were you when they were happening?" Nana D was skirting a dangerous line given they both had reason to keep the details of those incidences from being available to the public—Nana D and Marcus Stanton had interacted with the killer and never realized what was going on behind their backs the entire time.

After a few retorts, Lara pushed them both to the next question. She asked Nana D, "What are your top three initiatives?" Given we'd prepared for it, Nana D would nail this question.

"First, we're gonna rid this town of red tape, bully politicians, and false promises. I'm not one to point out the current regime's faults, but clearly these shenanigans need to stop. Wharton County needs a mayor committed to staying true to this land's history. We've got to focus on re-building our downtown area and that includes the Finnulia River waterfront and shores at Crilly Lake."

The audience cheered when Nana D told them she intended to ensure the county would bring in three new big business opportunities to create jobs. She then promised to re-create the family atmosphere in Wellington Park when there were cherished afternoons eating delicious frozen treats, playing old-fashioned games with family, and relaxing in the beauty of the outdoors.

By the end of the debate, Marcus Stanton earned some wins when he pointed out Nana D's lack of experience and her age. It was ironic given he was in his early-sixties and right on the cusp himself of being eligible to move to Willow Trees. He suggested forming a council of the community's elder population to advise him on how to help make Wharton County a better place. He even proposed Nana D step down from the mayoral race to be his right-hand woman running such a council. When the debate ended, Lara wouldn't declare anyone a winner but assured us she saw excellent points from both sides that day. As Marcus stepped off the stage, he snubbed Nana D and went into his private limo. I quickly pointed out his disgraceful attitude to the cameraman who was grateful to capture it on video.

"I think I did well," Nana D exclaimed when she found me thirty minutes later.

"You got in a few curveballs, Nana D. I'm proud of you," I said embracing her as the cameras snapped some photos of us. It would be good for the campaign if nothing else. Or maybe a silver-framed photo for her upcoming seventy-fifth birthday.

When I got back to Nana D's place, I noticed I had a voicemail from the executive producer at the network back in LA. After firing my boss a few weeks earlier, they'd told me they were planning to take the show in a different direction but weren't sure how or where I'd fit in. They'd recently finished their initial discussions with some investors and the top brass at the network who decided to put *Dark Reality*, our television series, on hiatus for one year. During that time, I was free to work for another television show, but in one year, when they were ready to start production on their next season, they'd be in contact with me to discuss potential roles. In one way, it was good. It meant I could try to convince them to take the show in a direction where

I could focus on true crime instead of the mock-crime-made-for-reality-television-series my former boss had insisted on.

It was also bad because that meant I had no reason to return to LA for the next year. I'd committed to staying in and teaching at Braxton for the next year, too. I guess it meant my professional life was settled for the short-term, but there was still a need to figure out the situation with Francesca. If I went back to LA as she wanted, I had no job. How could I afford to keep my house and raise Emma? The Castiglianos would surely foot the bill and be thoroughly thrilled if I moved in with them. It would mean they'd see Emma every day, and Francesca could be near us. But hiding with my in-laws and sneaking around to see my wife wasn't the life I wanted. I needed time to fully digest the news about my delayed contract at *Dark Reality*.

We got back to Nana D's house and had a late lunch. When we were finished, she called Dr. Betscha to find out more about Gwendolyn's death. I wasn't sure exactly how he and Nana D were related, but they both descended from the Betscha siblings who'd been founding members of Braxton and Wharton County over two hundred years earlier. Third cousins once removed by hopping branches and traversing leaves blowing in the wind via a stepladder and eighth re-marriage. Who knew? I just called him a cousin.

"You might be family, Seraphina, but I can't give you too many details. This is tied to a police investigation, and you're not the next of kin," Dr. Betscha said.

"Well, Eustacia is next of kin, and she informed me that she told you it was okay to talk to us," Nana D demanded of her cousin. "I'm only trying to figure out what happened to my poor friend. Something doesn't add up, and I'm willing to bet you know why, Alex."

"I've turned over a final report to Sheriff Montague as of this morning. I'll tell you a few things, but please don't let it slip to the sheriff," he replied.

"You're a solid man. Momma always told me your daddy was good to her. I can see it runs in the family. When we're all done talking here, you need to come by for dinner, Alex. I still can't believe you haven't been scooped up, yet. Forty and not married. What's this world coming to?" Nana D teased.

"I'm a confirmed bachelor, Seraphina. I've gone on a few dates from time to time, but I haven't met the right woman. Someday it might happen. Until then, let's leave it alone, alrighty?"

Nana D agreed. I didn't say a word, feeling grateful I wasn't the focus of her attention for once. Although, I did wonder whether I should set him up with Jennifer Paddington who was trying to have a child. He might be a prime candidate. "What can you tell us, Dr. Betscha?" I asked.

"Give us details. How does this work?" Nana D said unable to let him do the talking.

"Slow down, Seraphina. Gwendolyn was sick, probably sicker than she knew. She hadn't come in to see me in close to three months. A lot had changed during that time, and she wasn't a well woman. Her heart had begun to deteriorate, and she was developing clots. We could've controlled many of the symptoms, but given what I saw in her bloodstream, some recent infections, and the impact on her heart, the poor woman would've needed advanced medicine soon enough. The medication she'd been on already for years should've been keeping her system running a little better, but—"

"Are you saying she was going to die from something else?" I inquired feeling a twinge in my chest. Had Gwendolyn known how sick she was?

"I'm afraid so," Dr. Betscha remarked in a sympathetic tone. "But there's one key thing to point out. The blood tests did not show a good level of medications she was supposedly taking. I double checked it, if she was regularly following her prescribed medication plan, I would have seen it in the test results. Based on what I saw, either Gwendolyn stopped taking her medicine, or someone swapped a good chunk of her pills with a placebo. I told the sheriff I suspected she'd been swallowing fake sugar pills based on adding up everything found in her bloodwork."

I gasped. The shock of someone's intentional wickedness unnerved me. "Is there anything you can tell us about the placebos? Or whether her nurse, Brad, should have recognized any symptoms?"

"Perhaps Brad should have put a few things together based on the symptoms you mentioned. It's not uncommon for someone in their seventies to experience these same signs and have it be advanced age and existing illness."

"You're saying she would've thought it was only a need to change the amount of her medication? At least until she came to you, and you ran tests picking up the missing medications in her bloodwork," I noted.

"Correct. The cocaine definitely killed her, but lack of any real medication would've led it to happen relatively soon anyway."

When we hung up with Dr. Betscha, Nana D and I agreed it was time to have a detailed discussion with Gwendolyn's nurse, Brad. He would be able to shed light on how he managed her medication. He might also be someone who could've helped the killer plan Gwendolyn's death. Something must have changed in that last twenty-four hours to cause the killer to push his or her plan forward, so Gwendolyn was out of the picture much sooner.

* * *

"You're a lifesaver, big brother," Eleanor gleefully shouted into the phone the next morning. "I called the electrician Arthur suggested, and he's starting work today. He thinks he can get everything converted by Sunday. I might still be able to open early next week."

I pulled the phone away from my ear and looked at the time. Why did my sister feel the need to call me at six o'clock in the morning to share her good news? "That's awesome. Do you ever sleep? This is an uncivilized hour to call people, you know." Before she could respond, my phone beeped telling me I had another caller. This time it was Nana D. "Seriously? I need to learn how to shut my phone off at night. Can I call you back later, Eleanor?"

I switched back to the other line. "This better be important. I love you to pieces, Nana D, but I was dreaming about a warm, sunny beach full of calming waves and palm trees."

"Get your patootie out of bed. The sun is on its way up, and you've got a nurse to grill. Honestly, Kellan, I don't know what kind of lesson you're teaching Emma by staying in bed so late when there are major priorities in need of your attention." Nana D's voice was like a foghorn blasting at full volume in the middle of a tiny room.

"Emma is still sleeping. She gets up at seven o'clock for breakfast and then I drop her off at school. We have a routine. I thought we were meeting at the Paddington estate at ten o'clock today to talk with Brad?" Once we'd spoken with Dr. Betscha the night before, she'd cooked me dinner as an apology for getting me drunk on margaritas. Afterward, I'd gone home early, helped Emma do her homework, and caught up on sleep as I'd started feeling like I was coming down with a cold or had overworked my body during the last few days at the gym. I climbed out of my bed, threw on my robe, and checked Emma's room to confirm she was still sound asleep. "What changed?"

Nana D continued, "That's yesterday's news, kiddo. Finnigan Masters is coming by to review the will with Eustacia this morning at eight thirty. Meet me there, so we can find out who else has a motive."

"I'll do my best, but I can't promise I'll be there by..." I heard the phone click when she hung up. My grandmother apparently didn't care about my own plans this morning. I trudged down the hall to the shower and turned the cold water on full blast.

Within seconds my body startled out of hibernation as I reached for the shampoo. As I got myself ready for the day, I waffled on whether Brad wasn't a proficient nurse or he had something to do with the plot to kill her. There was a small chance he was innocent and had everything documented to review with Dr. Betscha, but the entire situation felt too suspicious.

Chapter 11

After dropping Emma off at school, I arrived at the Paddington estate shortly after eight-thirty. Bertha greeted me and led me to the Great Hall where Nana D, Millard, Eustacia, and Finnigan were having coffee.

"I see you chose to attend," Nana D teased. "We've discussed punctuality before, brilliant one."

"It's a shame what's happening this generation. They've no appreciation for getting up early to put in a hard day's work," Eustacia continued. "Today's youth will be the downfall of this society."

I wanted to defend myself, but pride over being called a youth despite being in my early thirties won out. Instead, I turned to Finnigan. "I'm sorry I missed you the other day. So glad to hear how well you're doing with the practice these days."

Finnigan was two years older than me. His tawny brown hair had begun to gray at the temples, but he still maintained a youthful appearance. His family was English and had moved to Wharton County when we were children. Traces of his accent made an appearance at times, but for the most part he'd been Americanized by now. Tall and thin, he and his brother, Liam, towered over me, yet they always seemed to try and shrink their appearance to blend in with the crowd. He wore a striped blue suit with a colorful tie that reminded me of a Monet painting I'd seen in one of the halls around the Paddington estate.

"Thanks, Kellan. I'm excited you're back in Braxton. Liam's hoping to find a few days to stop home in between hockey games," Finnigan said. He shared a picture of him and Liam at a recent game. I was glad to see they stayed close over the years. I wish I had that chance with my own brothers, but it hadn't worked out in the past.

"Shall we get started?" Millard said with a hint of nervousness in his voice. He sipped from his coffee cup while pruning one of the nearby lemon trees. Each time he brushed against one of the branches, a whiff of fresh citrus wafted by us.

Finnigan cleared his throat. "I'll make this as easy as possible. When Charles and Gwendolyn Paddington first came to see my father, I was recently out of law school and interning in the family practice. Dad handled the Paddington affairs, but he transitioned them to me shortly before Charles passed away. I met with Gwendolyn when Charles was diagnosed with pancreatic cancer, then again once he was gone. I tried to be as caring and gentle as possible with her during that difficult time to help prepare a new will."

Millard nodded. "Your father is an excellent attorney. He and Lindsey worked on many cases together in the past. Clever mind. He knew American law better than Lindsey did. I should call him to have tea soon."

"Yes, he insisted I study it even as a child. I still know very little about the UK because of his pressure to learn everything about our new homeland."

Eustacia pointedly banged her cane on the tiled floor. "I don't mean to rush you, but could we forego the details of your education and focus on the will? This ain't a remake of *Romper Room*."

Nana D pressed her fingers into my forearm as if to tell me to remain quiet. I was there to listen, I understood the message.

Finnigan blushed. "My apologies, I know this is a bit complicated given the circumstances. At the time, Charles and Gwendolyn had made the decision to exclude their son, Timothy, from the will. I wasn't privy to all of the detailed reasons, but Charles and Gwendolyn had chosen to split the estate among various charities and theater organizations, as well as with their daughters, Ophelia and Jennifer. It was a clean separation. Fifty percent was allocated as donations, and the remaining fifty percent was split equally between both women."

I watched Millard's expression as he turned toward us. He'd also been cut out of his parents will in the past. His face became quite pale, almost translucent. I needed to understand what had prompted such a decision.

"What can you tell us about the new will she discussed with you?" Eustacia said bluntly.

"It was also split with an equal portion being given to various charities, but the other fifty percent was allocated to different individuals. Unfortunately, I do not know whom Gwendolyn selected. She contacted me the day before she died telling me she'd had enough with all the drama in her family and needed to correct something that'd happened in the past."

"Have you found the new will?" I asked.

Finnigan shook his head. "We thoroughly checked her bedroom suite, but it's not in there. Neither Millard nor Eustacia had any knowledge of the revised will's location. I assume if it's finished, perhaps she mailed it to me. I'll give it a few more days before I unveil the current will to the rest of the family."

"Obviously something happened between Gwendolyn and her daughters. If she was changing her will, one or both of them were going to be removed as beneficiaries," Nana D noted.

"Or they stayed in it and someone new was added," Finnigan suggested.

"Were Gwendolyn's children aware of this will? Did they know Timothy wasn't going to inherit anything? Or that both daughters would?" I inquired. It was important to understand who was privy to the details of the inheritances.

"Gwendolyn mentioned that she'd never shared the decision with her children. In fact, she'd forgotten the details in the original will when we first spoke as it had been a while and she wasn't highly alert after Charles had passed on. My guess is none of the children knew who would benefit from her death," Finnigan explained while packing up his briefcase.

"Was anyone else aware she planned to write a new will?" Millard inquired.

"I can't answer that question," Finnigan replied while putting on his winter coat. "All I can tell you is that something happened last Saturday to result in her need to make an urgent change. I've only told the four of you about the potential existence of a new will. Unless Gwendolyn told the person or persons who would be the new beneficiaries, no one else knows about it either." He left with Millard who mentioned he had to get to the nursery to inspect some new arrivals. Nana D, Eustacia, and I continued talking as we weren't set to meet with Brad until he returned from running a few errands for Eustacia at ten o'clock.

"This is ludicrous," Eustacia whined and shook her head repeatedly. "How are we supposed to figure it out?"

Nana D said, "Don't give up, Eustacia. We've only just begun. Kellan will find Gwennie's killer. Let's go over the facts again."

"I'll do my best, but I have to agree with Eustacia. There are a lot of possibilities. It would help if you could tell me why Millard was left out of your parents' will." I began to wander around the Great Hall thinking about the dynamics among all the member of the Paddington family.

Eustacia explained that Millard had been groomed to assume responsibility for Paddington Enterprises. He'd earned an MBA at Columbia, worked in the family business for nearly twenty years, and had become a vice-president under his father. When he turned fifty, Millard realized he'd thrown his whole life away to run a large corporation but had no wife or children to love. He resigned from his position and took a job at a gardening center. Their parents were so upset they threatened to stop speaking with him over the embarrassment of the situation. Around the same time, Millard had befriended a young maid at the mansion. The family disapproved of the friendship since the girl was far beneath expected standards for a Paddington.

"It's hard to believe your parents were so old-fashioned. It was the early 1990s, right?" I asked.

Eustacia nodded. "You have to understand, my parents were considered high society, as were their parents before them. Braxton's a small town, people talk. My brother, Charles, and Gwennie had just finished raising their three children. Jennifer had graduated from college, Ophelia and Richard had become engaged, and Timothy had started working at the family business. They were seen as the perfect family. Gwennie was running around New York City with Broadway stars and the rich and famous. Millard threw it all away to grow flowers and trees. Our parents couldn't understand it."

"They disinherited Millard because he quit his job and had an affair with a maid?" I asked.

"There's more to the story. The maid was young, barely eighteen or nineteen. After a few months, it had become obvious to them she was pregnant. My parents were afraid of a scandal. They sent her away before anyone could find out. I thought I was the only one who'd learned the truth, but..." She seemed lost in thought and stopped speaking.

Eustacia's news shocked me. It wasn't like this took place a century ago. It'd been barely twenty-five years earlier. "What happened to the child? And why didn't Millard try to support the girl?"

"I don't think he or anyone else knew the maid was pregnant. Millard didn't care about the inheritance. He'd already made enough money working at the family company. That's when he traveled the world and focused on gardening," Eustacia said. It was clear the past had haunted her, but I wasn't certain how it would have anything to do with Gwendolyn's death.

Nana D added, "Millard's been so happy since he left Paddington Enterprises. I know he regretted never having had any children. How did you find out?"

Eustacia explained that she only knew about the baby because her mother had mentioned it on her death bed. Eustacia had never told Millard about the child. She felt guilty about keeping the secret even after their parents had passed away almost two decades earlier. Eustacia wanted to tell her brother many times but had no way to track down the girl or learn what had happened to her. She thought it would be a futile attempt that would only make Millard more upset to discover the truth.

"What was the maid's name?" I asked.

"We called her Hannah. That's all I remember about her," Eustacia said with a heavy sigh.

Nana D accompanied Eustacia to the restroom to help her splash some water on her face before we met with Brad. If Millard had a secret child, could that child have tried to get revenge on Gwendolyn if he or she discovered their true identity? If Gwendolyn had found out, could she have left money to this child as a way to right her parents' wrong when they'd excluded Millard from their will? It was a good theory, but until I could figure out whom the child was, it felt too fuzzy.

Just as the thought popped into my head, Brad entered the Great Hall. I nodded at him, then froze. "Brad, how old are you?" I asked, suddenly feeling alarmed at the potential connection I was about to make. "I, uh, apologize. I didn't mean to be too personal. I was curious. You look so young to have finished nursing school and worked several jobs already." Phew, epic save.

Brad was silent for a few seconds, then tilted his head. "No, you can ask. I don't mind. I turned twenty-five three weeks ago. Where is Ms. Paddington?"

"Eustacia will be along shortly, I'm sure." Maybe he'd tell me about his family thinking it was an innocent conversation. "You've got good genes, Brad. I guess you must have inherited them from your parents."

"My mother always looked young, too. I think it was pretty common on her side of the family," he said rubbing a few leaves of a nearby shrub looking away from me. "I'm happy to answer any questions you have about the list of Gwendolyn's medications I gave to everyone."

"How's the search for a job going?" I said, stalling until the others returned to the Great Hall.

"I have two interviews this afternoon. Eustacia set one up for me at Willow Trees, and the other is a private patient. I'm also waiting for a few calls back on apartments that looked promising." Brad sat on a bench near the pond. He looked tired and distracted by something weighing heavily on his mind.

I heard Eustacia's cane pounding the floor as she entered the room. "Pardon my absence. I see Brad's come down to meet with us. Have you started already, Kellan?" she asked. When I shook my head, Eustacia continued. "Brad, a few things have come to my attention regarding Gwennie's death. I should like to hear from you exactly what you—"

"If I may interrupt," he said standing to attention. "I've already been by to discuss it with the sheriff earlier this morning. I was stunned, as a matter of fact. I can't believe someone would intentionally try to kill Mrs. Paddington. I assure you, I had no idea."

"Surely, you have more to say than that," Eustacia admonished with a hard glare in his direction. "You were solely responsible for my sister-in-law's medication and gave her those pills moments before she died in the theater. While I'm not directly accusing you of having something to do with her murder, I hope you can understand I need to hear a lot more than '*can't believe someone would intentionally try to kill her*' as your only response."

Brad clasped his hands together. "The police took all of her medications and any glasses, cups, or utensils from her bedroom. I'm sure they plan to test them. If someone tampered with any of the medication I administered, we'll find out quickly. It certainly didn't come from me if that's what you're implying." He seemed to take offense at her tone and quickly responded by defending himself.

I wish I had a few minutes alone with Eustacia, so I could tell her about his age lining up with the baby the Paddington maid had supposedly given birth to. Possibly Millard Paddington's child. When Eustacia and Nana D turned to me, I took control of the conversation.

"Brad, this is definitely an awkward discussion. Please understand we are not accusing you of anything directly, but we need your assistance understanding some of the facts. Gwendolyn was acting strangely the last few weeks. We now know she was slowly being made sicker without proper medication. A lethal dose of cocaine was ingested moments before she died in the theater," I said pausing to make direct eye contact with him. He stared back with a chilled blank look that made me want to squirm. "You've spent the most time with her, and you gave her the medication she'd forgotten to take with her earlier in the day. Any reasonable person would want to understand what you think could've happened."

"But I had no reason to want Mrs. Paddington dead. She was my employer and truthfully, a confidante in the last few weeks. I'd been having a few personal issues she helped me deal with. Don't you understand? I have no job and home now. Why would I kill her?" he said in frustration, then threw his hands in the air. "I'm not in the habit of killing my patients despite what anyone has said in the past."

Nana D interrupted to put her arm around Brad's shoulder as if she were trying to play good cop to Eustacia's or my bad cop. "Brad, you've been a wonderful support to my friend in the last year. Was there anyone other than you that handled her medication, or had you seen anyone in her room that maybe didn't belong there?"

Nana D had a good point in terms of who had opportunity. We needed to know exactly what the sheriff had found during the search of Gwendolyn's bedroom to understand if the cocaine was in all of her pills or just the one dosage she'd taken at the theater. "Let's start with how you managed your patient's medication, so we can determine how the cocaine got put into those pills."

Brad perked up and explained that Gwendolyn took her medication three times each day—morning, afternoon, and evening. Some were gel-based capsules filled with the ground up medication and others were solid tablets. Each dosage contained a combination of pills, but Brad would prepare a weekly pill box separating each day's allotment. If Gwendolyn was going out for the day, she used a travel bottle to hold the next dosage while she'd be gone from the house. "Earlier that morning, she took her regular pills. At the same time as I gave her the morning pills, she took out her travel bottle for the afternoon dosage. It was too early to take that next dosage at brunch, so she planned to take it while attending the theater. I used the pills from the regular pill box that I'd prepared earlier that week and that contained the pills she'd taken a few hours earlier. There was nothing different about them."

"They couldn't have been tampered with in the early morning batch as nothing happened to her then," I concluded. If the killer had only switched a few pills in the batch, it would have been too coincidental that Brad had randomly chosen those same exact cocaine-laced pills from the whole supply when he'd brought them to her at the theater that afternoon. That specific tainted dosage had to have been swapped after the travel bottle was prepared that morning. "When did you give her the travel bottle?

And where was it from the point you gave it to her to the point you brought it to the theater?"

"I watched her put the filled travel bottle on her night table in the bedroom. It was sitting there while she showered and dressed. I suppose it was partially unattended while she was in the bathroom, but I was in my own room by then. At some point, she must have put the bottle in her purse and gone downstairs to the dining room to eat brunch with everyone. I don't know what happened during brunch until she sent Bertha to find me again," Brad explained.

"While we were eating brunch, we talked about going out for dinner with the whole family after the show ended. That's when she called Brad downstairs to ask him to have two travel dosages ready before she left for the theater," Eustacia noted. "Gwennie wanted us to all show up together for the first performance at the family theater. Jennifer and Millard were both at the house that morning. Ophelia and the kids, too. Richard was already out of town and couldn't make the *King Lear* performance. Timothy was nowhere to be found."

"I was there, too," Nana D interjected while snapping her fingers. "Brad said he would add the second dosage to her pills and put it back in her purse on the Edwardian console table in the hallway while everyone got ready to leave. He indicated he'd be done in less than fifteen minutes."

"Correct. So, I took the bottle out of her purse and placed it on the table next to her coat. I left it there while I went upstairs to get the pill box, so I could get the second dosage of all her medications," Brad said. "In retrospect, I should've taken the bottle with me, but I wasn't thinking straight."

"We sat for five minutes, then everyone went to the Great Hall to prepare to leave," Eustacia added before clearing her throat. "We were all in and out of that hallway using the restroom, getting our coats, and talking to each other. Anyone could've accessed the bottle to switch the pills."

"Jennifer left for the longest amount of time. Remember, someone joked about her always causing delays," Nana D mentioned.

While I wanted to explore Jennifer's extended absence, I had another important question. "I still don't understand how Gwendolyn left without the pills. Brad, you said you left the bottle on the table next to her purse when you went upstairs to get the additional pills. Then you returned and brought the additional dosage back down, right?" I questioned.

"When I got back to the hallway, her coat, purse, and pill bottle were gone," Brad said before biting his lip. "I thought we had a miscommunication... that she no longer needed the second travel dosage of medication."

"So, you knew something odd was going on that morning?" I suggested.

"Not really. I figured she changed her mind. It'd happened other times where she previously decided not to take an extra dosage of medication at the last minute."

"Didn't you try to find her to ask her?" Nana D said with an annoyed look.

"I asked Bertha where everyone went, but while I was upstairs, they'd left for Paddington's Play House," Brad explained. "I should've tracked her down, but I guess I made a mistake."

A potentially life-changing one. "What did you do then?" I asked.

"I put the extra dosage of pills back in the regular pill box, went for a long walk around the property, and did some laundry. Then I got Mrs. Danby's call that Mrs. Paddington wasn't feeling well and needed her pills. I was confused, so I went back downstairs to see if she'd accidentally left them somewhere else in the dining room. There they were on the table. I asked Bertha who said she'd found them on the floor under the table when she was cleaning. She assumed it was an older bottle and planned to give it to me later that day." When Bertha told him how she'd found them, Brad assumed they'd accidentally fallen to the floor and that Gwendolyn must've thought he'd already put them back in her purse before she'd left. "Timothy was also in the kitchen talking to Bertha. He offered to bring the pills to his mother, but it was my job. I didn't think much of it at the time and rushed to the Play House to drop off the pills."

Nana D squeezed the bridge of her nose. "Someone must have changed the first travel dosage of pills after Brad had filled them that morning but before everyone left for Paddington's Play House."

"Would Gwendolyn have left without validating she had all her pills?" I asked.

Eustacia responded, "I can see it happening. Gwennie was behaving oddly that morning. If she was changing her will, she might not have been paying full attention and didn't verify whether he'd already added the second dosage to her travel bottle. In the rush, she probably grabbed everything she saw and left assuming Brad had added the second dosage into the bottle and put it back in her purse."

Nana D added, "I vaguely remember hearing something fall to the floor when I returned from the bathroom, but I didn't think anything of it at the time. I thought it had come from another room."

"I'm not sure we'll be able to figure out who slipped into the hallway or bedroom and switched the medication that morning. At least we know when it happened, but unfortunately everyone had access. I'm sure it's even possible someone else was able to sneak in and swap them," I said trying to figure out if there was any way to narrow down the list of suspects. "In theory, with no one watching, it only takes a minute to remove a few pills and drop in the cocaine-laced ones."

Brad agreed with me, then explained he had to get to an interview. After he left, I started to develop a headache. I'd find time to verify what he'd said with Bertha. I didn't think he was lying but needed to confirm his explanation. Timothy's sudden appearance and Jennifer's lengthy disappearance seemed highly suspect. We were definitely missing something important.

Chapter 12

Eustacia asked Bertha to prepare a light lunch for Nana D and I. We devoured a Caesar salad with grilled chicken breast, battered prawns, and homemade croutons. In my mind I was expecting a grilled cheese sandwich or a bowl of tomato soup, but I wasn't going to complain about a free meal.

"I still don't agree with you for putting my brother's name on the list. He didn't have any reason to kill Gwennie," Eustacia argued. Her hands and arms waved about feverishly to make her point.

"I understand it doesn't seem logical to you, but if Millard found out he might have had a child and that Gwendolyn could have known something about it, he might have been too angry to stop himself," I explained as simply as I could.

"Kellan has a point. If that's his logic, maybe we should also put Eustacia on the suspect list," Nana D suggested looking serious and determined.

Eustacia gasped. "Me? Have you lost your mind, Seraphina? I had no reason to want my sister-in-law dead."

"Perhaps she discovered you'd kept the secret from Millard, and you killed her to keep it quiet," Nana D said with a flourish. "It's as plausible as Millard being the murderer. We've gotta look at this from every angle. I don't think you did it, but we should consider anyone who had the opportunity or the means.

Although the motive might not be clear right now, we can't rule out those with immediate access to Gwennie."

While Nana D and Eustacia engaged in a battle of wills, I absconded to Brad's room. I'd heard Bertha say goodbye to him a few moments earlier which meant his room was unoccupied. She led me through one of the back hallways to the servant's quarters. While we walked, she corroborated his story about the pills falling under the table in the hallway. "That's his room on the far left, near the laundry facility," she said with a nod. "I must get back to the table to clean up."

Brad's door was unlocked when I turned the glass-covered knob. His living quarters were at least twelve by twelve and situated in the far corner of the wing. He had two pairs of double windows on the east and south walls, a queen-size bed with a muted blue comforter tucked neatly on both sides, and a small French country writing desk and chair set. I decided to check the desk drawers first which like the room were spotless and organized. Other than a few current bills with minimal expenditures and a normal amount of debt for someone his age, nothing seemed out of the ordinary.

It was in the night table where I found something of interest. Hidden beneath a folder marked job opportunities and a crossword puzzle book was a framed photo of a little boy and a woman at the beach. I stared at the picture trying to decide if the child was Brad from years ago, but I couldn't be certain. There was a strong likeness but none of the clothing or furniture in the background suggested the time frame when the photo had been captured. I set it on the night table and took out my cell phone to take a picture for future reference. The velvet-covered cardboard flap holding the picture upright gave way and the whole frame fell to the floor.

When I picked up the picture, an obituary card slipped out. It read:

March 14, 2017, Hannah Shope

Hannah Shope, 45, of Boise, Idaho, passed away after a long battle with MS. Hannah had been active in the St. Francis Catholic Church up until her diagnosis several years ago when she became unable to leave her house. She is survived by a loving son, Brad Shope, who took care of his mother in the last few years. Hannah was an only child who'd moved to the area nearly twenty-five years ago from Pennsylvania where she'd worked in domestic services. She will be missed by all her friends in the rosary group and at Sunday morning mass. May she eternally rest in peace.

I snapped a picture of both the photograph and the obituary card before quickly shutting the drawer and verifying everything was left exactly as I'd found it. I dashed back to the dining room where Nana D and Eustacia were still arguing about the potential suspects.

"What if it was the mail carrier? Maybe he snuck into Gwennie's bedroom every morning and swapped the pills. Honestly, Seraphina, you're pulling these ideas out of your crotchety old—"

"Ladies, I found something," I said with a zest of energy. "Didn't you say the maid's name was Hannah? Look at this." I handed my phone to Eustacia and Nana D who huddled around the table's corner.

"I don't remember the name Shope, but that's definitely her. I now remember what she looked like and can't believe I didn't see the resemblance with Brad before."

"Do you know who introduced Brad to Gwendolyn at the rehabilitation facility?" I asked.

They both shook their heads. "I haven't the foggiest clue," Eustacia said rubbing her fingers together. "But I'll call that whippersnapper Lydia Nutberry, she knows everyone."

I'd spent much longer at the Paddington mansion than planned and escaped to The Big Beanery. As I stood in line to order, I heard a pair of familiar voices talking in the nearby corner. I leaned in their direction and saw Connor speaking with Sheriff Montague. After picking up my dark roast coffee and slice of coffee cake, I saddled up to their table and plopped down on an empty chair in exaggerated fashion. "Top of the morning to you!" I said with a giant grin.

"Little Ayrwick, did you misunderstand our silence as an invitation to interrupt? I can only assume you've been drinking already and must be heavily impaired," Sheriff Montague chided while crumpling her napkin and tossing it into the garbage pail behind me.

"Kellan," Connor said with a quick nod of his head. "What can we do for you?"

"Well, it's what I can do for the sheriff, that is, if she's at all interested in discussing the Paddington case," I teased while staring directly at April Montague. "Have I got some shocking information for you!"

"Let me guess. You've realized wearing tighty-whities cuts off all circulation to your brain and felt obligated to share your golden ticket discovery with every man or woman in the tri-state area? Or did you finally realize it is possible to walk and talk at the same time without forgetting to breathe?" The sheriff had a knack for delivering each and every word with such a disinterested and bland tone, I decided she'd make a good straight man in a comedy team.

"For your information, since you seem to be obsessed with my choice in underwear, I wear boxer briefs." For added delight, I stood up, peeled away the bottom section of my long-sleeve Henley and pulled up the black waistband of my underwear. "If you're so inclined to need further proof, I'm sure that can be arranged. Also, I've been walking and talking since I was two-years-old. Since you've already deemed me along with my nana the biggest gabbers in all of Wharton County, you should be careful not to contradict yourself when trying to crack a joke at my expense. Emphasis on *trying*."

Connor's eyes opened wide. He obviously thought I was overstepping some invisible line that dictated I should be afraid of the sheriff. Given the abuse I'd already taken from her, I wasn't going to let it become the norm. "Dude, nice eight pack," he said.

"Are you saying you don't find me funny?" the sheriff inquired while cocking her head to the left and smiling like a clown. "Because I think it'd be hilarious to slap a pair of handcuffs on your wrists and take you down to the station for a few hours."

"I've done nothing wrong. You can't arrest me, unless that's your way of trying to flirt with me. In which case, I'm compelled to remind you... emphasis on *trying*." I wasn't sure what had come over me. Maybe after having been home for close to a month as well as realizing I was starting to make decent headway into another murder investigation, my confidence had grown stronger.

"We could banter all day and night. Sure, I could arrest you for something, but then I'd have to deal with the paperwork. You're not worth my time. I have five minutes and will listen with full attention if it means you'll go away faster." Sheriff Montague growled and slurped the muddy remnants at the bottom of her coffee cup.

"I've unexpectedly come across some information about the Paddington family's wills and a few instances where certain members have been left out. I also discovered someone who might have a connection to the Paddingtons, but I can't figure out if it has any bearing on Gwendolyn's death." I didn't want to give away all the information I'd learned and chose to drop enough hints to see what the sheriff responded to.

"If you're referring to Gwendolyn's will, I'm already in contact with Finnigan Masters to discuss when it will be available to read. As far as these clues you're dropping about other wills and connections, spill it." The sheriff pulled out a pad and begin writing down a few notes.

I explained what I'd learned about Millard having been excluded from his parents will, then Brad's arrival a few months after Charles died. I left out the missing new will just so I had leverage for later. "There must be a connection somewhere. Brad's mother, Hannah, died several days after Charles died. It could be a coincidence, yet that's when Brad went to work for Gwendolyn. What if Millard is Brad's father and one or both of them have some sort of diabolical plot to flee with the family money?"

"It's odd, I agree. Careful with your allegations. I'm not sure what that means, but doesn't Millard have his own money? He's a world-famous landscaper and used to run the family company decades ago." Sheriff Montague cracked her knuckles and pushed her chair back from the table.

I nodded. "I couldn't make heads or tails of that myself. Any chance you've heard from Timothy? Eustacia has been trying to track him down for almost six days, but she can't find him. She'd like to hold the funeral service this weekend but hoped to find him. He was Gwendolyn's son."

"Timothy's been located and is currently a person of interest. As you're aware, he was seen arguing with his mother at the theater less than thirty minutes before she was murdered."

Connor said, "I've viewed the security camera footage in the lobby. The only two people who touched Gwendolyn's drink in the lobby were Brad and Timothy. I'm sure someone else had access inside the theater where we didn't have any cameras. And the cashier who poured the iced tea is a student who has impeccable references and no known connection to Gwendolyn.

The sheriff cleared her throat. "We've run tests on everything we pulled from the theater. There was no trace of any drugs in any beverages, containers, or any of the surfaces in the refreshment stand where she'd gotten the iced tea. It had to be introduced in the actual pills and not the glass that had been given to the victim. I'm waiting for the results on the remainder of the pills from the house."

"Can you tell me where you found Timothy?" I asked.

"I'm not sure that's something he'd want the general public to know. Besides, I expect within the next twenty-four hours, Timothy will no longer be there and will be in my custody," the sheriff said with a pointed stare.

"Are you saying he's your prime suspect?" I inquired. While everything pointed to Brad or Millard based on what I'd learned, not knowing where Timothy had been hiding out left me at a disadvantage. "What about the news I've just shared?"

"I'll be following up on it. In the meantime, if anything else pops up, be sure you alert me."

"And stay out of your murder investigation... yeah, yeah, got it. I understand," I said lying through my teeth. I needed to find out where Timothy was hiding, but I was supposed to meet Arthur. I said goodbye to Connor and the sheriff, ordered a coffee to go, and walked over to Paddington's Play House. As I entered, my phone vibrated with a text message. It was uncanny how timely she could be.

Nana D: *We've found Timothy. You'll never guess where he is.*
Me: *At a hotel on a bender?*
Nana D: *Nope, the complete opposite.*

I had no idea what Nana D meant by her last comment and couldn't understand her cryptic clues. I looked up and saw Dana Taft waving at me.

Me: *Gotta go. Just tell me.*
Nana D: *You've got a lot to learn about being a detective.*
Me: *Fine, pretty please with sugar on top. Can I know the secret, too?*

Nana D: *That's better. Timothy checked himself into rehab.*
Me: *For drug abuse?*
Nana D: *And gambling. He apparently went there right after his fight with Gwennie at the show before she died.*

Wow! What did that mean? I had no time to respond once Dana interrupted. "Hey. It's Kellan, right?" she asked while blinking a few times at me. "Arthur will be right over."

"How are you holding up?" I said.

"Oh, you know how it is. Trying to keep up with classes and the show."

"And losing your grandmother, I'm sure, has been painful." I winced at how quickly she seemed to forget or ignore Gwendolyn's death.

"We really weren't close," Dana noted. "No one liked her very much."

"I thought she and your brother, Sam, were very close," I countered.

"Oh, he fooled you, too, huh?" Dana obviously had something she wanted to share with me.

While I didn't care a whole lot about Dana given her attitude and the way she'd behaved with Arthur in the past, Sam didn't deserve his sister's reproach. "I may not know your family, Dana, but I'm generally a good judge of character. Sam was devastated the day she passed away."

"You're clueless! She and Sam had a huge fight the day before. I heard them arguing when I stopped back at the house to get something from my bedroom," Dana whined. "He tries so hard to look innocent, but he's hiding something from everyone."

"Is there something you're trying to tell me, Dana? Because to be honest, right now, it feels like you're acting a little jealous and immature." I wasn't sure whether it was the childish tone she spoke in or the dismissive gestures she'd made with each retort, but Dana's attitude angered me. I didn't know Sam from Adam, but the kid was genuinely devastated by his grandmother's death.

"I don't need to listen to this from someone like you. If you don't believe me, ask Sam yourself. I distinctly heard him tell Grandmother that she was being a judgmental sourpuss. Then he slammed the door and told her he wouldn't back down. I have no idea what he meant, but he's been super-secretive for the last few months and refuses to talk to anyone about it." Dana demanded that I leave her alone and stomped off as Arthur walked up to us. She apparently liked making a spectacle of herself.

"I've seen that look before. What did you do? Tell her you weren't interested?" Arthur teased.

"If only. It's a bit more complicated than that. How well do you know her?" I asked.

"I never met Dana before this show, but she's a wily one. If you don't push back, she tries to worm her way into every minute of your day," Arthur noted. "I hesitate to say this but be careful you're never alone with her. She's very hands-on and easily misconstrues a situation."

"I appreciate the advice. Listen, thank you for sending us the name of your electrician. He saved the day for my sister and might help her open the Pick-Me-Up Diner on schedule," I said shaking his hand. He'd done me a solid, and I definitely owed him a favor in the future.

"That's what friends are for, Kellan. I know things got outta hand when I came back to Braxton years ago, but all that's under control now. I've got my life back in order again." Arthur's posture was more relaxed than the last time I'd seen him.

"How've things been around here the last week? I can't imagine it's been easy with the dress rehearsal's cancelation last Sunday."

"Myriam and I worked out some of our differences, but ultimately, the show must go on, right?" he said with a flourish and a bow. "The cops suspected I had something to do with Gwendolyn's death. Called me in for a *conference*, as that unctuous sheriff put it."

"Par for the course. I had to talk with them, too. Was it because of your past differences with Gwendolyn?" I asked.

Arthur nodded. "Someone told them I threatened to kill her last week. I don't remember saying it, and even if I did, I'm an actor. I say things I don't mean all the time," he quipped. Arthur could be putting on a performance for everyone's sake. I asked him to tell me more about his time working on Broadway hoping to find any potential hole in his account of the past. I learned nothing of importance.

Arthur later explained he had little interaction other than once a week where Gwendolyn had met with all the staff at the Play House to discuss current and future projects. She'd also stop in at rehearsals from time to time to provide direction to him and Myriam. It often resulted in tentative compromises or highly caustic arguments, but Gwendolyn always got what she wanted. He'd begun to learn that's how it was with the powerful woman. He'd been to the Paddington house once earlier that month when she invited the whole management team over for a brunch, but he knew the bare minimum about the estate. Arthur finished his coffee and returned to rehearsing the final act with the rest of the cast.

I'd made little progress other than conjecturing potential reasons for almost anyone to have been the killer. It was time to collect Emma from school, then transport her to the library for an after-school reading program. I dropped her off for the ninety-minute activity, then took advantage of the unallocated time to get in a run since I'd had no opportunity earlier that morning once Nana D demanded my presence. As I navigated the steep hills of the Wharton mountains, I continued to search for a solution to my problem with Francesca's re-appearance.

Marriage was about living with both the good and the bad. Was I the kind of guy who could abandon my wife because I couldn't see myself hiding under cover for a few years? Instead of being grateful she hadn't died in the car accident, I was angry about being put into an impossible situation. It wasn't fair to keep Emma from seeing her mother, but if it put my daughter in any amount of danger, I reasoned out it was acceptable to stay far away from LA. I didn't see how I could rebuild the trust and love with Francesca if we lived nearly three-thousand miles apart. Others had made long-distance relationships work but never with the added complication of death threats and mob interference.

Feeling generally satisfied with my decision not to return to LA, I knew I'd made Emma the priority in the whole sordid affair. Unfortunately, it would also make things much harder for me. Even if I found a way to forget how much I loved Francesca, we'd always be married in the eyes of the law. There could never be another woman in my life as long as she was still out there somewhere. It was an impossible decision to force someone to make. I finished the last mile of the trail and pulled up outside of the library. Emma rushed from the lobby entrance when she saw me.

After hugging me, Emma said, "You smell like the dirty laundry basket, Daddy. I think you need to shower for a very long time tonight."

I took a quick sniff, then made a fake gagging sound for effect. "Oh, I'm worse than a wet dog who rolled around in the mud," I teased. Then I realized it was the wrong thing to say as Emma would never let me forget it.

"When are we getting a puppy, Daddy? I think since you're making me sit in this car when you're so stinky, you owe me big time!" Emma buckled her belt in the back seat and grinned so widely I feared she'd split in half.

I tugged on the seatbelt to be sure it was properly connected, then waved my dirty towel in her direction. "You think I stink? Wait until you have to clean up after the puppy, baby girl!" As

I started the engine and looked in the rearview mirror, I caught Emma rolling her eyes in exactly the same way I did.

"Nu uh! That's your job. I'm there to entertain the puppy. You have to keep it clean!"

If she were a little older, I might have said *touché*, but she needed a few more years before I could let her mimic my sarcasm.

Chapter 13

I woke up the following morning and decided to continue my cozy time with Emma by shopping. Fighting traffic to get to the mall on a Saturday morning was never an issue in Wharton County. Emma and I parked the car—she insisted on choosing the exact spot and helping navigate from the back seat—and skipped all the way to the north entrance. We played a few games of *Frogger* and *Pac-Man*, both of which Emma said had very poor graphics—evidence of the downside to a child being brought up on iPads and other digital technology. She giggled as the ghosts captured me in a few corners and told me I must be getting old if I couldn't run away from a ghost floating as slow as molasses. Since children hardly know enough to sugarcoat anything related to an adult's age, I tousled her hair and told her she was precious.

"Maybe Nana D can teach you how to play better. She beat me at *Candy Crush* this week!" Emma cooed as we left the arcade and headed to pick out a new puzzle for the upcoming week. When I noticed the floor tiles were randomly covered with pastel-colored stickers for spring, I challenged her to only walk on ones with blue or pink, and I took orange and green. She was so excited I almost felt bad when she got stuck too far away from the toy store entrance without any tiles to step on. I waved to her from inside the store. "I guess I'll have to choose the puzzle by myself, huh?" I teased.

Emma squinted at me, then gave me an evil eye that made her look so much like Nana D, I caught myself choking. I'd been so shocked I also hadn't heard someone call my name from further inside the store. Once I told Emma she'd won the game, she beelined it for the entrance. I caught her midair as she jumped in my arms. As I turned around, Jennifer Paddington walked toward me. After introductions, Emma asked if she could check out the puzzles in the back of the store. I let her go knowing I could see her in the reflection of the giant mirror on the side wall.

"She looks like such a happy girl, you should be proud," Jennifer noted while tossing two baby blankets over her left shoulder and kneeling on the ground near the shelf. "I didn't realize you had children. How long have you been back home?"

"Just Emma. We only moved back to Braxton a few weeks ago," I replied remembering what Eustacia had told me about Jennifer's previous miscarriages. What'd brought her to the toy store?

"Children are a blessing. We've not had any babies in the family for a long time." A cloudy gaze descended upon Jennifer's spirit as she spoke. I couldn't imagine desperately longing for a child only to lose the pregnancy.

"Shopping for a gift?" I asked hoping to keep her from growing too distant or sad.

"Oh, sort of. I stop in the store every so often. I... I don't have any children of my own, but I'm hoping someday soon," Jennifer said in a faint almost-whisper. She folded up one of the blankets and placed it back on the shelf next to the entrance.

"I hope it works out for you. My sister mentioned seeing you at a doctor's office the other day," I said praying it wasn't perceived as an invasion of privacy. If Jennifer had mentioned wanting to have a baby, it felt acceptable to bring up what Eleanor had seen at the gynecologist.

"Hmmm... I didn't see her. When was this?"

"A couple of days ago, I don't remember exactly. I think she was there for a check-up." After verifying Emma was still combing through the puzzles, I turned back to Jennifer. "I could be wrong."

"Well, I have been to the doctor's a lot, but the only one in the last few weeks was the in-vitro fertilization clinic. It wasn't my regular doctor," she explained. "It's not impossible to conceive on my own, but I need all the help I can get when fifty is much closer than forty these days." She tried to make light of the situation, but I could tell it was painful for her to discuss.

I nodded feeling uncomfortable about asking too many personal questions. "That must be tough. Maybe something unexpected will work out soon for you."

"It's not looking too positive. All the procedures are expensive. I've got to put them on hold until I can find more money," Jennifer said as her eyes began to swell and redden.

"I don't mean to pry, but couldn't your family help with the financial aspect? The Paddingtons seem to have more than enough to go around," I said feeling my heart reach out to the woman. I was curious how much her family knew about her current predicament.

"No, it's not like that in our family. My mother wasn't supportive of me trying to have a child on my own. I'm not very close with Timothy or Ophelia either. We just sort of tolerate one another the last few years." Jennifer folded the other blanket and put it on the lower shelf.

"Again, I'm sorry to hear that." Could Jennifer have been desperate enough to push her mother into an early grave knowing she'd inherit enough money to pay for the procedures? "Maybe things will be different now. Have you spoken to your Aunt Eustacia about your mother's estate?"

"No," she said tersely. "Aunt Eustacia said we needed to hold the funeral service tomorrow, then we'd meet with the lawyers next week. Something about it taking time to verify the final version of the will." Jennifer retrieved her cell phone from her purse, then noted she needed to get going.

Eustacia was savvy in keeping the family on hold while Finnigan tried to track down the supposedly new will Gwendolyn might have finalized the night before she was killed. "Have you spoken to anyone about the specific cause of your mother's death?"

Jennifer pulled away. "She was old and had a heart condition. I assumed it was the heart attack that finally did her in. Why do you ask?"

Hmm... I didn't want to be the one to tell her the truth. She looked genuinely surprised at my question, but I couldn't be sure if she was a good actress. "Just curious. Sometimes it helps the grieving process to know what happened to a loved one in the end," I said remembering some of the questions I wanted to ask but never did when Francesca died. Or supposedly died.

Jennifer thanked me for the suggestion, and I wished her success in finding the money to schedule another in-vitro fertilization procedure. As she left, a huge lump appeared in my throat. If Jennifer wasn't at her regular doctor when she saw Eleanor, it meant Eleanor had also been visiting the in-vitro fertilization clinic. Was she trying to have a baby on her own? I knew how important it was for my sister to have children, but she hadn't ever said she'd look to alternative methods. Could I ask her? Or was it just an initial conversation to understand her options? I'd have to think about the best way to approach the topic ensuring I didn't alienate or upset Eleanor.

Emma returned to the front of the store with two puzzle options. I went with the *Frozen* theme knowing she was obsessed with Disney as much as she was with getting a puppy. We paid for our purchase and took off for Grey Sports Field to attend Braxton's baseball game. After a quick tour of the campus, we bought hotdogs and French fries at the concession stand, then skipped to the center condiment stand to stock up on napkins and catsup. As we finished loading our trays, Emma waved at Nana D who stood a few feet from the restroom entrance talking to Marcus.

"Nana D looks a little busy, honey. Let's give her a minute to finish her discussion." Emma shoved a few fries into her mouth while I innocently listened to their conversation.

Nana D said, "No, I'm not ready to have our next debate on Tuesday. We agreed to all these dates in advance. You're not moving it up, Stanton!"

"Come on, Seraphina. I'm only asking to change it by three days. When we agreed, I had forgotten about my family's vacation beginning next week. I can't cancel it so close to the trip," Marcus replied. "Besides, I've already got the staff setting up the hall for us to discuss the campaign issues."

"What? We *also* agreed to hold the next debate at Wellington Park. Can't you keep any promises you make? That explains why the homeless shelter lost its funding this year," Nana D argued.

"That's baloney! They lost the money because the state reduced its contribution. I had nothing to do with it," Marcus challenged in a louder voice.

A few people stopped and listened to them fight. Nana D threw one hand to her hip and poked Marcus in his chest with the other. "You're a liar and a thief. We're having the debate on Friday as we previously agreed, and if you try to change it, I'll tell everyone what a fraud you are." Nana D continued to poke him extra times. She was a smart woman. By focusing on his attempt to change something they'd agreed to, it made him look far worse. At least fifteen people had begun to crowd around.

I grabbed Emma's hand and walked in their direction hoping to temper their argument. "Hello, Councilman, Nana D. It's gonna be an exciting game today. Why don't we go take our seats and watch the pitchers warm up?"

"Yeah, Nana D. I need to tell you all about how bad Daddy lost at *Packer-Man*," Emma teased while leading her great-grandmother toward the stands. Nana D winked at me as she walked away deeply engaged in conversation with Emma.

I turned to Marcus. "Diffusing that situation seemed ideal."

"Hmmm, probably a good plan. That grandmother of yours is one ornery gal. She's determined to hold me accountable for every little thing we discuss. Sometimes changes are necessary," he said trying to rationalize his behavior and pretending I wouldn't automatically support family before him.

"You two have been at each other's throat for years. What started it all?" I asked always having been curious about the past. Nana D would never reveal what'd happened between them which made me even more determined to discover their secrets.

"Nothing I'm going to discuss!" Marcus tightened both fists and shook them with gusto. "You'd do best to mind your business when it comes to the past, Kellan."

"Well, if that's how you feel, I'll give it some consideration," I consented knowing it wouldn't be the only way I could find out the truth. "I see Striker is pitching in today's game." Striker was his stepson and he'd effectively raised the kid for most of his life when Striker's mother passed away.

Marcus had stopped paying attention to me and instead focused on a pair of twenty-something girls walking by us. I'd only caught them from behind, but I saw more of one girl's legs than I had of the strippers at my bachelor party. Although I'd tried to stop my colleagues from throwing me a posh shindig at a LA-based gentlemen's club, I'd eventually caved and behaved myself! Whoever the girl was that had sashayed by the town councilman and I clearly thought dental floss was appropriate attire at a baseball game. Okay, it was more than dental floss, but Emma would never be allowed to dress like that!

"Excuse me, Kellan. I need to discuss something with Miss Taft," he said waving me off.

I realized it was Lilly and her sister, Dana, who'd trotted by. Dana wore the risqué outfit while Lilly was much more conservative and pretentious in dress. "Wait, councilman. Lilly Taft? What do you have to discuss with her?" I asked.

"What business is that of yours?" Marcus cocked his head in my direction and held a sour expression with one raised eye.

"None, really. I've been getting to know the family. Now that I live in Braxton, it's important for me to connect with my roots, that's all." I hoped it was enough not to raise any suspicion, but I was curious about anything that had to do with the Paddingtons these days.

"Lilly graduated with my youngest daughter. I know her family well. She's been looking for investors for some new business she wants to open."

Interesting. What could she be trying to do? "Are you lending her money?"

"It seems I no longer have to," Marcus replied taking a step away from me.

"Wait, how did she get the money?" I asked despite having no reason to interject myself into their business transaction. If she didn't need the money anymore, why was he trying to track her down?

"I haven't a clue. I told her I'd think about it the last time we discussed the opportunity, but then Lilly told my daughter this week she no longer needed my help." Marcus began walking away, then stopped and turned toward me. "Perhaps your time would be better spent if you'd focus on controlling that flaky grandmother of yours rather than obsessing over the daily activities of the Stantons and the Paddingtons. We're a little out of your family's league, Kellan," Marcus quipped as he rushed off in pursuit of Lilly.

I couldn't follow them without being noticed, nor did I have any idea where they were going. I ignored his derogatory remarks about my social status and pondered the information I'd learned. Lilly had either found an investor or thought she'd be coming into money. I needed to bring it up to Eustacia. Hopefully she had knowledge of Lilly's entrepreneurial undertakings.

The announcer asked everyone to stand for the national anthem being sung by the college's choir. After its dazzling finish, I made my way to our seats and watched the game with Nana D and Emma. At the end of the game, Emma was so excited the Braxton Bears had won, she begged to go home with Nana D for a sleepover. When Nana D agreed, I accepted knowing it meant I could get a majority of the work done for my classes on Monday since Spring Break would be over. As Emma left with Nana D, I walked to the parking lot and turned down the row where I'd left the SUV. I noticed Sam Taft waving at someone who'd pulled out of the parking spot next to him.

"Hey, Sam. Showing some school spirit today?" I said.

"Kellan, oh... hi... did you just see... um... never mind. Yeah, I volunteer at the hospital." Sam looked alarmed and confused. He again refused to look directly at me.

"For what?" I imagined him conversing with various senior citizens for some reason.

"What do you mean?" he said tossing his hands into his pockets and swallowing noisily.

"You said you volunteer. I was asking what you volunteered for," I explained. People had always felt relaxed around me. I'd never been known to worry someone so much in the past. Sam was either easily frightened, or he had something to hide from me.

"Right. I bring sick children from the Wharton County General Hospital to some of Braxton's sporting events. Helps get them out for a few hours, so they can maybe forget how ill they are," he said perking up a little.

"That's such a thoughtful thing to do," I replied. "It's good to see how generous you are with your time." Sam didn't behave like the rest of the Paddingtons or Tafts. There was a genuine down-to-earth quality about him. "I saw your sister, Lilly, a little earlier. She was meeting with Councilman Stanton."

Sam bit his lip. "Oh, really? Yeah, she's friends with his daughter." He started walking toward the driver's side door.

"The councilman mentioned something about investing in a business opportunity with your sister. Do you know anything about that?" I asked hoping he'd share whatever he knew.

"Oh, that... yeah, she's trying to start up a digital advertising agency. Lilly's all about social media and marketing partnerships. I think it's going well, but we don't talk that much." When Sam pulled his hand from his pocket to open the door, something fell to the ground.

I walked closer to him and bent down to pick it up at the same time as him. "I'll get it," I said.

"No, leave it." Sam reached for it first, then shoved it back in his pocket before I could figure out what it was.

"Um, is everything okay, Sam? You seem rattled." I noticed his face begin to fluster and redden.

"Yes, I gotta go."

As Sam pulled away, I shook my head. He was private and closed-off from everyone, including me. I barely knew him, but it was easy to see even in the three or four times we'd crossed paths. Whether it was lack of confidence from being surrounded by the vultures in his family, or a potentially dangerous secret he was hiding based on Dana's theory, the kid was close to exploding soon. I needed to find out whom he trusted in the hopes that person might be able to clue me in as to what made Sam tick. As I drove home, I called Eustacia to see what she might know.

"I've no clue how Lilly could've come up with the money to open her business. I only know she was trying to find investors because Brad mentioned it," Eustacia said after I told her what I'd discussed with Marcus.

"I wasn't aware Lilly and Brad knew each other well," I countered. Lilly lived at the Paddington estate, but she didn't seem to be the type of girl who'd hang around with the help. "What can you tell me about that relationship?"

"Beats me. I don't know what the kids are doing these days. Why don't you ask them? I happened to see them talking a few times in the hall this week whenever she made it home," Eustacia noted with disdain. "That girl comes and goes more than my hot flashes. Well, when I had hot flashes. Now I have lukewarm ones followed by these dang constant shakes. It's like my battery is dying or something."

If we couldn't track down any revised copies of Gwendolyn's will, then Eustacia and Finnigan would have to proceed with the one he had on file. Maybe Lilly thought she was getting the money from her mother who was set to inherit a lot of cash upon Gwendolyn's death. I ignored Eustacia's random musings about her body temperature since I didn't want to have mind-damaging nightmares that evening. "How about Sam? Do you know much about him? He always seems flustered whenever I run into him," I asked Eustacia. "Even just now, he dropped something and acted odd when I tried to pick it up.

"Could it have been his web pen?" Eustacia asked. I could hear in the background Bertha advising that dinner was being served. "The kid can't eat anything without blowing up."

Web pen. Blowing up. What was she talking about? "Huh, is Sam sick?" I asked remembering back to the first time I'd seen him holding something in his pocket. Did she mean an epi pen? Whatever he had that day would've been the same size and shape. Could he be carrying around medicine in case his body went into anaphylactic shock?

"I guess you could say that. He's allergic to a lot of things, so he's gotta carry that doohickey around to stab himself if he can't breathe or he passes out," Eustacia noted before telling me she had to hang up. "Sam's always been a nervous child. He's the gentlest and most respectful kid I've ever met, but he's secretive. He's vague whenever you ask him direct questions. I'm not sure what it's about, but it's probably because he was always afraid of getting sick."

Chapter 14

Several minutes after returning from a run the next morning, I found a note from my parents indicating they'd gone to Sunday mass and planned to meet some friends for brunch. I'd just peeled out of my sweaty gym clothes and turned the shower on when the house phone rang. I looked at the caller id noticing my brother, Hampton, was calling. Other than a few summers and major holidays, we'd spent little time together as adults. He'd grown more conservative and closed-minded once he connected with his wife's oil tycoon father and focused on building his own empire.

"Howdy! How's my favorite hampster doing?" I teased answering the phone. When we were young kids, my brother had brought home his class pet, Houdini, to care for it over a long holiday weekend, but the hamster went missing. While feeling sad and embarrassed at losing the school pet, my brother collected his laundry to give to the cleaning lady before we left for school. As she bent down to lift the basket, the furry creature popped his head out of the laundry pile scaring the poor woman into quitting. Knowing Hampton was going to collect the laundry, I neglected to tell him that I'd found his school pet and instead, I placed Houdini underneath the top layer of clothes a few minutes before the cleaning lady picked up the pile. To this day,

Hampton still didn't know what I'd done. If I told him, I wouldn't be able to use his hated nickname, The Hampster, anymore.

"I see you're still as childish as ever, Kellan. I guess I couldn't expect you to grow up knowing you're still sponging off Mom and Dad by living at home," Hampton scoffed on the phone.

"I'm here temporarily while I decide what to do. I haven't sold my house in LA and am considering renting it for a year. I think that's a fairly astute thing to do, ya know?" I tried to appeal to his cheap side by highlighting an opportunity to be fiscally responsible.

"Let's have this conversation again in a few months to see if anything's changed," he replied. Hampton constantly told everyone about his 401Ks, pensions, IRAs, bonuses, summer home on the Maryland shore, and anything else that clearly demonstrated how well-off he was. "How's that teacher's salary working out for you?"

"I'm sure you'd be pleased to know I negotiated a nice package for myself. I'm really working two jobs by helping develop the program to expand Braxton," I noted feeling proud at myself for simply stating the facts rather than going after him for his less-than-kind attitude.

"No doubt because of something Dad pulled to make that happen, I'm sure. Is he around?"

I wasn't sure why I even tried to impress my brother. It was a losing battle no matter what path I took. "No, they're at brunch with friends. May I ask you a legal question?" I leaned against the bathroom wall watching the steam build up around me, perhaps inside of me as well.

"I suppose I can give you one free consultation. Are you about to be arrested for something? I'm not as familiar with criminal law as I am corporate and business law." Hampton sighed, then laughed when he finished speaking.

"Estates and inheritances are what I need to know more about. I'm helping one of Nana D's friends who passed away recently. Do you remember Gwendolyn Paddington?"

"You're helping her? The Paddingtons are well-off. I'm sure they have plenty of attorneys to handle it, Kellan. Why are you inserting yourself into a situation where you have zero qualifications? Mom could handle it better than you would. Or Nana D."

"Quit being so sarcastic. I haven't said a single thing to you on this call to deserve your ruthless jibes. Talk about not ever growing up, big brother."

"Fine. What do you need to know?" he asked. I couldn't be sure if he genuinely wanted to help or preferred to hang up as quickly as possible.

I explained the situation about the missing will and noted I was still uncertain if it even existed.

He replied, "It's completely legal if Finnigan drew up the will and a few names were handwritten in the proper places. Assuming it's been signed by two parties who aren't named as beneficiaries, and it's dated after the previously written will, the new one would be upheld in any court in Pennsylvania."

I made a throaty noise that indicated I agreed. "I'm concerned someone's holding on to it until the funeral is finished, then he or she will claim they mysteriously found it."

"Have you asked around? Maybe one of the staff members at the Paddington estate served as a witness. It's likely no one in the family acted as a witness, assuming Gwendolyn left her money to the family. Witnesses should be disinterested parties."

The Hampster made a solid point. The staff might not have thought it was their business to disclose anything, or they believed the will was being handled already with the lawyers. "Speaking of family, Eleanor and I were talking the other day. Neither of us have heard from Gabriel. Have you?"

"Nope. As far as I'm concerned, he abandoned this family when he took off years ago. If Gabriel doesn't want to stay in contact with us, then I've no desire to waste any time thinking about him."

Ah, the brother I knew had returned after letting down his guard for just a few minutes. "I heard you had some news recently. Are you ready to share it with me?" Eleanor was convinced his wife was pregnant again. I thought it was something bigger.

"That's why I was calling Dad. I suppose I can tell you, but please let me be the one to tell him when he returns my call. You will let him know that I called, right, Kellan?"

"Of course. What's going on?" I asked hoping it was something positive. As much as I enjoyed teasing him, I wished only the best for my brother. We may not have much in common anymore, but with Gabriel gone and Penelope living in New York, we were losing siblings left and right.

"Natasha's expecting a fourth child this summer. We've also decided to move back home to Pennsylvania. Her father has located a new well up near the Betscha mines he thinks might be lucrative. He wants me to help him run the operations side of the business this time. I think he's considering leaving his companies to Natasha and me rather than his son who doesn't seem interested. Or competent. It'd be almost as bad as if he'd given them to you."

After I hung up with Hampton, I finished showering and dressing for my third visit to a funeral home in the last several weeks. Nana D called as I climbed into the SUV to let me know she'd dropped Emma off with Eleanor at the Pick-Me-Up Diner. Eleanor had agreed to watch Emma as she needed to stay at the diner while the electrician finished all the work in her kitchen. She planned to have Emma help her decide the final menu with Chef Manny. They'd kept many of the original dishes, but Eleanor wanted the new diner to reflect her personality as well as the history of the beloved eatery. Knowing Eleanor's love of astrology, I pictured new dishes with names like "Random Luck Fish" and "Crystal Ball Pancakes."

I arrived at the Wharton Whispering Pines funeral home ten minutes later. There were only two funeral homes in all of Wharton County, and for some reason, all three recent funerals had been held at this one. I entered the building and greeted the director, Lydia Nutberry, a third-generation mortician, who recognized me by now. "Room three down the hall, same as last time, Kellan," she said.

Although Gwendolyn was well-known in Braxton, the family decided to keep the service private. A separate memorial would be held the following week at Paddington Enterprises for any staff or colleagues who'd known Gwendolyn, and there would be a similar one for her at Paddington's Play House at the end of the *King Lear* production for any of her fellow theater comrades. I'd emailed Myriam suggesting we have a special dedication to Gwendolyn at the opening performance and was pleasantly surprised when she supported the idea.

Since today's service at the funeral parlor was an invitation-only event, Eustacia and the rest of the family had made a specific list of who could attend. Exceptions were cleared only through Ophelia who'd deemed it her right to limit the guest list. While it seemed peculiar at first, Nana D pointed out that people in Braxton often went to funerals just to hear idle gossip and consume free coffee and desserts. Given there were two separate services being held to allow friends and others to properly grieve, I kept my mouth shut. It might also be easier for me to observe the family's movements and reactions to one another once they were all finally in a room together.

After a quick discussion with Lindsey, Millard, Eustacia, and Nana D, I scanned the room to get a feel for who'd already arrived. Dana spoke with her mother in a corner near the back of the room. There was an older man with them, but I didn't recognize him. It might have been Richard Taft, Ophelia's husband and Dana's father. He had his arm around Dana in a parental-sort-of way. Gray hair was closely cropped to the side and top of his head, and he wore a pair of silver, wire-framed glasses. He wasn't particularly tall and had a few extra pounds in his gut area. He nodded at Lilly when she started walking away from Jennifer and toward me.

"You're Kellan, right?" she said with her nose held high up in the air. She wore a respectable yet on-trend, dark gray dress with her shoulders and arms covered by poufy sleeves. Lilly's shiny black hair was tightly pulled across her scalp in a French braid and fastened against the back of her head. She crossed her arms together and said, "I hear you've been around the manse lately, asking a lot of q's about me. What gives?"

Who'd said that? I suppose Marcus Stanton could've mentioned I inquired about her. I doubted very much Eustacia or Millard had said anything. Perhaps Sam or Dana, maybe even Jennifer, had brought up my name. I didn't think I'd talked to Brad about her, but all the conversations were starting to blur together given the number of adversarial and unclear relationships among the Paddingtons.

"Oh, really? I must have indicated I hadn't found a chance to speak with you after your grandmother passed away. Please accept my condolences on her loss," I said with a brief dip of my head in her direction.

"Yeah, thanks. So, I'm used to people talking about me. I'm usually at the center of things. You've found me now. What is it you want to know?" Lilly shifted her weight as if she'd been compelled to listen to me for some miniscule amount of time but wanted to be anywhere else.

"I don't think there's anything specific I wanted to know. Since I'm spending so much time with your family and representing them at the Play House, it seemed appropriate to learn a little more about everyone," I noted while watching the man who'd been standing with Ophelia and Dana kiss them both on the cheek, then take off toward the exit. "Would you know whom that gentlemen is?" I said pointing toward the gray-haired man I suspected was Richard Taft.

"Shouldn't you have figured that out already? I mean, if you're going to be our representative at the Play House, whatever that actually includes, you need to get with the program, Kellan. I can't see what Aunt Eustacia sees in you if you're this unaware of the family members." Lilly huffed loudly and walked toward the table to pour herself a cup of tea.

I followed her. "I assume it's your father, but I've only been acquainted with your family for the last few days. He hasn't been around as far as I can tell, has he, Lilly?" I tried to be as polite as possible, so I didn't isolate a potential lead, but the girl spewed venom like her mother and grandmother. Nastiness or uncivil attitudes definitely ran in the family.

"Yes, that's Daddy. He travels for work, but not much longer. If you haven't heard, he's going to be the new head of the family company." Lilly looked pleased with herself, obviously a daddy's girl. Could this be where she thought she'd find the money to launch her new business?

"Oh, Eustacia hadn't mentioned it to me, yet. I suppose that's a good thing for your family. I had been under the impression your Uncle Timothy was only on a temporary leave of absence from Paddington Enterprises."

"That drugged-out loser? Ugh, please. Yesterday's news." When Lilly poured milk into her tea, it spilled on the table. Before walking away, she said to me, "Get that, will you, love?"

I wiped up the mess laughing to myself about her lack of manners and impertinent countenance. When I caught up with her, she was looking around before zeroing in on Brad as he entered the room.

"I understand you and Brad are friendly," I said hoping to stir a reaction.

"I'm not sure that's any of your business. If you've nothing else to ask me, then I think we're done here," Lilly said waving her hand at me. Before she stepped away, she turned and handed me her paper cup. "That goes in the trash, if you don't mind, love."

I accepted the cup but gently held onto her wrist for a moment. "Oh, certainly. I don't mind at all, but we're clearly not finished, *love*. Tell me more about this little project you're trying to find investors for." I'd previously dealt with many girls like her in LA. If you let them walk all over you, they always did. Sometimes you had to push back even if it meant risking the relationship or your opportunity to find answers.

"It's not a *little* project. I have a brilliant team ready to execute solid marketing plans and unique approaches to better sell products and services. I'm the queen of social media, and this is going to be huge when it gets rolling," Lilly replied flicking my hand off her wrist. "I'll thank you not to paw at me."

"My apologies, I only intended to continue our conversation, not to make you feel uncomfortable. I'm fascinated by the science behind advertising data and research. I take it you've found some investors?" I said with a fake smile.

"Not exactly, but I'll either be coming into some money soon, or my father has offered to have Paddington Enterprises fund the entire launch. My mother was unwilling to help until he stepped back into our lives. She's quite useless when it comes to any sort of business matters. I know enough not to end up like her. I'm surprised she hadn't tried to knock off Grandmother before now." Lilly blinked several times, then walked away displaying exorbitant and unwarranted pride in herself.

I stood in silence reflecting on Lilly's ill-mannered behavior when I was interrupted. "What did my daughter want with you?" a shrill voice said behind me. I grimaced when I turned around as Ophelia stared at me with panicked eyes and pursed lips. "And don't give me the run-around, I know all about the questions you've been asking the rest of the family. My son, Sam, mentioned you'd been harassing him several times throughout the last week."

"First of all, I certainly wasn't harassing your son. We ran into one another while out on a run near the Wharton mountains, then again in the Grey Sports Field parking lot. He was tense and upset over losing his grandmother. I shared my own history losing a loved one hoping to comfort the kid."

"I'll suggest you leave my family alone. I'm not sure why Aunt Eustacia insisted you be given full access to the estate and the Play House, but that will all change soon when the will is read and I'm responsible for things going forward," Ophelia noted looking more and more like Cruella deVil. "In the meantime, if you have any questions about my family, you can direct them to me. Leave Sam, Dana, and Lilly alone. They're quite young and haven't a clear understanding of what's going on here. They don't know someone might have tampered with my mother's medication, nor do they need to know anything about it. Am I clear?"

What was with the Paddington family? They'd all made me their whipping boy in lieu of learning how to have a civil conversation with a normal person. "My only intention is to help Eustacia understand what happened to Gwendolyn in the last few weeks. She was getting sicker, and no one did anything to remedy it nor did they realize what was going on in the background. But the fact remains, someone switched her heart medication with placebos, then overdosed her with cocaine."

"All you're doing is restating the supposed facts. I've had enough of it from that invasive sheriff," Ophelia replied while fixing a stray hair that had come lose from her perfectly styled coiffure.

"Pardon my saying so, Ophelia, but few people in the family seem concerned about who might have tinkered with your mother's medication. Everyone's more interested in having the will read and moving on from the whole ordeal. What if it's your sister or one of your children? Or do you already know whom it is?" I assumed it would be controversial to suggest such a theory, but at that point, the only way to combat the derisive lashings I'd been receiving was to return fire. I didn't like being cruel, but I'd been backed into a corner.

"How dare you! No one in this family murdered my mother. I'm sure there was a mix-up with her medication. As for the drug overdose, I can't explain it. Call the pharmacist! As I told the sheriff, leave this family alone to grieve. If you insist there was something shady, perhaps you should focus on that interfering nurse and that repugnant theater director who's had it in for my mother for over a decade." Ophelia shook her finger in my face but kept her voice low not wanting to create a disturbance.

"I'm looking at those angles. If you're so certain your family is innocent, why did Lilly say she thought you might have killed your mother? Your daughter doesn't seem focused on protecting you."

Ophelia pulled back, then guffawed at me. "Lilly is angry because I won't give her any money to open that confounded business she wants to start up. There's room for her in any one of the family's corporations, she doesn't need to look elsewhere." Ophelia promptly turned in the opposite direction looking for anyone else she knew and stomped away from me.

Well, that was fun. It was as if I'd been tag-teamed by a mother and daughter looking to take their anger and vengeance out on anyone nearby. Rather than try to engage with Dana, Jennifer, or Sam, I gave up and left the funeral parlor after stopping by Gwendolyn's closed casket to say my own goodbye. When I got into the car, my phone indicated I had a message. Please don't let this be another Paddington or Taft screeching at me.

Nana D: *Looked like you had fun. Learn anything?*

Me: *Not really. We need to find out if there is another will. If not, my money's on Jennifer or Ophelia being the killer. They stood to collect the most.*

Nana D: *You're in luck. I spoke with Bertha. She never saw the details, but she was one of the two people who signed it. It definitely exists.*

Me: *That's great news. Whom was the other witness? And where is the will now?*

Nana D: *She could only answer one of those questions.*

Me: *Which one? Out with it, Nana D. I'm tired of being dragged around and kept at bay today.*

Nana D: *You're the most impatient imp I've ever known. Brad was the second witness. Bertha wasn't sure where the new will ended up.*

Me: *Brad??? Where did Bertha last see it?*

Nana D: *In the mailbox. Gwendolyn sent it to herself. Clever girl.*

Me: *It's been a week. It should've arrived already.*

Nana D: *Unless someone found it and destroyed it, so they wouldn't lose out on the inheritance.*

Chapter 15

Classes resumed on Monday morning. After dropping Emma off at school, I drove to campus and held my first lecture for the day. While the students talked in groups, the pregnant maid who disappeared from the Paddington estate years earlier flashed front and center in my mind. If Brad were Hannah's child, had the discovery of his father been why Gwendolyn had died? I needed to convince Eustacia that we had to tell Millard what we'd learned, even if it caused him any heartache. While I didn't think he could've killed his own sister-in-law, maybe it was time for the truth to come out about Hannah giving birth to his child.

Once my second course was finished, I followed the students out of the classroom to grab another cup of coffee. I'd woken up too late and needed extra caffeine to push through the rest of the day. While I stood in line, Connor and Sheriff Montague stepped into The Big Beanery. I paid for my coffee and snatched a corner table, then waved them over once they'd finished collecting their orders.

"Kellan, good to see you," Connor said while sitting across from me. "The sheriff and I only have a minute, but we didn't want to be rude."

"I appreciate it. I'm sure you two have a lot to discuss about Gwendolyn's death. I understand you've located Timothy finally," I offered up as a way to focus the conversation. "I wanted to speak with him myself, but as far as I understood, he was refusing visitors at the rehabilitation facility."

"Yes, he's trying to get clean and fight his gambling addiction. Although I commend him for fighting his demons, it's certainly a convenient time to hide out," Sheriff Montague growled while stirring milk into her cup. When I handed her the tray of sugar packets, she raised the palm of her hand at me. "Connor's shown me the light about staying away from that stuff."

In the four or five times I'd seen the two of them together, I'd picked up on a growing crush. I don't think Connor was fully aware how often she stared at him or tried to casually flirt. I'd mentioned it once, but Connor, who's built like a brick wall, bluntly told me to keep my mouth shut. Not one to risk any unintended consequences, I'd heeded his advice and observed from afar April's behavior around him. There were at least two furtive glances and a clandestine brush against his arm when she sat at the table with us.

"What makes you think Timothy's decision to quit drugs and gambling is convenient?" I said.

"While his mother has a heart attack and drops dead in the middle of a theater performance from a cocaine overdose, he suddenly sees the light and checks himself into rehab? You don't see anything coincidental about that, Little Ayrwick?" She cracked her knuckles causing me to flinch when each successive pop reached my eardrums.

"I didn't see him at the funeral. You haven't arrested him, have you?" I asked mostly believing the sheriff wouldn't have kept a son from visiting his mother one last time before the burial.

"Timothy has not been arrested. We've questioned him hoping to understand more about his drug choices. It appears cocaine was also his downfall," Sheriff Montague said with a tone so shallow I could practically see what she was thinking. She thought Timothy had killed his own mother.

"Timothy was free to leave the rehab facility but apparently chose not to show up at the funeral parlor," Connor added. He placed both hands together on the table in front of him and began tapping. "Seems he didn't need to say a final goodbye."

"Maybe he found religion and made his peace with her death. Not everyone enjoys a funeral service." Personally, I found them tedious and frustrating. Most people showed up because they felt compelled to say goodbye to a body. While I had no clue where the spirit or the soul went after you died, I was much more comfortable talking to somebody I'd lost from the comfort of my own home or a quiet bench in the sanctity of the park. "Did he explain what they fought about at the theater during the intermission?" I still didn't know why Timothy had chosen not to attend yet showed up anyway.

"If you're so curious, why don't you go to the Second Chance Reflections rehabilitation facility yourself to ask him?" the sheriff directed.

I was glad she did since I hadn't known which one he'd checked himself into. Cha ching! "Just curious. There are a lot of people who thought they'd benefit from Gwendolyn's death."

Sheriff Montague said, "Well one of them went to a great length to swap just one dosage of pills with huge amounts of cocaine to kill her. There was no trace of any additional cocaine anywhere other than those pills Gwendolyn took at the theater. None of the rest we found in her house were contaminated either."

At least now I had confirmation the tainted pills were specifically swapped for that afternoon's dosage. "I guess until someone finds the new missing will, we can't determine who might be the culprit. I don't particularly like or trust anyone in that family."

"Excuse me, did you say a new will?" the sheriff said while her eyes brightened and a sour expression developed on her face. "I'm not aware of anyone searching for a missing will."

"Yes, Gwendolyn signed a new one the night before she died. No one's been able to locate it, but as I understand there were two witnesses who signed it. I'm sure they can vouch for its existence, as can Finnigan Masters, Gwendolyn's attorney." I smiled as I responded to the sheriff feeling smug that I'd known something she hadn't. It wasn't mature of me, but I accepted little wins from time to time.

"Okay, Little Ayrwick... let's backtrack a bit. Please explain whatever it is you know. I can tell by the nauseating grin on your face you like having your ego stroked. Please share your investigative prowess with the poor, unfortunate sheriff who seems to be one step behind you this time." She cupped her hands together in prayer mode and faked as though she were begging me to assist.

Was she really admitting that I'd been able to find out more than she had? "What's in it for me?" I stared directly into her eyes as I replied. "I mean, it sounds like you're looking to work together on solving this peculiar puzzle."

"In exchange for you telling me what you know, I will happily not cart your pathetic rump to the county jail for withholding evidence and disrespecting law enforcement." As she stood, one hand reached for her hip where a gun had been safely locked in its holster. Was she trying to intimidate me?

"I'm trying to find a way to partner with you, April, but you block me at every turn. I think you need to be more open-minded and flexible. At the risk of annoying you any further, what's the harm in a little pro quo if it helps find a criminal? It's not like I'm broadcasting what you say on the news. I haven't once done anything on this case to get in your way, have I?"

Connor's shock and trepidation clearly told me to back down. "Kellan, I'm sure the sheriff appreciates your help, but why is this so important to you?"

"Honestly, at first it was because Nana D asked me to figure out if someone was trying to hurt Gwendolyn, but less than twenty-four hours later, the woman was murdered. Every single time I talk to someone in the Paddington family, they berate me or treat me like I'm not worth the dirt they step on. I want to see whomever killed the woman go to prison."

"You're beginning to annoy me even more than usual, but obviously, once again, you have an ability to get close to all the key players in this murder investigation. I'm not going to pretend having you on the inside isn't a benefit, but we need to establish some ground rules. I'd rather not have to put you in prison while that crazy grandmother of yours is in the lead to become the next mayor."

"I can respect rules if they're fair and mutually beneficial," I added. There had to be a way I could stay clear of causing any additional friction with the sheriff yet also still help Eustacia learn who killed her sister-in-law.

After explaining everything I knew, the sheriff asked me to give her twenty-four hours to process the updates. "Don't give any information away to anyone in that family right now!" she bellowed before walking out the door.

"You need to tread a little more lightly, Kellan," Connor noted after she left. "You've always been nosy, but you seem to be getting a lot more confident and pushier than I remember."

I hadn't thought of it that way. I saw myself as capable of getting answers, and my intellect and curiosity were intrigued by investigating real life crimes. I'd always wanted my own show focused on historical cases, but the adrenaline rush over something current or connected to people I knew was exciting me. "I don't mean to act cocky. I just think I have natural talents in this area. Why should I let them go to waste if I can find the right balance between observing the laws and discovering the truth?"

"Until you get killed because the murderer is smarter and more prepared than you. Have you thought about how Emma would feel losing both parents at such a young age?" Connor sniped.

I closed my eyes to prevent myself from saying something I knew I couldn't. Or shouldn't. When I felt relieved enough to respond, I said, "I know you're right. I promise to be more careful."

"If you're committed to staying in Braxton, I'd like to suggest maybe we could re-build our friendship. Get back to college days," Connor replied punching me in the arm. "I've been on my own for too long and miss having a best friend."

"I do, too," I said pushing down the emotional ball of stress trying to project itself from my gut. As much as Eleanor was helping me try to understand what I should do about Francesca, talking to Connor about it had been something I desperately wanted to do for days.

"Let's get back to having drinks and dinner more often. Maybe we could go for a few runs together?" Connor stood and slapped my shoulder twice. "You've got a little catching up to do, buddy."

I laughed knowing I could use the motivation. "Speaking of dinner, Eleanor mentioned you guys were going out tomorrow to talk about whatever happened between you last Christmas."

"Yep. I'm not saying it's gonna work out between her and me, and I'm still interested in Maggie, but I promised you I'd talk to Eleanor. She's an amazing woman. Who wouldn't want to date her?"

Although I knew he was right, she was my sister and I still hadn't asked her about why she was at the fertility clinic. After Connor and I made plans to go running that weekend and said our goodbyes, I taught my three-hour lecture and reviewed my upcoming lesson plans. The sun was beginning to set and although I wanted to get in a workout, I needed to find out from Brad what he knew about signing Gwendolyn's will. When I pulled out my phone to find the number for the Paddington estate, I noticed several missed messages from Eleanor.

I had forgotten today was the final meeting with the inspector to see if she could open for dinner service. I quickly checked in with her and learned she'd passed with flying colors. Eleanor was thrilled to finally have everything fall into place. I told her I would stop by in a couple of hours with Emma for a late dinner. My grandmother had also left a text message for me.

Nana D: *Emma is here with me. We're baking dessert since you had a rough weekend.*
Me: *You're the best. I'll be by at seven, so we can go to the Pick-Me-Up Diner's opening.*
Nana D: *Did you speak with Brad?*
Me: *On my way now, that's why I'm running late.*
Nana D: *Then stop bothering me and go accomplish something for a change.*
Me: *Speaking of getting things done, do you have the plan ready for Friday's debate?*
Nana D: *Did anyone ever tell you that you're a smug little devil?*
Me: *Yep. A crotchety woman I rather like being around even if I don't admit it often enough. It goes to her head too easily. And we've all had enough of that experience for a lifetime.*
Nana D: *Does that mean you'll be moving in with me? Your parents need their privacy. They need to be empty nesters, so they have some space to get their groove on. You're cramping their style. I imagine they haven't made whoopie since you returned.*
Me: *We're done. Thanks for giving me an image I'll never erase from memory. If you understood emojis, I'd share a picture of a frog throwing up. Since you don't, I'll settle for saying BARF!*
Nana D: *You're so immature. I didn't raise you to be so weak.*

I shook my head to detach any images the conversation had conjured up. When I called the Paddington estate, Bertha informed me that Brad had left for an interview at the hospital. I ran through a list of contacts who might know where his interview was being held, then settled on a former high school classmate who worked in the Human Resources department at the Wharton County General Hospital. Ten minutes later, including a promise to take Lydia Nutberry's daughter, Tiffany, for coffee the next week, I knew the time, location, and contact Brad would be meeting with. I'm sure her revealing the information was a violation of some law, but it was likely nothing Sheriff Montague could arrest me for. I promised the sheriff I'd stand down for twenty-four hours. Having an itty-bitty conversation with my new friend, Brad, about my old friend's will couldn't possibly lead to trouble.

I unfortunately hit a bunch of traffic while driving downtown during rush hour. By the time I arrived, I had three minutes to catch Brad before his interview started. I left my car on the third floor of the parking garage and took the elevator to the administrative wing. Wharton Country General Hospital had been built twenty years earlier in the center of the county, so it was easily accessible from all four towns. With generous donations from the Grey family, it served the needs for most illnesses and injuries, but any major surgeries or risky procedures were transferred to Philadelphia. Located near the sheriff's office and court buildings, the hospital stretched two blocks wide and two blocks long.

I rushed out of the stairwell—the elevator was taking too long—hoping the interview would start late and jogged down the final hall to the place Brad was supposed to be. I stopped outside the frosted glass door to catch my breath. Despite running several times per week, I must not have been used to racing up and down stairs as I thought I was having my own heart attack. When I entered the room, my throat seized up for an entirely different reason. Brad wasn't in the room. The sheriff was.

"Little Ayrwick, are you here to interview for a role as a nurse? I'd pay top dollar to see you in a pair of scrubs," she said with a large grin. "Surely, you couldn't be here to try and track down a potential person of interest in one of my murder investigations."

I could have lied. I could have said I was there for any other reason. Except nothing came to mind. Instead, my mouth hung open and a drop of drool oozed out of the corner of my lips. I took a deep breath, then said, "I'm awful. I don't know how to listen. I was trying to make your job easier. I thought if I could find out what Brad knew about the will, it would be one less person you had to find time to deal with. Is there any chance of me getting out of here with my—"

"Outside, now!" she shouted. As I slithered through the door, Tiffany whispered '*sorry*' at me. I shrugged my shoulders preparing to accept whatever punishment would be thrown in my direction.

"Can you just overlook this one time? You don't even know exactly what—"

"Shut. Your. Mouth. Before. I. Shut. It. For. You," Sheriff Montague said with a distinct pause between each word. Is that how it sounded when I taught Emma how to pronounce big words? I waited in silence until we got to the end of the hall and sat in a small waiting area. If she was going to arrest me, she would've done it in public, not a room where we were alone.

"Brad Shope signed the will at the same time as Bertha Crawford. Neither one of them were shown the specifics of who inherited anything upon Gwendolyn Paddington's death. He was under the impression Gwendolyn planned to give the will to her lawyer the following week. He assured me he didn't kill her, not that I'm inclined to believe him yet."

"Why are you telling me this and not kicking my—"

"I asked you to be quiet, Little Ayrwick. Are we going to do this the easy way or the hard way?" the sheriff said in an obnoxious manner. When I didn't respond, she said, "I asked you a question."

Was I supposed to respond or shut up? How did this keep happening to me? I decided to type my response on my cell phone's notepad. I would be able to acknowledge that I preferred the easy way, but I didn't actually need to speak the words. When I finished typing, I handed her my phone.

April read my message and broke out in an unexpected chuckle. "You are the most sarcastic and obstinate man I've ever met!"

I typed on my phone in response: '*Can I speak now?*' When she nodded, I said, "Did you ask about his mother's obituary or if he knew his father's identity?"

"No, I didn't. Since our earlier chat, I decided it would be better for you to handle that angle. I'm not sure it has anything to do with Gwendolyn's death. Brad will be coming by to see me in two days. I didn't want to inhibit his chances of getting the job he was interviewing for."

"Okay, so you want me to talk to Millard to find out if they are father and son?"

"Yep, call me as soon as possible, so we can discuss it. And do not think I've forgotten you disobeyed direct orders. I hope you will see this chivalrous act of kindness as the tiniest of olive branches. We shall discuss this further once you find out something useful."

I watched the sheriff walk toward the elevator and step inside the car after the doors opened. As they closed, she stared through the diminishing crack holding two fingers first to her eyes, then pointed at me mouthing what I was pretty sure were the words '*I'm watching you closely, Little Ayrwick.*'

Chapter 16

"Are you sure it was really the sheriff? Maybe there was an invasion of body snatchers earlier today. I smelled something funky in the air this afternoon," Nana D said in an exaggerated alien-sounding voice causing Emma to laugh like a hyena. "What do you think, kiddo, did some nasty, green-colored four-eyed creature from outer space tell your father to keep investigating?"

Emma giggled again and slapped her forehead. "Aliens don't visit the Earth during the winter, Nana D. It's waaayyy too cold for them. They need hot air to breathe. Didn't you watch *Avatar*?"

"Oh, honey, I don't know what an avatar is or what it does, but if you met that sheriff, you'd know she's full of enough hot air she could support an entire space alien planet," replied Nana D bugging her eyes out so fiercely she fell forward on the table from putting so much pressure behind them.

"Nana D, you're gonna give yourself an aneurysm. Quit it while you're ahead of the game," I said. We'd just sat down in a cozy booth Eleanor had reserved for us in the front corner of the Pick-Me-Up Diner. The grand re-opening had sent the entire town out in droves. We were lucky to hold on to it despite Mayor Bartleby Grosvalet showing up last-minute without a reservation. Eleanor found a space for him at the bar and comped him several martinis. The mayor liked to drink heavily.

"What's an anarysm, Daddy?" Emma placed her menu back on the table and announced she was ordering steak Diane.

"Aneurysm. It's kinda like when you consume too much ice cream and you get a headache only a whole lot worse," I explained, then suggested she might not like eating a woman named Diane.

"No, silly. Diane is the name of the goddess of hunting. I'm not going to eat anybody. My name's not Hannibal." She stuck her tongue out at Nana D who promptly returned the gesture only it contained some childish noises in her attempt to up the ante. How did my daughter even know whom either of those people were? *She's only six years old* I repeated several times inside my head.

"I'm not sure who's more mature between the two of you," I scolded. Judging by the competition currently occurring at the table, I was the most mature and that wasn't saying very much. "As for the sheriff, I wasn't gonna press my luck to find out what led to her generosity. I hightailed it out of there and called Millard. He's meeting us here in twenty minutes."

My phone rang before anyone could respond. It was my mother-in-law, and I wasn't letting her go to voicemail. "Be back shortly," I muttered to Nana D and Emma who were still making outrageous faces at one another.

I passed Eleanor walking near the kitchen and pointed to the phone. "The she-devil's calling me, I'm hiding out in your office." After I shut the door, I clicked accept to stop the theme song from Jaws ringing on an endless loop. "Hi, Cecilia. I'm at my sister's diner having dinner with Emma. I only picked up because we need to talk about this ridiculous mess. Can I call you back in a little while?"

"Time is almost up. Have you come to your senses?" she said without any other greeting.

"I left several messages for you over the weekend. I need to speak with my wife," I said through gritted teeth realizing she wasn't going to cooperate. I unclenched my jaw when thinking about being forced to see the dentist if I'd broken one. It was on my top five list of places never to go again unless necessary in order to prevent death.

"The Castiglianos do not answer to you, Kellan. I've made it quite clear that you cannot speak with her. I also remind you that while this may be a secure line, please stop using her name." Cecilia had always been headstrong, but for many years, she knew Francesca wouldn't tolerate her parents treating me poorly. It seemed she now had the upper hand and felt no need to hold back.

"Why are you doing this to us? Do you have any remorse over what pain you've caused Emma? Forget what it's done to me, but you and your husband's dirty businesses have robbed a precious girl from growing up with two loving parents." Emma had bounced back from her mother's death, but there would still be a permanent impact on her future. I'd never forgive them for what they'd done to her.

"I'm not going to re-hash another conversation where you tell us we're bad parents or we should be in prison. You've made your point. You do not respect our business, the decision we made, or the need to ensure our future safety. It's rather selfish of you, but I always told her you weren't good enough to marry." Cecilia huffed loudly causing me to pull the phone away from my ears. If I hadn't been in a public place, I would've lost my cool and shouted back at her.

"Do you have any solutions other than living in some secret wing of your mansion? How do you see this working out long term, Cecilia?"

"I don't have all the answers. But what I do have is enough history and knowledge of the potential dangers involved if you don't return to LA. My daughter will not give up. She's been angry ever since this whole situation blow up in our faces years ago."

"I can't live in seclusion. Can't you get the police involved? How many members of the Vargas family are we expecting to still be angry years later?" I knew little about mob policies and etiquette. Were we talking about waiting for one ancient godfather-type to kick the bucket? Or were there hordes of irate Vargas relatives looking to stick dead horseheads in every member of my family's beds?

"It's not like that anymore. We run everything like a business. There's a fine line to keeping status quo among all the different territories. If anyone found out we tricked the Vargas family, everyone would begin to draw lines, form alliances, and execute retaliatory tactics," Cecilia replied in a demeaning tone. "I'm doing the best I can to help you both, Kellan. I don't want to see anyone hurt."

Fat chance! She practically threatened me when she was in Braxton the last time. "I've got a few more days, but I can tell you one thing for certain. I refuse to make any decision without talking to my wife again. If you think there's any chance of me listening to you, then you better find a way to cut me some slack here," I hissed. One half of my body burned as if fire coursed through my veins while the other half froze with a chill that might never regain normal temperature again. I stared at the cell phone screen watching the call length increase. I couldn't take another second and hung up on Cecilia. For added effect, I also turned the whole device off not wanting to talk to the woman anymore that evening.

I stomped back to the table at the same time Millard arrived. After introducing him to Emma, I asked her to find her Aunt Eleanor to help prepare our dinners. I didn't want Emma to overhear any part of the conversation with Millard.

"So, Kellan, what was so urgent that you had to meet with me tonight?" Millard asked while scratching at his moustache. Emma found it so funny, she'd called him Yosemite Sam after one of her favorite cartoons.

"Mr. Paddington, I need to talk to you about something in your past. I don't know you all that well, so this might be a little tough. Are you the kinda guy who likes to slowly peel away a Band-Aid to avoid pain? Or are you a rip it off, scream once, and get it over with kinda guy?" Personally, I was a rip it off and scream *several* times kinda guy. I wasn't giving him that option and judging by the number of scratches on his forearm from pruning holly trees earlier that day, he wasn't going to scream anyway.

Nana D's head cocked to the side. "Stop being a fusspot, Kellan. Just ask him if he knew Hannah Shope had his baby twenty-five years ago. He's a big boy, I think he can take it." Not usually known for her tact, Nana D threw both hands into the air between her and Millard waiting for his response.

Millard stiffened against the booth's back padding. "I would have said rip the Band-Aid off, Kellan. Seraphina knows me well enough." He paused and went deep into thought. While I waited for his response, I studied the distant look in his gaze knowing he was remembering happier days of his past.

"Take your time, I'm sure this isn't easy," I added.

"If she had a baby twenty-five years ago, it sounds to me like you're saying she was pregnant when she left Braxton. More specifically, when she quit working at the Paddington estate," Millard said. His left hand shook with a few tremors before he rested it against the stable one on the table's surface.

"That's what I've come to understand, if I've done the math properly. I gather from your expression this is not something you'd been aware of. I'm sorry to be the one to tell you about your long-lost child. But I think I know whom he is. As do you," I said slowly hoping not to agitate Millard more than necessary.

"You've always wanted to be a father, Millard. I suppose this might give you an opportunity to make up for the past. He may be a fully grown adult, but there's still time to connect with him," Nana D responded as she cupped his hands with hers. Despite a relationship not working out between them in the past, her affection for a friend was evident.

A confused look settled on Millard's face. "You think I was the father of Hannah's child?"

Nana D and I looked at one another. "Of course. Weren't you the reason she was fired? I know your parents weren't tolerant and forgiving of anyone getting involved with the staff."

"Oh, Seraphina, you might know my family well, but clearly you must think I'm just as bad as them." Millard shifted toward the end of the bench. "I couldn't have been that child's father."

I thought I'd heard him incorrectly. "I don't understand why not."

"Hannah and I were never intimate. We were friends. I needed someone to talk to about wanting to quit the family business and take up gardening. She helped keep me sane in that loony bin," Millard said with a chuckle. "I need a bit of fresh air if you don't mind. I think I'll take a rain check on dinner. Please extend my apologies to your daughter and your sister, Kellan."

As he rifled through his wallet and dropped cash on the table, Nana D spoke. I was too confused at what he'd just told us. "Millard, what do you mean? If you weren't the child's father, who was?" Nana D whispered. It was rare she kept her mouth quiet, but she seemed not to want anyone to overhear the question.

"In return for supporting me, I also lent my ears to Hannah those few months she worked at the mansion. She'd found herself attracted to someone in the house and had apparently developed sincere feelings for him. It wasn't exactly someone she should've been involved with either, but it certainly wasn't me. I merely counseled her to let it go if she wanted to keep her job and not incur the wrath of someone in my family." As he started walking away from the table, he turned back and looked at Nana D. "I can't believe you think I would have seduced a young girl. I could have been her father, Seraphina. We had a very different kind of relationship than what you've implied today."

I called out before he got too far away. "Mr. Paddington, is there anything you can tell us about whom could've been the child's father? We're afraid it's the reason Gwendolyn was murdered."

"I can't. Hannah never told me whom she'd fallen for. I didn't want to know either. I needed to get away from my family. They also thought I was fooling around with that poor girl which is why they let her go. I never had a chance to say goodbye. That same day I quit the family business and she was fired, my father informed me I was cut out of the will for making the choices I did. I guess he thought it was a fair and just punishment."

As Millard left the diner, Nana D turned to me. "I can't believe you made such a huge mistake, Kellan. We need to find a way to make it up to that man."

Me? She should've told me he wasn't the type to do something like that. "I don't understand. If it wasn't him, was Millard saying it could've been his father, Timothy, or Charles?"

"Millard was over fifty at that point. I can't imagine it was his father. Old man Paddington was close to eighty! And not the kinda spry eighty I'll be one day. He was knocking on death's door."

We both shivered thinking about an eighty-year-old and an eighteen-year old being intimate. "Do you think Charles could've cheated on Gwendolyn with a maid?"

"I don't know. But if Brad is actually a Paddington…" Nana D noted.

"It would have angered Timothy, Ophelia, and Jennifer who thought they were supposed to get all the money," I said feeling confident Brad's parentage had something to do with the reason Gwendolyn died. "Something still doesn't make sense. Brad couldn't have been left anything by Gwendolyn if he also signed the will as a witness. The Hampster had confirmed what Finnigan told us. Pennsylvania law might leave a bit of wiggle room for the beneficiary to also be a witness, but Finnigan clarified he told Gwendolyn to be sure she didn't do it."

Nana D reminded me that not everyone knows the specifics of those laws. Once Emma returned, we finished our meal choosing to leave the murder investigation out of our discussions. Eleanor and Maggie stopped by to ensure our meals were good but couldn't stay to chat. They had hundreds of other guests to check with on their opening night.

As we finished saying our goodbyes and leaving a generous tip—our meal had been free since we knew the owners—Myriam arrived at the diner. I checked my watch and was surprised to learn it read nine thirty. I needed to get Emma home to bed. Hoping to sneak past Myriam without her noticing me, I pushed Emma and Nana D out first, so I could stand on the other side of them. After they exited, I attempted to leave too, but Myriam's penetrating gaze zeroed in on me.

"Kellan, I thought I'd stop by to sample the cuisine at the new Pick-Me-Up Diner. The *King Lear* performance ended a little while ago, and I was hungry," she said lifting a single finger to let the waitress know she needed a table for one. The harried server asked Myriam to wait several minutes for a table to be cleared.

"I appreciate you throwing a little business my sister's way, thank you," I said walking through the doorway. I smiled knowing she had to summon an ability to be patient before she could sit at a table, too. She hated to be kept waiting for any reason.

"You should know I didn't come by because she's your sister. I thought it was important to support my colleague, Maggie Roarke. I believe she's a co-owner here, correct? I didn't choose this place because of your family. I'd have thought you knew that already," Myriam grunted.

"Of course. I should have guessed. Please accept my humble apologies, but I need to catch up with my daughter." I was keenly aware Myriam severely disliked my family but given the ultimatum Ursula had given us in regards to working together, I thought she would have attempted to play better in the sandbox.

"Ursula has been detained by Braxton's Board of Trustees this evening, so I'm grabbing dinner alone. I'd like to schedule time with you in the next few days to discuss your role as the Paddington family member's voice at the Play House." Her nose wrinkled in irritation clearly revealing how she felt about the entire situation.

"Certainly, perhaps tomorrow? I need to discuss your decision to terminate Arthur. If I understand correctly, you gave him two weeks' notice. Perhaps we could find a way to re-consider." I remembered that I'd promised Fern I'd try to help save her son's job.

"I'm usually open to discussion on many topics. That is not one of them. Engaging in lewd behavior in a dressing room on public property is assuredly not acceptable in my book. Arthur is lucky I didn't fire him on the spot without any additional pay." Myriam grabbed a menu from the wall cubby and lifted her glasses onto the bridge of her nose to begin reading.

What was she talking about? Arthur said he'd been avoiding Dana's overt flirtations the last few weeks. "Are you sure it was Arthur? Or for that matter... was it definitely two people engaging in—"

"You don't need to articulate any further descriptions. It most definitely was Arthur because I saw him leaving the dressing room twenty minutes later," Myriam replied pursing her lips.

"May I ask when this was?"

"A month ago. Why is that important? Isn't the fact it happened enough to agree with me?" I expected you to support me on this decision, but I can see your morals are nearly as impious as his."

"Honestly, I can't discuss this right now. I'll be happy to talk further tomorrow. If he and Dana were behaving inappropriately, then I can understand the decision to fire him," I said reaching back for a mint from the countertop. I suddenly had a sour taste in my mouth.

"I positively didn't say it was Dana. I'm not sure who was inside the room with him, but I insisted it be fumigated by the janitor that evening. As for Dana, she's a smart girl. I doubt she'd get involved with that joker. She was the only person who could locate the fake medication we needed for this summer's next production." As Myriam finished speaking, the waitress told her the table was ready.

"Hold up. What did you say about fake medication?" My heart nearly stopped when she said the word *fake*. "Tell me exactly what that means."

Myriam explained that she'd been searching for various sorts of pills and medication bottles for a future hospital scene. Since Dana was responsible for props, she'd been assigned the task. Within twenty-four hours, she had various options for Myriam to choose from. Dana had stumbled upon the placebos on a website used by theaters and television shows to locate hard-to-find props. As Myriam left, she turned and said, "*So farewell to the little good you bear me. Farewell! A long farewell, to all my greatness!*"

If I remembered properly, that was from Henry VIII. Cardinal Wolsey, an ambitious and arrogant man, had delivered the lines. "Myriam, are you proud of the similarity you just exhibited to a man who supported one of the most abominable kings in English history?"

Myriam stopped short in her path and without turning around to face me directly, replied, "You always go for the obvious, Kellan, don't you? Perhaps you need to convince the tiny, little, miniscule, uneducated gray cells in your brain to look past the words being said and find the true meaning."

As she continued walking away, Eleanor appeared. "She's got a point, big brother. Sometimes you have tunnel vision."

"Why are you supporting her?" I asked feeling my frustration levels increase.

Eleanor's shoulders shrugged. "She's a paying guest. You're not. I know where my bread's buttered."

I closed my eyes humming loudly as a way to distract myself from exploding at the next person who said anything rude, mean, or negative to me. When I opened them, Emma stood in front of me. "Are you coming, Daddy? Nana D complained you always take too long. She sent me back inside and told me to tell you something."

"What's that, baby girl?" I braced for a litany of Nana D's ridiculous comments.

"She said, '*Tell your father he owes Mr. Paddington an apology. And as punishment for making unsuptions, there won't be any dessert again for two weeks.*' What did you do now, Daddy? How come you always get yourself into trouble when I leave the room?" Emma led me outside and to the parking lot, so I could drive home and forget the whole evening. "I'm tired, and I have school tomorrow. You really shouldn't keep me out so late next time, Daddy."

After buckling Emma in the back seat, I shut the door and opened my own. A large, menacing man stood nearby looking in my direction. "You Kellan Ayrwick."

I nodded.

"I've got a message for you." He reached into his pocket.

I gulped and backed up against Emma's car door. "From whom?"

"She says you should never hang up on her again. Nor should you turn off your cell phone. The line should be kept open for whenever the boss wants to speak with you."

My mother-in-law had tracked me down at the diner. Within an hour. She had contacts nearby who were willing to do her dirty work. "I'll take that under advisement." I felt my legs weaken but was confident Cecilia would never do anything to hurt Emma. Like killing me in front of my daughter.

"I know the boss pretty well, Mr. Ayrwick. She only warns someone once. I believe you've exhausted that count a few times. I suggest you do more than *take it under advisement*." Although he disappeared into the darkness, I could hear his heavy shoes pounding the pavement and a bubble bursting in his mouth from the gum he'd taken out of his pocket.

Chapter 17

"I barely slept last night, Nana D. It's a good thing I don't have to teach any classes today. Maybe I'll swing by Danby Landing after tracking down Timothy. I need to know what he and his mother talked about just before she died." Nightmares about my mother-in-law's henchman had haunted me nearly every hour while I'd laid in bed trying to forget our encounter in the parking lot. My restless body twitched every time a tree branch scratched the roof or the wind whistled through the eaves. Sleeping in the attic bedroom had both its benefits and its downsides. Last night was definitely a downside.

"Good boy, that's the priority for today. I'll ask Eustacia to come by for tea at three o'clock. It'll do her some good to get out of that mansion. It's sucking her dry worse than an evening listening to your father talk about himself. And that old bat needs to quiz me for the debate on Friday." Nana D was familiarizing herself with what type of jobs people held in Wharton County and what policies had changed over the last decade under Mayor Grosvalet and Councilman Stanton.

After agreeing to meet them for tea, I dropped Emma off at school and drove to campus to experience my weekly harassment with Myriam. I was able to convince her to let Arthur remain working until the end of the King Lear run, then we'd re-evaluate his position at the end of the semester. She ended the meeting quickly, citing the need to complete some research. I was pleasantly surprised by her more hospitable attitude, but it only reminded me she was likely sugaring me up to execute a sneak attack as all spiders do.

With my work activities on track, it meant I had time for a run. There were a few hidden trails scattered throughout the western section of Wellington Park which also happened to be close to the Second Chance Reflections rehabilitation facility where Timothy was recuperating. I'd never been there before, but a few people I'd gone to college with had sought their help after turning to drugs and alcohol. It had been built in the 1970s after an excessive amount of addictions cropped up in Wharton County. We'd been a dry county for most of our existence, then granted licenses to a few establishments shortly after World War II ended. Unfortunately, as the years passed, the county government lost control of the situation and citizens turned to dangerous substances as distractions once the financial crisis hit.

Timothy had voluntarily checked himself in, but it was still up to him whether he accepted visitors. I stopped at the front desk in the reception area before beginning my run. "I'd like to request a brief visit with Timothy Paddington. He's not expecting me, but his family asked that I talk to him for a few minutes today," I said to an older gentleman named Buddy who'd dressed in a comfortable-looking cardigan, beige t-shirt, and brown corduroys.

"Has he put you on the approved list of visitors?" Buddy had a gentleness about him that made me think I stood a chance of getting inside.

"Probably not, but it's important. His mother passed away recently, and his family is worried Timothy's taking her death very hard. His aunt and uncle aren't doing well themselves. They're in their seventies and having some health problems." I appealed to Buddy's humanity and the need to protect the patients. Perhaps it would win him over.

"Timothy's a good lad, but he's struggling. I knew the boy back in high school. I was the school doctor and checked him out a few times. Now I'm here trying to make ends meet. Not easy. This town is all messed up when it comes to protecting its senior citizens," Buddy said veering off into an entirely different topic.

I needed to get him focused before I lost my chance to get inside. "I wasn't aware you knew Timothy. He's had a rough life from what I understand."

"He played on the football team. Quarterback in his senior year," Buddy said with a nostalgic gleam in his eye. He told me more about Timothy's days back at Braxton High School, explained how tough it was to grow up in the Paddington family, and offered his sincere hopes that Timothy could wrestle with his current demons. Buddy agreed to check if Timothy would grant me a few minutes even though it was against the facility's rules for random guests who weren't on the list to be admitted.

"I'm grateful, Buddy. I know his family would be, too." As Buddy walked away, I remembered seeing him in my first year of high school. I didn't play any sports, but I also thought he had retired that year. He'd probably completed his years of service to the high school, collected his pension, and found a new part-time career to earn some additional income. Like most other places across the country, teachers and school administrators weren't paid properly and had difficult times surviving after retiring from their positions.

While Buddy disappeared behind a locked entrance to the main part of the facility, I perused a pamphlet about Second Chance Reflections. I found some information noting how they were funded both from government assistance and private contributions. I also stumbled upon a few metrics I thought might be helpful for Nana D to use in her campaign plans that would benefit her and the patients at Second Chance Reflections. I slipped the pamphlet into my back pocket as Buddy returned to the reception area.

"You're in luck. Timothy needs your help. Follow me, and I'll get you set up in one of our visitation rooms. The South Room has the best view of the gardens. They're not maintained well, but at least you're not staring at the back of the bus station or the parking lot." Buddy verified my identification, entered me into the system, and navigated us through a narrow hallway. Although the facility was clean and organized, the décor hadn't changed since the 1980s. I suspected the funding they received from the government didn't cover the look-and-feel, given it wasn't a large amount of money to begin with. I was certain Nana D could convince the garden club to donate a few hours of time each week to spruce up what looked like it was once a grand landscape.

When I arrived at the South Room, Buddy opened the door for me and returned to the reception area. Timothy greeted me while standing near two wooden chairs and a small, lime-green Formica-covered table with a few chips in the surface. The room was no more than forty square feet and looked remarkably similar to the county prison's visitor rooms minus the bars and glass partition. Its walls were a dimly painted white and littered with scratch marks. Several water marks stained the ceiling. I wouldn't exactly call it a dump but give it another year or two without any tender loving care, and that's where it would end up.

Timothy looked about the same as when I'd briefly noticed him at Paddington's Play House on the day Gwendolyn was murdered. His face was pale and withdrawn, he was at least a month overdue for a haircut, and his clothes were a size larger than his body required. He'd apparently lost weight, likely from his drug addiction, and couldn't afford a higher-end rehabilitation clinic since he'd also suffered with a gambling and debt problem. I'd seen a picture of him as president of Paddington Enterprises a few years ago when Lara Bouvier had done a special report for the local news network. It was like a whole different man occupied the room with me now. Unfortunately, not in a good way.

"Kellan, I was surprised to hear you came to visit me," Timothy said shaking my hand and telling me to take a seat. "I know your parents, but I haven't seen you since you were a toddler."

"I appreciate you agreeing to meet with me. I told Buddy that your family asked me to visit, which is true, but not the whole reason." I folded my hands on the table and smiled at him. This wasn't going to be an easy conversation.

"Buddy's been taking care of me. I didn't want the royal treatment. I screwed up in the last year, and part of my recovery includes living like a regular guy. I can't expect people to go out of their way because I'm a Paddington." Timothy's legs must have been shaking underneath the table because I could feel the heavy piece of furniture vibrating. "Before sharing why you came, how's my family?"

I wasn't sure which members he cared about, so I told him about the funeral and my interactions with Millard and Eustacia. "I know they both are worried about you."

"Aunt Eustacia is one in a million. She's a tough cookie, but that woman has been there for me more times than I care to remember," Timothy noted clutching the end of the table with both hands hard enough to turn his knuckles a blotchy mix of white and red.

I wasn't sure if I should jump in with my questions or let him talk for a few minutes. He was nervous, and his eyes darted around the room a lot. Was he going cold turkey or gradually decreasing the amount of drug usage to wean him off everything? "Do you want to tell me about how you ended up here? I'm not family, but I can listen if there's anything you need to get off your chest." I didn't know him all that well yet he clearly was suffering from everything swirling around him.

"That'd be great, you're a good guy. Not many people would come visit me here. I chose Second Chance Reflections for two reasons. One, I'm broke and they were the cheapest place available. Two, no one in my family would visit me here. It's not like I don't ever want to see them again, but... well, I've come to realize part of the reason I'm so messed up is because of my family."

Timothy explained that he'd been placed under a microscope ever since he was a child. His parents expected him to be a perfect child, perfect businessman, and a perfect family man. He'd spent so much time focused on meeting Charles and Gwendolyn's expectations that he'd forgotten his own needs until he couldn't handle the pressure anymore. It sounded a lot like Millard's story, and that's when I realized how lucky I had it in my own family. Despite feeling pressure from time to time, I'd never felt as if I'd been scrutinized so closely I needed some sort of medication or drugs to escape. I might've run all the way across the country to disappear from them, but that was different. At least that's what I told myself to get by each day.

"The year my father retired, I was on top of the world. But it soon went downhill. Every minute became consumed by the family business. I worked sixteen-hour days and traveled all over the world never knowing what time zone I was in. I had no one by my side to have a better work-life balance. I began sneaking out for thrills just to feel something shocking and different." Timothy stood, walked to the window, and stared into the desolate garden. "It started out as making wagers on silly things. Even when I lost, I still felt alive. That's when I fell in with the wrong crowd and started using too many drugs that I eventually lost track of night and day. My father convinced the Board of Directors to put me on temporary leave insisting I couldn't come back to work until I finished therapy."

"Is that what led you to finally check into Second Chance Reflections last week?" I asked knowing it wasn't the full picture since it'd had been almost a year between the two events.

"No, I escaped for a while. Spent all my money," he said turning back to look at me. I could see him visibly shaking. "Ever since I stopped the drugs last week, my body is always freezing cold. Raw."

"You're doing the right thing, Timothy. You've got to get sober and find a better path in life. There's a lot of time left in your future to make things right again," I added thinking he might have a son to get to know.

"Exactly. I promised my mother the day she died that I'd fix things." Timothy wrestled with his conscience while rocking in his seat. I could feel the pain and fear emanating off of him.

Although I wanted to help him, my purpose for the visit was to determine if he could be Brad's father or whether he might've killed his mother. "What did you talk about at the theater?" I asked.

Timothy clenched his fist. "It was the night before when everything changed. I only stopped by the theater to say goodbye. I had already contacted Second Chance Reflections to check myself in."

Timothy explained what had happened the weekend before Gwendolyn passed away. He'd gone to Philadelphia and gotten outrageously wrecked. When he was walking back to his hotel after drinking in a bar, he stepped off the curb and was nearly hit by a car. Someone tried to help him, but he pushed the Good Samaritan away and berated her for no reason other than he was plastered. He woke up the next morning sleeping half on the sidewalk and half in the street covered in mud, littered with garbage, and lying next to a drugged-out teenager. His wallet and shoes were missing, and he had a large open wound on his forearm. "I'd hit rock bottom. I went home that Saturday evening to tend to my cut, sober up, and apologize to my mother. I told her that I was planning to get help."

"What time was this?" I asked trying to figure out the chronology of events.

"Late. She'd just gotten home from a friend's place. It might have been your grandmother's. I was still out of it, but I remember most of the conversation. I cried in my mother's arms for the first time since I was a kid. I didn't even cry at my father's funeral. I was high on cocaine and pot the day he was buried." Timothy shielded his face with his hands to hide the shame of the past. He explained how grateful he was to have that last chance to make things right between them before she died.

I realized by the way he spoke, Timothy was under the impression his mother had a heart attack and died from natural causes. I didn't want to be the one to tell him she was murdered. I would confirm with Sheriff Montague to be sure she'd never told him about the results of the autopsy. Timothy hadn't seen anyone else, and the sheriff smartly kept the news out of the papers until she could find the killer.

"What did your mother think about you getting treatment?" I wanted him to focus on something positive, but I also needed to know how they'd left things.

"She was supportive. We had such a great conversation that night. Mother even told me she would put me in her will again once I proved I could get back on the right track. I didn't care about the money, I wanted to fix things with her. She's my mother, and I screwed up too many times."

I nodded at Timothy. He knew he wasn't in the old will, which meant he had no financial reason to kill her. "I'm sure that night meant a lot to her. Do you... I'm sorry to have to ask you this, but do you know if she ever got around to putting you in a new will?"

Timothy shook his head. "I don't know. I left her house shortly afterward and went home to pack my stuff, so I could come here the next day. We didn't speak again until the following afternoon."

"She was at the Play House watching the show with me," I explained.

"Right. I'd gone to the estate to say goodbye but had missed her."

"Did you see anyone else at the house?" I needed to know if he'd admit to seeing Brad in the kitchen. If he lied, I thought that could mean he'd been up to something bad like swapping the pills.

"I came in the front door and went directly to my mother's room. I knocked but she didn't answer. I thought I heard her moving around in there, but I didn't want to just walk in. She was a private woman. So, I went downstairs to see if Brad or Mrs. Crawford were around."

"Were they?" I asked beginning to feel as if I might be about to learn important information.

"Mrs. Crawford was in the kitchen talking to the cook about meals for the upcoming week. Brad came in a few minutes later to say he had to go up to the Play House to bring my mother's medicine."

"Could Brad have been whom you heard in her room?" I asked wondering if Timothy had still been drugged out of his mind that morning. When he shook his head, I asked, "When did you leave for the theater?"

Timothy began to rub his temples. "I offered to drop off the pills for my mother, but Brad said he was in a rush. About an hour later, I guess. Is there a reason for all these questions? Did Brad do something wrong?"

"No, sorry. I didn't mean to alarm you. I was trying to understand the timing."

Timothy nodded. "I was supposed to check in here at four o' clock. I went to the Play House to catch my mother during the intermission to thank her and to say goodbye. I originally wasn't going to see visitors for a month once I arrived at Second Chance Reflections. I needed to focus on my recovery and to think about my future. But something else happened, and now you showed up today."

"You looked upset while you were talking to your mother at the theater. What happened?" I asked trying to understand the full picture. I'd ask what he meant about *something else happening* next.

"She didn't want me to leave until after the show. She wanted to go with me, but I insisted I had to do this on my own. We argued about it, but I told her I'd see her soon. That's when she touched my arm, and I felt the pain from my wound. I pushed her wrist away and told her she had to trust me."

"And then you came here?" If he and his mother hadn't been on bad terms, there was little chance he'd killed her. It would make no sense, and he didn't appear to be lying to me right now. There was genuine pain and heartache in his demeanor, and if he was truly coming off years of drugs, his body and mind weren't strong enough to create some elaborate ruse for me to believe.

Timothy said he was starting to get tired and needed to be alone. "Before you go, there was a reason I agreed to see you. I need your help based on what happened."

"Sure, what can I do?" I also wanted to find out if he'd ever been romantically involved with Hannah, but I'd let him ask his favor first.

"Can you give this to Aunt Eustacia? I'm not allowed to send or receive mail from here while I'm going through this early recovery stage. It's a thank you letter. She recently paid my gambling debt for me, so that I can start fresh when I finish the program." He handed me a small envelope from his pocket.

"Of course. She loves you and wants to see you get better," I said feeling nothing but respect for the cantankerous woman who loved to berate me. She might be difficult at times, but Eustacia was truly an admirable woman. "Before I leave, one more question. Do you recall a young maid that worked at your family's mansion about twenty-five years ago?"

Timothy smiled. "Sure, Hannah. She was only around for less than a year. Why do you ask?"

"I ran into a family member of hers, and he was looking to learn more about Hannah. She died a year ago." I didn't want to say too much. It'd be better to let Timothy tell me what he knew.

"She was the newest maid right after I started working at Paddington Enterprises. The former one had retired, and my parents accepted the first girl who applied. I still lived at home with them and my grandparents at the time. I didn't know her all that well, to be honest. I probably couldn't help whomever was asking about her."

"I thought maybe you and Hannah were closer… um… since you were about the same age at the time, you know…" I hesitated to say anything that might upset Timothy, but I needed to know if he could be Brad's father.

"You thought Hannah and I were together?" Timothy laughed for the first time since I'd arrived at Second Chance Reflections. It softened him and showed me he had a possibility for a better future. "No, definitely not. I was too caught up in being the perfect kid. If Father or Grandfather thought I was messing around with one of the family servants, they'd have read me the riot act and punished me for years. I guess that ended up happening anyway, huh?"

If Brad's father wasn't Millard or Timothy, that left Charles or someone else I didn't know about. "I appreciate it. I'll let Hannah's family know. Do you remember whom she might have been close with?"

"Not off the top of my head. If I think of anyone, I'll let you know," Timothy said before shaking my hand and leaving the room.

Although I'd learned a vast amount of information by meeting with him, it only eliminated suspects from my list. I left the rehabilitation facility and went for an hour-long run. After I finished showering and changing, it was lunchtime. I grabbed some food at Braxton's cafeteria and stopped at my office in Diamond

Hall to meet with a few students who had questions on an upcoming paper. In between their visits, Maggie and I caught up.

Me: *How's the library today?*
Maggie: *Good. I'm putting the finishing touches on the invitations for the masquerade ball.*
Me: *For the new building? When is the ball?*
Maggie: *In May right after graduation. It'll be the first of a series of events to raise money.*
Me: *Great! Reservations Friday at eight at the new French restaurant on the Finnulia waterfront.*
Maggie: *I'm looking forward to it. We have lots to talk about. Got a meeting. See you soon.*

I put my head on the desk to nap. Luckily Emma would be at a play date after school, so I could rest my eyes for a few minutes before going to Nana D's for tea. I had only a few more days to let Francesca know if I was going to come back to Los Angeles. Could I tell Maggie what was going on? Would she be able to help me without any personal feelings getting in the way? With no answers to any of my questions, I forced myself to drive to Danby Landing. I needed the distraction and Nana D would provide the best way to make me feel better—dessert!

Chapter 18

When I arrived, Eustacia and Nana D were setting the table for tea. Nana D had baked a chocolate cheesecake with peanut butter frosting. It looked and smelled so delicious, I could barely stop myself from picking crumbs off the top and sides. Nana D smacked my hand a few times. "Leave it. Wait until the tea is done steeping. Let's talk about Gwennie."

"Yeah, what have you learned, Kellan? You're not as good of an investigator as your grandmother made you out to be. Why don't I have answers yet?" Eustacia chided me.

After telling them all about my visit with Timothy, Eustacia gave me points for making some progress and confirmed she'd paid his debt. "I can't see my brother, Charles, cheating on Gwennie, but I guess anything's possible," Eustacia said while slicing into the cheesecake.

"I want to talk about your great nephews and nieces. I haven't been able to get a good reading on them. As far as we know, they could've been included in the new will. Let's pretend for a minute Gwendolyn chose to leave one or more of them the Paddington family fortune."

"Good idea. What might the little rascal's motives be?" Nana D added while pouring tea into three cups.

"Dana told me Sam was fighting with Gwendolyn about something in the days before she was killed. Anyone know why?" I asked.

"Sam's always been a good boy. Gwennie thought he'd look after her if she ever got too sick. I'm not sure what they could've been fighting about," Eustacia explained struggling to drink her tea without spilling a few drops on the table. The lack of answers was wearing her down.

"Who's he closest to? Someone needs to ask him, but I don't see it being me. The kid runs away whenever I try to talk to him," I noted while handing Eustacia a napkin.

"I'll do it," Nana D said. "I'm good at talking to young guys. They seem to confide in me."

Nana D had a good point. I spilled my secrets to her in the past. Failing to tell her about Francesca being alive was the only thing I'd ever kept from her, and it was nearly killing me. "Tread lightly. He might be dangerous, we still don't know enough."

"Gwennie used to complain about Lilly all the time. She got herself into trouble years ago when a friend of hers died in a skiing accident. It was right before her grandfather passed away, but he thought Lilly was capable of pushing her friend down that mountain. Gwennie always thought Charles' grasp on reality was starting to fade near the end. She believed Lilly was difficult, but not pathological. I'm inclined to agree with her on this one."

"I've seen Lilly be nasty, and she was quite rude to me at the funeral. From what I understand, Lilly believes she's found the money to get her new business started," I said scooping up my first piece of cheesecake. "This is amazing, Nana D."

"Of course, it is. Nothing I do is ever short of perfect. Now, about Lilly... I saw her and Brad talking several times in the past few weeks. She seems to like him, but I don't know what they've been talking about," Nana D said. "It didn't look romantic, but I couldn't say for certain."

"Lilly and her mother never got along. She blamed her for Richard's frequent disappearances. She's been much better now that Ophelia and her father are back together."

"Could Richard have loaned her the money? Someone told me he's going to be the new president at Paddington Enterprises," I asked contemplating how to locate him.

"With Timothy out of the picture in rehab, Richard's the only one left in the family who knows enough about the business. The Board approved him as the new president for a one-year term. He might be investing in Lilly's business. And if that's the case, then she had no reason to kill her grandmother to get the money," Eustacia said slamming her fist on the table. "Then there's Dana."

"Yes, she's a handful, too. I've heard a few people talk about the way she chases after guys. There was an incident in the library once, and I suspect that Dana was involved with Arthur in the…" I stopped when I realized my audience. I was telling two seventy-something year old women about the risqué actions of a young girl they knew.

"Well?" Nana D shouted. "Don't leave us hanging. What did she do?"

"Kellan, my grandniece is a bit of a trollop. I'm aware of her behavior. If you have something to say, out with it," Eustacia commented before handing me her cup to pour more tea.

"I'm sorry. I wasn't sure how to say it. She's been excessively flirtatious, but my understanding is Arthur initially rejected her advances. Something doesn't add up," I explained thinking about how Dana was also the one who'd found and ordered the placebos.

"Arthur was outraged with Gwennie. Maybe Dana convinced Gwennie to leave the fortune to her, and she helped Arthur get revenge."

"Did she realistically have access to swap the pills with cocaine the morning Gwennie died?" Nana D asked tapping her fingers on the table.

"Dana was with us at the theater, not at brunch at the mansion. She lives on campus, right?" I said. "Could she have come home to the estate on Sunday morning to steal her grandmother's medicine, swap it with cocaine, and return to the theater without anyone knowing?"

"Probably not, but that's where Arthur could've helped out," Eustacia said.

"I'll ask Myriam. I'm certain Arthur couldn't have left Paddington's Play House before or during the dress rehearsal. He was running the place and had way too much to do," I explained.

"I'll ask Bertha if Dana was around at all over the weekend. You find out from Myriam," Nana D instructed. She began cleaning up the plates while we were talking. "You know what you have to do, Kellan."

Me? What was she talking about? "Umm, what did you have in mind?"

In unison, Eustacia and Nana D shouted, "The sheriff, Kellan. Go see the sheriff."

Although April Montague had softened the last time we'd chatted, I didn't think she'd share any important news about the case with me. I did need to update her on my discussion with Millard about his non-intimate relationship with Hannah, but was that going to help any? "Fine, I'll take one for the team again. But I'm not gonna like it."

"That's life, Kellan. At least until you reach our age," Eustacia scoffed.

"And then you can make everyone else do the real work!" Nana D added with a high-five in Eustacia's direction.

After Nana D's, I picked Emma up from her play date. In the car ride home, we told each other about our days. I left out the part about the murder investigation, although part of me wondered if she might have an interesting take on the possible culprit. Children often weeded out the extraneous information and pointed out the one thing you'd missed all along. Should I try?

I was considering it when my father's name appeared on my cell phone as we pulled onto their street. "Hey, Dad. What's going on?"

"You have a visitor. I thought you might want to return home as soon as you could," he said in the same way he used to nudge me to come home for dinner more often to see my mother while I was in college. I pulled up in front of the house.

Given the motorcycle parked in the Royal Chic-Shack's driveway and my dumb luck, it was probably the sheriff. For a really long moment where even Emma had to remind me I was still on the phone, I considered passing the house as if I'd never been there. That's when I heard the knock on the passenger's side window and hung up the phone.

"Daddy, some lady cop is here to see you. And she looks angry. Or like she swallowed a bunch of nasty lima beans. Ewww!!!" Emma squealed in a high-pitched voice.

"Just don't look into her eyes, baby girl. She's not a real cop. She's a mean demon, and you don't want to get on her bad side, okay? Pretend you don't see her and back slowly into the house like you're scared of her. She'll ignore you." I muttered while smiling at the sheriff through the closed window. Before getting out of my own seat, I reached around to unlock Emma's seatbelt and told her to rush inside to see Grandpa. After shutting the car door, Emma decided not to follow my instructions and instead marched toward the sheriff. "Can I see your badge? My dad said you're a fake cop, but I don't believe him. You look like a real one. Just a mean one. Did you eat something bad just now? Cause your face looks like it. Are you trying to hide your monster fangs? I'm confused, but I'll sort this out."

April looked from Emma to me. I could guess what was on her mind by the subsequent twitches in the corners of her lips. She was awful at hiding her feelings. "Kids. They say the strangest things, huh?" I said shrugging my shoulders and pointing toward the house. "Inside Emma."

"But Dad, if she's truly a monster, I'll wave a magic spell on her and send her far away. And she didn't answer my question. That's rude!" Emma threw her hands to her hips and stared at the sheriff. "My friend Shalini at school says boys pick on you when they want you to be their girlfriend. Are you mean to my daddy because you want to be his girlfriend?"

April's eyes opened so wide she looked like she'd stuck her finger in an electric socket. "Is she for real, Little Ayrwick? Did you rent a smaller version of yourself for the day?"

I had no choice but to introduce Emma to April. "She's six and sometimes doesn't know when to keep her mouth closed. I'm not really sure what my daughter's saying half the time."

"I can see the resemblance," April said to me, then turned to Emma. "It's a pleasure to meet you, Emma. I'm not a monster, but I am a real cop. I might've looked a little angry because your daddy was supposed to call me earlier to tell me something important. He was also not supposed to talk to anyone else about it. For some reason, he seems to have forgotten what we discussed recently. I'm a stickler for rules, and I expect others to follow them."

"I like rules, too. Daddy's forgetful sometimes. I think it's because he does too much. I guess you wouldn't want to be his girlfriend. He'd probably forget your birthday. Although, he's never forgot mine. I wonder if he needs a girlfriend to help keep him in line. That's what Nana D told me the other day," Emma announced walking toward the house to see my father.

"I think you've got your hands full with that one, Kellan," the sheriff noted.

"Kellan? I think that's the only time you've called me by my first name." I made a mental note to read my nana the riot act for saying something about getting a girlfriend in front of Emma.

"Yeah, well... based on what you're dealing with between your nana and your daughter, I might be able to take it easy on you from time to time. I certainly don't want to be the one to cause your complete and utter breakdown," the sheriff said while pulling out her notepad. "As for the revealing comments you apparently shared about me in front of your daughter, at least I know where we stand. And to think I was going to try to be a little more forthcoming with you in the future."

"Perhaps there might have been a wee bit of exaggeration. Can you honestly tell me you haven't said something equally controversial about me? Surely, Connor's been a good sounding board at some point in the past. I've seen the way you look—" I said with enough sarcasm to prove my point but was stopped mid-sentence.

"Let's move on. Neither one of us want to have that discussion. So, what did you find out from Timothy? I feel the need to remind you that you were only supposed to discuss Hannah with Millard. I'm not at all sure how you thought you had approval to hunt down Timothy. I was only joking when I told you where he was and that you could check for yourself." Sheriff Montague walked toward the garage to avoid the chilled wind whipping by us.

We agreed to disagree on my approach, then I updated her on everything Timothy had told me at Second Chance Reflections. "He doesn't know his mother was murdered, I take it?"

"Nope. I was trying to keep that as quiet as possible, but Eustacia told several members of the family. She's a piece of work, ain't she?" Sheriff made a note on her pad, then continued after I nodded in agreement at her remarks. "We were able to confirm that the cocaine given to Gwendolyn was nowhere else in the house, nor in any of her other medication. We did find some in

Timothy's apartment, but I'm not certain we'll be able to prove that's the source where it came from. Dr. Betscha isn't an expert in recreational drugs, but he's doing his best."

"As for Brad's father, I'm at a loss. Could we attempt a DNA test?" I said.

"I couldn't get a warrant for it at this point. We can't prove Brad's done anything wrong," the sheriff explained. "However, I did learn something interesting when I was poking around Brad's background."

My curiosity piqued. "Can you share it?"

"If you promise to follow all of my instructions going forward, yes, I can," she said narrowing her eyes. "This is against my better judgment, but if you step out of line, apparently all I need to do is talk with your daughter to put you back on the straight and narrow."

"Scout's honor," I replied with one hand showing the proper gesture, and the other behind my back crossing my fingers. She also didn't need to know I was never a scout.

"Brad Shope doesn't have a nursing license. He's completed most of the coursework, but he never received his formal certification. Apparently, he failed one of the exams, and then he was released from a prior position after there was a mix-up with several patients' medications." When the sheriff's phone rang, she stepped away to take the call.

It was unexpected news. What was he hiding? Maybe Eustacia could talk to Dr. Betscha about a DNA test. Whether Brad was guilty of killing Gwendolyn or not, if he was a legitimate member of the family, everyone would have to know. Or should know. They probably didn't want to know.

"It seems there are several large withdrawals the Paddington's accountants knew nothing about. I'm on my way to find out more," Sheriff Montague said upon returning. "Don't speak with Brad about any of this. I will let you know when I have any additional information about his background."

"Can I suggest a DNA test to Eustacia?" I asked.

"Yes, but that's all. By the way, your daughter is adorable. I can see you're a great father. Maybe I will re-consider letting you call me April instead of Sheriff Montague," she said before jumping on her motorcycle and tearing off down the driveway.

I stepped inside with a smile. Maybe Emma did know exactly the right things to say! We spent the rest of the evening together with my parents eating dinner, baking cookies, and watching an episode of Emma's favorite television show. Normally she wasn't allowed to watch it during the week, but she deserved a reward. Then we read a bedtime story and discussed getting a puppy. She was winning.

* * *

On Wednesday after teaching classes, Fern had a working lunch to prepare our first major presentation on the structure of the new communications department at Braxton University. Once finished, she asked, "Have you talked to Myriam yet about letting Arthur stay on?" Fern looked like she needed to hear good news. Her head hung a little low and her eyes looked weary.

"Temporarily through the end of the show. I'm going to check again with her this afternoon. She asked for a few days to consider my input. I'll let you know what I find out." I unwrapped the plastic from the double fudge brownie I'd bought in the cafeteria and offered half to Fern.

"I needed it, thanks," she said accepting the dessert. "Arthur's gotten himself into some sort of trouble again. He called last night to tell me things had gotten complicated, but he wouldn't say why. I'm hoping it's not something with the Play House or the show. He needs to stay focused on his career."

"You're a good mother, Fern. Arthur's a little too dramatic sometimes. Maybe he's exaggerating about how complex things are." I'd already seen his outburst on a few occasions since I'd been back home. I was also certain his news had something to do with Dana. There was more going on there than I could put my finger on currently. "Is he dating anyone?" I asked.

"Not that I'm aware of. He was seeing someone in New York before he came home, but that ended. I didn't know anything about the person either," she said careful not to say the gender of his former significant other. "He's generally secretive about whom he's dating."

Living in LA had exposed me to a much larger community unlike our small town where people were still fairly quiet about revealing their sexuality. I wasn't sure if Arthur dated men or women, but his reaction to Dana and his secrecy led me to believe that his preference had something to do with why he stayed clear of her. It wasn't something I felt comfortable bringing up to Fern, especially if his mother wasn't aware.

"Has Arthur said anything about Gwendolyn's death? I know they weren't always angry with one another, but how has he been reacting lately?" I asked with a tentative approach.

"Kellan, we've known each other for years. I'm also aware you were investigating the two deaths on campus last month. Are you asking because you think Arthur had something to do with Gwendolyn's death? I thought it was a heart attack," Fern said with concern rising on her face.

"I won't lie. We need to work together and trust one another. I've heard rumors there was foul play with her medication and that her family might be involved. I know Arthur is friendly with one of her granddaughters, Dana. A thought or two has crossed my mind if he might have been coerced into doing something… and now that you mentioned he is in trouble, well…" My stomach cramped up knowing I was turning our meeting into something uncomfortable.

"I doubt it. Arthur can be difficult, but he's not a killer. He also stands up for himself, and if someone in that family tried to push him into doing something illegal, Arthur wouldn't have allowed it," Fern said with a hint of doubt lingering in her voice.

"Are you sure? I don't think he did either, but I can't rule it out. I've heard he's been... how shall I say... intimately involved with someone recently."

"I know my son. He's never been able to lie to me before," Fern said while collecting our trays. "And don't think I am upset with you for asking. I understand why you're doing it. You've always been a stand-up guy, even back when you used to fight for your fraternity when you were a student here. I admired your courage and strength then, and I admire it now."

"Thank you, it means a lot to hear you say it." After Fern left, I noticed a missed voicemail from an unknown caller. Who wanted something now?

Chapter 19

I listened to the voicemail only to learn I'd forgotten to reschedule my annual exam with Dr. Betscha. I had to cancel it when I'd gotten Francesca's letter and couldn't push myself to do anything for a few hours other than sulking and reminiscing. Knowing I also needed to talk to him about Gwendolyn, I called the office and picked a new date and time. "Is there any chance he's available to speak?"

"Sure, he's got a light afternoon today. He was supposed to be offsite at a conference, but the schedule changed last-minute," she said before putting me on hold.

A few seconds later, he picked up. After we caught up on the big things going on in our lives, he said, "So, what can I do for you today, Kellan?"

I told him about the possibility of the Paddington's maid giving birth to a child that might have been fathered by someone in their household. He was unusually quiet before finally responding.

"I'm sorry, I needed to give the question proper thought. Someone in the Paddington family recently asked me the same question," Dr. Betscha said. "I suppose now that she's gone, I'm not breaking Gwendolyn's confidence, especially if you're helping the family figure out who killed her."

His news surprised me. "Did Gwendolyn ask you for a DNA test on Brad Shope?"

"Yes. She'd apparently come to find out the same thing you've learned about Brad. I got her in contact with a friend of mine who runs a DNA testing laboratory over in Woodland. I don't think she had time to get the final results, but she did have two different tests run if I understood correctly. It was only a couple of weeks ago," Dr. Betscha said.

"Did she say whom she suspected of being his father?"

"No, but she wanted to know if he was or wasn't a Paddington. I believe she was fond of the lad." Dr. Betscha put me on hold to speak with another patient who demanded the doctor make himself available. "Sorry about that, Kellan. I'm not sure how you deal with those Paddingtons all day long. That was one of them begging for a minute of my time this afternoon," he replied. Dr. Betscha was a good doctor, and he made as much time for his patients as possible. Sometimes he didn't know how or when to say *no*. Which Paddington was calling him? I didn't think I could ask him to reveal that, too.

"I won't keep you much longer. Can you send me the same info you sent Gwendolyn? It's a last resort to understanding who might have wanted her dead. If a relative thought she was going to add a new beneficiary or take someone else's name off the list, I'm worried that person might have killed her."

"It's a theory. There were lots of people in that family who disliked Gwendolyn. Even her daughter, Jennifer, threatened to kill her, and she was often the most level-headed of the whole bunch. At least she was before the incident, that is." Dr. Betscha coughed, then began to say his goodbye.

I wasn't sure what incident he was referring to. "Wait, is that something you can share?"

"I probably shouldn't, but it wasn't said to me in confidence. I just happened to learn about it through conversation with Jennifer one day afterward. Apparently, the reason she suffered the last miscarriage which ultimately ended her engagement was a fight with her mother. Gwendolyn accidentally pushed Jennifer down a flight of stairs during an argument at the mansion."

"Really? I knew about the miscarriages but not the rest. Did she tell many people?"

"No, it wasn't like that. At first, she told the emergency room it was an accident. When she came to see me a few hours later, I had a consultation with her ob/gyn. We told Jennifer she might have difficulty conceiving a child again, and she became quite upset. That's when she started ranting and raving about her mother pushing her down the stairs."

"Do you think that's how it happened?" I asked suddenly seeing a stronger reason why Jennifer might want to hurt her mother.

"Jennifer was angry and upset at the thought of not having a child. We never said she couldn't, just that it would be more difficult from some of the damage. You might want to talk to her about it. It's been four or five years, and I don't know how she felt about the situation anymore." Dr. Betscha hung up to deal with his other patient.

The Paddington family was full of so much drama, hatred, and long-held grudges. Any one of them truly could have snapped at some point in the last few months and concocted a plan to murder Gwendolyn. I wasn't going to be able to solve it unless we could find the missing will or force someone to confess out of guilt. Maybe the best next step was to call a family meeting and put all the cards on the table. Could we trigger the murderer to say something that would reveal his or her identity?

After unsuccessfully trying to reach Nana D and Eustacia following my conversation with Dr. Betscha, I went to the library to do some research on how to have someone re-declared alive after they'd been previously declared dead. Surprisingly, there were quite a list of articles and a few books on the extraordinary topic. Most of what I'd learned focused on the financial and legal side of being declared dead when there wasn't an actual body to prove it. That wasn't my problem. There was definitely a body, it was just alive. And I was dealing with a crazy mob family who bribed cops and a coroner to issue a death certificate. Who was going to believe me?

Three hours later, after banging my head on the desk several times causing a small red bump to appear, I took some aspirin and drove home. My mother had picked Emma up after school and gone to a friend's daughter's birthday party which meant I was on my own for dinner. No one else was around. I either needed to get myself some additional friends or take advantage of an early night given I felt like my body was fighting off a cold. I texted my mother that I was going to sleep and she was responsible for getting Emma to bed. I also told her that I owed her big time. She agreed and sent me the number of a florist with a hint that she could use a little something for her office. I ordered two large bouquets of Easter lilies and conked out listening to an episode of the Great British Baking show.

* * *

On Thursday morning, I awoke with a congested head and frustrating cough. The clock on the bedside table read nine o'clock. A note next to it from my father said he'd taken Emma to school that morning. When I hadn't woken up even when Emma tried to nudge me, they knew I was in no condition to get through the day on my own. I sent my parents each a text message thanking them for being the best parents in the world. My father replied saying he'd kept track of the favors I'd needed since returning home and that I should expect a bill at the end of the month. Was he being facetious? Why could I never tell with that man? My mother replied saying the flowers were delivered at precisely eight thirty and smelled so fragrant, everyone in the admissions building stopped by to check them out.

After foregoing my run and workout, I showered and had a leisurely breakfast. Nana D called to tell me I was off the hook if I needed to skip the mayoral debate. She'd heard from my mother who said I was on my death bed. I'm not sure how it went from a cold to almost dying, but the game of telephone between my mother and her mother often went off the rails easily. I let Nana D know I'd be at the debate as soon as I dropped off my dry cleaning, made a few phone calls, and picked up some decongestion medicine. Thirty minutes later, I found myself sitting at a tall table in The Big Beanery for a cup of tea to alleviate my throat which was getting scratchier.

I connected with the DNA testing facility and left a message that I was inquiring on behalf of Gwendolyn Paddington who'd recently passed away. I wanted to see if they could provide the results to me or to her lawyer, whichever they felt comfortable doing. I knew it would go to the lawyer, but I had to try. Finnigan would undoubtedly share them with Eustacia, so I'd ultimately see them. As I sulked over feeling like I'd been hit by a truck, and wishing I could crawl back in bed, I heard a familiar voice. I turned around and saw Sam Taft sitting at the booth to my left. I listened to his conversation.

Sam said, "I never expected this to happen, but ever since I met you, everything seems so much better in my life. You're amazing. I can't wait to see you again."

His voice was so full of glee and bliss, I could feel it a dozen feet away. Was Sam seeing someone new? If so, I was happy for him, but whom was it?

Sam continued, "I understand why you don't want anyone to know right now. It's complex, I get it. I'm not asking you to share the news until you're ready. Sure… yeah, I can do that."

Was his girlfriend trying to keep it under wraps? I felt bad listening in, but it was an opportunity to learn more about him. The kid had been secretive and standoffish whenever I was near him.

Sam laughed, then said, "I'm falling in love with you. I don't care what anyone thinks. My family might not be okay with it, but who needs them? Grandmother was the only one who listened to me. I still can't believe she and I fought over telling the others about you. Then she died without closure."

Interesting. I'd learned two things from Sam's phone conversation. One, why would he kill his grandmother if she was the only person who seemed to care about him? Two, he had a secret lover. Did Dana not approve of whom he was dating and that's why she told me about the fight?

Sam said, "I think Kellan knows. He's shown up a couple of times when I didn't expect to see him. I know we need to keep this a secret right now. But what do we do if he figures out what's going on? I'm already freaking out that my grandmother died because of what's going on."

What did that mean? As I considered everything I learned, I wondered if Sam didn't have a girlfriend. Could he have a boyfriend and be scared to come out of the closet? And if the guy he was talking to also wasn't ready to tell anyone, could it be someone Sam's family knew? I gasped when another thought crossed my mind. Was it Arthur or Brad? I hardly knew anything about Brad's personal life, but that would be incestuous if Brad turned out to be a Paddington. My mind was busy racing all over the place and processing all the information that I never heard Sam approach me.

"Kellan, I didn't see you there. Did you overhear me?" Sam said intently biting his lower lip.

Should I say yes, or pretend I didn't? "Um... I... noticed you, yes, but... I didn't want to interrupt when I saw you on the phone."

"It's not what you think. I didn't want to keep it hidden." Sam's eyes narrowed to the floor.

"I didn't hear much. Is there something you want to tell me?"

He shook his head. "I was talking to a friend, that's all."

I decided to throw out a little bait to see if he'd bite. "Ah, that wouldn't be Brad, by any chance, would it? I need to speak with him and couldn't find him this morning."

Sam looked at me with a puzzled expression. "Brad who?"

"Your grandmother's nurse," I replied.

"Oh, no. It wasn't Brad. I barely know him. I thought he was done working at the mansion already," Sam noted haphazardly gathering up his school bag.

"Brad's helping your great Aunt Eustacia with several things. I believe he's staying on a few more days," I explained searching Sam's face for any sign or clue.

"Well, I gotta run. Can't help you on Brad. By the way, I know you said you didn't overhear anything, but if by any chance you did, please don't tell anyone. I'm not ready to share the news. I'm still dealing with it myself, and well, it's only half my news to share. There is someone else involved, too. I'm sure you understand why it's important to wait until we're all ready to sit down and discuss it, right?"

I nodded only half understanding what he meant. Was he concerned I would reveal that he was gay? Or that he had something to do with Gwendolyn's death? "Sure, it's not my place to say anything. I want everyone involved to be happy."

"Thanks. I figured you of all people might understand, Kellan. Maybe I'll see you around again." Sam tossed on his coat and left The Big Beanery looking partially relieved.

I needed time to process the whole conversation, but I was fairly certain Sam's attitude toward me had suddenly changed. Maybe he'd seen I wasn't bothered by his news and didn't need to worry about hiding the truth from another person. Or maybe he was cleverly keeping me confused, so I wouldn't discover what'd really happened to his grandmother. I stood from my seat realizing I had to get to the debate. Nana D had forced Marcus to stick to the original date and location despite his every effort to change both.

Twenty minutes later, they both took to the stage alongside Lara Bouvier in Wellington Park. We sat in an outdoor amphitheater protected from the cool weather by dozens of heat lamps. Lara asked both candidates to share a personal message to the constituents. Marcus talked about how his family had been in Wharton County for over two hundred years, highlighting all the donations they'd given to build the hospital, promote the concert hall, and re-develop the Finnulia waterfront. Nana D countered with all the benefits her ancestors, the Danbys and Betschas, had given to everyone including creating jobs at the Betscha mines, developing the farmland, and organizing all the volunteer programs. She even cited the new opportunities she would commit to, including the suggestions I'd made to help clean up the Second Chance Reflections facility.

For almost the entire debate, they were neck and neck. Until it came time for the audience to ask questions. The first speaker asked Marcus how he would handle addressing growing concerns about the environment. Crilly Lake was starting to shrink due to limited water from mountain run-off properly draining off into its basin, and several of the older chemical companies in the area had been dumping toxic waste into the Finnulia River. A few had been caught but the latest readings on the cleanliness of the water showed a major focus was soon needed. The councilman had already been researching the impacts on the environment in the county and announced several plans he would put in place to stop the current offenders and increase the fines on future ones.

When it came time for Nana D's speaker to ask her question, she focused on Wharton County inhabitants who were worried that as the county grew more populous and offered opportunities for bigger businesses, how would it impact the percentage of funding we'd receive from the state in the future. Unfortunately, Nana D's full grasp on the political structure within the town of Braxton, Wharton County, and the state of Pennsylvania was still limited. While she was aware of what the county's citizens needed in terms of more jobs and less red tape, she hadn't learned enough about the risks of increased profits and revenue impacting the balance of what the state contributed to the county. She misspoke a few times about what she thought we should do, and Marcus called her out on it in his rebuttal. In the end, Nana D's supporters still rallied for her, but she took a painful step backward in the eyes of big business and corporate groups who had yet to reveal which candidate they planned to back.

As the debate ended, I listened to a few conversations and the news didn't bode well for Nana D. As much as the county's inhabitants wanted change, they were afraid of money being taken away from them as well as supporting a candidate whose experience wasn't as strong as they needed. I comforted Nana D who barely spoke on the walk back to the car. When we reached the parking lot, we saw a woman standing near a car and trying to keep herself from falling over. As we got closer, I realized it was Jennifer Paddington. I grabbed her hand and steadied her against my body. "Are you okay?"

"Kellan, yes, thank you," she mumbled. After regaining her composure, she handed me the keys to her car. "Can you grab the bottle of water from the bag on the passenger seat, please?"

I gave the keys to Nana D who opened the door and reached for the bottle. When she got back to Jennifer and me, Nana D reached into her purse. "You look like you could use something to eat, too. Here, have an apple," she said after taking a Macintosh from her purse."

"What happened, Jennifer?" I asked when she leaned against the side of the car.

"I was feeling a little faint. It must be the morning sickness," Jennifer said looking green.

"Um, are you pregnant?" Nana D asked.

Jennifer nodded. "Yes, I only found out a couple of days ago. It was a complete surprise."

"But I thought you were going to the fertility clinic, Jennifer?" I said feeling dumbstruck by her last statement and our discussion at the toy store.

"I'd been going for the last year, but I ran out of money after the last one. I was shocked when I took the home test earlier this week and it said I was pregnant. I went to Dr. Betscha who confirmed it. I'm six weeks pregnant," Jennifer said with the beginning of a smile forming on her lips.

"Congratulations! I guess the procedure must have taken after all," Nana D added.

"No, that's not what happened. I know for sure the last one didn't work out. I got pregnant the old-fashioned way this time. I'm sorry to be so blunt," she said wiping her cheek. "I'm still shocked!"

"You must be thrilled," I added wondering what it all meant.

"Yes, definitely. Don't get me wrong. My body's been through a lot. It's trying to adjust to different drugs, getting pregnant, and my mother's death. I need to go home and rest, I think," she said while getting into her car.

"You shouldn't be driving right now, Jennifer," Nana D demanded as she looked at me. "Kellan can take you home. I'll follow him and we'll come back for his car afterward."

"No, really. I can't trouble you both. I'll be okay," Jennifer replied.

"If you think you can drive, that's fine. I'll follow you until you get home to be sure everything's okay. Is that alright?" I said. Jennifer nodded, and Nana D left for her car. As I got into mine, she texted.

Nana D: *What was that all about? You're not the father, are you?*
Me: *What is wrong with you? Of course, I'm not.*

Nana D: *I'm just sayin'. I wouldn't blame you if you needed to address that side of your life.*
Me: *What side's that? Having children with a strange woman who might have killed her mother?*
Nana D: *Don't be a fool! If it's not you, then who's the father?*
Me: *I haven't a clue! I'm not even sure what this means in regards to Gwendolyn's death. Or will.*
Nana D: *By the way… are you seeing anyone? I think it's time you moved on. Emma might like a baby brother or sister one day. She'll stop asking about that puppy.*
Me: *This is none of your business. Especially right now. Go do some research for your campaign.*
Nana D: *Sometimes you can be a bad grandson. I've got a nerve to leave you outta my will now!*
Me: *Not funny! Maybe I ought to get you a glass of iced tea?*
Nana D: *Do you need another margarita lesson?*

That shut me up quickly. When I got back to the house, I spent the rest of the afternoon and early evening updating my '*Who killed Gwendolyn?*' chart. I had more questions than answers, but at least everything was written down. As I got ready to pick up Emma from gymnastics class, my phone rang. It was likely going to be the rotten cherry on the pinnacle of my bad day. "Hello, Myriam."

"Good evening, Kellan. I just received the mail for the department," she said in a perfectly normal voice. There wasn't a hint of sarcasm coming from her. Was she preparing for a sneak attack?

"Is there a reason you called to tell me this?" I asked as pleasantly as possible.

"Correct. There's a package addressed to someone who doesn't work here, but I believe you are the best person to handle it," Myriam replied. Still no rage or peculiar Shakespeare quotes.

What could she be talking about? "Okay, I'll come by to pick it up in the morning. Who's it addressed to?"

"Gwendolyn Paddington. It's also from Gwendolyn Paddington. It appears she sent herself something at Paddington's Play House," Myriam noted.

There was only one thing I thought it could be—we finally found her revised will!

Chapter 20

Another night passed with hardly any sleep since my cold had turned into something much worse. While living in LA for nearly a decade, I'd avoided every possible germ and illness there was to catch. A month back in Braxton's harsh winters, and my body was ready to abandon me. I suppose that wasn't the only reason I couldn't sleep.

Once Myriam notified me about the package Gwendolyn received at Paddington's Play House, I immediately thought about rushing off to collect it. Then I realized it was probably a violation of federal law to open someone else's mail even if the person was no longer alive. Actually, it was Myriam who brought up that last part. When I'd told her that I'd stop by to get it last night, she discreetly tried to explain why she couldn't give it to me without proper approval. When I asked whom she expected to provide said consent, I listened to a litany of possible ways to legally transfer the document. I wanted to suggest holding a séance where Eleanor could contact Gwendolyn's ghost and ask her to haunt Myriam until she caved in, but I was certain that would send my vindictive boss to Second Chance Reflections for therapy. Even I knew that wouldn't be very nice of me.

Myriam had been too busy with the *King Lear* performance to discuss next steps, but she agreed to give me the document this morning if I had approval from both Gwendolyn's attorney and her estate's executor. Finnigan and Eustacia were kind enough to send me an approval via email while I'd been sleeping. All I needed to do was show them to Myriam when I went to teach my courses at Braxton. Except I felt so awful, I moved as slow as a snail with a hangover and broken shell. But my hangover wasn't from drinking alcohol, it was from a combination of cough medicine and various over-the-counter drugs I'd bought in a mad dash raid at the Nutberry Pharmacy the day before. Not only did they run one of the funeral parlors, but the Nutberry family also kept us well-medicated in life. I was still trying to avoid one of Nana D's infamous cures. She probably wants me to drink some worm root and ground-up eucalyptus leaves. I'm only hazarding a guess as to her holistic cures as the last time I had a four-day leg cramp from running, she made me drink the most awful concoction ever. I still had freakish hallucinations and swore to myself I'd never again accept her brand of medicine.

I re-planned my lecture on the drive to campus, settling on showing a thirty-minute film and organizing the class into groups for discussions. I could walk around and comment as they were discussing it, then request a one-page paper summarizing their thoughts. It was not the way I preferred to teach, but there was little chance I could make it through the entire day when my body was in need of more sleep.

I called the sheriff to let her know about the package at Paddington's Play House. She asked me to meet her at Finnigan's office that afternoon to open it while she was present. I printed the emails—including signatures—after I finished teaching both classes and stopped in Myriam's office. "Good afternoon. How's your day going?" I said followed by a loud sneeze and several unattractive sniffles.

"Better than yours, Kellan. You look worse than usual. Out partying too much? I'd hoped you would take this job much more seriously and stay in good health. The students depend on us to educate them using our full potential," she said while opening her desk drawer. She pulled out a small package of disinfectant towelettes and began wiping her desk as though I'd sneezed on her belongings.

"I'm not in any shape to engage in our usual combat fighting. And your wife asked us to play nice," I said while handing her the printed approvals. "Signed by both Finnigan Masters, esteemed attorney for the recently deceased Gwendolyn Paddington, and Eustacia Paddington as the executor. I assume this will be sufficient for you to give me the package you received yesterday?"

"Leave them there on the desk. When I have a pair of gloves, I will sanitize them and put them in my files. *It seems there is a plague upon both your houses.*" Myriam's lips frowned as she stood and walked to the other side of her desk to read them.

Both my houses? Either she'd become more obtuse than usual or my various symptoms were playing games with my hearing. "Come again?"

"Not only are you riddled with some sort of disease you've brought on campus, you're caught up in another one at the Paddington estate with drugs and murder. I spoke with the sheriff this morning. She told me Gwendolyn didn't just die of a heart attack. There's murder most foul in the air." Myriam used a pencil to move the top copy away from the bottom print-out, so she could finish reading the approvals.

"I guess you felt the need to double-check my work. Shouldn't there be a stronger sense of trust between us?" I asked followed by another sneeze. I was certain I covered my mouth, but Myriam jumped so far away from me, I couldn't tell.

"I trust no one. Your papers appear to be in order. If you don't mind, please take your virus-ridden presence elsewhere. The package is over there," she demanded and pointed to the corner chair.

"Well, you're a haven of comfort in a sick man's time of need. A regular Mother Theresa and Florence Nightingale all wrapped up into one generous human being," I snarled before grabbing the package and leaving her office. As I turned the corner, I caught her nose wrinkle in anger and shock. There was no visible guilt or sorrow in her expression, only a satisfied repugnance I wanted to slash with a cleaver.

Although I had several administrative tasks to complete, I left knowing I couldn't focus on anything to save my life. As I drove by North Campus, Maggie texted to tell me she was looking forward to our date. My stomach sank when I realized I might not be well enough to socialize with her. I decided to first meet with Finnigan, Eustacia, and the sheriff, then go home to take a nap. If I felt as bad as I did now once I woke up, I'd re-schedule the dinner with Maggie.

As I was leaving, the DNA testing facility called me back to indicate they weren't authorized to tell me anything, but they would be in contact the following week with the person Gwendolyn had named as the individual to receive the results. They couldn't give me any additional information, which made sense given the need for privacy and security in the current day and age.

Thirty minutes later, I entered Finnigan's law offices at the base of the Wharton Mountains. He'd inherited the practice from his father who didn't want to be in the middle of all the action in downtown Braxton. He'd instead chosen a charming converted log cabin as his law offices, so they could bask in a gorgeous landscape each and every day. When we all assembled in Finnigan's conference room, I handed him the package. Finnigan explained that he would need to authenticate the document by verifying signatures and ensuring it was the exact text copy he'd sent to Gwendolyn. He reminded us that all she was supposed to do was fill in a few names next to each of the bequeathals, sign the document in a few places, and obtain signatures from two non-interested witnesses.

Eustacia stared at him hard. "Just open it, will you. We've been waiting centuries for this dang document to show up." She banged her cane on the wooden floor. As it reverberated against the walls, Finnigan tore open the package with fervor.

"I will need a copy of that," Sheriff Montague said pulling her chair closer to the table. "It may not have any bearing on the case, but I always keep my records clean and up to date." She turned to me as if I needed to be reminded of her keen attention to detail.

"Excellent point," I said followed by another sneeze.

Eustacia handed me her handkerchief when I appeared to be in need of one to stop the drip threatening to explode from my nose. "You should talk to your nana. She's always got those miracle cures. Just last week, she fixed this rash I had on my leg. I don't know where it came from, but Lord Almighty, it wouldn't go away. I kept scratching for weeks until she saw it all red and puffy like a rampant fungus. Seraphina fixed me up in less than forty-eight hours."

I choked on a small amount of bile that had propelled up my throat. "I'll do that." When Eustacia looked toward Finnigan, I rolled my eyes wincing from the exerted pressure on my face.

The sheriff stifled a laugh as she leaned over in my direction. "You really do fit right in with your nana's friends, don't ya, Little Ayrwick?"

Finnigan cleared his throat. "I'll skip the normal approach when I read a last will and testament. Shall I focus on just the particulars?" he said looking around the room. We all nodded in agreement.

"Get on with it, Masters. I could die before you spit everything out. I'm not paying you by the hour on this one," Eustacia snarled. Two more bangs of her cane on the floor.

Finnigan smiled and clapped his hands together. "Certainly. Let's see... okay, Gwendolyn Paddington split her fortune in half. Fifty percent was left to various charities and Paddington's Play House at Braxton. The remaining fifty percent of her estate was split equally among three people."

Interesting. She'd included someone new since the prior version. Eustacia coughed. "Go on."

"Millard Paddington, her brother-in-law. Timothy Paddington, her son. And Sam Taft, her grandson. She mentions leaving behind another letter that's meant to be read aloud at the final will reading. She explains why she made these decisions," Finnigan clarified. His gaze swept across the room starting with the sheriff, then me, and ending with Eustacia. "Apparently, she left it with you, Eustacia. This note says it's safely hidden in something you depend on greatly to keep you living each day."

The sheriff stood. "I think we need to read it, Ms. Paddington. That letter might let us know who would be angry enough about her decision and want to kill her. Hand it over."

Eustacia withdrew. "I don't have any letter. I'm not sure what she's talking about!"

Sheriff Montague replied, "Well, give it some thought while we read through the rest of the will. This is important."

"What do you depend on, Eustacia?" I asked while walking toward her in confusion.

"Maybe it's somewhere back at my place in Willow Trees. I'll check tonight," Eustacia noted while squinting her eyes and tapping her cane against the floor. "Confounded woman."

"Who were the witnesses?" I asked thinking that might help us move forward in the meantime.

"Brad Shope and Bertha Crawford," Finnigan replied. "The will appears to be in good condition. My legal secretary will match it word-for-word, but this is what we can use to probate the estate."

"Bertha signed it with no vested interest. She's just an employee who probably did Gwendolyn a favor that night by helping her get the new will finished. I'm more concerned about Brad being the other witness," the sheriff noted while twisting her fingers together.

I wasn't sure where the idea came from, but I suddenly thought of a way to lure the killer out of hiding. "What if we inform the whole Paddington family that the new will has been found. We tell them that Gwendolyn mailed it to herself and it's in Paddington's Play House, but we are waiting for the proper approvals to open it."

"Go ahead, I think I understand where you're going with this, Little Ayrwick." The sheriff had the early formation of a smile.

"If the killer wants to keep this new will from being found, he or she might sneak in to steal or destroy it. The murderer probably thinks it was either lost or thrown away, but if the will were to show up, the killer would need to do something to protect their interests." I felt my face flush, uncertain if it was the medication kicking in or the excitement over discovering a potential way to solve the case.

"Set a trap is what you're saying," Eustacia noted. She attempted to stand up but couldn't push the chair away from the table. "That's a smart idea. I can get the family together tomorrow to tell them we are reading the will. Then we can tell them about the new one!"

Finnigan rose to help Eustacia. "I'll play along if the sheriff thinks this will potentially help."

Sheriff Montague consented. "It's a strong possibility. Let me think through how I want to handle it. But go ahead, let's schedule it for ten o'clock tomorrow morning at the Paddington estate."

After we agreed on the basics, everyone left Finnigan's office. The sheriff pulled me aside in the parking lot. "I discussed everything with the Paddington accountants. It seems Ophelia was responsible for those unexplained withdrawals from Gwendolyn's accounts. She had access for years but had never used it until recently. I'm assuming Gwendolyn never realized her daughter was able to withdraw money when Charles died last year. Ophelia might be the person we're after."

"She's been cagey about the entire situation throughout the last week. Now that her husband is back and he's head of the company, it looks like everything's coming together for her," I remarked. "If she was removed as a beneficiary with the new will, killing her mother before the new will turned up is definitely the opportunity and motive we need. Maybe we'll catch her tomorrow."

The sheriff was surprised at how quickly I had thought of the idea to bait the killer. "This approach is the best chance we have to getting close to solving the case. We don't have a weapon to trace nor any alibis to confirm or deny. This kind of murder is always difficult to pin down."

"I'm glad I thought of it. We might solve the investigation together," I noted with a smile despite a desperate need to crash in my bed for a few hours. I decided to push my luck. "You're welcome, *April*." Sheriff Montague nodded at me as she got on her motorcycle and left the law office parking lot.

On the drive home, I called my parents to thank them for bringing Emma to Philadelphia. Emma had convinced them to take her to the zoo for the afternoon, and since her school was closed for a teacher conference that day, my parents offered to watch her. I pulled into the driveway at the Royal Chic-Shack dragging myself upstairs to take a nap. When I got to the top landing, my bedroom door was open and a light shined through the crack. I knew I'd left the door closed and no one else was home.

I turned the corner while calling out, "Hellooo..." In retrospect, knowing the Castigliano family had sent a goon to scare me in the Pick-Me-Up Diner's parking lot earlier that week, I shouldn't have walked in the room without worrying. Maybe it was the medication I had taken or the illness zapping any remaining common sense I had left. When the door swung fully open, I saw someone sitting on the edge of my bed. She looked back at me with a devious yet comforting grin and said, "Surprise."

"What are you doing here? Someone could've caught you!" I stood almost paralyzed.

"Your parents are gone for the day. I knew I could hide out here until you got home," Francesca said walking over to hug me.

"But how did you know? When did you get here?" I said feeling lightheaded.

"My mother bugged the house the last time she was here. She's been listening to all your conversations to see if you'd said anything about me being alive. I overheard you and her talking the other day, and I caught a flight out here the next morning." Francesca explained that she'd stayed at a hotel the previous day waiting for the right moment to reveal herself. I was glad to see her, and we needed to talk despite me not feeling well enough to focus. "But don't worry, I disconnected the listening devices in your room when I got here."

My body started to weaken. Just as I realized I'd never eaten breakfast or lunch, and that I'd probably overdosed on too much medicine trying to knock the original cold-turned-whatever-virus out of my system, I fell to the floor. The last thing I remember before passing out was Francesca leaning over me saying, "It's okay… you get some sleep. Let your wife take care of you."

* * *

As I rolled over onto my back, a stream of light hit my face. I was in my bedroom, but I had no idea what day or time it was. I felt around the night table for my glasses, then stared at a clock that read seven thirty. Something didn't feel right. I lifted the covers and felt a sudden chill. When I looked down, I had nothing on but a pair of boxer briefs. I didn't remember getting undressed. Then I realized if it was seven thirty in March, the sun had already set. Why was light coming through the window? I sat up in the bed and wrapped myself in an extra blanket lying nearby. That's when I remembered Francesca was in my bedroom. I was about to jump from the bed when the door creaked open.

"Good morning, sunshine. How are you feeling?" Francesca asked with a huge grin. "I'm so glad you slept through the night. I was worried when I took your temperature and you had a high fever." She set a breakfast tray on the desk across from my bed and brought me a cup of coffee.

"What happened? How did you... where's Emma?" I said. Then I remembered my parents had taken her to the zoo in Philadelphia and were staying overnight. But I also remembered I was supposed to meet Maggie for dinner. If it was morning, I'd missed the whole evening.

"Calm down. Don't get yourself even sicker. You were in bad shape last night and passed out. I had to drag you into the bed and get you comfortable," Francesca said while sitting on the edge of the mattress and feeling my forehead. "No more fever."

I pulled the covers away and verified I really did have underwear on. "Did you take off my clothes, too?"

"You're acting like this is unusual. I am your wife, right?" Francesca patted my lap and kissed my cheek. "You're looking pretty amazing, hon. I missed snuggling up with you at night."

"Did we... do anything..." I asked urging my brain to recall what'd happened the previous night. "Where did you sleep?" I wasn't sure that it mattered since she was my wife.

"You were way too sick to do anything like that, Kellan. I got you all tucked in by late afternoon. You've been asleep for almost sixteen hours. Not that I didn't want to, of course, but I prefer you to be awake enough to remember our first time together again," she cooed. "I slept next to you for most of the night to be sure you were okay."

"Where's my phone?" I asked hesitantly and feeling a weird grogginess in my head. When Francesca handed it to me, I unlocked the security code and checked what I'd missed. I had over twenty missed calls and multiple voicemails from the sheriff, Nana D, Eleanor, Maggie, and my mother.

"Your phone kept ringing, so I turned it off while you slept. I tried to access it, but you must be using a different code now. I couldn't unlock the infernal device," Francesca noted. She grabbed a slice of toast from the tray and handed it to me. "Eat something, hon. You need your strength."

I suddenly felt a pit in my stomach growing so large I couldn't even swallow a bite of toast. "Does anyone know you're here?"

Francesca explained her mother was horrified and incensed that she'd run off, but Cecilia ultimately backed down as long as Francesca would return that evening. "I called Eleanor, too. I let her know you were with me and not feeling well. I asked her to let Nana D know were fine. Your grandmother kept calling before I turned the phone off. I didn't want her to worry."

"Thanks," I mumbled while scrolling through all my text messages. I could respond to everything later except for the sheriff and Maggie. But I couldn't call Maggie with Francesca in the room. "Could you get me some ice water? I need something cold for my throat."

Once Francesca left, I dialed Maggie's number to apologize to her. She didn't pick up. Her voicemail and text message didn't sound like she was angry I'd bailed on our dinner, but I wasn't certain. I left her a voicemail apologizing for not calling. I told her I'd been so sick, I intended to wake up to call her but slept through the night. I'd fix it the next time I talked to her. Then I rang the sheriff.

"Where have you been? We need to discuss the plan for the meeting with the Paddington family? I thought I could trust you based on our last conversation," she yelled through the phone.

"I'm so sorry. I will be there soon. I'll explain everything later. Is it still ten o'clock? I'll arrive a little beforehand to talk with you." I managed to squeak out a quick apology before sneezing again.

"Fine. But you've taken quite a step down in my eyes, Little Ayrwick. I'll be watching the security camera at the Paddington estate to get a reading on everyone's facial expressions and comments," Sheriff Montague growled. She was beyond angry with me.

When I hung up, Francesca ambled into the room and handed me a glass of water and more medicine. "Take these. It's the same pills you took last night. The directions said every eight hours, but you missed a dose while you were sleeping. I didn't want to wake you."

For a moment, I debated whether to swallow them. Someone had been messing with Gwendolyn's medication, and it killed her. Francesca surely wouldn't do that to me, but I wasn't feeling like myself given everything that had happened in the last day. "Thanks. I need to be somewhere important in two hours, but we should chat."

"That's why I'm here, Kellan. Let's talk." Francesca climbed into the bed and snuggled against my chest. "It's like before the accident. We're wrapped up in each other's arms discussing our future."

I swallowed the pills with a big gulp of water, told myself I'd thoroughly considered all my options, and prepared to have a very difficult conversation with my wife.

Chapter 21

"You know how much I love you, right? It absolutely breaks my heart to think about where we ended up after everything we've been through together," I said to Francesca as we held hands sitting on my bed. I was slightly more certain of my decision than I had been the prior day. Despite how well she took care of me, and the moments of happiness I felt being so close with her, Francesca's re-appearance in my bedroom helped confirm the correct next steps.

"We're soulmates, Kellan. From that first day we met at the pier in Santa Monica, I knew you were the one. I can't wait to bring Emma back home, so I can see her all the time." Francesca kissed my cheek and squeezed my hand.

"I've thought about us a lot lately. Ever since I found out you were alive, I dreamt about cooking Sunday morning breakfasts together, teaching Emma how to read with you, and walking on the beach holding hands as we look for buried treasure." And it was the truth. For a little while, I was caught up in all the amazing things we could do as a family once Emma was a little older and we were back in Los Angeles. Then I realized how scared and nervous I was with Francesca in my parents' house.

"Let's go home today. My flight leaves in a few hours. I'll go ahead now, and you can meet me there with Emma later. I'm sure there will be two seats available for you both," Francesca said looking as beautiful as always. The hope and desire in her face was as contagious as it had ever been.

I changed positions on the bed, so I could look directly at my wife. "But I've also felt scared and angry the last couple of weeks. Maybe even angrier than I was the first year after I thought you had died. When I wanted to kill that drunk driver and had almost no will left to live without you. The only thing that kept me focused was knowing I had to protect our baby girl. Emma needed me no matter what I was feeling." I found my strength and prepared to tell Francesca what I'd decided.

Every nerve in my body was on high alert. What if someone walked in on us? Could the Vargas family suspect something was going on if Emma and I returned? Were we being watched already? I couldn't live like that. As awful as it sounded and felt, letting my daughter think her mother was dead, even if the smallest chance existed to try to make this bizarre situation work, was the best solution. How could anyone be expected to know the right answer?

"I know it hurt you, but I'll make it up to you. We'll figure it out as long as you're back in LA. I promise this won't be forever," Francesca said with tears rolling down her cheeks. When she reached forward to hug me, I felt a few begin to drop from my broken eyes as well.

"I'm so sorry," I whispered in her ear. "But I can't do it. I'm not going to move back to LA and take any risks with Emma's future. I know it means you won't get a chance to see her, but that's my final decision. I'm so sorry, Francesca."

At first, she was quiet. I could feel her body tense up then quiver as if she'd been going through shock. I mumbled more words to try to explain how I felt, probably still trying to convince myself that I knew what I was doing. Francesca eventually reached the point of anger and lashed out at me.

"You can't, I won't let you. She's my daughter!" Francesca screamed pushing me away from her. We continued to search for a solution but one didn't exist. At least none that would work for the both of us. For a few seconds, Nana D's advice remained steady in my head. '*If you love something, let it go. If it's meant to be yours, it will come back to you.*' I didn't dare say those words to Francesca because I didn't know in this situation who was truly letting whom go.

When my phone rang and Francesca saw it was my mother, she went to grab it thinking it was Emma calling from Philadelphia to say good morning. She was about to hit the accept button, then stared back at me. "You have to answer it."

"I'll put it on speakerphone, so you can hear her voice, too." Francesca and I sat together listening to our daughter excitedly tell us about her trip with her grandparents. When we hung up, I grabbed Francesca's hand. "Maybe one day things will change. And we'll figure out a way for you to see her. I'll come back on trips to LA and stay with your family, so you know what's going on with Emma."

"It won't be enough," Francesca cried. "I want my life back. I deserve it. You deserve it." Her warm, quivering lips kissed me with years of longing reminding me why I'd fallen in love with her. As she rushed from the room and down the stairs, I felt each of her steps bouncing in my chest breaking my heart into tiny little pieces. I had caused this pain by deciding not to put our family back together. I'd have to live with the consequences of lying to our daughter. If we ever found a way for Francesca to come back to life again, would Emma forgive me for what I'd done? I could hardly forgive myself.

* * *

An hour later after a long cry and an even longer shower, I made it to the Paddington estate with a cloudy head. Although I should've stayed in bed, I'd grown accustomed to putting myself in uncomfortable situations and needed to draw out Gwendolyn's killer. In a weird and cathartic way, the potential to close the door on Gwendolyn's pain might alleviate my own.

Eustacia and I chatted with the sheriff on the drive over to establish protocol for the family meeting. April and I would be listening in from a nearby electrical closet. At first, I was not pleased about being locked together in a small space with the sheriff for an hour. Then I learned that an electrical closet in the Paddington estate was larger than my entire bedroom at the Royal Chic-Shack. April and I would have the comforts of plush recliners, sound-proof padding, so no one could hear us talking, and a large video screen to monitor the Paddington family's every move and word.

Twenty minutes later, Bertha snuck us through a servant's entrance and led us to the electrical closet. When she closed the door, April turned to me and said, "Certainly not my idea of a fun way to spend a Saturday morning. Just keep quiet and do your part when the time comes. Don't veer from our script. I'm still not sure I can trust you after your disappearance last night."

My energy was so non-existent, I didn't even try to continue the repartee I'd come to enjoy the last few weeks. "Okay, I'll be ready. You don't have to worry. I'm truly sorry."

"Wait, who are you?" April replied with a confused glance. "Did Martians kidnap the real Kellan Ayrwick and replace him with the automaton I'm stuck in here with?" For added emphasis, April walked across the room toward me like a robot swinging her arms in exaggerated slow motion up and down.

"I knew you could be witty and sarcastic, but I never expected regular, old-fashioned jokes," I said trying to rouse a tease out of myself. I wasn't ready to laugh. "Sorry. It's been a rough morning."

"Well, I much prefer the old Kellan, even if he's a pain in my tuchus. The kind where it's so aggravating, I feel it radiating in every single limb to the point I want to throttle you with my bare hands. But of course, as the sheriff of this fine county, I would never do such a thing." She tilted her head and smiled at me.

I felt myself emit a tiny giggle. Was she trying to make me laugh as a way to help me feel better? "I didn't realize you were Jewish. Or did you borrow one of their words to make an eloquent point?"

"Born and bred. My mother would tan my hide if she knew I was working today. It's the sabbath, you know."

"I assume criminals don't stop doing bad things because it's a Saturday, huh?"

"They're worse on weekends. If I got paid for the number of times I took a call between Friday evening and Sunday morning, I'd be a rich lady," April replied with a smirk. "Hopefully whatever's got you down will dissipate soon enough. We've got a murder to solve today. And as much as I like to berate you, I don't like seeing this side of you, Little Ayrwick. It's like kicking a puppy. And if I ever saw someone do that, I'm take 'em down with old Betsy here," she said tapping the gun in her hip holster.

April raised the volume on the television monitor and indicated Eustacia was starting to talk to her family. We both took seats in the recliners and watched them carefully. I had my cell phone in my hand ready to call at the appropriate time.

Eustacia sat at the head of the table looking calm and collected. Millard, who had no idea that we were hiding nearby or that this was part of a set-up, sat to her right pruning a small plant on his lap. He either had little interest in the will or was trying to distract himself. With each clip, there was a delicate touch and clear sense of dedication to his craft.

Further down that side of the table were Jennifer and Sam engaged in a quiet conversation. I couldn't hear their words, but based on Jennifer's caress of her belly, I assumed she'd told her nephew about the pregnancy. When Sam smiled, her eyes opened wide and she whispered '*shh*' to keep him from saying anything. It seemed she didn't want to make it a major announcement at the family meeting.

"What's going on over there?" demanded an irritated Ophelia. From past experience, she never let anyone keep her from knowing what was going on, nor did she like when her children had gotten too close to other people. She sat across the table from Jennifer to the left of her husband, Richard.

It was the first time I'd seen him other than the brief moment at the funeral parlor when I was focused on other things. He scrolled through something on his cell phone looking up every ten seconds to see what was going on around him. He neither smiled nor frowned. He looked more disconnected and bored, if anything.

"That Taft fellow is certainly interesting, don't ya think?" April said as Eustacia asked everyone to settle down. "I've been doing some research on him. He makes frequent trips out to Los Angeles in support of the family business. Have you ever met him?"

I shook my head. "No. Contrary to popular belief, us Braxtonites don't all know each other!" I managed a smile, so she knew I was starting to feel a little better.

"Yeah, well, I never trust those west coasters… a little too… well, let's just say it's different than a place like Wharton County where we're rooted in old-fashioned values and beliefs," she said.

"Like murderers?" I knew April hadn't meant it as a dig about LA, so I let it go. She was just used to our comfortable mid-west surroundings. "Never been there, I take it?"

"Nope. But I might have to head out there soon enough. I stumbled upon a connection between Paddington Enterprises and an import/export business out in California called Castigliano International. Ever heard of it?" April casually shared while changing the position of the recliner, so she could relax.

I refused to look at her. Was she trying to hint about my connection to them? Did she know about Francesca turning up? "I've heard of it. How does it connect to the Paddingtons?" I asked feeling my heart begin to race.

"I'm not sure. I received an anonymous tip last week about a business transaction between the two companies from a year ago while Timothy was in charge. The informant apparently thought there was something illegal going on and wanted me to investigate it."

We both stopped talking as Eustacia addressed the family. April's message had unnerved me. What did my in-laws have to do with Paddington Enterprises? If it'd happened a year ago, that's roughly when Charles died and Timothy was about to be removed from the company by the Board of Directors.

Lilly was the first to speak after Eustacia told everyone they were there to discuss Gwendolyn's will. She sat next to her sister, Dana, on the other side of their father, Richard. "What's this all about, Aunt Eustacia? I don't understand why you called us last-minute and demanded we show up today. This better not be a waste of my time."

Ophelia leaned over Richard to pat her daughter's arm. "Let's wait to see what she wants, hon."

Dana asked, "And where's Uncle Timothy? How come he gets to avoid this meeting?" I thought it was a good question despite the arrogance oozing from the girl.

"Your grandmother died, young lady. The least you can do is keep your mouth quiet while we discuss her final words before she got called back to Heaven. Honestly, Ophelia... your daughters are both as spoiled as you were as a child. My parents are rolling over in the graves at what you've let them become." Eustacia banged her cane on the floor and shouted again, "Enough! I don't want to hear from any of you until I've shared some important news."

Eustacia informed everyone that a second, newer will had been located. As she told them about Gwendolyn's last-minute changes the day before she died, April and I searched everyone's faces and mannerisms to see if we could learn anything they might be trying to hide.

Ophelia reached for Richard's hand and leaned forward with a semi-shocked expression on her face. He gently pulled her back and patted her wrist. It might have been a normal reaction to learning unexpected news. Millard's ears perked up, and he stopped pruning the leaves on the plant. He opened his mouth to speak but then thought better of it. Jennifer looked disinterested. Sam, Dana, and Lilly all sat back in their chairs with alarmed expressions.

"Unfortunately, there will be a delay in getting to read the new will," Finnigan added. He was sitting opposite Eustacia at the other end of the table with his back to the camera. "Gwendolyn mailed the will to someone else, but I assure you it is valid. I reviewed it with her the day before she died. She wanted to make one final change that night, which she did. I asked her to drop it off the next day, but she was worried about being able to meet me on Sunday since she was attending the opening of *King Lear* that afternoon. Instead, she mailed it to a friend for safekeeping. I'm not exactly sure why she didn't mail it to me, but we'll need to get the final version from him." It was a long-shot explanation, but we had to try it.

"That's outrageous," Lilly stood and yelled. "Why would she do such a stupid thing?"

Richard reached for his daughter's hand. "Your grandmother was a bit of an eccentric. Let the lawyer talk, so we can find out what happens next."

"Eccentric? She was a certified nutcase. You should've had her committed years ago," Dana added while crossing her arms and huffing as she slid down the chair into a sulk.

"Don't say such repulsive things, Dana" Ophelia chastised. "No one in this family belongs in a psychiatric ward!"

It was my queue to call. Eustacia placed the office phone on speaker, so everyone could hear. "Hello, is that you, Kellan?"

"Yes, I'm here. Is this still the right time?" I replied.

Eustacia confirmed and explained to everyone that the package was locked in Paddington's Play House office but had been addressed to me. Jennifer laughed when she heard the news, then turned to Sam to shrug her shoulders. Richard and Ophelia whispered something I couldn't hear.

"I received the package last night when I stopped at Paddington's Play House. When I realized it was Gwendolyn's will, I called Finnigan to let him know what I'd found. Unfortunately, I left it locked in the office and had to head out of town for today. I'll be back tomorrow and can drop it off with him."

Finnigan added, "Correct. I will validate the will and we can re-convene again on Monday to go through it once I've had a chance to understand the final updates Gwendolyn made."

"Can't Kellan tell us what it says? That makes more sense," Sam added. He sounded genuine, but I hadn't been able to get a solid read on him since we'd met the previous week. "It's already hard enough thinking about Grandmother being gone, but to delay this any further seems a little excessive."

"I agree. I don't understand what he has to do with our family anyway. I'm the one in the theater. Why couldn't Grandmother make me the representative. Why's Kellan in our business so much these days? Is he trying to steal the family money?" Dana growled.

"Exactly! This is ridiculous. Do something, Daddy," Lilly exclaimed. "I'm done here. I don't want to hear anything else until the situation is under control. Mom's the oldest, she should be in charge."

Millard rushed over to stop Lilly from leaving. "Listen, young lady. I've been through this many times before. I know how hard it is, but your behavior is inappropriate. I suggest you sit down and wait until we have further instructions." He turned to Finnigan and said, "Can't someone else get the document right now, so we can close this out today? It seems urgent."

"Unfortunately, that won't work. Gwendolyn's will was enclosed in another envelope specifically addressed to Finnigan Masters. I didn't open that one," I said looking back at the sheriff and nodding. "I asked Finnigan the same question, but since the initial envelope was addressed to me, I need to hand it off to Gwendolyn's attorney or executor, so there isn't any question about the authenticity of the will or that anything was altered since my receipt. I will be back tomorrow to hand deliver it to Finnigan."

I hung up the phone after listening to everyone disagree and express their frustrations. They were all planning to attend the *King Lear* performance that afternoon since they'd never gotten to see it in its entirety the first time when Gwendolyn died during the second half. The sheriff remained behind to finish listening to the conversation, and I rushed off to Paddington's Play House. I was meeting Officer Flatman to hide out in the office in case anyone tried to break in to steal the will.

On the drive, I called Nana D to let her know what had happened. "I'm proud of you, brilliant one. You put yourself in the middle of this debacle and found a way to trap the killer," Nana D said.

"Let's hope. I couldn't get a feel from the room. Everyone was upset, but it could've been that we wasted their time or they didn't care about the money," I replied pulling into the parking lot.

"What about Brad Shope? Have you talked to him yet?"

"I'm going to call him after I hang up with you and ask him to meet me at the theater. He doesn't know anything about the will, but if Brad's working with someone in the family, he or she probably notified him already." If Brad was conspiring with someone, he might be concerned that I wasn't out of town, but I'd find a way to dance around that issue if he brought it up. It would tell me someone went running to him as soon as the meeting had finished.

"Do you think Brad will try to steal the will or ask questions about it while he's with you at Paddington's Play House?" Nana D asked.

"The sheriff couldn't come up with a way to tip off Brad about the new will, so she told me to invite him over afterward. It covers all our bases, but it might not amount to much in the end."

Nana D repeatedly made an excited noise. "I almost forgot to tell you. I talked to Sam. He's definitely hiding someone. He had a date and couldn't chat, but he wanted to talk about something. He said his grandmother told him to trust me if he ever needed help."

"I wonder what that's about. Do you think he accidentally did something to Gwendolyn and might confess to you?" I asked not wanting to believe he had crossed such a horrific line.

"I don't think so, but he had something important he wanted to share. Let's see what happens as a result of this trap you've set. Besides, if you don't solve it today, we'll come up with another plan. I'm starting to like solving crimes with you, Kellan," Nana D teased.

"It is exciting, huh? Although, the sheriff seems to know something she's not telling me. I have a feeling she already knows the killer's identity. She mentioned something about the Paddington family doing business with the Castigliano family." I still couldn't figure out the connection, but I knew it was important. Part of me wanted to call my in-laws, but I worried it could cause a bigger issue. I also assumed Francesca had already told them I wouldn't be returning to LA. Incurring their wrath was not something I looked forward to.

"It's a good thing you decided to move back to Braxton. It's a better thing you're getting away from those people. I never cared for them much. They'll bring you down, and no one hurts my grandson except me!" Nana D laughed once she finished speaking. I desperately wanted to tell her about Francesca being alive. She would tell me I did the right thing by staying in Braxton.

"I gotta go, Nana D. The sheriff is calling," I said before hanging up to accept April's call. "Everything okay?"

The sheriff said, "Yep. You did well. Richard and Ophelia left together. Sam's outside talking to Eustacia. Jennifer and Millard went to that room with the flowers. I saw them as I sneaked outside."

"You mean the Great Hall. What about Lilly and Dana? Did you hear their nasty remarks?" I said.

"I've got a name for people like them," April taunted. "But as a lady, I refuse to say any more."

I kept my mouth shut. It wasn't that I didn't think April was a lady. I was still having a hard time figuring out that fine line between annoying her and staying on her good side. "I'll let you know what happens at the theater, April. I'm looking forward to my time with Officer Flatman."

Chapter 22

When I entered the lobby of Paddington's Play House, I saw Arthur walking into the Box Office. I checked my watch and confirmed it was almost time for the theater to open for ticket sales. There was only a matinee performance today since they were still in pre-show for another two days. "Wait up, Arthur. I'll follow you inside," I yelled jogging toward the door.

"Kellan, what are you doing here? I sent you a bunch of tickets for opening night next Monday." Arthur held the door as I approached. He wore a dark suit and tie highlighting Braxton's colors, burgundy and blue. There was a relaxed sense about him now that I'd convinced Myriam to let him keep his job at least through the end of this show. Based on how the whole run turned out, we could extend an offer for him to manage the next production or let him leave on a high note. Unless he turned out to be the killer which was still a minor concern floating around the cobwebs inside my head.

"I'll be there, thank you very much. I'm bringing Emma, my parents, and my sister with me. They're all looking forward to it, but that's not why I'm here today." I was curious about his indiscretion in one of the dressing rooms and how it fit into the entire overall puzzle. I closed the door behind me noticing it no longer got stuck. "I guess they fixed that door?"

Arthur nodded while he flipped on the lights in the Box Office. "Earlier this week. Remember the electrician that helped your sister out? Same crew, they're jack-of-all-trades."

We chatted about the performance before I realized I needed to contact Brad. "I'm gonna hang around in the Paddington office while the show is on stage. Just wanted to verify you didn't mind," I said searching his expression for any concerns.

"You've got carte blanche. My mother told me you spoke with Myriam to save my job. I still can't believe how vindictive that woman can be. Thank you." He looked calm and grateful, no trace of fear about me being in the office. It didn't appear as if he knew about the will. I had the package with me now but had to slip inside soon. I wasn't sure how quickly someone might dash over here from the Paddington estate. "It's unlocked. I was in there to drop off some mail. I need to go back and lock up, but I wanted to grab a few ads I'd left in here first. Maybe you can take them with you?"

"Sure," I said taking the envelope. "Can you tell me what Myriam was so angry about?"

"Umm, well... I had brought a friend with me that afternoon to the theater... and we ducked into a space I thought was private, but... well, Myriam overheard us sorta... well... you get the picture," Arthur said as his face reddened. "It was unplanned. Myriam made a huge deal out of it and the next thing I know... she's blasting me with some silly quote from *A Midsummer Night's Dream*. That woman is so thickheaded, she's worse than dealing with the DMV!"

"You gotta be more careful with Dana," I said despite knowing Myriam thought it was someone else. I needed to see if he'd tell me his partner's name. I was certain it had to be Sam.

"Dana? No, I told you last time. I'm staying clear of that tart. She's straight up crazy! I'm more interested in a quieter, calmer... well, never mind. The point is, I owned up to my mistake, and I won't do it again," Arthur explained before telling me he needed to verify there was enough cash in the Box Office windows for the ticket sellers.

I followed him out and walked down the hall toward the Paddington Office. Along the way, I called Brad who said he would drop by shortly to talk with me. He didn't seem to know I was supposed to be out of town. I also ordered a pizza since I hadn't eaten lunch. I verified the will was in my briefcase, tossed the strap over my shoulder, and walked into the far corner. When I approached the office, I saw Officer Flatman and waved in his direction. I was going to call out to him, but my phone rang. It was Maggie, and I couldn't let it go to voicemail. I had a massive apology to convey.

I picked up the phone and said, "You have absolutely every reason to be angry with me, but I truly have a valid excuse." I felt my forehead to verify the fever was still gone. My head was loopy from the medicine, and my eyes were sore from crying over Francesca, but my health was improving. I explained what'd happened with the medicine causing me to crash.

"I understand. You're worrying too much, Kellan." Her voice was gentle and caring, but I knew Maggie well enough to guess she'd been disappointed by my no-show. "Connor filled in. I figured there was no reason to waste the table, so he popped over. I've thought about us a lot this morning."

I felt a twinge of jealousy when she indicated Connor had taken my place. I wanted to tell her the truth, but I also knew I'd had an exhausting and emotional day already and needed to be careful in what I shared. "Me, too. I was excited to have some time alone with you. I've only been back a few weeks, but it feels like we hardly had a chance to connect."

"I feel the same way. I realized this morning that we've tried to have dinner several times, yet something always gets in the way. Maybe it's Eleanor rubbing off on me, but could the universe be trying to tell us something?" Maggie laughed at the end just enough to reveal her discomfort. I could picture her playing with her earlobes, guessing how nervous the conversation made her.

My heart was feeling stabs of pain as she spoke and I prepared my response. I knew what I had to do. "I'm inclined to agree. You're still figuring out how you feel about Connor. You only just moved back to Braxton, too."

"Same for you. And Francesca's death is much fresher than my husband's death. I know what you're going through. Reaching out in the middle of the night just to feel if the other side of the bed is warm. Buying things she used to love, then not having the strength to return them. It gets easier, Kellan." Maggie always put other people first. She was trying to comfort me despite the fact that I'd been the one to cancel on her.

"You're an amazing woman. I've loved you for so long, but maybe we're both not ready to jump into anything," I said burying my face into my free hand hoping it could stop the inevitable.

"And you're a terrific guy. You need time to figure out how to raise your daughter in a new town. Even though you've been back a few times, Braxton's different than it was a decade ago." Maggie sniffled through the phone. I imagined her dabbing her cheeks with a tissue but smiling as though we were right next to each other.

She was right. I was still married in the eyes of the church and in my heart. The law might think Francesca was dead and allow me to move on, but it was only a fantasy or a façade the Castiglianos had created for the world to believe. "Let's agree to focus on rebuilding our friendship, Maggie. And maybe in a few months or a year, we'll be ready to talk about something else."

"I think that's perfect, Kellan." As she hung up, I reminded myself of Nana D's advice about things coming back once they'd been set free. I still wasn't certain whether it applied to Francesca or Maggie. I also had little time to indulge myself in anymore grief or loss in my personal life.

Officer Flatman arrived with the pizza. "I believe you ordered this? The guy said it was paid for, but I gave him a couple bucks tip."

"We needed something to eat. We could have a long afternoon ahead of us," I replied. He declined reimbursement for tipping the delivery guy. We walked to the Paddington office and scarfed down a few slices. While we ate, we talked about the case.

"Sheriff Montague met with the Paddington accountants again. That's where she learned the details about the transactions with the Castigliano family. Someone at Paddington Enterprises was using their services to import goods into the country. She's trying to find out exactly who was involved and what exactly it was," he explained. "Apparently, it has something to do with hiding drugs."

I was about to respond when Brad's number appeared on my cell phone. I picked up, and he told me he was in the main lobby. Officer Flatman shut off the lights and hid in the closet in the corner of the room. I placed the will on the desk, then went to find Brad.

As I led him back to the room, I said, "I appreciate you coming by. I had a few things to discuss with you, but I needed to stick around the theater this afternoon as the family's representative while the show is in production."

"I understand, and it's kinda funny. Something came up that I should talk to you about, too," Brad replied as we entered the Paddington office. I saw him look at the desk and assumed he'd noticed the will.

"Listen, I need to get rid of this pizza box and bring something to the Box Office," I said to Brad as I walked back toward the hall. "Can you hang around for a few minutes? I'll be right back." Officer Flatman watched through a small crack in the closet door. If Brad tried to leave with it, he'd stop him.

I left and tossed the pizza box in the garbage. I wandered the main reception area watching a few guests head into the theatre as the show started. After five minutes passed, I walked back to the Paddington Office. "Sorry about that. All clear, we've got some time to talk alone." The will hadn't been moved. He'd either looked through it and put it back in the same place I'd left it, or he hadn't even bothered to touch it.

"No sweat. So, you first?" Brad said.

"Sure, I wanted to ask you a couple of things. I'm not gonna beat around the bush, so pardon if I'm being a bit blunt," I explained hoping to catch a reaction from him.

"That's the best way to be. My mother taught me never to keep secrets nor to waste people's time. Money was precious to her, she worked hard to support me and had little freedoms." Brad leaned against the desk with his hands buried in his pockets.

"Great. So... first, it's come to my attention that you were the second witness when Gwendolyn changed her will the day before she died. I'm not sure why you didn't share that piece of information with me at any point."

"Oh, well, I—" Brad began but I held my hand up.

"Let me talk first, then you'll have a chance, Brad," I said. When he nodded, I continued. "Then, I learned you do not have your official nursing license or certification. You were denied after something happened at a previous hospital or nursing home with a mix-up on several patients' medications. Ironic given that's exactly what led to Gwendolyn's death." I watched him carefully, but he only opened his mouth to interrupt again.

"That's not how it happened. If you'd let me—"

"Please let me finish, this will be a lot easier," I said knowing I came across like a tyrant. Desperate times called for desperate measures. "I'm also aware that your mother, Hannah Shope, used to work at the Paddington mansion twenty-five years ago. In fact, she probably conceived you while she was employed there as a maid. It seems Gwendolyn had run a DNA test to determine if you are related to her family."

Brad turned white, but he didn't speak. He tapped his foot and swallowed with heavy force.

"When I add all these things together, you must realize, it makes you look guilty of something. Whether it's murder or conspiracy to commit murder with someone else, I don't know. But I don't get that vibe from you. You're hiding something, that's for sure." I stepped toward him to grab the will in case he tried to do anything hasty. "Before I update the sheriff with all this news, is there anything you want to share with me?"

Brad nodded, then pulled his hand out of his pocket. He unfolded a piece of paper and handed it to me. "That's the DNA test. Gwendolyn helped me find someone to conduct it. If you'll give me a minute, I'll tell you everything I know. But right up front, I assure you, I had nothing to do with her death. There was no reason for me to hurt the woman."

I looked at the DNA results but couldn't understand any of the medical jargon. I didn't know which sample belonged to which person. "Okay, go ahead." I knew Officer Flatman was listening to the whole conversation, so I didn't worry about missing anything important related to the murder. I wanted to figure out how Brad fit into the Paddington family.

"I previously worked for someone who kept pressuring me to go on a date with her. After I said no and threatened to report her to the hospital and the medical board, she finally backed away. I was weeks away from obtaining my nursing degree when one of my patients got sick. A few days later, another patient passed away. Something didn't feel right, but I didn't want to jeopardize my chances of finally reaching my dreams to become a nurse. I knew the woman wanted to get revenge against me, but I couldn't prove anything. She essentially caused my license to be detained." Brad shook his head with contempt and frustration. He shared that the other girl had been the one playing games not him.

"That's awful you were taken advantage of like that, I'm sorry. How did you end up in Braxton?" I said.

"When my mom was near the end, she talked a lot about growing up in Braxton. With no job or family left, I moved here and got a new job as a nurse. I just need to get my formal certification."

"Okay, but that doesn't explain how you met Gwendolyn," I said.

"I'd been working at the rehabilitation facility where she was recuperating. I didn't work in her wing, but she was friendly with one of my patients. I'd told my patient that my mom had worked at the Paddington household years ago. Next thing I know, Gwendolyn called and asked if I would be interested in becoming her private nurse. My former patient had told the story to Gwendolyn. I was upset at first, but it turned out to be a big help."

If Gwendolyn had been aware of the baby, she might have realized Brad could be related to her. That's probably why she hired him, so she had access to get a sample of his DNA and find out more for herself. "Did you tell Gwendolyn about your mother?"

"I didn't have to. A few weeks after I began working for her, she brought it up. I wasn't interested in finding out whom my father was, but she kept pressuring me. She told me that a mistake had been made years ago, and if my father was whom she thought he was, I would want to know him." Brad looked deeply upset. His face began to shrink and wrinkle as though he had little control over his feelings in that moment.

"Did she take this DNA test with your consent? Or behind your back?" I asked.

"I eventually agreed to. I was never interested in the money, just knowing more about my father and his family. Gwendolyn and I became friends the last few weeks. She didn't need a nurse anymore. Just someone to talk to. Someone to keep her from being lonely and bored in the house. You've seen how awful that family is."

By the way he said *that family*, I began to believe he wasn't one of them. "I've seen them behave like animals. What do these results prove?"

"I'm not a Paddington. She thought Millard was my father, but he can't be. I don't share any DNA with Millard or Ophelia. Gwendolyn wasn't a Paddington by blood, so they couldn't try to match hers."

I was shocked at the response. He didn't appear to be lying. "Did she figure out whom your father is?"

Brad shook his head. "If she did, Gwendolyn didn't tell me. We got the results from that first DNA test the day before she died. She told me she had ordered a second one based on a hunch, but then she died the next day."

"How did you come to be the witness to sign her new will?"

"After she got home from your grandmother's house, she called Bertha and me into her room and asked us to sign the will. She filled in the new names, but I didn't see whom she left the money to. And then I left."

"So, you have no idea whom your father is?" If it wasn't a Paddington, who else had been in the house that might have been Hannah's lover twenty-five years ago?

"Nope. For a while, I tried to get to know everyone in the family. I hoped maybe I would be related to them, not because I liked them but because I have no other family. Ever since my mother died, I've been on my own. My mother had no siblings, and her parents passed away before I was born."

Brad had no reason to kill Gwendolyn. "Thanks for sharing the DNA results with me. Is that what you meant when you said you had something to talk to me about?"

"Yes, I've been keeping it a secret from everyone because I didn't want the family to think I was trying to insert myself once Gwendolyn had passed away. Then Eustacia hired me to be her part-time nurse, and I started feeling guilty. I thought I'd talk to you first to help decide what to tell them."

I informed Brad that the DNA facility had told me they would be in contact with him soon with the results of the second test. I knew Brad's parentage wouldn't matter to the Paddingtons, but it was more important to figure out what this meant in relation to Gwendolyn being murdered over the change in her will. When he left, Brad pulled the door closed, and it automatically locked. I checked with Officer Flatman who confirmed that Brad never touched the will while he was alone in the office.

We sat pondering the entire situation. After an hour, we both heard someone trying to open the door handle. Officer Flatman looked at me with large, excited eyes, and whispered, "Maybe that's the killer trying to get the will?"

I agreed and gently tossed the will back on the desk. I quickly shut out the lights, then quietly rushed into the closet and pulled the door shut. As we stood in the darkness, I worried the person trying to enter the room was just an employee but remembered this was a private office the Paddingtons kept locked at all times. Besides the cleaning crew, Myriam, and Arthur, no one else had a key.

A few seconds later, we heard the door unlock. Someone turned on the lights and walked toward the desk. I couldn't determine whom it was initially because he or she had been quick to get to the desk before there was enough light in the room. When the person turned around, I let out a quiet gasp. Everything made complete sense once I saw who'd shown up to steal the will. How could I have been such a fool not to realize who'd killed Gwendolyn?

Chapter 23

Richard Taft went directly to the desk and inspected the envelope. He didn't know that it was a fake copy I'd made that morning before leaving my parents' house. I didn't want to risk the real will being stolen, so I'd opened the envelope addressed to Finnigan and replaced the contents with a letter that read *'Surprise, this isn't the will you've been searching for!'*

As Richard opened the envelope and read the note, he muttered out loud, "What kinda trick is that Ayrwick dimwit up to?" He rifled through the rest of the papers on the desk but found nothing else. The real will was sitting in Finnigan's hands, as I'd given it to the sheriff before I left the Paddington estate. She'd promised to give it back to Finnigan on her way out. Richard paced through the office grumbling and slamming his fist on the desk. "That woman tried to chase me out of town for the last twenty-five years, but I got rid of her first. I'll find that will if it's the last thing I do!"

And that was my cue. I hadn't expected him to confess to the crime, and maybe it wouldn't hold up in court, but Officer Flatman and I both heard him say he'd done something to Gwendolyn. Flatman told me to step out of the closet first, and he'd stay behind to keep listening from his hidden vantage point. I heard a round of thunderous applause coming from inside the main theater which meant the intermission was just beginning. I had a few minutes left to get a full confession out of Richard.

I stepped into the office while his back was to me, then closed the door almost all the way. "Did you find what you were looking for, Richard?"

He turned around with a snarl on his face and practically spit at me. "What's going on here? Where's the will? This isn't any of your business."

"Isn't that the will in your hands? Surely, it's what you came here looking for," I said calmly. "I must admit, you weren't on my radar for the last week. You've done a fantastic job coming and going so often that you were pretty much background noise. Until now." I stared him down like I was preparing for a kill shot.

"You don't have any clue what you're talking about. I just thought I'd help out since I was at the show. What kind of games are you playing here telling us you left the will in the office and went out of town. You're right here, and this is a stupid note from an even stupider woman!" He stepped toward me with a panicked yet dangerous look spreading across his face.

"I'd say Gwendolyn was pretty smart to change her will when she did. You might want to look in the mirror before you throw stones, Richard. Did you kill her, so Ophelia would inherit all the money? Is your wife in on this with you?" I sized him up as I stood there realizing he was several pounds heavier than me. I didn't see any sort of weapon, but I couldn't be certain.

"I guess I can tell you the whole story. It's not like you'll be around to share it with anyone else," he replied in a menacing tone while his gaze narrowed. "How much do you know already?"

As long as I stayed adjacent to the closet door, Officer Flatman could jump out at any moment to stop Richard from hurting me. I dug deep to play a role and get the answers in case he got away from us. I remembered Eustacia telling me Ophelia had just gotten married and she and Richard were living in the Paddington estate when the new maid had started working there. I'd forgotten it until now. "Were you friendly with a woman named Hannah Shope right around the time you got married? Perhaps twenty-five or twenty-six years ago sounds familiar?"

"It seems you've found out a lot of personal information in the last few days. Too bad it's not gonna help save you." He clenched his hands into giant fists.

"Let me see if I understand what happened," I said imploring him with my mind to give me a chance before he attacked me. "You and Hannah were having an affair even though you'd just married Ophelia. When Hannah told Gwendolyn she was pregnant, Gwendolyn thought it was Millard's baby. But it wasn't. It was yours. Only you didn't know until recently."

"I had no clue Hannah was pregnant. The Paddingtons sent her away without telling anyone. I came home one night, and she was gone. Gwendolyn said Hannah had quit and left no forwarding contact information. I tried to find her those first few weeks, but I couldn't. That's when I realized I was stuck with Ophelia." Although I could empathize with his pain, I'd never commit murder because of it.

"Here's where I'm a little confused about what happened. You stayed married to Ophelia and had several kids but kept taking assignments out of town because you couldn't stand to be around her. Why did you suddenly feel the need to kill Gwendolyn now?" I knew it had something to do with the DNA test and Brad mysteriously showing up, but I couldn't pinpoint exactly what had changed.

"For years, Charles doted on his wayward son. Timothy got the family business. Timothy was set to inherit the family estate when Gwendolyn died. But behind the scenes, I was doing all the work. I secured new lines of business. I kept the operations running at Paddington Enterprises. I accepted my role until one day when Timothy and I were out at a club, and he started using recreational drugs. If he was going to hurt himself, maybe it wasn't so bad if I made it a little easier for that to happen. I decided to push him into trying different kinds until he became addicted. Cocaine was his downfall."

"And then he started gambling and screwing up several deals at the office because he was high or at various casinos betting too much?"

"Exactly. When Charles had the Board remove Timothy, I thought it would finally be my chance, but no, it never happened. Charles put Timothy out on a one-year leave of absence while he turned the company over to a silly leadership team who knew nothing about the organization. I was ignored just as they'd ignored Ophelia all those years. That pompous fool's a drug addict and almost lost the company!"

"And you wanted revenge?" I could see Richard unraveling in pieces.

"Charles died, Timothy was out. Gwendolyn had been depressed, broken her hip, and checked into the hospital. I should've been given the keys to Paddington Enterprises. Then Gwendolyn confronts me about the affair with Hannah from years ago. She'd found out about it and threatened to tell Ophelia. I thought it was buried."

"When the first DNA test failed to prove Brad was a Paddington, Gwendolyn realized it was you. That's when she had the second DNA test to be certain before telling anyone." I asked assembling the whole sordid picture together.

"And my pre-nuptial agreement with Ophelia stated I got nothing if I had an affair." A wicked grin smiled back to me. Richard Taft was a cunning man. "I couldn't acknowledge Brad as my son."

"So, you started to switch Gwendolyn's medicine with placebos. Is Dana in on this deceit with you?" I worried he wasn't the only person in the family who'd tried to kill Gwendolyn.

"No, my daughter had no idea I stole them from her. It was a coincidence when she told me she'd located them for the next show at the theater. The sun was shining on me that day. I could slowly kill Gwendolyn and watch her suffer the way she made me suffer all these years. It just took too long."

"That's when you concocted a plan to overdose her with the cocaine?"

"I told her I couldn't go to the show. I went to LA for a quick deal and returned early Sunday morning on a private plane. I made it look like I'd taken a flight back after I heard the news Gwendolyn had passed away." Richard had little shame or remorse over his actions. He assumed no one would request an autopsy, and if they did, it'd probably point to Timothy.

"How did you get the cocaine?"

"Hah! That's easy. One of the lines of business I started with Paddington Enterprises is a front for smuggling drugs in and out of the country. I took some from the shipment and gave it to Timothy, so he'd have a long supply to keep destroying his life. I kept enough to put in Gwendolyn's medication that morning."

"When did you make the swap?" I asked.

"I snuck into the house Sunday morning after my plane landed and when everyone was still sleeping. I hid downstairs while everyone had been eating brunch." Richard stepped closer to me looking around the room for a weapon.

"That's when you saw the bottle sitting on the table in the hallway. You knew Gwendolyn would be taking them sometime at the show, so you dropped the replacement ones laced with cocaine into the bottle," I added realizing he'd had an advantage sneaking around and knowing all the hiding spots.

"Unfortunately, that interfering grandmother of yours was coming back down the hall, and in the rush, I knocked the pill bottle to the floor."

"Clever… to think you almost got away with it." I said suddenly recalling the company he was working with was Castigliano International. That meant my in-laws were involved in smuggling drugs. Did Francesca know anything about this dastardly side of the family business?

"I will get away with it. Just as soon as you tell me where the new will is. As it stands, Ophelia inherits a quarter of her mother's estate with the old will," he said with the smile of a devil growing wider each moment that passed. "Now hand it over, and I'll be very gentle when I kill you."

Officer Flatman stepped out of the closet with his gun pointed directly at Richard at exactly that moment. "I don't think so. Put your hands up."

Richard grabbed hold of a bookcase on the wall to his right and pushed it toward us giving him enough time to rush down the hall. While Officer Flatman and I shoved the books and the shelves out of our way, Richard opened the door and ran into the hall not realizing guests were beginning to leave the performance. As he tried to dash toward the lobby exit, Eustacia stuck out her cane causing him to fall to the ground. The sheriff rushed across the lobby pushing a few guests out of her way and aimed old Betsy at Richard. Officer Flatman and I soon followed and surrounded them, so there could be no available escape route.

Eustacia guffawed. "That's the fool responsible for Gwennie's death?"

"Yes, ma'am," I said leaning against the side wall. In the scuffle, I'd lost my breath and began to feel sick from over-exertion. It was wearing me down to the point I was almost going to pass out again.

Ophelia and her children dashed over to see why Richard was being put in handcuffs. Officer Flatman said, "He confessed to killing Gwendolyn while we were in the office. Not only that, he admitted to having an affair with Hannah Shope twenty-five years ago."

"And Brad is Richard's secret son," I added watching Ophelia's eyes glare like a laser.

Lilly looked at her father and shrieked. "He's my half-brother? How could you do that to Mom?"

Dana turned to Jennifer who stood nearby. "I don't understand it. How could he never tell us?"

When I caught my breath, I saw Nana D, Lindsey, and Millard comforting Eustacia. Ophelia rebuked Richard as Sheriff Montague handed him off to Officer Flatman to read him his Miranda rights. Sam looked shocked and devastated. He wasn't sure whom to turn to and kept shaking his head. When I walked toward him to ask if he was okay, he took off and never looked back.

Sheriff Montague approached me. "Excellent job, Little Ayrwick. Flatman informs me you convinced Richard to keep talking, so he could tell you exactly how everything happened."

"For some reason, I wasn't surprised to see him show up in the office when he did. It took putting him in the right environment for me to realize he'd been behind everything the whole time." I watched Eustacia turn to Lindsey, then I noticed Nana D's response. She still cared for Lindsey even though she'd been backing away to let Eustacia have a chance with him. It was rare to see Nana D look disheartened, but I knew it wasn't the first time.

"Don't feel bad. He wasn't on my radar at first either. Then I got a tip about the Paddington and Castigliano business connections. That's what led me to seeing who signed the deal between the two companies. It was Richard," the sheriff noted as she idly ran a hand through her bristly hair. "If those drug deals happened in Wharton County, I'm going to make it a big focus in the coming weeks to nail those dirty traffickers. I read up on that Castigliano mob. They are one vicious family, but I'm not afraid of them. I'll take them down one by one if I have to." April's determined stare shot right through me.

All I knew is I needed to get some sleep. "I'm sure if anyone could take down the Castiglianos, it'd be you, April."

"Yep. Maybe I'll have to call on you for help. I don't like to admit when I'm wrong, but this is twice in a row you've stuck out your neck to protect our town. I'm not saying I misjudged you, so don't let that pretty boy head of yours swell up any larger than it already has. I'll call you next week to discuss my plans a little further." As the sheriff left Paddington's Play House, I shook my head in disbelief. I kept telling myself I wanted to prove to that woman I was better than her. Now she wanted to talk with me about working together. What was wrong with me? It's like I wanted to repeatedly punish myself. Wasn't there a support group for those kinds of people?

"Kellan! What took you so long to figure this one out? I could've told you Richard Taft was a no-good loser," Nana D chided as she stepped away from her fellow septuagenarians and sidled up next to me to share her diatribe. "You look like death. Here, take this bottle of juice. I just opened it."

"Thanks, Nana D." I was tempted to ask her if she put cocaine it, but it was too soon to crack such a joke. "Just juice, right?"

"Would I poison you? Seriously, drink it. You really need to listen more closely. I told you that family was trying to kill poor Gwennie from the first day it came up at Danby Landing. But no... you wouldn't take it seriously until she keeled over in your lap. What kind of sleuth are you?"

Now I understood why I was constantly subjected to relationships like the ones I had with April and Myriam. I was surrounded by sassy women who liked to torture me. If I loved Nana D, did that mean one day I'd grow to love April and Myriam, too? My stomach began to grind and churn. I feared if I didn't do something soon, we'd have a situation in the lobby of Paddington's Play House. I was about to drop to the ground to take a well-deserved nap when an unexpected commotion brewed nearby.

"Jennifer, I heard what happened. I was stuck backstage. I'm so sorry. Are you okay?" Arthur rattled off before reaching us and hugging her. "Please tell me nothing happened to you or our baby!"

"Baby? Arthur is your baby daddy? You're cheating on me with my aunt? She's like ancient and close to my mom's age. I can't believe it," Dana shouted and beat Arthur's chest.

"I'm going to be a grandmother," Fern said covering her mouth in shock as she joined the group.

Arthur grabbed Dana's wrists and stopped her from attacking him. "Enough, Dana. I've told you from the first day you tried to seduce me, I'm not interested. You're a little girl who throws temper tantrums when she doesn't get what she wants. You've heaved yourself at every guy within a five-foot radius. You'll never be anything like your aunt and need to stay away from us and our baby."

"You're a monster. I can't believe I ever liked you," Dana snarled while looking around, but her mother had already left with Officer Flatman when he'd escorted Richard Taft to the precinct. "I'll get even with you, Aunt Jennifer! This isn't the end of it. I'm a Paddington, too!"

As Dana stomped off, Lilly grabbed her sister's wrist. "Dad was just arrested for killing Grandmother. We have a new half-brother named Brad. Sam's taken off, and we don't know where he is. I think our family has enough to deal with, little sister. Grow up and stop being such a child!"

While Lilly's words were highly appropriate, she hadn't been the best role model in the past. As Lilly and Dana left the lobby, I nodded at Fern hoping she interpreted my mixed show of congratulations and sympathy for her. Fern and Arthur would now be forever tied to the Paddington family.

I said goodbye to Nana D and drove home to finally get some sleep. I checked with my parents who confirmed they were staying over in Philadelphia one more night and would bring Emma back the following evening, so she'd get plenty of rest before school on Monday. I verified Francesca's flight had taken off which meant she was mid-air back to Los Angeles. I had no calls from the Castiglianos threatening me. Francesca likely hadn't told them my decision yet. Perhaps I would wake up with a brand-new focus and outlook on my life.

As I pulled into the driveway at the Royal Chic-Shack, Ursula Power stepped out of her car and waved me down. What was my boss doing at my house on a Saturday evening? After stepping to my car window, Ursula said, "Something urgent has come up, and I need your advice. Don't tell anyone, especially Myriam. She can't know how much trouble I'm in. You're my only hope."

I wasn't sure how to respond, but I needed downtime before I could take anything else on. "Sure, can we meet tomorrow. I'm about to pass out."

Ursula hesitated before leaving. "Yes, but this is important. My past has come back to haunt me, and I don't know how long before it explodes again."

"I promise. We can meet for dinner tomorrow if you'd like."

Ursula nodded and got back into her car. Before shutting the door, she turned toward me and said, "If I may speak freely, Kellan… you need a haircut. That mop on your head is ridiculous. I've been waiting weeks to see if you'd fix it, but I need to step in before it gets any worse. You're looking like a punk eighties rock star and not in a good way." Ursula pulled out her phone and typed something. "Check your text messages. I've sent you the name and number of my stylist. He'll be able to save you from further embarrassment."

Chapter 24

I woke up on Sunday morning to a flurry of messages and what felt like an entirely new body. All the over-the-counter drugs I'd taken must have finally kicked my cold symptoms to the curb. I was glad I didn't develop a full-on flu, as I had no time to rest with everything suddenly heating up in Braxton. Even though I'd solved the latest murder, I couldn't help but worry the hits were going to keep on coming. Something in the air told me I was only given a temporary reprieve and that I should prepare for a bigger battle. Eleanor would tell me the stars were warning me to stay in bed all day. I went through my missed messages, then got in touch with everyone to organize my day before seeing Ursula for dinner. Nana D was the first person I followed up with.

Me: *I'm a whole new man this morning. Life is good.*
Nana D: *I knew you just needed one of my special cures to fix you.*
Me: *What are you talking about?*
Nana D: *You didn't think that was just juice yesterday? I added a few things.*
Me: *You drugged me? I knew you were up to something. Wait, why didn't it taste bad?*
Nana D: *Surely you don't expect me to give away all my secrets?*

Me: *You should be locked away somewhere. There's something wrong with you.*
Nana D: *Eh, I'm not gonna argue with you based on what I did last night.*

I replied and called a few times, but Nana D didn't explain her last line. I assumed I'd see her soon at the Paddington thank you brunch being held in my honor. I showered, dressed, and headed to the Paddingtons fearing whatever first disaster awaited me. Bertha greeted and led me to the Great Hall. "Is my nana here, too?" I asked.

Bertha shook her head. "No, Kellan. Eustacia and Seraphina had a little disagreement last night. She won't be attending brunch today."

I suspected it had to do with Eustacia turning to Lindsey at the theater. "Are you able to share what caused this little disagreement?"

"Well, I'm not exactly certain how it began this time. They were fine yesterday when Seraphina came by for dinner. Until Councilman Stanton showed up. Things got a little ugly," Bertha said as she buried her hands in her face. "It took me three hours to get those stains off the wallpaper in the dining room last night."

"Um... are you saying they had a food fight?" I pictured Nana D throwing a handful of asparagus or broccoli at the councilman. She didn't know when to stop and would get herself locked up again if she didn't learn to control her distaste for that man.

"If only it were that simple. It all started out calm, but then Lindsey said he agreed with one of Councilman Stanton's new political plans. He was making a donation to the campaign, it seems. Seraphina wasn't too happy about that."

"I don't blame her. I thought the Septuagenarian Club was supporting my nana!" What could've gone wrong to cause such a change?

"That's when Seraphina grabbed the whole pot of meatballs and sauce I'd put on the table. It was buffet style last night since we weren't originally expecting company, but then they all showed up. Seraphina is stronger than she looks!" Bertha wiped her hands with the bottom of her apron.

"What exactly happened?" I asked, alarmed over how the night had ended up.

"I'm not sure how to tell you this, Kellan. Seraphina started racing around the room throwing meatballs at everyone like it was a war zone. One by one, she picked them out of the sauce pan and tossed them like little water balloons. When she was all out of meatballs, she dumped the whole pot of sauce over someone's head."

"Over Lindsey's head? Or the councilman's? Either way, that's horrible!"

"No, Kellan. Over Eustacia's head. Seraphina told her it was payback for inviting the devil into their little party and being a ruthless jezebel trying to steal Lindsey again. I don't know what she was talking about, but your nana was a possessed woman." Bertha and I reached the Great Hall. She stopped before I stepped toward the fountain and pool. I couldn't help but think about the water wheel plant and its need to keep eating meat.

"I guess Eustacia wasn't too happy with my nana, huh?" I said feeling the need to stifle my laughter. The devil was likely Marcus Stanton, which made sense, but to call Eustacia a jezebel in front of everyone was not productive nor a very kind thing to do.

"Nope. Apparently, Eustacia set the whole thing up as a trick to convince the councilman that he had the Paddington support, then they would rip it away from him at the next big debate. Eustacia just forgot to tell Seraphina in advance," Bertha said before she walked toward the kitchen. "Silly women!"

And now Nana D had started her rivalry back up again with Eustacia. This was going to be quite a mess for me to solve. "Why do you do this to me?" I said out loud looking up through the glass dome at the sky. I didn't expect anyone to respond, but when a voice did, I startled.

"You're the only one who can control her, Kellan." Millard had been standing in the Great Hall not too far away and had heard the whole conversation. "There's not much time left. We need to get Seraphina and Eustacia talking again if there's any hope for your grandmother to win the mayoral race."

"I believe you're right, Mr. Paddington. I'll talk to Nana D this afternoon. You convince Eustacia to give her another chance. We'll get them together tomorrow to figure it out," I said shaking his hand.

"I'm glad to see you today. I wanted to thank you for helping out my family. I think we're in for some rough times in the near future, but ultimately, it's the best thing to happen to us in years. With Richard out of our lives, and Timothy finally getting help, this family might have a chance to reclaim the power and respect we once had." Millard and I took a seat near some of the fruit trees to his right. The scent of lemons and limes was overwhelming yet comforting in a way I desperately needed.

"What's gonna happen at Paddington Enterprises now?" I asked.

"I will step in and help for a few months. Just until Timothy finishes his recovery at Second Chance Reflections. Once he gets back, we'll talk about getting Ophelia's son and daughters involved in the family business. They're still young, but I think we can get them focused." Millard ruffled his moustache when he finished speaking.

"Sounds like a good plan. What about Brad? How does he fit into all of this? He's not a Paddington, but he's tied into the family now," I asked feeling bad for the nurse. He finally learned whom his father was only to discover the man had murdered someone to keep the news quiet.

"Brad's staying on to help Eustacia. She's gonna sell her place at Willow Trees and run the Paddington estate for a while. At least until she decides if Ophelia or Jennifer will step up to the plate for this family."

"Speaking of Ophelia, I had a question about something I saw the other day. You handed her an envelope that looked like it was from a bank." I felt awkward asking Millard about a private affair but leaving it unaddressed would bother me forever.

"Yes, that... I believe Gwennie's final letter should explain everything. Eustacia found it last night after everyone left. It was inside her cane, that's what she meant by Eustacia *needing it to live* each day. When she dropped her cane last night, the bottom part fell off and out rolled the letter. My sister-in-law always did know how to motivate the rest of this family. I suppose Gwennie lost confidence in herself after Charles died, but this shows she would've gotten us aligned again. As much as it hurts, Gwennie's death serves a purpose," Millard noted handing me the letter she'd mentioned in the will.

To my family...

Ever since I lost Charles, my life hasn't been the same. His death impacted me in ways I never expected. We did the best we could to raise our three children and lead by example for our grandchildren. On some levels, we were successful. On others, we were not. I'm not sure how much time I have left on this planet but should anything happen to me before I've had a chance to fix things, I leave behind these final thoughts.

Millard, you've been a wonderful brother-in-law to me and uncle to my children. You had a soft spot for my girls ever since they were rebellious teenagers and hoped one day to teach them how to be better people. While I didn't like finding out you'd been giving money to Ophelia, so she could support herself and that fool of a husband, I know it was done with good intentions. It needs to stop until she learns how to help herself. I also need to correct your father's wrong when he left you out of his will. I've left behind a portion of the estate for you to administer on behalf of my daughters and to use at your own discretion. When they grow up and stop their immaturity, you can share some of the inheritance with them. Do something nice for yourself, too. Thank you for always being there for us.

Timothy, I'm glad you decided to get help. You screwed up in the past, but of all my kids, you're the one finally doing something to get better. I'm thrilled you've checked yourself into the rehabilitation facility and can't wait to see your progress. It was a mistake to remove you from the will years ago, so you're back in. Take care of your sisters. Find yourself a wife and maybe have some kids. You're not getting any younger, but I think this is just the start of your new life.

Jennifer, I'm truly sorry we fought so much in the past, but you need to stop blaming me for your mistakes. I will always regret slapping you that day on the stairs, especially since it led to you falling and losing your precious child. Now is the time to get your life in order. If you want to be a better person, get a job and stop chasing after no-good men. Find someone worthy of you. Once you've proven to Millard that you can stop being a whiny little girl, he'll share the inheritance, so you can have another chance at becoming a mother through that ridiculous fertilization clinic. It doesn't make any sense why you can't do this the old-fashioned way, but good luck to you.

Ophelia, your husband is a louse. Someone's been stealing money from our accounts, and while I don't know if it's you or him, it needs to stop. I've ordered a DNA test to prove he cheated on you years ago. The results will be sent to the gentleman I believe is his son, but in case anything happens to me, I wanted you to know what he'd done in the past. You need to grow up and set a better example for your children. I'm teaching you a lesson here, and you better pay attention. Leave Richard. Be a better mother. Work at the family company. Millard will get you a position, so you can turn your life around, and maybe then he'll give you some of my inheritance. I believe in you.

Lilly and Dana, there's not much to say right now. You're both spiteful and spoiled. So was I at your age. Grow up. Stop relying on men to make you happy. Make something out of yourselves and maybe your lives will amount to something better. If Lilly's business has that much potential, prove it to Millard. Work together on it, and he'll guide you through all the necessary steps.

Sam, of everyone in the family, you've always been the most precious to me. Not a day went by when you didn't sit with me at the hospital or at the estate during my recovery. You're the future of this family. You need to make those sisters of yours see reality. You need to find a way to love your mother more, even if she's been difficult with you. I know you're struggling with a big decision, and I'm sorry we fought about it before I died. This family's not exactly open-minded, but in time, they'll be okay with what you have to tell them. And based on what you'll eventually tell them, I suspect things are gonna get a lot more complicated. I'm leaving you part of my estate because I believe you'll be the one to steer this family back to greatness. Don't disappoint me, or I'll haunt you from beyond.

Eustacia, you've been my best friend in the family for most of our lives. It's your job to keep this family on the right track. That's why I left this note in your beloved cane. Your lifeblood. Everyone should have the right to live at the family estate, and I want you to oversee the place. You decide what happens to it on your own time. Perhaps someone in this family will step up and show us they're worthy.

Gwendolyn must have known she was getting sicker, or she truly believed someone was going to kill her. She died without confirmation that Richard was Brad's father which meant she probably never knew it was Richard who was trying to kill her all along. After I handed the letter back to Millard and we said our goodbyes, Brad walked into the Great Hall. We exchanged a quick greeting, then he thanked me for helping him find his father. Eustacia had called him after the arrest at the theater to reveal the secret. "You've been a good friend. I need some of those if I'm going to stick around this town and live with the knowledge Richard Taft is my father."

"You've got two half-sisters and a half-brother to get to know. I think maybe you'll be a good influence on them. At least Lilly and Dana. They've been left to their own devices for far too long. Sam's a good kid. I just can't figure him out," I said hoping Brad might take his younger brother under his wing.

"Sam's a cool guy. He confided in me this morning that he's met someone and previously told Gwendolyn all about it. She was accepting of his life choices, which was a good thing to see. Not all families are supportive when someone comes out of the closet." Brad would be a good role model for his younger siblings with that attitude. "I'm meeting with the DNA facility tomorrow. They will have the second test completed, but it looks like I already know the answer. Huh, Richard Taft, a murderer!"

"I'm so sorry it turned out this way. I wish you luck getting your nursing license. If I can help, my late wife used to be a nurse. I know a little bit about what it takes to get that completed," I explained before saying goodbye. Brad and I made plans to grab drinks the following week to discuss everything. I needed to make some new friends, and now that he was cleared of any suspicion, he'd be a great guy to hang out with.

Since the brunch was cancelled due to last night's catfight and meatball extravaganza, I headed to my favorite eatery. I pulled into Pick-Me-Up Diner's parking lot at the same time as Maggie. We walked inside together doing our best to abide by the conversation we'd had the prior day.

"So, we're friends, right?" she said with a giant grin.

"I think so. I'm ready to reconnect and do things together like other friends do," I said.

"Friends hug one another, right?" Maggie said.

"They certainly do," I replied and stepped closer toward her. When we embraced, I knew there would always be something between us, but I also knew it wasn't the right time to explore it again. "Come on, let's go inside and see how your new diner's doing since opening last week."

Maggie went in to talk to the chef while I tracked down Eleanor. "Hey sis, tell me all about your day. I think it's time we stopped talking about me and started talking about you."

"Wow! I lead a pretty dull life. I don't have a back-from-the-dead wife, killers trying to do away with me, or mayoral campaigns blowing up in my face. I'd say you're the one with the stuff to talk about," Eleanor teased with a mouth full of sarcasm and a piece of apple pie.

"Really? You don't call visiting a fertility clinic *something to talk about*? It might not be any of my business, but I've been telling you everything about my life. So, spill it. What's going on?" I said pushing her into the office and shutting the door.

"You can't tell anyone," she said barely able to contain her glee. "I've decided to have a baby. I know it's a crazy idea, but I want a child. And I'm not getting any younger. I'm only thirty, but this feels like the right time. I could wait until I find the right guy and do everything the old-fashioned way, but the stars have been pointing me in this direction for months. I finally listened."

"And what exactly did they say?" I wasn't sure how I felt about her decision, but she was my sister and I'd support her in any way she needed.

"They said I should stop waiting for things to happen and go after what I want. I'm gonna do it. I've just got to figure out who's gonna be the father!" Eleanor tossed her hands in the air and did her version of a happy dance that looked more like a drunken macarena to me. "What do you think?"

I wanted to tell her she was doing too much at once between assuming ownership of the diner, going after Connor, and trying to become a single mother. But if I could do it, so could she, I ended up deciding. "I think it's fantastic. I don't want to know any of the details on how you get pregnant."

"You really need to grow up. Didn't I already tell you this recently? Nana D is right, you can be a giant baby sometimes," Eleanor chided, then asked me to go with her to the clinic the following week to discuss her options. She needed to pick out a sperm donor and wanted my input. The things I did for my family were getting way too weird.

As I stepped into the parking lot, I cleared my head of everything except heading home to spend the afternoon with my parents and Emma once they arrived. I walked to the last parking row and was about to unlock the SUV with my remote when I noticed Sam talking to someone near the sidewalk.

At first, I looked the other way not wanting to intrude and knowing how uncomfortable he'd been around me. I had no idea why I made him so nervous, but if he didn't want to talk with me, I had no choice but to respect his wishes. Then I had to step into the space between my SUV and the car next to it, so I could leave. As I turned, I found myself close enough to see Sam lean in to kiss whomever he'd been speaking to. It was the kind of kiss you only see in movies when two people who love each other finally give in to their passions and don't care what the world has to say about it.

Given I could be as nosy as Nana D, I might have stared longer than I should've hoping to catch a glimpse of the guy he was making out with on the pathway. If it wasn't Arthur or Brad, I was clueless. When Sam pulled away, I got the shock of my life. Sam Taft was kissing someone I knew—my brother. Not only was Gabriel back in Braxton and hadn't told any of us, it seemed he'd been keeping another big secret, too. I stood there paralyzed for a few seconds. Should I interrupt them? Was I supposed to hide, so they didn't see me? Maybe that's why Sam had been so nervous around me. He knew I was Gabriel's brother. Before I could decide what to do, my cell phone rang.

I knew they'd heard it ring, so I dropped to my knees and hid on the side of the SUV. I glanced at the phone's screen only to curse when I saw it was Cecilia Castigliano. I grudgingly pressed accept and whispered, "Hi. I can't talk right now. I'll call you back in a few minutes. I'm guessing Francesca told you what I decided."

"No, Kellan. She didn't tell me anything because she never got on the flight back home. Francesca is missing, and I blame this entirely on you. What did you do to my daughter?"

About the Author

James is my given name, but most folks call me Jay. I live in New York City, grew up on Long Island, and graduated from Moravian College with a degree in English literature. I spent fifteen years building a technology career in the retail, sports, media, and entertainment industries. I enjoyed my job, but a passion for books and stories had been missing for far too long. I'm a voracious reader in my favorite genres (thriller, suspense, contemporary, mystery, and historical fiction), as books transport me to a different world where I can immerse myself in so many fantastic cultures and places. I'm an avid genealogist who hopes to visit all the German, Scottish, Irish, and British villages my ancestors emigrated from in the 18th and 19th centuries. I frequently blog and publish book reviews on everything I read at ThisIsMyTruthNow via WordPress.

Writing has been a part of my life as much as my heart, my mind, and my body. I decided to pursue my passion by dusting off the creativity inside my head and drafting outlines for several novels. I quickly realized I was back in my element growing happier and more excited with life each day. My goal in writing is to connect with readers who want to be part of great stories and who enjoy interacting with authors. To get a strong picture of who I am, check out my author website or my blog. It's full of humor and eccentricity, sharing connections with everyone

I follow—all in the hope of building a network of friends across the world.

When I completed the first book, *Watching Glass Shatter*, I knew I'd stumbled upon my passion again, suddenly dreaming up characters, plots, and settings all day long. I chose my second novel, *Father Figure*, through a poll on my blog where I let everyone vote for their favorite plot and character summaries. It is with my third book, *Academic Curveball*, the first in the Braxton Campus Mysteries, where I immersed myself in a college campus full of so much activity, I could hardly stop thinking about new murder scenes or character relationships to finish writing the current story. Come join in the fun!

List of Books & Blog
Watching Glass Shatter (October 2017)
Father Figure (April 2018)
Braxton Campus Mysteries
Academic Curveball - #1 (October 2018)
Broken Heart Attack - #2 (December 2018)
Flower Power Trip - #3 (Early 2019)

Websites & Blog
Website: https://jamesjcudney.com/
Next Chapter author page:
https://www.nextchapter.pub/authors/james-j-cudney
Blog: https://thisismytruthnow.com/

Social Media Links
Amazon:
https://www.amazon.com/James-J.-Cudney/e/B076B6PB3M/
Twitter: https://twitter.com/jamescudney4
Facebook:
https://www.facebook.com/JamesJCudneyIVAuthor/
Pinterest: https://www.pinterest.com/jamescudney4/
Instagram: https://www.instagram.com/jamescudney4/
Goodreads: https://www.goodreads.com/jamescudney4
LinkedIn: https://www.linkedin.com/in/jamescudney4

Dear reader,

Thank you for taking time to read *Broken Heart Attack*. Word of mouth is an author's best friend and much appreciated. If you enjoyed it, please consider supporting this author:

- Leave a book review on Amazon US, Amazon (also your own country if different), Goodreads, BookBub, and any other book site you use to help market and promote this book

- Tell your friends, family, and colleagues all about this author and his books

- Share brief posts on your social media platforms and tag (#BrokenHeartAttack or #BraxtonMysteries) the book or author (#JamesJCudney) on Twitter, Facebook, Instagram, Pinterest, LinkedIn, WordPress, Google+, Tumblr, YouTube, Bloglovin, and SnapChat

- Suggest the book for book clubs, to book stores, or to any libraries you know

You might also like:

Flower Power Trip by James J. Cudney

To read first chapter for free, head to:
https://www.nextchapter.pub/books/flower-power-trip

CPSIA information can be obtained
at www.ICGtesting.com
Printed in the USA
BVHW061313270321
603571BV00005B/917